Matt [...]ful action adventure novels. As a journalist, he has worked for *The Sunday Times* for many years and now writes a column for Bloomberg in the US and is a regular contrib[...] *Spectator*.

DEATH FORCE

MATT LYNN

headline

First published in 2009
by HEADLINE PUBLISHING GROUP

First published in paperback in 2009
by HEADLINE PUBLISHING GROUP

1

Cataloguing in Publication Data is available from the British Library

ISBN 978 0 7553 4495 6 (B Format)
ISBN 978 0 7553 4898 5 (A Format)

Typeset in Hoefler by Avon DataSet Ltd,
Bidford on Avon, Warwickshire

Printed in the UK by CPI Mackays, Chatham, ME5 8TD

Headline's policy is to use papers that are natural, renewable and
recyclable products and made from wood grown in sustainable forests.
The logging and manufacturing processes are expected to conform
to the environmental regulations of the country of origin.

HEADLINE PUBLISHING GROUP
An Hachette UK Company
338 Euston Road
London NW1 3BH

www.headline.co.uk
www.hachette.co.uk

To Leonora

Acknowledgements

First and foremost thanks to Ken, Mitch and Colin, all men experienced in fighting with private military corporations, for taking the time to explain how that world works. Any mistakes are my fault, not theirs. Thanks to Martin Fletcher at Headline and Bill Hamilton at A.M. Heath for their advice and encouragement and to Chris Ryan for the Foreword. And, of course, to my wife Angharad, and daughters Isabella and Leonora, and, naturally, Claudia, who, despite being born around chapter eighteen, didn't hold up the writing of the book for more than a couple of days.

Matt Lynn, Goudhurst, Kent.
February 2008

Foreword

THE WORK IS ROUGH, HARD and dangerous. You get shipped out to some of the most brutal, unforgiving places in the world, given the worst jobs, and often left on your own with none of the kit or back-up that regular soldiers can expect.

But it is also well paid. And it provides men used to the non-stop action of the military with a second career. Maybe that's why private military corporations, as the men who for centuries were called mercenaries have restyled themselves, have become a booming business.

They are, in reality, the real face of twenty-first-century warfare.

Two or three decades ago, mercenaries were small groups of washed-up soldiers who got mixed up in toppling governments in dodgy Third World dictatorships – and often got themselves into a lot of trouble as well. Now, all that has changed. The mercenaries have become a legitimate part of the defence industry.

Just take a look at a few of the figures.

According to industry statistics, the private security industry was worth less than $900 million globally in 2004.

It is worth more than $2.5 billion today. It embraces quoted companies such as Britain's Armor Group, as well as substantial privately held companies such as Aegis, Olive and Saladin. The giant of the industry is America's Blackwater. They are making money on big, lucrative contracts from the American and British governments.

They've grown for two reasons.

One is that the peace-keeping operations the British and American governments are now engaged in require a lot of men on the ground – and those men need to know how to fight. There isn't much point in trying to build electricity systems or schools if all the kit is going to be blown up. You need guys to protect it. Regular armies don't have the manpower, and that means the PMCs are doing the job instead.

Next, there's been a huge boom in commodity prices. A decade ago, oil cost $10 a barrel. Now it is $100. The same is true of precious metals. Most natural resources are found in brutal, lawless countries. As companies pour money into opening up new oil fields and gold mines, they are taking teams of professional soldiers along with them. They know it is the only way they are going to survive.

But no one should underestimate the risks that PMC men take. In May 2007, for example, four British contractors guarding a management consultant were kidnapped in Baghdad, along with the man they were meant to be protecting. In 2004, four operatives working for Blackwater in the Iraqi city of Fallujah were dragged from their vehicles, beaten, then hacked to death, before their bodies were hung from a bridge. It was in response to that attack that the US Army kicked off what became known as the Battle of Fallujah.

Those are just the examples that hit the headlines.

Every PMC loses men. Sometimes they go down trying to protect a client. Other times they get caught up in a fire fight.

Either way, they have none of the security that comes with a uniform. Terrorists will hesitate to take on a British soldier. Why? Because they know they'll face massive retaliation from the army. Take down a PMC man, and nobody cares. Nor is there any support. An army unit that gets caught up in a skirmish, and finds itself pinned down, can call up air support. They can bring up reinforcements. PMC guys don't have that luxury. If they are wounded, there is no emergency medical care to call upon. There aren't any choppers to be scrambled to pick up a man that has gone down. And you can't expect to be whisked off to a high-tech hospital.

The PMC men are fighting on their own. And they are fighting for money.

The brutal truth is, they run far greater risks than mainstream soldiers. And their casualties can be high.

Even so, there is no shortage of recruits. The regular army doesn't pay that well any more. And defence cuts mean there isn't the room for promotion that there once was. Men come out of the armed forces in their mid-thirties, expertly trained and still in the prime of life. Even if they can find a civilian job, sitting behind a desk all day isn't much of a life for men who are used to being in action. Lots of good soldiers can't adjust to civilian life. The PMCs offer them a way of getting back into action – and on better wages as well.

There is no sign of terrorism abating. Nor is there any sign that the number of chaotic, failed states is getting any fewer. That means the power and influence of the PMCs is only going to grow. If the twentieth century belonged to big, public armies, then the twenty-first century is likely to belong to small, private ones – not so different to the ones portrayed in this book.

Chris Ryan,
February 2008

One

THE SWEAT AND SMOKE AND stench of a Baghdad brothel at two o'clock in the morning are enough to turn even the strongest stomach. Steve West could feel the hot, fetid air clogging his eyes. The beer bottle was so clammy it was clinging to his fists, and his lungs were choking on the thick aroma of Turkish tobacco that wafted around the room in small, angry clouds.

'You want something, baby?' said Ludmilla.

She was twenty-two, twenty-three maybe, with smooth, dimpled skin, and long blond hair that even in the pale light had a brightness and vigour to it that was completely out of place. A Ukrainian, reckoned Steve, judging by the harsh way the vowels rolled around her lips. There might have been thirty guys in the place, but only five women. A couple of eastern Europeans, two Moroccans, and a black girl from somewhere on the other side of the Sahara, all of them controlled by a big, fat, ugly Turk who sat in the corner trying to break the world lung-cancer record and perfecting his impression of Jabba the Hut.

'Sure,' said Steve.

Her fingers started to twist round the stem of his bottle.

She prised open his hand, took the bottle and curled her lips provocatively round its cap. A flick of the tongue, then another, and Ludmilla took a swig of the beer, swallowing hard. 'I'll get a room.'

Steve grabbed hold of her forearm, and for a brief moment a look of anger flashed across her deep green eyes. 'I'm looking for a man,' he said.

The 'Red Zone', as it was affectionately known among the soldiers and mercenaries, was a bar, a pool hall and a few bedrooms on a street running directly parallel to the official 'Green Zone' which housed the government and whatever foreign diplomats were mad or stupid enough to stay in the Iraqi capital. The Red Zone wasn't as safe as the official compound, one of the diplomats had warned Steve when he directed him to the place. Then again, the 'Green Zone' wasn't that safe either. Nowhere in Baghdad was.

Earlier that day, Steve had touched down in Kuwait on the British Airways flight from London, then caught the Hercules C130 that three times a day ferried the men from the private military corporations to Baghdad International Airport. It was always a rough flight. The South African next to him said all the guys were now sitting on their body armour during the descent into Baghdad after some insurgents sprayed a Hercules with gunfire and took out an Australian with a bullet that went right through the skin of the aircraft, through the bloke's backside, and lodged itself in his lungs. After hearing that, Steve sat tight on his Kevlar breastplate, which made the two-hour flight even more uncomfortable than usual. He hated Baghdad; he'd seen too many good men die here in the past year to hold the city in anything but contempt. But he'd been told to find Ollie Hall, and that was what he planned to do. Find the bastard, sign him up, then get the hell out of here.

Steve tried to focus through the cigarette smoke.

'Wrong zone, baby,' said Ludmilla. Her faced creased up into a giggle, and for a moment you could see the younger girl behind the make-up caked thickly across the white skin of her face.

'Not that kind of man,' snapped Steve. 'Guy called Oliver Hall. He hangs out here somewhere.'

Ludmilla put down the beer bottle. 'Ollie?' She rolled her eyes, and held up the smallest finger of her left hand. 'His dick is this big.'

Steve laughed. 'I don't care about that. I need to talk to him, that's all.'

The Red Zone was the only brothel operating anywhere near the government compound, indeed probably the only brothel anywhere in the whole of Iraq, and it attracted a brutal crowd of mercenaries, hustlers and gamblers. The American soldiers were under strict orders not to come here, and most of them were too frightened to venture off their heavily fortified bases. Most of the customers were Arabs, or Russians, with a sprinkling of British and American guys from the PMCs operating around Baghdad. Every hustler in the city passed through here at some point. Ollie Hall had been a major in the Household Cavalry, but that was two years ago. Since then, he'd resigned from the army over his drinking and gambling debts, spent six months in the City failing to re-establish himself in finance, and for the last six months had been failing to get his own private military corporation off the ground in Iraq. When it came to failing at things, Ollie was the world expert. The way Steve heard it, you could now find him most nights at the Red Zone, trying to hustle up the price of a plane ticket home. With a pool cue and not much else.

Certainly not brains, thought Steve, looking around at the shabby interior of the place.

There were a pair of bouncers on the door. Only handguns were allowed inside the club and Steve kept a Magnum Research Desert Eagle Mark XIX pistol visibly tucked into his belt. With a 0.5 calibre shot on it, the Desert Eagle was the biggest, nastiest handgun ever built. You saw them all the time in the movies. As a weapon, it was virtually useless; it had the accuracy of a tipsy schoolgirl, and the kickback from its recoil was more likely to take your arm off than cause any damage to your opponent. Still, it looked menacing, and Steve kept a slim Beretta 92 tucked into his boot in case he actually had to shoot anyone.

He walked through to the pool hall, scanning the faces of the men crowding round the green baize. At the table, an American was lining up the cue, looking to pot the yellow. An Arab was standing next to him, putting a fifty-dollar bill down on the side of the table. The winner would collect the money. Around them, a group of Lebanese mercenaries were offering odds of three to one against the American, laughing as they did so.

Steve remained in the background, behind the Lebanese mercenaries. Twenty yards away, Ollie Hall was putting down a twenty-dollar bill. He was a tall man, over six feet, with jet-black hair, and a tough, muscular face, but he looked worried. Like a man who wasn't betting for fun. His eyes were darting between the two players, calculating the odds. That twenty dollars means a lot to him, decided Steve. There's not much left in whatever wallet that came out of.

One tap of the cue, and the yellow fell neatly into the pocket. Ollie collected sixty dollars.

That's probably the most money he's made since he's been here, thought Steve.

The mercenaries were starting to fall silent now. Their eyes turned away from the Moroccan girl who had just emerged from one of the upstairs bedrooms, and towards the table. One of them laughed. Ollie put the sixty dollars he'd just won back down on the green baize and picked up the cue. He was betting the table that he could pot a blue which was half obscured behind a black. The shot would need to cannon off the cushion, and that was always tricky. Ollie leant across the table, the cue steady in his hands. His eyes narrowed; a single bead of sweat ran down his forehead. About two hundred dollars was at stake, reckoned Steve. And Ollie needed to drop that ball.

Steve glanced around. He could hear a commotion at the door. The Red Zone was protected by thick steel doors and the two three-hundred-pound Liberians who kept guard outside. There was one exception to the handgun rule: Lebanese mercenaries were allowed to bring in their AK-47s. They never went anywhere without them, and they spent a lot of money on the girls. But no Semtex, hand grenades, or RPGs. Even the management of the Red Zone, which didn't really take a moral view on anything, drew the line at high explosives – at least unless you were willing to check them in at the door.

A shot.

Steve ducked, holding himself rock steady. He'd learned during his first weeks in the SAS how to remain composed under fire, and in the few days earlier in the year when he'd been fighting in Iraq he'd heard more gunfire than in a decade in the Regiment. The rattle of machine-gun fire filled the city the way the honking of traffic and the hum of air-conditioning filled other places. But he hadn't learned to get used to it yet, and he wasn't sure he ever wanted to.

A cry. A man was shouting something in Arabic.

Ollie was nervously holding on to the cue.

Christ, thought Steve. He's trying to make the shot. Even as the whole place goes down.

Steve looked around. One of the door guards was lying flat on the ground, a trickle of blood seeping out of the side of his head. A man dressed completely in black knelt down on the guard's chest and delivered one bullet, then another. Behind him, six men had lined up, each one holding an AK-47. Their guns were pointing straight into the centre of the club.

A single word escaped Steve's lips.

'Shit.'

A burst of gunfire rattled through the building like a sudden hailstorm. The noise was deafening, breaking into your eardrums. Bullets crashed into the cheap plaster, kicking up clouds of dust. Steve could hear screams all around but he could no longer see anything. The Desert Eagle was in his right hand, the Beretta in his left, but it was impossible to focus, let alone shoot. He threw himself to the ground. At his side, Ludmilla was cowering against the frame of the table, her hands shaking. Steve looked around desperately, trying to see what had happened to Ollie.

'Who in the name of Christ are they?' he shouted.

Another volley of machine-gun fire filled the room. There were more cries and screams, Arab, African, even a few American voices. Steve climbed back on to his feet and pushed his way through the dust clouds towards the pool table. There were bodies everywhere, and it was impossible to see more than a foot ahead. He knocked a couple of bleeding men away from the edge of the table. Behind it, Ollie lay on the ground. A trickle of blood was seeping out of his forehead, and the pool cue was still in his right hand.

'Christ, man,' muttered Steve, grabbing hold of his left wrist to see if he could feel a pulse. 'You really are a loser.'

Ollie blinked and looked around the room, letting his eyes adjust to the pale sunlight streaming in through the open window. He was lying between crisp white sheets, in a room that measured twenty feet by twenty-five. His throat felt dry and parched, his head was throbbing, and there was a thick bandage round the top of his skull. Bugger it, he thought. Where the hell am I?

'You awake?' said Steve.

Ollie tried to focus on the man. He looked in his late twenties, with big strong shoulders, a harsh, broken nose, and skin that was tanned and hardened like leather. He spoke with a soft south London accent, but there was a hint of menace underneath it. A scar ran down his left cheek, pointing towards a mouth that seemed permanently set in a wry, amused smile.

'I said, you awake?' he repeated.

Ollie nodded. His mind was still hazy, but he thought he recognised the guy. He'd seen him somewhere before. He rifled through his mental filing cabinet, racking his brains. School? No way. The guy was too rough. Sandhurst? Not an officer, not with an accent like that. One of the squaddies? Maybe. Ollie reached for the side of the bed, grabbed hold of a plastic bottle of water, and started to drink. His head began to clear. A battlefield, he decided. About six, maybe seven years ago, when they were peace-keeping in Kosovo. A unit of SAS guys, running around as if they were saving the world single-handedly, blasting away with their guns and their mouths, getting in the way of the real soldiers.

Steve West.

'What the hell are you doing here?' he asked sourly.

Steve got up and crossed the room to the end of Ollie's bed. 'Good morning, Mr Hall, and welcome to Sadr City. Not much of a neighbourhood. No parks, no proper shops, nothing much to eat, and only the suicide bombers for entertainment. But for the moment, it's home.'

'I said, what the hell are you doing here?'

Steve shrugged. 'I live here, mate, at least for a couple of days. The real question is, what are *you* doing here?'

Ollie thought about it. His head throbbed and he couldn't remember very much about what had happened last night. If it was last night, that is. He'd been out cold; the blow he'd taken, he could have been unconscious for two or three days. He knew he'd been getting drunk over at the Red Zone. He knew there had been an attack. The sound of gunfire was etched in his mind, and he could still see the corpses tumbling to the ground. After that, it all went hazy.

'You tell me,' he said.

'Get yourself cleaned up, then we'll talk.'

Ollie struggled into the bathroom. His jeans had been washed and ironed, and there was a new white-T-shirt folded next to them. He slipped into the shower and turned on a jet of cold water, ignoring the bandage on his head. Steve West, he thought to himself. How did I wind up in his apartment in Baghdad?

Back in Kosovo, when Ollie had still been in the Household Cavalry, and Steve was in the SAS, there'd been a Croatian girl, and they'd got into a fight over her. Ollie rubbed soap over himself. Jagoda, that was her name. He had knocked around with her for a week's leave, then Steve took off with her. It was the kind of thing that happened all the time. Ollie was struggling even to remember what she looked like, but the blow Steve had delivered to his jaw was still vivid and fresh in his memory. There were a lot of people from his time in the army Ollie would be happy never to see again. Steve West wasn't top of the list but he was definitely on it.

Ollie scraped a razor across his chin and put his clothes back on. The bedroom led on to a small sitting room, with a TV, a sofa, and a microwave and kettle perched in one corner. Sunlight was streaming in through the one window, and outside Ollie could hear the scream of a siren, and somewhere far away the low, insistent rumble of machine-gun fire. Steve had brewed up some thick, strong coffee and on the table was a plate of dried French toast and some jam. Ollie sat down opposite Steve. The shower had revived him, and as far as he could tell, apart from some cuts to his forehead, he didn't seem to be in bad shape. Bruised, maybe. Confused, for sure. But physically OK.

'I heard you were dead,' he said.

Steve grinned, poured out two coffees into chipped mugs and stirred in some powdered milk.

'That's just for the Inland Revenue,' he said. 'I've got a bit of a rash, but I think I might have picked that up at the gaff you've been drinking at. Otherwise I've never felt better.'

'You were out in the Far East somewhere after you came out of the SAS, that's what I heard.'

Steve took a sip of coffee. He'd kipped on the sofa after patching up Ollie's wounds and tucking him into the single bed and it hadn't been the best night's sleep he'd ever had.

He'd only flown into Baghdad twenty-four hours ago, and he was still jet-lagged. He wasn't even sure why Bruce Dudley wanted the guy so much. Ollie Hall might have been a capable soldier once, but there were plenty of those knocking about. There were dozens of others out there who would be just as good, and you didn't have to pick them up from the floor of a brothel and clean them up before you could put them into action.

'You heard wrong,' he replied, looking at Ollie.

From his expression, he didn't want to discuss it. The way Ollie had heard it, Steve West had been killed on a botched hostage rescue in Papua New Guinea. But the guy looked like he had blood running through his veins now.

'What happened last night?'

'I came out to the Red Zone looking for you,' said Steve. 'I've been searching for you across Baghdad, and I heard you were so down on your luck, you'd washed up there. I'd only just got there when the place was raided.'

'By who?'

Steve shrugged. 'This is Baghdad, it could be practically anyone. Al-Queda, the Mahdi Army, the Malik Ibn Al Ashtar Brigade, or any one of a dozen different groups of Islamic nutters. Or maybe just some gangsters with a grudge. It doesn't really matter. They could have been trying to kill someone in particular or take out the lot of you for having a drink and meeting some girls and generally being a bad bunch of boys. Just after I got there, the whole place was shot to pieces and there were a dozen different corpses lying on the floor, but knowing what that place is like they'll probably have cleaned it all up and be back in business by this evening.'

'Thanks,' said Ollie, taking a piece of dried toast and spreading a thick layer of jam on it.

'Don't mention it,' said Steve. 'I'm sure you'd do the same for me.'

'Don't count on it.'

Steve laughed. 'Anyway, I hauled you into a car and got you back here. The outfit I work for keeps this place for when their men are passing through Baghdad, which is too often, for my liking. There's some grub in the fridge, and some medical supplies. Antibiotics, bandages, even some blood plasma, although I think the last bloke who stayed here might have mistaken it for a vodka shot and drunk the stuff. I got you cleaned up, and put you to bed. You'd taken a nasty blow to the head, but it was concussion, that's all. There must have been a hundred rounds of ordnance flying around that place last night, but somehow you managed to keep clear of all of it. You were lucky.'

Ollie shook his head, chewing on the toast. Luck didn't come into it, he reflected. I dropped to the floor as soon as the shooting started.

'What the hell were you doing there, anyway?'

'Looking for a guy who might give me some work.'

'Christ, man, that's no way to look for a job. You were at Sandhurst . . .'

No need to rub it in, thought Ollie. 'I needed the money,' he snapped. 'I still do.'

'Then I've got a gig for you,' said Steve. 'If you're interested.'

Ollie drained the dregs of his coffee and poured himself another cup. 'What kind of men are you looking for?'

'Dead ones, preferably.'

Ollie laughed. 'You won't be needing a full CV then.'

'No,' replied Steve. 'If I was, I wouldn't be talking to you, would I? Even in the grand tradition of fuck-ups coming out of the Household Cavalry, you're in a class of your own.'

'What's the job?'

'Black op,' said Steve. 'Off the record, off the books, no questions asked.'

'Where?'

'Which of the three words "questions", "no" and "asked" are you having trouble understanding?' said Steve, a scowl crossing his face. 'There's three million dollars on the table for each man, and you're either in or out.'

Ollie hesitated. What are my options? he thought. He was thirty-one, and his life was already washed up. He'd drunk and gambled his way out of the finest regiment in the British Army and was stuck in Baghdad without so much as the price of a ticket home. He was supposed to be getting married in six months but couldn't even afford to rent a morning suit, never mind support a family. He owed so much money, he couldn't even get a credit card.

'It's your call,' said Steve. 'But if you're coming, we haven't got much time to lose.'

'If I could think of anything else to do, then I'd do it,' said Ollie. 'But as it is, count me in.'

TWO

STEVE PUT A GLASS OF pineapple juice down on the table.

'I thought I asked for a beer,' said Ollie.

'You should stay off the booze, mate,' said Steve. 'You'll only get yourself into more trouble.'

Steve took a sip of his drink and glanced through the lobby of the Jumeirah Beach Hotel a big glass and steel building right on the waterfront. The place was one of a series of massive luxury resorts that had sprung up along the Gulf in the last decade. When he had first been to Dubai on a training course soon after he'd passed through the punishing selection process for the SAS, it was just a few oil trading houses and a gold souk, but now it was more like Benidorm reinvented: big blocks of hotels mainly filled with British and German families grabbing some guaranteed sunshine.

'So who are we meeting?' asked Ollie, looking across at Steve.

Both men were dressed casually in cargo pants, polo shirts and dark glasses. It had been a long journey down from Baghdad. A Hercules had been hit by a surface-to-air missile the night before, and Baghdad International was closed while they cleared the runway and rolled out some fresh tarmac. If you wanted to go south, you had to take the roads. Steve had hired a car and driver who'd run them down to Basra overnight, then they'd picked up a lift in a minibus that was taking some Filipino construction workers through Kuwait and on to Dubai. It was another day's drive across some baking hot roads with only an open window for air-conditioning but Steve had decided it was best to travel with the locals, whatever Ollie might have thought. The Filipinos were dirt poor, and whatever money they made, they wired home to their wives, so even the insurgents who roamed around the Kuwait-Iraq border looking for businessmen to kidnap weren't going to bother with them. It wasn't a comfortable way to travel, but as Steve pointed out to Ollie, if you tried to get across the border in any kind of normal vehicle and your skin was white, you might as well bring your own orange boiler suit with you. It would save the insurgents the trouble of dressing you in one before they cut off your head and posted the whole thing on the web.

They had arrived at the hotel this morning and checked straight in; it wasn't half-term, and there wasn't a sales conference on, so the hotel was far from full. Both men had slept for a few hours, showered, then met up again in the hotel lobby. In front of them, a diamond-blue ocean stretched into the distance. The sun was fading, and people were drifting away from the pool. I could get used to this, thought Steve. If I had the money.

When I have the money.

'What's the name of the outfit?' asked Ollie.

'DEF,' Steve replied. 'Dudley Emergency Forces. But most of the guys on the payroll call it Death Inc.'

'Shall I ask why?'

'I wouldn't if I were you.'

Ollie took a sip of his juice. He could use something stronger; it was forty-eight hours now since he'd put the last beer down his throat back in the Red Zone. Maybe later, he told himself. He needed this gig. If he went back to Katie and told her he'd spent three weeks out here and come back with nothing more than some bruises and another cancelled credit card, then he could kiss goodbye to whatever remained of their engagement. He'd called off the wedding once already on account of a lack of ready funds; another postponement and the relationship had about as much chance of surviving as a brand new Mercedes parked in downtown Baghdad.

'Mr Hall? I'm Bruce Dudley. I've heard all about you.'

Ollie glanced up. Bruce Dudley was dressed in pale chinos and a green Ralph Lauren polo shirt. Ollie knew the name, but he'd never actually laid eyes on the man before.

Once you started tracking the private military corporations, there was no way you could avoid hearing about Dudley. Like a kind of Keith Richards in khaki, he'd started out on the wilder fringes of the industry but had now moved into the mainstream. Or maybe the mainstream had moved to him, thought Ollie. From the outlaw mercenary who was written up in the tabloids as the madman of Chad a few years ago, he was now so close to the British government he was practically a subdivision of the Ministry of Defence. If there was anyone who knew what made this industry tick, it was Bruce Dudley.

'Some of it good, I hope,' said Ollie.

Bruce shrugged. 'Not enough.'

He nodded across to Steve, but the two men just glanced

at each other, as if they preferred not to speak. Bruce still had the manner of the SAS sergeant he'd once been, noted Ollie. All spit and polish and parade grounds. Back in the Blues, there were plenty of men like Bruce, and you'd put your life in the hands of any one of them, but they were always stoically deferential towards officers. Out here, among the PMCs, it was different. The sergeants were running all the shows, and they didn't give a damn what anyone else thought. Maybe, reflected Ollie, that was because they were the real heart of the army all along.

Bruce took a long swig of the beer the waitress had just put down in front of him. 'Steve here works freelance for me,' he said. 'He puts together teams, he helps to train the new guys, and he advises on missions. We've got a job . . .' He paused, glancing towards the sea. 'And I think you two guys would be just right for it.'

'What is it?'

'I need ten good men,' said Bruce.

Ollie noted the way he avoided the question.

'Guys who can work together, who trust each other, can fight hard, and can dig their way out of any hole they find themselves in. And I need them in Afghanistan in less than a week.'

'What kind of men?' asked Ollie.

'The desperate and the damned,' answered Bruce. 'But the payday will be a good one. This is going to be rough, hard work, and you'll be risking your lives, and I don't expect you to do that for nothing. You find your own guys, men you feel you can rely on, can fight alongside, and won't ask questions.'

'And you won't tell us what the job is?'

'Not until you get there, no,' said Bruce. 'But like Steve

told you, there should be three million dollars at the end of it for every man. If someone else is offering you even a quarter of that, then I'd take that job instead. If they're not, then the gig is yours if you want it.'

Ollie didn't hesitate. 'When do we start?'

'Tomorrow morning.'

Bruce pushed a brown A4 envelope across the table towards Steve. 'Here's two tickets for the Emirates flight back to London that leaves at eight tomorrow morning. There's also ten thousand pounds in cash which should cover your expenses. Anything over fifty quid, I want a receipt for it, and if you think the Mahdi Army up in Baghdad are scary, wait until you see the old Scottish lady who runs our accounts department.'

Steve picked up the envelope and tucked it under his arm. 'So, you're in, are you?' he said, glancing at Ollie.

Ollie nodded.

Steve stood up. 'Then get yourself a good night's kip,' he said. 'And for Christ's sake, try to stay out of any card games you find being organised in the bar.'

Bruce shook Ollie by the hand and looked him straight in the eye. 'Maybe your luck is about to turn, Mr Hall. Let's hope so anyway.'

Steve could smell the woman's perfume clinging to the collar of his polo shirt, a smoky mixture of honey and whisky that he already knew would linger in his mind much longer than the girl who wore it.

He pulled the shirt over his head, glancing towards the shower. Orlena had been in there for ten minutes already. Washing her hair, perhaps. It certainly looked like it took plenty of maintenance. A thick, lustrous mane that tumbled around her neck and shoulders, she wore it the same way some guys drove around in a new sports car: as a way of commanding attention from the opposite sex. It worked. He'd spotted her last night serving drinks in the hotel bar, and the place had been quiet enough for them to strike up a conversation. It turned out she'd only been working there for a couple of days. She was Byelorussian and had flown in from Minsk the day before because she felt like working abroad for a year, and it was never a problem for a good-looking girl to find bar work in the Dubai hotels. They'd chatted, then gone for a swim in the sea after she finished her shift, grabbed some Thai food at one of the late-night restaurants, then wound up in his room together at about two o'clock in the morning.

I should have got a decent night's sleep, thought Steve, as he pulled aside the blinds on the fourth-floor room and looked out across the Gulf coast. That's what the handbook says. Then again, I'm about to be sent to Afghanistan, on a job that even Bruce Dudley regards as dangerous. I sure as hell won't meet any girls out there. Even if I did, I wouldn't be able to see them behind their burqas.

He opened the door on the second knock. Bruce was standing there, and from the bead of sweat on his forehead, Steve guessed he'd already been for the five-mile run with which he started most mornings. Bruce poured himself a glass of orange juice from the breakfast tray.

'You need to be at the airport in an hour,' he said.

Steve strapped on his watch: a Luminox Navy Seal diving watch, originally developed for the American special forces. His uncle Ken had given it to him the day he was accepted into the SAS.

'I'll make it,' he told Bruce. He grabbed a coffee, and

poured it down his throat, waiting a second for the caffeine to kick in. 'Why are we taking the dickhead?'

'You don't rate him?'

'Out of ten, I'd given him one for being able to tie his own shoelaces, although he can probably only do that when there isn't a stiff wind blowing,' said Steve. 'He's just another useless tosser of a Rupert. He's probably fine when he's got a platoon of decent blokes to do the actual fighting for him. Ask him to do the business for himself, and he'll go to pieces. You send me all the way out to Baghdad, and all I'm doing is hauling some drunken tosser out of a brothel. He's a loser, Bruce. A waste of space. We'd be better off without him.'

Bruce poured himself a coffee and walked towards the window. 'Ollie Hall was once one of the brightest prospects of his generation,' he said. 'Top of his class at Sandhurst. One of the youngest officers in the Household Cavalry. They talked about him as a certainty for general one day, maybe even field marshal. Ten years ago, the British Army had no brighter young prospect. The best of the best, and all that.'

'So what the hell happened?'

'Drink, and the gaming tables,' said Bruce. 'All soldiers like to gamble, we wouldn't be any good at the job if we didn't like taking a risk every now and again. But Ollie took it all too far. He was hanging out at casinos, going to the race tracks, organising card games back at the barracks. He'd lose all his money, then drown himself in booze to try and forget about it. Eighteen months ago, he quit, and they weren't sad to see the back of him either. If he hadn't resigned, they'd have thrown him out soon enough, and he knew it. He managed to use the old boys' network to get himself a job in the City, but he hated it, and that only lasted eight months. He's engaged, and he's put down a deposit on a place in

Dorset, but for the last few months he's been trying to put together his own PMC.'

'I've seen enough blokes like that,' said Steve. 'They sail through school and their regiments, but they can't cut it by themselves. They aren't worth the aggro.'

Bruce turned to look at Steve. 'He's looking to redeem himself, and that can be a mighty powerful force within a man. He was a good soldier once, and I reckon he knows better than anyone that he didn't manage to live up to his potential. Didn't even get close. I reckon if he can find even a tenth of what he once had within himself, then he'll be more than worth having on the team.'

Steve was about to reply when Orlena stepped out of the bathroom. She was dressed in the white hotel dressing gown, and her black hair was tied back around her neck. Her green eyes flashed across to Steve. She smiled, helped herself to a glass of juice, and spread a thick layer of jam across a warm croissant. Bruce looked at Orlena, then back at Steve. There was nothing on his lips, but you could see the smile in his eyes.

'There's another guy I want you to meet when you get back to London,' he said to Steve. 'A bloke called Ian Murphy. Decent guy. I reckon you'll like him.'

'I thought we were choosing our own team for this gig.'

'You are. But Ian's good.' Bruce pushed across a slip of paper with an eleven-digit mobile number written on it. 'Call him.'

Steve nodded.

'And don't miss your flight.'

Steve shut the door behind Bruce and finished off a second cup of coffee. Orlena was standing close to him, and she smelt of soap and shampoo. 'You're some kind of soldier, no?' she said.

'Some kind,' said Steve.

'The British Army?'

Steve nodded. 'I used to be. These days, I freelance. We're just putting together the team for a new job.'

'My brother, Maksim, he's a soldier too,' she said. He could see most of her leg outside the white towelling of her robe. 'Five years in the regular army, then three years in the Spetsnaz.'

'I thought you were from Byelorussia,' said Steve. He didn't rate Russian soldiers, not even the Spetsnaz. Russia's special forces were brutal all right. If you had a small central Asian country you wanted wiped off the map, they were the right men for the job. But they were mostly psychos. Their tactics were rudimentary, and they were as careless with their own lives as they were with other men's.

'The Byelorussian Army is a joke,' said Orlena. 'The Russian Army is the only place for a proper soldier. But he's left now, and he's looking for work. Freelance work, the kind that you do. You could take him with you.'

Steve shrugged. 'Maybe.'

He started to run his hands across her creamy white skin, and felt her tongue on his neck.

'You've still got forty minutes until you need to be at the airport,' she said huskily.

Three

STEVE RAN HIS HAND ALONG the glistening metal bonnet of the Austin Healey 3000. A 1961 Mark 1 model, with front disc brakes, and a roaring three-litre engine, it was sitting proudly on the forecourt of West and Hallam Motors, its chrome fenders and wheel arches just catching the remnants of the early evening sun. There were a lot of fine-looking cars in the world, reflected Steve, just the way there were a lot of fine-looking women. But an Austin Healey 3000 was like your first love: it might be matched, but it could never be replaced in your affections.

'They're going up in price like a bomb,' said Ken, walking across the shaded tarmac that stretched out in front of the garage. 'I paid fifteen grand for that six months ago from a lady up in Cheshire who seemed too bloody keen to get rid of it when her old man dropped off the perch. I've patched up the paintwork, and put some oil in the gearbox, and I've been on the phone today to a Yank who's offering me sixty thousand dollars for it.'

'Run OK?' asked Steve.

Ken grinned. 'Well, like I always say, if you actually want to get somewhere, then there's a bloke down the road who can sell you a two-year-old Toyota. But if it's romance you want, there's no better car in the world.'

There were eight cars on display in the forecourt: three Austin Healeys, two Jaguars, two Triumphs, and one Aston Martin DB5 which, if Steve was forced to start compiling a list, was probably the second finest car ever made. Inside the workshop, there were at least another five cars, their innards being gutted and their leather, walnut and chrome being polished, ready for a sale. You could smell the engine oil everywhere, a rich, earthy aroma that dug into your skin, and was, in its own way, as intoxicating as any perfume.

'I'll see you in the pub in ten minutes,' said Ken. 'After we've closed this place up.'

Steve walked across the narrow High Street towards the Three Crowns. He'd touched down at Heathrow after a seven-hour flight from Dubai just after lunch, hired himself a car, and come up here. He'd meet up with Ollie back in London tomorrow morning and start putting together the unit they'd be taking out to Afghanistan, but tonight he needed to talk to his uncle. The text he'd received in Dubai said there was a sale in the works, and that couldn't be ignored. Ever since he was a kid, Steve had dreamed of buying the dealership one day. There was no better centre for vintage British cars in the whole of the East Midlands. Now that it was up for grabs, there was no way he was letting some other guy get his hands on it. It even had his name above the door. All he had to do now was raise the cash.

Steve blew the froth from the top of his pint. As he'd driven up from Heathrow, he'd reflected how it was always his uncle Ken he came to see, not his mum or dad. It was his uncle he felt closest to. Steve had grown up in Bromley, where his dad worked in insurance and his mum worked as a nurse in the local hospital. His older brother Rob was working in the City now, and had bought himself a big house in Orpington, and his younger sister Louisa was married and looking after her first kid. Steve had been desperate to get away: he could feel a splitting headache coming on as soon as he set foot in a leafy street lined with semis and Mondeos. I must have been built from the same DNA as my dad's brother, he told himself; Ken had spent ten years in the Royal Engineers before setting up the dealership.

'It's time to sell,' said Ken, pulling up a chair next to where Steve was sitting, a pint in his hand.

Ken was greying now, but you could still see the strength in him that must have made him a fine soldier once, Steve judged. He was built like one of the jeeps he used to fix back in the army: practical, rugged, easy to maintain, and good on rough terrain. His skin was rough and worn, but that was just the upholstery; the engine was as tough as it had ever been.

'You've plenty of life in you yet.'

'It's not me, it's Ritchie,' said Ken.

Ritchie Hallam was Ken's partner in the business. A local property developer, he'd helped Ken set up the dealership, mainly because he loved vintage Aston Martins, and he helped out with the books. But he was never more than a sleeping partner.

'He's found a buyer,' continued Ken. 'One of the big dealerships up in Birmingham. The guy is buying Ritchie's stake.'

'So you'll have a new partner,' said Steve. 'Maybe someone who knows about cars this time.'

Ken shook his head. 'There's a clause in the original contract between Ritchie and me that says if either of us sells our stake, the other person has to offer his shares as well at the same price.'

'So West and Hallam is going to get sold?'

Steve could see a momentary flicker of hesitation in Ken's eyes. The plan had always been that Steve would take over the dealership one day. They hadn't spoken about it for at least ten years, not since Steve had left school and joined the army, but it was there as an unspoken agreement all the same. It was one of the reasons Steve had quit the Regiment and gone freelance. So he could put together the kind of cash he'd need to buy a stake. He knew he'd have to settle down one day, and he also knew he could never spend his life in an office the way his dad and brother did. There were cowboys, and there were deskmen, and Steve had always known which side of that line he'd been born on. But if he had to settle – and the truth was most men had to one day – then the dealership was a life he might be able to handle.

'You'll need a hundred grand,' said Ken. 'That's what the guy up in Birmingham is paying. If you can match it, then the business is yours.'

He could see in his uncle's eyes that he didn't believe for a second Steve had that kind of money. He knew what the army paid, and it wasn't much. He had a pretty good idea what guys were making out in Iraq as freelancers, and even though it was a lot better than what the army stumped up, even five hundred a day tax free didn't put a hundred grand in the bank.

'How long have I got?'

'To get a hundred grand—'

'How long?'

Ken shrugged. 'How much time do you need?'

Steve thought for a moment. They had three days to put

the unit together, starting tomorrow morning. Another day to get out to Kabul. And then? A few days to plan the job, maybe five at most. You wouldn't want to hang out in a rat hole like that any longer than necessary. A couple of days to get the loot out. Then, if it all went according to plan, he'd have three million dollars to play with. He could buy the dealership and he still wouldn't be making any kind of serious dent in his stash until he bought himself a yacht to go with it.

'Two weeks,' said Steve.

Ken laughed. 'Where the hell are you going to get that kind of money in a couple of weeks?'

'There's a job.'

Steve could see a shadow of suspicion crossing his uncle's face. There were Regiment boys who joined up with some of the South London gangsters, and Ken knew a few of their names; they'd roll up at the dealership sometimes, with suspiciously large wads of cash. Why not? a few of them asked themselves. The government taught them how to blow a safe, and shoot straight, then it paid them nothing and told them to get lost with a pension that was worth even less. It wasn't really surprising that some of them started helping themselves.

'Nothing like that,' said Steve. 'It's a government job – well, sort of. Off the books, black op, and all the usual rubbish. But legit, at least as legitimate as anything out in Afghanistan is these days.'

'You can get the cash?'

'For sure.'

'Then you've got two weeks,' said Ken. 'I can hold Ritchie off until then.'

Steve drained the last of his pint. Sometimes life just

clicked into place, he reflected. He needed some serious cash, and now here was a job that was likely to pay off big time. Just got to make sure I don't screw it up, that's all.

Katie was twisting the ring on her finger, a single diamond on a strip of white platinum. Ollie had bought it at Tiffany a year ago, just after he left the Household Cavalry and just before he started the job in the PR department at one of the very few investment banks left in the City where a good school and a decent regiment on your CV still got you an interview. It had maxed out yet one more credit card, but at least that one had made someone happy. For a while, anyway. She'd already tossed the ring back in his face once, and was constantly threatening to do it again. Maybe that was why she played with it all the time.

'The house won't wait,' she said. 'The wedding won't wait either.'

Ollie tried to smile but he felt as if he'd just taken a bad punch to the stomach. They were sitting in Oriel, a bar on Sloane Square, just a couple of hundred yards down from where Katie worked for a PR company. She was wearing a black dress and leggings, and her auburn hair tumbled down the back of her neck and shoulders, melting into her olive skin the way the leaves blend into the countryside during the autumn. She might drive me crazy, but she could still snap a man's heart in two at a hundred yards, reflected Ollie. Turn that into a weapon, and you'd score an easy victory on any battlefield in the world. They'd been together for three years now, engaged for one. The wedding had already been cancelled once, due to Ollie's lack of ready funds, but had been scheduled again for the autumn. Or at least, so Ollie had been told. He didn't like to push for details. The house

Katie wanted was a big Georgian place down in Dorset that belonged to her godmother. Complete with thirty acres of farmland, in today's market it was a steal at a million. The godmother had promised Katie she could buy it from her privately, but they still had to raise the cash, and right now Ollie had about zero chance of being approved for a mortgage. If they didn't move fast, they'd lose it. And then they'd be lucky to buy a small flat in Tooting. It was hard to imagine Katie even opening those pages of the A-Z, even harder to imagine her living there.

'We have to get a move on,' she persisted.

Christ, thought Ollie to himself. There's not a lot of waiting going on here. 'I've fixed something,' he said tersely.

Her eyes instantly mellowed. It was moments like that which made it all worthwhile. He'd called her as soon as he and Steve touched down at Heathrow. There had been a lightness in his voice that he hadn't been able to disguise. When he'd set off for Iraq telling her he was planning to set up his own private military corporation she'd seen him off with barely disguised contempt. She clearly didn't rate his chance of succeeding, and in that at least, Ollie reflected, it would be hard to dispute her judgement. But she could tell from his tone that he'd got somewhere. Maybe I've earned myself another chance, he thought.

'What?'

'I can't say.'

'Why on earth not?'

I don't bloody know, thought Ollie to himself. That's why. I'm flying out to Afghanistan in three days' time, and I don't even know what the mission is. It's my last shot, however. I know that much. He held her hand across the bar. 'This time it's going to be OK, Katie,' he said. 'Trust me.'

'Where are you going?'

'Afghanistan.'

'Christ, isn't that dangerous?'

Ollie laughed. 'Not as dangerous as telling your mother we might have to postpone the wedding again.'

Four

THE STARLIGHT CAFE WAS ONE of the few remaining places you could still get a decent full English for less than a fiver – at least, the only one Steve knew with an SW at the front of its postcode. He ordered sausage, bacon, eggs, beans, a couple of slices of fried bread, and an extra large mug of tea, and kept an eye on the window, waiting for Ollie to arrive. They had arranged to get together at nine, and it was now three minutes to. I'll give him until five past, decided Steve. Enough time to polish off this grub. Then I can get on with putting together this job. My way.

Steve had driven down from the Midlands last night, and kipped down at a flat Bruce Dudley maintained over the river in one of the new apartment blocks that had sprung up along the Battersea side of the Thames. The last job he'd been on had been a long body-guarding gig out in Brunei, and he'd given up the flat he'd been renting in Clapham and moved his few belongings into a self-store warehouse. It wasn't much to show for thirty years: a medal from the invasion of Iraq; a solid gold bath tap he'd 'liberated' from Saddam's Palace in Baghdad and planned to put in his own house if he ever got around to buying one; a football signed by Kerry Dixon in the year he scored as many goals for Chelsea in the league as Gary Lineker did for Spurs; and a collection of repair and valuation manuals for Austin-Healeys, Astons and Jaguars dating back to models that had been produced in the early thirties. Still, it was a start, Steve had reflected to himself as he'd carted the boxes into the smallest room they rented in the storage depot. It was the memories that counted more than the stuff and he had enough of them to fill the whole warehouse.

He'd been thinking about the dealership on the drive down. A hundred grand was a lot of money. Whether the business was worth it, Steve had no way of knowing. Ken never seemed to be rolling in money but he made a decent living, and nobody was taking pot shots at him, which suited Steve just fine. He'd raise the money. One last battle, he told himself, spearing a sausage on the end of his fork. That's all it's going to take. And at least the payday is going to be a decent one this time.

'I'll have what he's having,' said Ollie, pointing to the plateful of food.

It was one minute before nine, noted Steve. Ollie was freshly shaved and showered, and was wearing a well-creased pair of jeans, and a blue denim shirt. From the grin on the guy's face, and the lightness in his step, Steve reckoned Ollie's fiancée had made up with him again. At least somebody had had a good start to the day.

'How long have we got?' Ollie asked, sitting down.

'Three days,' said Steve. 'We fly out to Kabul on Saturday afternoon, and meet up with Bruce Dudley on Sunday morning.'

A plate of breakfast was put down in front of Ollie. He'd already polished off a bowl of Waitrose luxury organic muesli back at Katie's flat over the river in Clapham, but that had hardly put a dent in his appetite. He pierced the eggs first, then mixed them up with the beans. 'So what kind of skills do we need?'

'The usual,' said Steve tersely.

Ollie looked up at him. Steve had finished his breakfast and was sipping his tea. 'And what kind of job is it?'

'Like I said, black op.'

'But doing what?'

'Bruce will tell us when we get there,' said Steve.

'Then we can't judge what kind of men we need.'

'Good ones,' said Steve. 'Have you fought in Afghanistan?'

'For three months, up in Kabul, after we first went in after nine eleven.'

'Then you should know what it's like,' said Steve. 'The cesspit of the universe. Anything can happen out there. Once you get outside Kabul, there's no laws, no government, not much in the way of infrastructure. If something can go wrong, it probably already has. That means we need ten guys who we'd trust with our lives, men who can deal with whatever the country can throw at them, and won't start whingeing if it gets rough.'

Ollie nodded. 'All-rounders.'

'That's it.'

'Who do you have in mind?'

'Two blokes . . .'

Jeff Campbell was lifting weight in the Lewisham High Street branch of Fitness First. It was eleven o'clock when Steve and Ollie walked into the training room, and there were only four people in there, although the hall was equipped for at least thirty.

Jeff didn't notice them as they walked in. He was lying flat on his back, sweat glistening off his toned black skin. Ollie had seen plenty of fit-looking guys back in the Blues but Jeff was in a class of his own. He was at least six feet two tall, with a barrel of a chest, and arms that were like the girders on a building site: great big chunks of steel locked solidly into place. He was wearing only a pair of tight blue trunks, and next to him was a tub of magnesium carbonate, used as chalk by weightlifters, and a half-drunk bottle of Lucozade Sport. He closed his eyes, then took a firm grip on the bar. Ollie glanced at the weights. He was using a standard Olympic bench press bar, which measured 2.2 metres and weighed 20 kilograms. On both sides was a 100 kilos in weights, making a total of 220 kilos for the bench press. That was a long way off the world record – it currently stood at 324 kilos for a raw bench press – but it was still a big weight to push into the air for an early-morning workout. Jeff gripped the bar, took one lungful of air, then pushed the weight up, holding it effortlessly in place, as if his mind was temporarily on something else.

'You're getting soft, mate,' said Steve, looking down at Jeff. 'Didn't you used to do this with one hand?'

The weight stayed held perfectly in place, and Jeff's eyes remained closed.

He shuffled his hands along to the middle of the bar, his palms upturned slightly. Then he gradually withdrew one hand, so that the bar was balancing on his right hand. It wobbled slightly, and for a brief second Steve could see the muscle's in Jeff's shoulder start to tremble under the weight of the load pressing down on them. One momentary loss of grip and the bar would come crashing down, snapping Jeff's neck into two like a pane of glass. The risk of losing control of the bar was the reason why you were always meant to wear a protective metal collar when taking on big weights for a bench press.

'That good enough for you?' said Jeff casually.

Jeff's left hand shot up, took control of the bar, and lowered it gently to the ground. He sat up, took a swig of the Lucozade, and wiped his hands on his towel. He wasn't even out of breath, noted Ollie. If any heavy loads needed shifting out in Afghanistan, there was no mystery about who was going to be doing it.

'Want a go?' asked Jeff.

'Ollie here could use a turn,' said Steve.

For the first time, Jeff turned to look at him. He had an open, handsome face, noted Ollie. Big eyes, a straight nose, and a jaw that looked as if it was sculpted from ivory. On the way down, Steve had filled him in on some of the details. Jeff had left the Paras two years ago and had done two six-month tours with a PMC out in Iraq. He'd done one tour guarding an oil rigging convoy heading down to the southern oilfields and another working in close protection with a BBC camera crew. But he was back in London for a few weeks, working out at the gym, and doing some bouncing at one of the New Cross nightclubs. Steve felt certain he'd be up for this job. Back in the Paras, Jeff would always talk about setting up a boxing club for the boys who grew up on the estate where he still lived between jobs. If they could pull this job off, he'd have the money – after he'd blown a few hundred grand on a red Ferrari, a full Armani wardrobe, and his own personal nightclub, that is.

'I'll give you a trial of strength,' said Jeff, looking at Ollie.

Steve smiled. 'We've been waiting to see what the guy is made of.'

Ollie knew he didn't stand a chance but he wasn't going to let the challenge remain unmet. He'd done plenty of weight training back in the Blues, and he'd always been able to get a tidy load up into the air. True, he'd lifted nothing heavier than a credit card statement since he'd left the army, but he still ran five miles a day and reckoned he was in fair physical shape.

Ollie lay down on the mat, next to the press.

'No way,' said Jeff. 'Proper weights.'

The kit was ten yards away, up against the back wall of the gym.

'Snatch or clean and jerk?' asked Ollie. At least I know the lingo, he thought to himself. A 'snatch' was when you lifted the bar clean above your head in one single movement. A clean and jerk was when you lifted it first to chest height, then pushed it above your head.

'Snatch,' said Steve. 'We haven't got all day.'

He was already lining up the weights, slotting 100 kilos in cast-iron discs on to either side of the barbell. Ollie took his shoes off, dusted some powder into his hands, and walked on to the mat. He glanced down at the lump of metal. Like any sport, he knew that weightlifting was mainly about mental discipline and self-belief: as long as you focused, you could lift it. He knelt down, filled his lungs with air, and gripped the barbell. With one swift yank, he lifted it high into the air, above his shoulders. He steadied himself for a second, tightened his grip, then lowered it back down on to the ground.

'Your turn,' he said to Jeff.

Jeff lifted it as if it was a feather.

Ten minutes later, Ollie could feel the sweat pouring off his face. And his arms felt like they'd been mangled through a car crusher. It was going to be a couple of days before he lifted anything heavier than a slice of toast. And Jeff had still beaten him easily.

Jeff drained the last of his Lucozade. 'So what are you boys here for, anyway?'

'There's a job,' said Steve. He glanced around the room. Nobody could hear them, and it wasn't likely they would be interested anyway. 'Out in Afghanistan,' he continued. 'Might take a week, might take two. But there's a big payday. Three million dollars for each man, if it all goes according to plan.'

'Since when did it ever go according to plan?'

'Never,' said Steve with a grin. 'But this is . . . on the level.'

'And the chances of getting killed?'

'No worse than usual.'

'That bad, eh?'

Steve laughed. 'You'll be all right.'

'So when do we leave?'

'Saturday. You in?'

Jeff glanced at Ollie, then back at Steve. 'Steve West's big payday,' he said, smiling. 'He's been talking about it long enough. I wouldn't miss it for the world.'

Five

THE HOUSE LOOKED AS IF it had seen better days. It was a big Victorian building on New Brent Street, just around the corner from Hendon Central tube station. What remained of the front garden was filled with weeds and rubbish, and the stone of the front step was chipped and broken. It had been divided up a dozen different ways at least two decades ago, but it didn't look as if anyone had finished the job. Steve rang the doorbell three times, but either it was not working or else nobody was bothering to answer. He fished his mobile from his pocket, and when Chris Reynolds answered he told Steve tersely to let himself in.

Chris was a 'Recce' and even among military men they were considered an elite. The South African special forces had fought one of the longest and most vicious of modern wars against the African National Congress in their own country, and against the Soviet-backed insurgents in Angola and Namibia. In Steve's judgement, even the average guy in South Africa was pretty tough; to make it into the special forces you needed almost inhuman levels of strength and endurance. Chris certainly had those. And that meant age didn't matter.

The flat was on the fourth floor. Except flat was probably too grand a word. As they walked up the stairs, Steve could hear the sounds of at least three different babies screaming, and you had to climb over small piles of phone directories, estate agent leaflets and unpaid bills. Even the property sharks of north-west London couldn't be bothered with buying up this place and redeveloping it. Steve held his breath against the fumes of rotting food drifting out of each apartment.

'I reckon he'll be happy to get out to Afghanistan just to get away from this place,' said Ollie as they arrived on the fourth floor. 'A Taliban jail would be an improvement.'

Chris had already opened the door. He was a solid bull of a man, with deep-tanned skin and murky blue eyes the colour of a rough sea. He was wearing jeans and a black sweatshirt, and there were a couple of tattoos on his thick, muscled forearms. He nodded towards Steve, but didn't say anything as the two men stepped inside. Steve had met Chris during a stint out in Iraq, and rated him highly. There were plenty of South Africans in Iraq, some of them trained soldiers but many of them former policeman or security guards or even farmers who were struggling to make a living now that the white minority had lost its grip on the economy. Most of them were just hoping to make some quick cash and pay the cost of relocating to Britain or Australia. Not Chris. He was the genuine article, a member of what had once been the most formidable fighting machine on the planet.

'How's things?' said Steve, taking the mug of tea he was offered.

'Bloody terrible,' muttered Chris. 'I've had my papers.'

'What papers?'

Steve only knew the sketchiest details of the history of

the South African Special Forces Brigade, as the Recces were formally known. The brigade had been formed in 1971, during the vicious struggle between South Africa and its allies in Angola and Namibia, and the Soviet-backed South West Africa People's Organisation (known as Swapo) which was attempting to bring communist-sponsored black rule to the region. They weren't just fighting the black nationalists, although they would have been tough enough. The border wars became one of the underground battles of the Cold War, with the Soviets pouring in men and equipment as part of a plan to create puppet regimes that could control the whole of southern Africa. There were Russian special forces soldiers – the Spetsnaz – running around the region, but also Bulgarians and East Germans and at least one battle-hardened platoon of former Vietcong fighters who'd already bested the cream of the US Army and didn't reckon the South Africans should give them any trouble.

The Recces might have been based on the SAS, but they took it a step further. For Steve, the selection regime for the Regiment might have been the toughest few weeks of his life, but compared to getting a place in the Recces it was a stroll in the park on a Sunday afternoon, with a trip to the cinema afterwards. For the selection week, candidates were not allowed to sleep or eat for seven days, while being pushed through a gruelling series of physical and mental tests. Some years, only one or two candidates passed. Some years, none at all. Nobody ever got selected just to make up the numbers. If you weren't good enough, the Recces didn't want you.

'Papers,' said Chris tersely, 'from the government.'

Chris wasn't a great talker, Steve remembered that from the time they'd met in Iraq. Most of the time, he'd said nothing at all, and the one time they'd got him drunk in an attempt to loosen his tongue, he retreated into monosyllabic grunts, then fell asleep.

'South Africa is the only country in the world that stops its citizens from fighting in private military corporations,' Chris explained. 'It's illegal.'

'You can't stop a man from getting a job,' said Ollie.

'In South Africa you can,' Chris looked sharply at Ollie, scrutinising him for the first time. His eyes were suddenly piercing and clear, then he retreated back into himself. 'They are frightened of us, you see. They think all the white boys are going to go off around the world fighting in the PMCs, then one day we'll get together and go back home and see if we can't take charge again.' Chris chuckled softly to himself. 'And they're bloody right to be frightened as well. Because we just might do that.'

'So they're on to you?' asked Steve.

The apartment was just one room. There was a futon rolled up in one corner, a single, cheap sofa on which a couple of springs seemed to have broken, and a pair of bean bags. Steve and Ollie were sitting on the sofa, while Chris was resting with his back on one of the bean bags.

'The letter just asks me if I can tell them what I'm currently doing, and reminds me about the law,' he said. 'It says the letter is sent out routinely to all former members of the South African Defence Force. But I don't believe it. I think it means they're on to me.'

'Because there's a job,' said Steve. 'Although I'll understand if—'

'I bloody need it, I can tell you that,' said Chris. 'But it better pay well.'

Steve looked closely at him. He looked older than forty.

There were battle lines etched into the skin drawn tightly across his face, and although the grit and determination were there, like the seams of iron threaded through a lump of ore, you could also see the first, ugly traces of defeat. He didn't look like a man with much hope left in him.

'This will,' said Steve quietly.

'How much?'

Briefly Steve explained how much money was on the table. And what they had to do to get it.

'You're not worried about the South African government?' he asked.

Chris chuckled. 'I'm not taking orders from those bastards,' he said. 'If anyone asks, I'm just out in Afghanistan talking to a few dope dealers. The government doesn't have anything against drug traffickers. It's just white mercenaries they don't like.'

Six

'SO WHAT THE HELL IS this stuff about Steve West's big payday?' asked Ollie.

Steve could see Ollie looking at him coldly.

He steadied the rented Astra. There was an elderly couple in a VW in front of him chugging along at fifty and there was no way he was going to get past them on this road.

'It's a vintage car dealership, up near Northampton.'

Ollie was unwrapping some boiled sweets he'd bought at the garage. 'Vintage cars? You mean you're going out to the biggest hellhole in the known universe just so you can flog a few rusty old bangers? What are we talking about here? A Capri?'

'We're talking Austin Healey 3000s, DB5s, the Jag Mark II.'

'Cars worth dying for.'

'Believe it,' said Steve with a grin. 'My uncle Ken runs this place that restores them and sells them on. He's planning on selling up, and I need a hundred grand to buy out his share of the business.'

'So that's why we're off to Afghanistan?'

'It's no stupider than doing it because some piece of posh

Matt Lynn

totty wants a big day out with a nice ring and a white dress.'

Ollie was silent.

'Every man has a big payday,' Steve added. 'It's just that some of them haven't even figured out what it is yet.'

'So what's mine?' said Ollie finally.

'I don't think you know yet. A man who drinks and gambles the way you did hasn't found his payday, but it's not that Katie bird, I'll tell you that for nothing.'

Steve pulled the Astra up outside 12 Baslow Road. It was a row of modest 1950s bungalows, all of them whitewashed, most of them with neatly trimmed but small gardens in front of them. The next road up had views of the sea, but not Baslow Road; you could smell the sea, but not quite see it. A place to retire for people who had almost made it, but not quite, thought Steve as he climbed out of the car and walked through the gate.

Ganju Rai was the first of Ollie's two suggestions. A 31-year-old Gurkha, Ganju had served for eight years in C Company, in the 2nd Battalion of the Parachute Regiment, which is primarily staffed by Gurkhas. Ollie had got to know him when the Household Cavalry had been on a joint mission with C Company in Kosovo. Ganju's brother Lachniman had been killed out there, when C Company had stormed a position held by the remnants of Milosevic's army. Ollie had been impressed at the time by the dedication and bravery of the men. Back in his tiny home village of Lamjung in Nepal, Lachniman had left behind his wife Kani, his son Gurung, and his daughter Israni. Kani was now struggling to bring up the family on the miserable pension the army paid her. It was far less than the British soldiers, or their widows, received, and even that wasn't very generous. It was a point that rankled with the Gurkhas as much as it did with the soldiers they fought alongside. Soldiers didn't ask for much, and they didn't object to dying if they had to, but they did like to get paid.

Even in the SAS, reflected Steve as he rang the bell, the men had nothing but respect for the Gurkhas. The name derived from the ancient Nepalese city state of Gorkha. The British in India had fought a long and bitter war with Gorkha along the frontier and by the time a peace treaty was signed in 1816, the Gurkha soldiers were allowed to sign up for the East India Company's army. After India became independent in 1947, the four Gurkha brigades were transferred to the British Army. They'd served it with uncompromising bravery and distinction ever since. 'Better to die than be a coward,' was the Gurkha motto, recalled Steve. And just about every man of them he'd ever met took that literally. Maybe too literally.

He'd seen men from the Gurkha brigades storm positions that even the SAS would have regarded as impregnable. So when Ollie suggested signing up Ganju for the mission, Steve hadn't disagreed. In truth, if there was one type of soldier he'd want alongside out in Afghanistan, it would be a Gurkha.

The only problem would be getting him on board. Gurkhas fought for their regiment and their flag. They didn't fight for money. Among the thousands of private military contractors that had poured into Afghanistan and Iraq in the last few years, there were hundreds of South Africans, Argentinians, Poles, and Russians. There were men from every dark corner of the world. But despite their formidable fighting skills, there were hardly any Gurkhas. They fought for honour, and there wasn't much of that to be found escorting oil rigs into Basra or protecting a bunch of pampered United Nations busybodies in Kabul.

'Talk to his grandfather,' said Ollie, as they rang the bell. 'If we can win the old man over, then Ganju will sign up.'

The door was opened by a man who, to Steve, looked to be at least eighty. In fact, Gaje Rai was eighty-three. Gaje had served with the 9th Gorkha Rifles, a unit that traced its history back to 1817. It had fought in the Anglo-Sikh war, and had first seen action in Europe during the First World War. Gaje had fought his way through the Second World War in both North Africa and Italy.

'Come inside, come inside,' said Gaje politely.

The house was small, just two bedrooms and a sitting room and kitchen, but it was immaculately tidy. Tea had already been laid out on the small table next to the gas fire: ham sandwiches, a plate of Jaffa cakes, and a pot of tea.

'You keeping well?' said Ganju, greeting Ollie warmly.

'Well enough.'

He wasn't a big man, no more than five feet seven, but Steve noted at once that like all Gurkhas he had presence. So, too, did his grandfather; he looked as if he might have been an inch taller when he was in his prime but had started to shrink as he moved through his seventies. Together, they filled the tiny room; you felt they were ready to burst out of the place.

'How is Kani doing?' Ollie asked Ganju.

'She's OK . . .'

Steve was watching him as he answered, and he could tell at once that 'OK' wasn't really the word to describe how his sister-in-law was surviving. Dignity was everything to a Gurkha, so he wouldn't dream of disputing the point, but if they wanted to sign Ganju up, that was his weak point. The man could look after himself, but it wasn't going to be so easy to look after his brother's wife and children. That would take money, and they were probably the only people likely to offer him anything more than a few hundred quid a week.

Steve started to explain why they were there, aware of the silence greeting him as he ran through the mission.

'How can a soldier make three million legitimately?' asked Gaje when he'd finished.

The question was direct, piercing.

'Trust me, he can,' said Steve flatly.

'It's too much money.'

'As somebody once said, you can't be too thin or too rich.'

'But you can be too dead,' said Ganju.

Steve was silent.

'My brother's wife needs me,' said Ganju quietly. 'She's already lost her husband and the father of her children and she's relying on me for support. For myself, I don't mind, but if my name's on a bullet, she has nothing.'

'Like I said, it's soldiering,' Steve said. 'I could tell you there weren't any risks, but I'd be lying, and that's no use to anyone.'

'But three million . . .' said Ganju.

The sentence trailed off as he thought about it.

'You'll have my answer by tomorrow.'

It was another two hours' drive up towards Woking. David lived in a modern, three-bedroomed house in the village of Worpledon, about five miles from the centre of the town.

'No special drill needed with David,' said Ollie as he climbed out of the car. 'This bloke needs money the way an alcoholic needs a drink. He's got more overheads than Chelsea Football Club.'

Along the drive up from Eastbourne, Steve and Ollie had discussed their chances of getting Ganju on to the team.

They needed him, Steve knew that. Ten white blokes in Kabul were going to stick out like a group of nuns on the terraces at Millwall on a Saturday afternoon. They could use scouts, but at some point they were going to need a man who could blend in. That was Ganju. There wasn't anyone else. Ollie seemed confident enough; the man needed the money, and he was up for the adventure, but Steve wasn't so sure. In his experience, mercenaries were men without any responsibilities, and Ganju had plenty.

He wasn't so sure about Ollie's second choice either, for the same reason. From the brief rundown Ollie had given him, he sounded like a fine soldier. Now thirty-eight, David Mallet had served eighteen years in the army. He'd been with the Irish Guards, a regiment that had originally recruited in Ireland and in the Irish districts of the larger British cities. Now it mainly drew its officers from the big Catholic public schools, such as Ampleforth and Stonyhurst. Ollie himself had been at Sherborne – a school, he liked to point out, that counted no fewer than five Victoria Cross holders among its old boys – while David had been at Stonyhurst. He was a few years older than Ollie, but they had got to know each other on the old boys' rugby circuit.

'Good chap,' said Ollie on the drive. 'But he's got a rough hand to play right now.'

'How rough?' asked Steve.

'He's got two kids from his first marriage, but he split up with Laura three years ago,' Ollie replied. 'Now his new wife, Sandy, is having twins. And I don't think the guy has any idea how he's going to pay for all of them.'

The door was opened by an attractive-looking blonde woman. About thirty-five, Steve judged, with soft blue eyes, creamy white skin, and a figure that would have been a lot more shapely if it wasn't for the massive bump in her stomach. There was a buggy in the hallway, and the smell of something tasty cooking in the kitchen. 'I'll get David,' she said quickly.

After introducing Steve, they walked to the village pub. Life had, indeed, dealt David a rough hand, Steve decided, as the guy unburdened himself over a pint. His ex-wife was pressing him for more alimony, his eldest kid had just started his first term at Stonyhurst, and the fees were fourteen grand a year even for day boys. Since he had left the Irish Guards four years ago, he'd done a year in Iraq, commanding some of the convoys. Then he'd joined up with one of the big American PMCs but hadn't been able to handle all the politics. After that, he'd set up his own PMC with three other former Guards officers. But, as Steve well knew, it was hard to get a business like that started. You needed capital to buy all the kit and get the men on the ground, and you had to spend it all before the cash started rolling in. Guys went into the industry thinking they only needed military expertise, then discovered they needed to know how to run a business as well. And if they didn't learn fast, they didn't survive.

It sounded like David had learned that the hard way.

His last job had been three months' bodyguarding on the Algerian oil rigs and, as Steve knew from the guys who did it, that was very close to the bottom of the barrel. You'd spend six weeks straight out on an oil rig, in charge of a crew of Moroccans who did nothing but smoke the strongest, cheapest tobacco you ever smelt and watch German porn DVDs. They weren't a bad bunch of boys, and there were hardly ever any attacks to worry about, but within three days your head was numb with boredom and there were still another five and a half weeks to go. After that, you got ten days back at home before they shipped you out there again.

A man working the Algerian rigs was ready for change, reckoned Steve. No matter how desperate the odds.

'Blimey, twins,' said David, burying his face in his hands. 'You should have seen me when we went in for the scan. I'm glancing up at the bloody screen, and Sandy and the scan girl are all going ahhhhh, it's a real baby, and all that rubbish women go in for, and I'm sitting there thinking, when can we get out of here? And then I look up, and see what looks suspiciously like two mad tadpoles, and at first I'm just kidding around, saying it looks like twins. And then she says, that's right, it is twins. Bloody hell! I practically fell out of my chair.' He took a long pull on his pint. 'Of course, Sandy was thrilled about it. Then I told Laura, and the mad cow practically bit my ear off. She's not compromising on what she spends on Harry and Emily, if I want to start another family . . .'

Jesus, thought Steve. This guy needs to get out to Afghanistan just to get some peace and quiet.

'I think we're the answer to all your problems,' said Ollie.

For the first time since they'd sat down, David seemed to cheer up. The pub was a quiet, cosy place, with oak beams, a real fire in the hearth, and a landlord who greeted David by his first name. He was a muscular, fit man, with jet-black hair cropped close to his head, and the rugged build of a rugby player. His blue eyes were set deep into his face, and even though his nose had one break in it, it was straight and thick.

'Somebody has to be,' said David. 'Because I sure as hell don't know what I'm going to do otherwise.'

Steve started to explain the mission with words that were beginning to feel well rehearsed. He could see David's jaw slackening as he listened. It was like telling a man on death row you'd just found a crucial piece of new evidence. At the end, David drained his pint.

'One favour,' he said, 'and I'm in.'

'Just ask,' said Steve.

'We need to go back and tell Sandy that we're doing something completely safe, like escorting some oil rigging out into the Gulf,' said David. 'If she knows we're in Afghanistan, she's going to worry herself sick. I don't want to put her through that. The pregnancy has already been rough on her.'

Ollie punched Steve playfully on the shoulder. 'This is your man,' he said. 'Steve's been telling fibs to girls ever since he persuaded Kylie or Chlöe or whoever to play doctors and nurses with him back in Bromley Juniors. He's got it down to a fine art by now.'

'Thanks, mate,' said Steve. 'I'll do the same for you one day.'

He finished off his drink, and grabbed the car keys. I'm not sure I like this, he thought to himself. We need ghosts and corpses. Men without hope, or expectations, or responsibilities. The living dead. Because where we're going, that's the kind of bastards we're going to be up against.

Seven

STEVE WAS ENJOYING ANOTHER breakfast at the Starlight Cafe when Ollie sat down next to him. It was just after eight in the morning. They had a little over seventy hours left to play with before they had to catch a plane to Afghanistan.

Not much chance of a decent breakfast out there.

'We've got six men,' said Ollie. 'Ganju called. He's in.'

'Which means we need four more,' said Steve.

There was a newspaper on the table opposite, with pictures of two young guys from the Mercian Regiment who'd lost their lives in Helmand yesterday. There were so many casualties out in Afghanistan right now that Steve didn't want to read about them. He didn't even want to flick through the pages, fearful of what he might find. They might be someone he knew. They'd certainly be someone who was just like the guys he knew.

And one of these days it might even be me, he thought.

Ollie pulled out a notepad and jotted down a series of names. 'The way I see it is this,' he said. 'We've got Jeff to cover transportation, and Ganju to cover camouflage. David can take care of logistics, planning and tactics, and Chris will give us stealth and battlefield experience. We've still got boxes to tick, however. We need explosives capability, long-range sniping, and communications.'

'We'll improvise on the ground,' said Steve.

'Improvising is no bloody use if you haven't got the right men in place,' said Ollie.

Steve shrugged. I'm not a planner, he thought, never have been. Maybe that's why I joined the regiment. We go in hard and fast, maximum speed, maximum aggression, and then we run like hell. The Ruperts can take care of the planning. They learn all that stuff at Sandhurst.

'Who've you got?' he asked.

'I think I know the man.'

Within half an hour they'd polished off their breakfast and were heading down towards Fulham to meet up with Roddy Smarden. At twenty-seven, Roddy was another Sherborne old boy. He'd gone straight from school to Sandhurst, then into the Household Cavalry, but his speciality had always been communications and signalling. He'd left two years ago. One year had been spent with a PMC, including two three-month tours in Iraq, then three months in the company press office. For the last six months he'd been setting up 'The Big Adventure Ski Company' which, as its name suggested, took mainly City boys on black runs down some of the most difficult slopes in the world. One guy had suffered brain damage during a nasty run in Norway, which had received plenty of coverage in the press; as a result, business had slowed to a trickle.

Roddy was sitting in a cafe just past the cinema about halfway down the Fulham Road, a big latte and a pair of cinnamon rolls in front of him. He was wearing red jeans, a blue and white striped rugby jersey, and a pair of Police sunglasses, tipped up on his forehead. A good-looking enough guy, reckoned Steve. Brown hair, tanned skin, blue eyes, and a solid build: there was, no doubt, always a chalet girl ready to climb into bed with him. But there was no strength to the man, no substance; you could blow him away with a simple gust of wind, never mind an AK-47.

'You up for an adventure, then?' said Ollie, after they'd made the introductions.

'Damn right I am, old man,' said Roddy. 'That nasty incident out in Norway has done for us, I'm afraid. Anyway, it's too hot for skiing.'

'We're going to Afghanistan.' said Ollie.

'Right oh,' said Roddy cheerfully. 'Splendid. Not much chance of any skiing, but I'm sure we'll find some way to amuse ourselves.'

'Black op,' said Steve.

'The blacker the better,' said Roddy. 'That's how I like it.' He chortled so much he blew some of the froth from the top of his latte.

Christ, thought Steve. This bloke is a danger to the planet. If the Taliban don't blow him to pieces, I might be forced to do it myself.

After leaving Roddy in the coffee bar, Steve and Ollie walked in silence along the Fulham Road, in the direction of the river. It was just after eleven in the morning, and they were due to meet the next man on their list at twelve over in Hammersmith.

'So that makes seven of us,' said Ollie.

'Does it?'

'Roddy larks around, but he's a good man.'

Steve remained silent.

'You don't like him, do you?'

'Well, put it this way, I'm glad to see that whoever came up with the phrase "total prat" wasn't wasting his time,' said Steve.

'He can do a job,' said Ollie. 'He's been through one of the best regiments in the whole bloody army, he knows his stuff, and he can make the comms kit work.'

'He's a tosser.'

'I say he's in.'

'And I don't fucking want him.'

Ollie stopped in the street. 'If we're putting together this bloody mission, then I get to choose the men just the same as you do,' he growled. 'And if you don't like it, I suggest you bugger off to Kabul by yourself.'

For a moment, Steve was ready to lash out. He could feel a surge of anger rippling through him. He'd never been able to stand being pushed around by the Ruperts. It was one of the reasons why he hadn't been able to stick the regular army, and the SAS hadn't been much better. His fists were curling into a ball, and he could feel his shoulder muscles stretching, ready to throw a punch.

He took a deep breath. Cool it, he warned himself. This is the big payday, the one you've been planning for years. This is the dealership.

'OK,' he said, a smile suddenly flashing across his face as he relaxed inside. 'I reckon every unit needs some cannon fodder. And we've got Roddy.'

'Good.'

'But if his nappy needs changing, then that's your job.'

Steve hailed a taxi and told the driver to take them up to Hammersmith. They were meeting in a pub on King Street, a dull strip of chain shops that headed due west from the Broadway. Ian Murphy was the man Bruce Dudley had recommended. He had a build that was half footballer, half bricklayer: short and round, with a low centre of gravity, and thick, bruising muscles. He had short brown hair that looked as if might turn orange if it was left out in the sun, and his face was marked with freckles. His skin was white and blotchy, and his nose seemed to be squashed into the centre of his face as if somebody had slapped it on in a hurry. Steve had seen plenty of ugly blokes in the army, but Ian, well, even his mum must have been tempted to close her eyes when she looked at him.

'Make mine a pint of Guinness,' said Ian as Ollie offered to get a round of drinks in.

'So how do you know Bruce?' asked Steve.

'From the circuit,' said Ian casually.

The circuit was the term used by former soldiers – special forces men, mostly, but also regular army – to describe the network of security firms that hired men by the day or the week to do the jobs that most ordinary mortals would have considered far too dangerous to contemplate.

'Which jobs?'

'A couple in Iraq, a couple in Africa,' said Ian. 'Bruce uses me as a specialist. For my particular skill.'

Ollie returned with a pint of Guinness and two bottles of Czech lager.

'Which is?' Steve asked.

'I'm a bomb-maker,' Ian said casually. 'Like, say you needed a firebomb. Well, you'd get some old-fashioned soap suds, the flakes your gran used to use. Then you mix it up with some petrol, and you roll it up into little gooey balls. The buggers will stick to anything. And they burn like hell.'

'We take our own kit,' said Steve.

'But you need to be able to make your own bombs,' said

Ian. 'A military unit that can't mix up its own explosives is like a chef who can't make his own mayonnaise. It's a bit pathetic if you have to start searching around for a jar of Hellmann's before you can start cooking.'

Steve nodded. He liked Ian already.

In the Regiment, they always believed in relying on total self-sufficiency. They could feed themselves off the land if they needed to. And they could arm themselves as well. That was what made them an effective fighting force. They relied on nobody but themselves.

'So what regiment were you?' asked Ollie after Steve had explained the mission.

'One of the Ulster ones,' said Ian. 'I'm from Derry.'

'And you can fly on Saturday?' asked Steve.

Ian nodded.

'Then you're on the team,' said Ollie.

'I'll pack some suntan lotion,' said Ian. 'Celtic skin, you see. Not built for Kabul in the summer.'

Steve grinned. 'And if you need to test one of your bombs, we've got a bloke called Roddy who'd be perfect for lighting the blue touchpaper.'

'Not Roddy Smarden?' said Ian. 'Or rather, Woddy the Wanker?'

Steve glanced at Ollie, and he could see his skin turning slightly red, but whether he was embarrassed or angry he couldn't tell.

'That sounds like the guy,' Steve said. 'You know him?'

Ian shook his head. 'I've heard of him, though. Bloody dangerous bloke, even without a gun in his hand, from what I hear. Could make you die laughing . . .'

Eight

'THIRTY HOURS TO GO, AND we still need two more men,' said Steve, looking up at Ollie.

He put the plane tickets down on the table. There were ten of them for the British Airways flight leaving for Istanbul at ten thirty tomorrow morning, landing there at four thirty local time. There were no direct commercial flights from London to Afghanistan, so they were flying to Turkey first, then connecting with an Ariana Airlines flight to Kabul.

Steve pushed aside his bacon, sausages and eggs. They were getting to be regulars at the Starlight Cafe; at this rate, the old hag who wielded the frying pan would start calling them 'pet' and offering them an extra sausage.

'I called a couple of guys,' said Ollie. 'But it's bloody short notice.'

Steve knew what he meant.

They'd done well rounding up eight men in the time available, even if one of them was Roddy. But they'd made all the easy hires.

'Ian called me with the details of a guy called Dan,' he said. 'An Aussie. Ex-special forces, and he reckons he might be up for it.'

'Then let's go,' said Ollie. 'We haven't much time.'

Dan Coleman had been kipping down on a mate's floor in a flat out in Acton. It was two weeks since he'd touched down in London, and most of his kit was still in a rucksack. 'Us Aussies haven't been able to afford Earl's Court since around nineteen eighty-three,' he said when he met Steve and Ollie at a Starbucks on Acton High Street at eleven that morning. 'So we've all moved out to Acton. And the way things are going we'll be out in bloody Osterley soon.'

He was a big man, at least six two, with broad shoulders, and a jaw so solid it looked as if it had been carved out of a piece of granite. He had dirty blond hair, and a rugged grin. His hands were massive, like pieces of wood, but he held himself gracefully. About once a year, at most, Steve met a guy he wouldn't want to get into a fight with. And Dan was one of them.

'I heard you'd been in the Aussie Army,' said Steve.

'That's right, mate,' said Dan, tucking into the first of two chocolate muffins he'd ordered for himself. 'SASR for five years.'

Steve knew a bit about the Special Air Services Regiment, as the special forces unit of the Australian Army was known. The SAS had been on joint training exercises with them, and had learned to respect the fighting determination of the Australians. The SASR had been formed in 1957, directly modelled on the British SAS. Typically it operated with four-man units, concentrating on behind-the-lines reconnaissance and sabotage and on counter-terrorism and hostage rescue. It was organised into three elite 'sabre squadrons', and had first been put into action alongside the British in the Malaya campaign of the 1950s. They fought with distinction in Vietnam, alongside the American forces. Since then, they'd been involved in covert wars close to Australia's borders in the Philippines and Indonesia, and formed the main Australian contribution to the wars in both Iraq and Afghanistan. Back in Hereford, they were considered at least the equal of the British special forces.

Which means he's good enough for me, thought Steve.

'What were you in the SASR?' he asked.

'An operator.'

From what Steve knew of it, all the men in the SASR were given basic special forces training but the majority of them specialised in support functions, such as transport, signalling, or munitions. A small minority were referred to as 'beret-qualified', on account of the fact that they were allowed to wear the regiment's traditional sand-coloured beret. They were known as the 'operators' and there were only about eighty in each of the three sabre squadrons, while the support staff were known as 'blackhats' because of the dark blue berets they were issued.

'You've been in Afghanistan?'

'Two years,' said Dan. 'Bloody rathole of a place it is as well.'

'So what are you doing in London?' said Ollie.

'Watching your boys getting a bruising at the cricket,' said Dan.

Ollie stiffened.

'Don't get him started,' Steve said. 'Ollie's bloody touchy when it comes to the English cricket team.' He looked at Dan. 'Would you be willing to go back to Afghanistan?'

'And we get to mallet the Taliban?'

Interesting, thought Steve. He glanced across at Ollie to see if he'd noticed. Dan was the first man to mention fighting the Taliban. He hadn't focused on the money, he'd focused on the enemy.

Maybe it wasn't over for him. Not yet anyway.

He'd known guys like that in the Regiment. For years they nursed grievances against the opponents they'd fought. There were men who still couldn't talk to an Irishman after the campaigns along the Ulster border territory. And if they met an Iraqi or a Kosovan, they might well lose it. The shrinks with all their post-combat stress bollocks told you to clear your head and move on. But for some guys, Steve knew well enough, it wasn't that easy. They'd seen their mates die on the battlefield, good men usually, who didn't deserve to have their life cut off in their prime. They'd been to see their wives and their mums to tell them what had happened, because that was the least you owed your mates, and they'd felt their hot tears on their shoulders. They'd told little kids they wouldn't be seeing their dads again. After that, it wasn't always so easy to move on. They didn't have that kind of forgiveness within them, just couldn't find it. And frankly, who could blame them?

'The ragheads will take a malleting, don't worry about that.'

'They fucking deserve it,' said Dan sharply. He wiped away a few chocolate crumbs from his mouth with the back of his massive fist. 'Animals.'

'So how come you left?' asked Ollie, leaning forward.

It was mid-morning, on a Friday, and there weren't many people in Starbucks. Just the local mums out with their buggies, and they weren't paying any attention to the three guys sitting by the window looking out on to the High Street.

'When do we leave?' asked Dan.

'Tomorrow, from Heathrow,' said Steve, wondering why

Dan had ignored the question, but he didn't have time to worry about that now. 'You think you can make it?'

Dan nodded. There was a smile on his lips. And Steve reckoned it was the thought of getting a Taliban soldier back in the sights of his gun.

'One condition,' said Ollie, standing up and shaking Dan firmly by the hand. 'You lay off our cricket team, and we won't make any sheep shagging jokes.'

Dan grinned. 'I think we're going to get along just fine.'

The landlord of the Three Crowns clearly hadn't heard of the smoking ban. Or if he had, he'd decided to ignore it. Along with most of his customers.

It was a dingy, dark pub in the network of tiny streets behind King's Cross and St Pancras stations running up towards Camden. Steve was familiar with this part of town. Lots of the small security firms that made up the circuit were based in offices around here. It was cheap, there were lock-ups nearby if you needed to stash some kit, there was good transport close at hand, and plenty of cheap hotels where you could doss down for a few days.

It had something else as well, reflected Steve. Anonymity. A man could slip right into the shadows in this part of London, which was where many of the guys on the circuit preferred to live.

Jock Livingstone had been freelancing for about five years now. Steve had never worked alongside him, but from what he'd heard, he was a decent enough bloke. They had one more berth to fill, and less than twenty-four hours to find a man for it. It hadn't been easy. Which left them with Jock.

Steve wasn't sure how old he was. Thirty-two, thirty-three

maybe. He'd served with the King's Own Scottish Borderers, a regiment that could trace its history all the way back to before the Battle of Culloden. It had been amalgamated with the Royal Scots in 2004. Jock hadn't served with any great distinction, not the way Steve heard it; he was a plodder who, even by the admittedly high standards of the Scottish infantry, spent his time whingeing and bellyaching. But he had come into his own when he quit the army and went to work for the PMCs. Some guys were like that, reflected Steve; they were better as freelancers than they were in the regular forces.

He was sitting in the corner, by himself, with a pint in front of him, and a packet of twenty Rothmans. He was a dark, craggy man, with the build of a serious drinker: thin and wiry and muscular, with drooping eyes and blotchy red skin. He looked as if the bulk of his daily intake of calories came out of a bottle, and the rest from a pub microwave. He glanced at Steve, but there was a blank look in his eyes.

'I'll have a Coke,' said Steve, when Ollie asked him what he wanted to drink.

Steve introduced himself, and Jock quickly added a pint of lager and a vodka chaser to Ollie's round even though the drinks in front of him were still half full.

'There's some money to be made out in Afghanistan, you say,' said Jock, thanking Ollie for the drinks, and draining the last of the pint that was already on the table.

He took a cigarette from his packet and lit up, creating a small cloud of smoke around his table. He smelt of booze and sweat, noticed Steve. Not that he minded about that. He was looking for men who knew how to fight, not guys who were studying the GQ grooming catalogue. If you could hold a knife, and shoot straight, it didn't matter what you looked like. But a drunk – that was different. A drunk was no use to anyone.

'What happened to you, Jock?' he asked, looking through the cigarette smoke into Jock's eyes.

'I'm on leave, man. I'm just having a few drinks, that's all.'

'A few drinks . . .' Steve gestured to the empty glasses on the table. It was still only three in the afternoon and the man was clearly trying to empty out a whole brewery.

'What is this, a bloody Salvation Army job?' snarled Jock. 'If you're on some kind of church mission, then you've got the wrong man. If it's a fighting job, then I'm the bloke you need.'

His eyes were runny and sad, but it wasn't the drink that was doing that to him, judged Steve. Like most Scotsmen, he was an angry drinker. It was the Irish blokes who started turning miserable on you once they got a few beers in their belly; the Scots just turned vicious.

'I said, what the hell happened?'

Jock took a hit on the vodka, lit another Rothmans, then started to talk. 'It was like this, you see, boys. I was out in Iraq back in February, doing a three-month tour for Palmerston. Eight of us, doing convoys mostly, along the highway that runs north out of Baghdad towards Kirkuk.'

'The Highway of Hell,' said Ollie.

'That's the bastard,' said Jock grumpily. 'It was a wages run, up to one of the American forward operating bases. We got into a fire fight with some insurgents. I reckon it was a set-up. They had a tip-off from one of the Iraqis that we were on that road, in that van, and they knew how much cash we had, because they were waiting for us. At least thirty of them.'

'But you must have fought,' said Ollie.

There was a simple rule among all the PMCs operating in Iraq. Don't get taken alive. It's far, far better to die with your boots on and an AK-47 in your hand.

'Two of us were shot in the fire fight,' continued Jock. 'Six of us were blindfolded, had plasti-cuffs snapped on us, and were bundled into a van. We were taken to some kind of cell. They nicked the money, of course. Then they put us up for ransom. A couple of days passed, then the executions started. One night they made us all line up, and they put out these six red-hot coals from the brazier. They made each one of us pick up a bloody coal in our right hand. First man to drop his gets his bloody head chopped off . . .'

At first Steve though he was joking. Then Jock held up the palm of his right hand, and Steve saw the burn mark on his skin.

Jock swallowed half his pint to steady himself.

'After about forty seconds, Ken dropped his,' said Jock. 'Ken Ashton. Nice bloke. His girlfriend Kelly had just had a kid, so they called him Keith just to stick with the Ks. The bastards dragged him away, tied his hands, set up a camera so they could broadcast the whole thing over the internet, got out the biggest fucker of a sword you've ever seen, then made him kneel down. Have you ever seen a man get his head chopped off?'

'It's not the kind of thing you see every day,' said Steve. 'Not even in Bromley.'

'Yeah, well, you ever get invited to a beheading, give it a miss,' said Jock. 'They yank the guy's head back hard, just to stiffen up all the neck muscles, then the sword smashes into the neck, but it isn't a clean kill. You can hear the metal crunching into the bone . . .'

Jock grabbed his pint and gulped more beer.

'Next night it was Pete,' he continued. 'Same routine, the hot coals. After that, we didn't feel like sitting around waiting until the rest of us had our turn. It was kill or be killed, simple as that. So we worked out our moves, waiting until we had our coals in our hands, then turned on the blokes, and let them have it.'

Jock chuckled to himself, and torched up another Rothman.

'Christ,' muttered Ollie.

'I'm OK now,' said Jock. 'The doctor says the hand is healing up. I'll have some bad scarring but I can live with that.'

'And you don't mind going back into combat?' said Ollie.

Jock grabbed the vodka. His hand was shaking, noticed Steve, but he paused before putting the glass to his lips.

'I need a job,' he said. 'Hair of the dog, and all that. It's like the way the best cure for a bad hangover is a double vodka, so I reckon the best cure for an experience like that is to get straight back on to the front line.'

Steve looked straight at Jock. 'You're in no state, pal,' he said tersely. 'Too much booze—'

'A man needs a second chance,' said Ollie, glancing angrily at Steve.

'There's only one rehabilitation slot on this job,' snarled Steve. 'And you've already taken it.'

He could see Ollie was stung by the remark.

Jock staggered uncertainly to his feet. 'I bloody need a job,' he said. His eyes were watery.

'I'm sorry, we need men we can rely on, you know that.'

Jock reached out and his hand rested on Steve's shoulder. His breath stank of stale beer. 'Listen, you bastard, I fucking—'

Ollie stepped behind him and took Jock's hand away. 'Leave it,' he said firmly.

He went to the barman and handed him a tenner. 'Keep this man in drinks,' he said.

Then Ollie looked at Steve and nodded, and the two men left the pub. They remained silent as they walked swiftly back in the direction of the Euston Road. The afternoon was drawing in, and they were getting close to the flocks of summer tourists searching for the museums when their silence was interrupted by Ollie's mobile going off. He flipped open the phone, spoke for just a couple of minutes, then said goodbye and snapped it shut.

'We're back down to eight men,' he said, looking at Steve.

'Christ, what now?'

'I called a mate of mine, Shane Fallows, an officer in the Royal Tasmanians,' said Ollie. 'He checked Dan out for me . . .' Ollie fell silent.

'And?' prompted Steve.

'He was court-martialled while he was out in Afghanistan for shooting two innocent children,' he said. 'He spent a year in a military jail, and now he's out on parole. One of the conditions is that he doesn't go back to the country.'

Steve ground his fists together. 'Sod it,' he muttered. Then he laughed, but it was threaded with anger. 'Maybe we should go back to Jock and get ourselves a drink. I certainly need one.'

Nine

STEVE AND OLLIE TOOK A cab to Paddington. It was after four o'clock and they were still two men short.

Sod it, thought Steve to himself. If we need to, we'll do this job with eight men. I'm not letting this one go.

They'd called Dan and left a message on his mobile telling him he was off the team. Right afterwards, Bruce called with another suggestion. A kid called Nick Thomas.

'A Welsh guy?' said Ollie, as they sat in the back of the cab.

'Bengali, mate,' said Steve drily. 'He's called Nick Thomas and we're meeting him off the Swansea train that arrives at Paddington at four seventeen, so yes, I'm only guessing here, but there's a possibility he might be a Welshie.'

'What do we know about him?'

Steve only had the sketchiest details from Bruce. Nick was a twenty-year-old from Swansea. He'd spent a couple of years in the Territorials but had never been a full-time soldier. He'd written to DEF a couple of times saying he wanted to sign up for a PMC, and Bruce had called him this morning to say that if he could get himself on a train to London and bring his passport with him, there were a couple of guys he could meet. He couldn't promise anything but . . .

'But he must be bloody crazy,' said Ollie. 'A kid with no proper training? Flying straight out to Afghanistan?'

Steve nodded. Ollie had a point. If Bruce hadn't already told the kid to get the train to London, Steve wouldn't have bothered to see him.

'I'd rather take the old drunk,' said Ollie.

And so, in truth, would I, reflected Steve. If nothing else, he might be able to hold a gun, at least when his hands stopped shaking. All the PMCs were receiving applications from young guys in towns like Swansea and Doncaster and Portsmouth. They'd read their Andy McNab books, and they reckoned making a bit of fast cash, and playing with some heavy-duty kit, sounded like a lot more fun than studying golf course management or whatever it was most of them did when they got shipped off to university. It would certainly impress the girls down at Weatherspoon's on a Friday night.

'We'll just talk to the kid,' said Steve.

Nick was waiting for them when they arrived at the station. He was a tall guy, at least six feet, with orange-brown hair, cut close to his head, and ears that stuck out so much that even Prince Charles might have felt embarrassed by them. His green eyes were solid enough, and he had enough muscle on him to suggest that he worked out in the gym regularly, but his skin was pale even though it was the height of summer, and, standing at the head of the platform, in his jeans and sweatshirt and with a rucksack on his back, he looked completely lost.

'Please look after this bear,' said Ollie.

'What?'

'He should have a tag on him, just like in the kids' story.'

Steve laughed. 'Do you think you can get any marmalade for him out in Kabul?'

They went to the Paddington Hilton directly behind the station. It had been built as the Great Western Hotel but had been sucked up by the chain a few years ago and had lost much of its charm. Steve had had a drink here ten years ago with his uncle Ken when he was catching the train down to Hereford for his SAS selection week, and he could still remember the old guy's words of encouragement, and his resentment that his own father was too dismissive of the Regiment and everything it stood for even to come and see him off.

'Do you have any idea what we do?' Steve asked Nick after ordering three coffees.

Steve could see how nervous the boy was but he felt no sympathy for him. We were all babies once, he thought to himself. We all do stupid things. I'm just not about to help him, that's all.

'It's a PMC,' said Nick. 'You fight.' He spoke in the lilting, fresh voice of the Welsh valleys.

'We're off to Afghanistan in the morning,' said Ollie. 'Ten men in the unit.'

Nick smiled nervously. 'I brought my passport.'

'Change of socks?' said Steve.

'My mum washed two pairs . . .'

Steve and Ollie caught each other's eyes and cracked into a peel of laughter. Nick's ears started to turn a brighter shade of crimson.

'Listen, we've no time for babysitting,' said Ollie. 'I don't question your commitment, but this is no place for beginners. Join the real army, do ten years square-bashing, figure out which end of a rifle is which, then maybe you'll be ready.'

Steve stood up and shook his hand. He liked the boy, but

there was no way he was taking him to Afghanistan with him.

But Nick was holding his hand, his grip surprisingly vigorous and strong.

'I'm the best shot you ever saw,' he said.

Steve grinned. 'I was SAS, mate. I've seen a lot of good shots.'

'Not like me.'

'We have to go,' said Ollie stiffly.

'I can prove it.'

'Where?' said Steve. 'Down at the computer game arcades?'

'Just one shot.'

Steve looked at Ollie. Neither man moved.

'You really think you're the best we've ever seen?' said Ollie.

He was still a member of the Stock Exchange Shooting Club over in Moorgate from his time in the City, and that was only twenty minutes away on the Central Line. The club had been running for over a century, a relic of the days when most stockbrokers were former army men, and many of them remained affiliated to their regiments.

Nick was largely silent on the way. Steve managed to find out he was an only child, had no idea who his dad was, and grew up with his mum Sandra on a council estate on the outskirts of Swansea. Sandra worked on the check-out at the local B&Q, the only job she'd ever had, and there had never been more money around than they needed to get by. Nick supported Liverpool at the football and, of course, Wales at the rugby. Whether he had a girlfriend, Steve couldn't find out; with ears like that, he suspected not. Even in Swansea, the girls must draw the line somewhere, and poor old Nick was on the wrong side of it.

The rifle club had a fifty-metre range. A real sniper could of course put a shot straight through a target at a thousand metres or more, but with a low-calibre weapon, fifty metres was more than enough to make an accurate assessment of a man's abilities. They handed Nick a .22 target rifle. A series of black and white concentric circles marked out the target.

'OK,' said Steve. 'Let's see what you can do.'

He noticed the way Nick handled the weapon. He was totally at ease with it, the way some guys are with a football, others with a car, or a woman. He held it firmly in his hand, assessing its weight and balance, before raising it to his shoulder. He paused for a second, shifting his feet, letting the rifle find its own position just below the neck, then looked through its sights. There were no telescopic rangefinders, just an old-fashioned metal sight at the tip of the gun's barrel. Nick squinted, took a breath, then took a single, relaxed shot.

Bullseye. And not just any bullseye, noted Steve. The shot was dead on centre. Not so much as a millimetre out.

And Nick repeated that shot again and again and again.

Steve glanced at Ollie. He could tell exactly what he was thinking. The same thing that was going through his mind. The boy can shoot. It was not just a talent. In this case, it was a gift.

'OK,' Steve said tersely. 'You're in.'

Nick grinned. 'I won't let you down.'

'We'll see you at Heathrow tomorrow,' said Ollie. 'Get a good night's kip.'

'And some clean socks,' said Steve.

Steve unwrapped the takeaway curry cartons. 'Jesus, what a pair of losers we are,' he said to Ollie. 'Our last night of freedom before we get shipped off to Kabul to face God knows what and we're staying in with a takeaway curry and watching Jonathan Ross on the telly.'

Ollie had had some kind of bust-up with Katie – he didn't seem to want to go into the details. She'd left work earlier this afternoon and gone off to spend the weekend in the country with her parents, which meant that Ollie didn't have anywhere to sleep. So Steve had offered him the spare bed in Dudley's Battersea apartment. They were still one man short for this job and he couldn't risk losing Ollie now; the idiot was besotted with Katie and, left to his own moronic devices, he was more than capable of running off after her and missing his flight.

Ollie was chewing on his food. He ate methodically, noted Steve, the same way he did everything.

'People keep using the words "Bruce Dudley" and "suicide missions" in the same sentence,' said Ollie. 'It's making me uneasy. And so is his reputation.'

'Which is?'

'A mean Scottish bastard who takes on the jobs that no one else wants because they pay well,' said Ollie. 'But he puts his men's lives at risk.'

'Listen, Bruce is a hard bastard, I'll admit that, and if he got put up in a courtroom for pushing his men too hard, I guess he'd be found guilty of that as well,' said Steve. 'But he's also the finest soldier and the finest judge of men I've ever met. He heard you were out in Iraq and when most guys would have written you off as a basket case, he reckoned it was worth going to the trouble of sorting you out and getting you signed up for this gig. He trusted you, so maybe you should think about trusting him.'

'I want to know what the mission is,' snapped Ollie.

'Bruce will tell us in Kabul.'

'It's bloody ridiculous,' complained Ollie. 'Going all that way when we don't even know what the hell we're doing.'

'I'll tell you what's bloody ridiculous,' said Steve. 'You sitting here having a curry with some bloke you hardly know while your so-called fiancée pisses off home to Mum and Dad for the weekend.'

The buzzer shrieked before Ollie could respond. He glanced angrily at Steve then got up and opened the door.

'As if we didn't have enough problems,' said Steve when he saw who it was. 'The bloody convict has turned up.'

Dan shut the door behind him. 'Any of that grub going spare?' he said, looking down at the cartons of Indian food spread out on the table.

'Help yourself,' said Ollie.

Dan sat down on the sofa. 'I know what you're going to say, guys, and I'd say it myself if I was in your shoes, but just listen to me, that's all I'm asking. I need this job.'

He looks rough, thought Steve.

'The way we heard it, you did some time in the nick for killing some Afghan kids,' he said, 'and one of your parole conditions was you're not allowed back into the country. We can't afford to take a chance like that.'

'I should have told you,' said Dan.

'You're bloody right you should have told us,' said Ollie angrily. 'I can forgive a lot of things in a man. But hiding stuff from his mates – I don't know about that.'

Dan opened up a bottle of beer, leaving just one left on the table. He took a long, thoughtful drink. 'Maybe if I told you what happened, it will change your mind.'

'You can tell us if you want, but rules are rules,' said Ollie stiffly.

'Just let me bloody speak, will you? We were out in Nawsad, in Helmand, patrolling in the borderlands between Afghanistan and Pakistan. We were meant to be rounding up any remnants of the Taliban, plus getting a fix on the al-Queda training camps in the region. We got wind of the fact that a unit of senior officers was holed up in one village, and we had an idea that if we could get hold of the bastards, put a bit of a squeeze on them, we might even get a lead on where Osama was hiding out. We had a feeling that if anyone was going to catch the fucker, it would be us Aussies. Show the Americans and the Brits how it's done.' He paused.

'The only problem was there were some UN observers in the village as well. Some bloody do-gooders from Sweden or somewhere. Otherwise we'd have just waded in there, shot the hell out of the bastards, then put a knife to the throat of whoever was left alive and asked them some questions. When the UN are around you have to go through all the Geneva Convention bollocks – read people their rights, give them a bite to eat, ask them if they'd like a lawyer. As it turned out, they knew we were coming, and they didn't fancy a fight. They gave us the slip before we got to them. We could see the fuckers making their escape in those Toyota SUVs they all drive around in. So we set off after them. The Toyota veered round a corner and I managed to lay down some fire which burst open its tyres and spilled the guys out on to the ground. There were two of them. Nasty looking blokes, with black beards, and dishdashas. I was all ready to bring them down when they ran into this house and came out with two little kids, a boy of about seven and a girl of about five. The next thing, the bastard with the beard has dropped the boy. Put a bullet straight through him. His sister runs towards him and the bastard is still firing, peppering her with bullets as well. So I open up with my own gun and let him and his mate have it, right into the head and the chest. The whole thing was over in a few seconds . . .' Dan's voice trailed away. He was staring at the ceiling.

'And?' said Steve.

'One of the UN wankers was this uptight Swedish bitch called Katerina. Whoever got the idea Swedish girls are sexy obviously hadn't met Kat. We called her UN Barbie, but it was just a joke. So the two Taliban and the two kids are dead, and I'm left standing. I was feeling numb, I don't mind admitting that. I don't know if either of you have ever seen a kid get killed . . . well, it's the most horrible thing in the world. So I'm feeling like shit already. Then it turns out Katerina has filed an official complaint. She says I opened fire on the Taliban and shot the kids as well . . .' Dan paused, screwing up his eyes.

'So you were done for,' said Steve.

'If it had been internal, the blokes would have accepted my side of the story,' said Dan. 'We've all been there, and we know what combat is like. It's chaos. Shit happens. Most fire fights go pear-shaped before they've even started. But the bitch had already filed the complaint with the UN office in Kabul, and once you're caught up in that machine, you're bloody toast. It's just lawyers and social workers. None of them have been near a battlefield, and none of them know what it's like.'

Steve glanced at Ollie, and Ollie nodded back. They didn't need to speak, they both knew what the other meant. Dan was an honest bloke who'd had a hard time.

'So, you see, I need this job,' said Dan, suddenly looking at Steve. 'I've done a year in a military jail, and I didn't enjoy one minute of it. So if there's Taliban that need slotting, then I'm your man.'

Steve grinned. 'You're back on the plane.'

'Good one, mate,' said Dan. 'I could tell you blokes were all right.' He stood up, shovelled the remaining rice and curry into a carton, and started eating again. 'I don't suppose there's any more of that beer going spare, is there?'

'If we'd known the sodding Aussies were coming, we'd have got a few more in,' said Steve.

Ten

WE'LL COUNT THEM ALL IN, thought Steve. And with any luck we'll be able to count them all back again in a couple of weeks' time. With thirty million dollars to split between us. If that isn't a prize worth fighting for, then I'd like to know what is.

He was standing at the British Airways check-in desk at Heathrow's Terminal One. Ollie was right next to him, and so was Dan. They'd all travelled up together on the tube after a last slap-up breakfast at the Starlight. Steve had ten tickets for the flight to Istanbul that left in two hours, with connections on to Kabul. All they needed to do now was round up the rest of the team, and then they were on their way.

To what? pondered Steve to himself.

The fight of our lives.

If he was being honest with himself, Steve always enjoyed the ride up to Heathrow at the start of every job. He'd sit and watch the rest of the passengers on the Piccadilly Line and think: you people haven't even started to catch on to what life is all about. You're going out shopping, or catching a football game. A few of you might even be flying somewhere, but it's probably a couple of weeks in some tourist hotel in Thailand, and for most of you it's a business trip to Zurich. But me? I'm about to test myself in one of the most dangerous jobs, in one of the most dangerous places in the world. And I'm the only person on this tube who's figured out that if you can't live on the edge, there isn't much point in living at all.

It was on those journeys to Heathrow that Steve remembered why he did what he did. And why he could never settle down to an ordinary life again, even if he wanted to. He'd miss the buzz too much.

'Clean socks, lad,' said Ollie as Nick bounded up to them.

Nick laughed but said nothing.

Steve handed him his ticket. 'You sure you're up for this?' he asked sharply.

Nick nodded.

'It's bloody dangerous,' he said. 'There's no shame in going home if you want to.'

'So you keep saying,' said Nick. 'Maybe it's you that's frightened.'

'That's a good one,' said Steve. But maybe I am nervous, he thought to himself.

Over the next twenty minutes, the rest of the team assembled around the check-in desk.

Jeff showed up first. He had a rucksack on his back, filled with body-builders' proteins, as well as an iPod Nano and a pair of travel speakers. The Nano, he explained, was filled with the collected works of Stevie Wonder, Bruce Springsteen, and Prince. 'If we pull this off, we're going to need a party,' he said cheerfully. 'And we won't want to be restricted to some crap Afghan music.'

'Bit ancient, isn't it?' said Nick.

'Classic, mate,' said Jeff. 'This unit fights with AKs and listens to Stevie Wonder. Why bother with any of the modern rubbish?'

Ganju arrived next: quiet, smartly dressed in chinos and a polo shirt, with his hair freshly cut. He shook everyone by the hand but hardly said a word. He was followed by David, who tried to say hello to each man in turn but was interrupted by a constant stream of calls on his mobile from both Sandy and Laura. We need to take that phone off him, decided Steve, as he watched the man's brow crease up. Or hope that there's no signal out in Kabul. The stress of dealing with those two women is going to stop the bloke from thinking straight.

Chris and Ian rolled up, joining the party. Chris had equipped himself with several packets of generic doxycycline, which he distributed to each man, along with instructions to start taking the tablets right away. 'It wasn't the Swapo bastards that did the real damage to us out in Africa,' he warned. 'It was the malaria, and they've got it in Afghanistan as well. A sick soldier is no bloody use to anyone.'

Ian was holding a radio-controlled Transformers car, still in the bag from Argos where he'd bought it.

'Glad you brought that along,' said Jeff suspiciously. 'Nick here will have something to play with before it's his bedtime.'

'It's for the roadside bombs, isn't it?' said David.

Ian nodded. 'Most terrorist groups don't have the money for any very sophisticated devices,' he said. 'They put some plastic explosive in the ground, then they hide themselves a couple of hundred yards away and use the radio controller from a kid's toy to blow the thing when you're driving past it.'

'And all the toys operate on the same bit of radio spectrum, right?' said Dan. 'So if you have one yourself in your vehicle, and keep it permanently switched on and transmitting, there's a good chance you can detonate any roadside devices before you get within a couple of hundred yards of them.'

'That's why you need a bomber on the team,' said Ian.

Steve nodded. He was glad to see that everyone was starting to hit it off. The most important thing over the next forty-eight hours was that the unit started to gel into a team. Unless they could do that, they could never fight together, and there was a tough war ahead of them, they could be sure of that.

He finished the introductions, making sure each man shook the other's hand.

'So we've got an Aussie and a Welshman,' said Jeff. 'Don't fight over the sheep, boys . . .'

Nick laughed.

'Nick, it's your mum on the phone,' said Dan, holding up his own phone. 'She wants to know when playtime's finished.'

'Leave it out,' snarled Nick.

'OK, everyone ready?' He handed out a ticket to each man. 'Don't worry, we can get a refund on the returns if anyone doesn't make it back.'

When he'd finished, there was still one ticket left in his hand.

'Where's Roddy?' he asked, looking at Ollie.

Ollie looked around, then his eyes flicked down to his watch.

You could tell what he was thinking.

Where the hell *is* Roddy?

'Probably at Gatwick, wondering where the fuck we are,' said Steve. 'I knew that bloke wasn't paying attention in the arse and elbow lessons.'

Ollie pulled his mobile from his pocket and punched a number on his contacts list.

He waited for a moment, then, when the phone was answered, said. 'Goddamit, Roderick, we're waiting for you.'

Ollie nodded a couple of times, then snapped the phone shut. He looked at Steve.

'Roddy's not coming,' he said firmly.

Steve stared at him. 'Not fucking coming? What the hell do you mean?'

'Apparently his girlfriend reckons it's too dangerous.'

'Too dangerous?' All the men could hear the tension in Steve's voice. 'Now he sodding tells us. With ten minutes to go before the plane boards.'

'I'm sorry, I shouldn't have asked him on to the unit,' said Ollie stiffly. 'He's let us down and, worse than that, he's let himself down.'

'Spare us the fucking Sandhurst crap,' said Steve. 'I don't give a toss whether he's let us or himself down. We're a sodding man short, and there's not much chance of filling that slot now, is there?'

'I said I'm sorry.' Ollie's face was reddening, and his fists were starting to clench.

'So how may more useless cowards have you signed up for this mission?'

'They're all here, aren't they?' snapped Ollie.

'No thanks to you,' said Steve. 'You can't pull sodding rank now. In the army, you can get away with being a useless bloody tosser so long as you went to the right school and you've got the right accent, but once we touch down in Kabul, you're only as good as the work you're doing, and right now I've seen fuck all from you.'

'Jesus, man,' said Ollie. 'Get the damned chip off your

shoulder. We should be fighting the Taliban, not each other.'

Steve was about to speak. But he took a deep breath and tried to calm himself.

Arguing wasn't going to get them anywhere. He turned away from Ollie, his ticket in his fist, and started marching towards the departures gate. As he did so, he looked at Nick who was walking alongside him.

'Welcome to bloody soldiering, mate,' he said. 'I hope you know what you've let yourself in for.'

Eleven

I F YOU THOUGHT LONDON PROPERTY prices were bad, Steve said as they waited for taxis at Kabul's airport, then you hadn't ever visited a Kabul estate agent. Prices had been shooting up by a couple of hundred per cent a year since the international circus of aid agencies, development consultants, international embassies, and the private security contractors they needed to look after them all had descended on the country in the wake of the invasion. Kabul hadn't had many decent buildings to start with, and the locals had been busy splashing some paint on what few there were and renting them out to foreigners for vast sums.

'Property speculation and drug trafficking, that's the basis of the Afghan economy,' Steve said.

'Then it's hardly surprising that a guy from South London should feel right at home,' replied Jeff.

They piled into two eight-year-old Nissan taxis which took them to a whitewashed villa on the Bagram Road, the central artery that led out of the city towards the air base that was one of the main fortresses for the American forces in the country. Bruce Dudley wasn't known for the opulence of the living quarters he provided for his men, but this time he seemed to have rented a decent enough place. Inside a thick pair of steel reinforced gates was a courtyard with a CCTV system that allowed you to monitor the street outside. There were six bedrooms in the house, and a couple of single beds in each one. It had originally been a diplomatic family's accommodation, built by the Soviets for one of the commissars who 'advised' the government during that country's occupation of Afghanistan, so it had air conditioning, and the electrics worked. There was a fridge, a cupboard full of tinned and dried food, and plenty of bottled water.

'Home sweet home,' said Jeff, putting his kitbag on the table. 'It's not much, but I'm sure we can turn it into something we're proud of.'

It was only mid-morning but they were all exhausted from the flight. Nick had suggested going out for some sightseeing – it was only the second time he'd been abroad, the other trip was a week in Majorca with his mum, and he was desperate to get out of the house. Don't be ridiculous, David told him sharply. Kabul was one of the most dangerous cities in the world, and with his pasty white skin Nick was hardly going to blend in with the locals. Ollie insisted they all get some kip. Dudley was arriving tomorrow morning to outline the mission. 'We all need to get as much sleep as possible,' he said, 'because we don't know when we might get our heads down again.'

The men helped themselves to some food from the kitchen and headed for the bedrooms. Whatever else, Steve reflected, they were all professional soldiers and the first lesson every soldier learned was to grab any food or sleep they could at any time of the day or night because combat didn't usually allow for either.

He took out his mobile. There was a text message from Orlena. 'Can you meet me at the Serena Hotel at eight,' it said. 'I want you to meet my brother.'

She'd said back in Dubai that her brother had been in the Russian special forces, the Spetsnaz. The text explained she'd stopped off in Kabul on her way home from Dubai to see if she could help her brother find a job.

Steve looked at Ollie. 'We're a man short, right?'

'We'll manage,' said Ollie.

'There's a Russian special forces guy in town. He might be useful.'

'The Spetsnaz? Bloody nutters.'

That's true, reflected Steve. He'd given the girl the brush-off in Dubai when she'd mentioned his signing up her brother. They might be a diverse bunch of men in this unit, but at least they were all from the same basic stock. A Russian? That was something different.

Then again, it would be good to see Orlena again. He'd thought about her a couple of times since he'd left Dubai. Even thought about sending her a text. After all, in a couple of weeks' time, he was going to be a rich man and he'd need someone to keep him company while he lounged around the pool of a five-star hotel, sipping cocktails. There were a lot worse candidates for that vacancy than Orlena.

'I'll go meet him,' said Steve. 'It can't do any harm to talk to the guy.'

'Then I'm coming with you.'

'I'll just have a chat . . .'

'We're not signing some madman just because you fancy shagging the bloke's sister,' said Ollie. 'Either I'm coming with you or we're staying right here.'

*

The Serena Hotel was one of the few classy places to stay in the whole of Kabul; the place was still far too dangerous for the Hiltons, Marriotts and Sofitels to set up in the city, so the Serena had the market largely to itself. Overlooking the Zarnegar Park, it was close to all the main embassies and only a twenty-minute drive from the airport. Built in 1945, it was set in its own parkland and had been extensively refurbished in the past couple of years since money had been pouring into the city. It was the one place in town where all the Westerners could be sure of running into each other. As soon as you stepped through its sliding glass doors and into the temperature-controlled lobby, you were out of the madness of Kabul and back in touch with civilisation.

For a few minutes anyway, thought Steve.

Steve and Ollie had grabbed a few hours' kip, showered, and were dressed in smart chinos and polo shirts when they stepped into the hotel. Orlena was already waiting for them in the Char Chatra bar, an ornate hotel lounge, filled with traditional Afghan rugs, animal heads, and tribal weapons. She was sipping a fruit cocktail. She looked even better than the last time he'd seen her, decided Steve as soon as he laid eyes on her. Her hair was fresh and light, and there was a subtle tan to her skin. She was wearing calf-length leather boots, short suede skirt, and a patterned blouse. Around her neck was a big chunk of amber that blended into her breasts.

'I wonder if the Spetsnaz nutter has any more sisters,' muttered Ollie.

'Big families out there,' said Steve. 'Maybe she's the ugly one.'

'I'm starting to warm to the Spetsnaz.'

'Watch it, I'll tell Katie.'

'Jesus,' hissed Ollie. 'You wouldn't, would you?'

They walked up to the bar.

'I missed you,' said Orlena. She stood up and gave him a kiss. To anyone observing them it would have looked like nothing more than a peck between business acquaintances but it packed as much sexual punch as the Spearmint Rhino training academy. Her mouth lingered on his cheek for a fraction of a second, and her tongue caressed his skin. Her perfume floated across him, the same smoky mixture of honey and whisky he remembered from Dubai.

'And I missed you too, babes,' said Steve. He looked into her eyes, and smiled. More than you probably realise.

At her side, Maksim was also standing up. He was a well-built man, six feet tall, with muscles that rippled through him. He had dirty blond hair the colour of dishwater, and he had tiny blue eyes, so dark they were almost black, and they tracked everything around him, moving constantly. He seemed tense, noted Steve, wired up, as if he was afraid of something.

'This is my brother,' said Orlena.

He shot out a hand. Steve shook it, wincing inwardly at the grip. Maksim squeezed his hand until the bones started to creak.

'Pleased to meet you,' he said, in faltering, uncertain English. 'Orlena says you are here to fight.'

Maksim already had a beer on the table, and Ollie signalled to the waitress to bring them a couple more.

'You were Spetsnaz?' said Steve, sitting down.

He was by no means an expert, but anyone who had been in the special forces was aware of the Spetsnaz. The name was an abbreviation of the Russian words *Spetsialnoye nazraniem*, which translated as 'troops of special purpose'. Unlike the SAS, it was a big organisation, with thirty thousand men in total, and it was controlled by the GRU, the Russian Army's internal intelligence unit. Through most of the Cold War, the existence of the Spetsnaz wasn't even officially acknowledged. But although they were used for combating terrorists and fighting behind the lines, they were more like shock troops than mainstream special forces. They all had training in foreign languages and were familiarised with all the major weapons of the world, with a particular focus on knives and hand-to-hand combat. They even had a few tricks of their own, such as the infamous NR-2, a knife with a gun barrel concealed in its handle, which could be fired secretly. They were tough, there was no question of that; the training regime for the Spetsnaz was among the most brutal in the world. But stealth? Tactics? Battlefield awareness? These were not the qualities they were famous for, Steve reminded himself, and yet that was what they were likely to need in the days ahead of them.

'Ten years,' said Maksim. 'From the day I joined until the day I left. And let me tell you, there aren't many men who come through ten years in that organisation.'

'Where'd you fight?'

'Chechnya mostly.'

'Which unit?' asked Ollie.

Steve glanced at him. At Sandhurst he reckoned they'd have had plenty of lectures on the Red Army, so the chances were Ollie knew one brigade from another.

'The Third Guards,' said Maksim.

'Which is based where?'

'In Samara Oblast.'

Ollie nodded, and Steve could tell the answers were straight enough. Either Maksim was telling the truth or he'd read up enough to bluff his way through.

'So what are you doing here?' Steve asked.

'Like my sister says,' said Maksim, his voice turning serious, 'I need a job, one that pays well, and pays quick.'

'Your skills?' said Ollie.

'I'm a solider, what skills do I need? I can kill a man with my bare hands.'

'Weapons?'

'AKs, of course. Knives, and ropes. And I did a special course in signals.'

Steve gave Ollie a look. 'Give us five minutes,' he said to Maksim.

Steve stood up, and walked towards the gents. Ollie was behind him. Steve stood in front of the urinal for a minute. The room was large, measuring twenty feet by five, with six cubicles, and black and white tiles on the walls. It was empty.

'So?'

'He seems OK,' Ollie said. 'I don't know how he'll fit in with the team.'

'He can fight well enough.'

'But if one man disrupts the group, then we're buggered,' said Ollie. 'We're only a few guys, so if we aren't all fighting for each other, we're done for.'

'I'll fit in,' growled Maksim.

Steve turned round. He zipped up his fly but kept his eyes fixed to Maksim's right hand. He was cradling a Nagent M1895 revolver, one of the sturdiest, most reliable handguns ever built. It had been developed in Liège but had been manufactured in Russia since before the Revolution, and stayed in production until the 1950s. It was still used by the Russian railway staff and by the more remote police forces.

Steadying himself, Steve took a step forward. 'What's that for?' he asked, nodding at the Nagent.

He'd faced men with guns enough times not to feel nervous around them, but there was a ripple of angry, pepped-up energy within Maksim that made him uneasy.

'Let me show you an old Russian Army trick,' said Maksim.

The revolver was sitting in his right hand. Lifting it up slightly, Maksim slotted a bullet into its cylinder and spun it round.

Steve knew instantly what he was up to.

Russian roulette. The traditional blood sport of the Russian Army. The men would fill the cylinder of a revolver with spent bullets, plus one live round, then spin it, and fire it into their own heads, gambling on whether they would live or die.

'Christ, man, leave it,' said Ollie.

Maksim shot him a look of pure contempt. And with his left hand he spun the cylinder again.

The characteristics of the gun made it uniquely suited to the game. The Nagent had seven chambers instead of the usual six, significantly increasing the chances of surviving, and the unique shape of its cartridges meant that as the cylinder was spun, it was impossible to tell which were spent and which one was still live.

The cylinder clicked to a stop.

Maksim cocked the trigger and raised the barrel to his head so that its muzzle was resting just over his earlobe. The perfect position for blowing your brains out, noted Steve. We might question the guy's sanity, but there's no doubting his professionalism.

'You're looking for brave men,' said Maksim. 'Men who don't mind whether they live or die.'

His small dark eyes were looking straight ahead, his skin

and lips were perfectly dry, and the fear and tension seemed to have evaporated out of him.

'Sod it,' growled Steve. 'Don't be a fucking idiot.'

Maksim glanced at him. A slow smile spread across his lips. Then, without a flicker of hesitation, he squeezed the trigger. Steve caught his breath as the hammer on the Nagent smashed into the cartridge. Maksim didn't flinch.

A still silence fell across the bathroom.

'The gun is filled with damned blanks,' snorted Ollie. 'You're not impressing anyone with that party trick.'

Maksim spun the cylinder again, waited for it to come to rest, then raised it in his right hand so that it was pointing straight at Ollie. 'You sure of that?'

'OK, OK, let's skip the aggro,' said Steve. 'You're in, OK?'

Maksim smiled. 'Really?'

'It's a bloody dangerous job, and we can't tell you what it is until the morning, but there will be three million dollars for each man at the end of it, and if you want it, the gig's yours,' said Steve.

'I don't mind danger,' said Maksim.

'Yeah, I think we got the general drift, mate,' said Steve.

'I still say it's a damned blank,' said Ollie sourly.

Maksim turned his right hand so that the Nagent was pointing towards one of the cubicle doors. He squeezed the trigger. The gun exploded, the report of the bullet echoing around the room. The wood of the door splintered and a small cloud of plaster spun out of the tiles on the back wall.

Maksim laughed. 'It's lucky you're not a gambling man.'

Ollie grinned. It was hard not to be impressed by the performance.

He stepped across to Maksim and handed him a slip of paper with the address they were staying at. 'Get your kit together, try and get a decent night's kip, and be at this address tomorrow morning at eight sharp,' he said. 'That's if you can manage to stay alive for the next twelve hours.'

Maksim nodded enthusiastically. 'You won't regret it.'

'I already am,' said Ollie. 'Now get the fuck out of here.'

After Maksim had left, Steve splashed some water over his face then dried himself. 'Christ, he's a madman, isn't he?'

Ollie nodded. 'But every unit needs one of those. I mean, he scares the hell out of me, so just think what he's going to do to the enemy.'

Together they walked back to the hotel bar. Maksim had already left, and Orlena was sitting by herself, her lips round the straw of her cocktail, and her legs crossed so that you could see several inches of her thigh running between her boots and her skirt.

'Fancy a tip, mate?'

'OK,' said Steve.

'I'd think twice about shagging that bloke's sister, no matter how much of a looker she might be. I mean, I hate to think what happens when the family's honour has been called into question.'

Fair point, thought Steve. But she is gorgeous. How's a man meant to resist?

'I'll look after myself,' said Steve with a grin.

*

Orlena's body felt supple and warm next to him in the bed. Steve was cradling her in his arms, aware of the way their sweat was mingling. Her head was lying across his chest, and he could feel her breath on his skin, and her nipples squeezed up next to him. It was close to midnight, and after a couple of drinks in the bar they had grabbed something to eat then come up to her room and made love for an hour. She was grateful to him for taking Maksim into his unit; just how grateful, he didn't discover until she took her clothes off.

Christ, he thought to himself. I could fall hard for this girl. I wonder if she's interested in vintage cars?

'So what's this job?' she asked.

Steve shrugged. 'We won't know for sure until the morning.'

'But are you really going to make three million dollars?'

Steve was certain he could hear her purring as the words rolled off her tongue. But why not? he thought to himself. A woman's entitled to have something to look forward to.

'That's the plan.'

'And then?'

'We should take a holiday together,' said Steve.

'Where?'

'We could go back to Dubai,' said Steve. 'Back to Jumeirah Beach. That's not a bad place to relax for a couple of weeks.'

Orlena pulled a face. 'I don't want to go back there, I didn't like the bar manager. The Burkj Al Arab is much nicer. It's where all the sheiks and the Russian oilmen meet.'

'Whatever you say.'

'It's expensive.'

'Don't you worry, it takes some serious luxury to make any kind of dent in the kind of stash we're going to be bringing back from this job.'

'You won't take too many risks?'

'None that I can't handle.'

Orlena reached down into her handbag and pulled out a rabbit's foot, carefully stuffed and preserved, and attached to a thin metal chain. 'Take this with you,' she said.

'What is it?'

'A good luck charm.'

'I'll be fine.'

Orlena grabbed hold of his wrist, her face suddenly anxious. 'Just wear it for me,' she said. 'It will bring you luck.'

Steve flicked his tongue across her stiffening nipples. 'I already got lucky.'

Orlena started running her tongue down Steve's abdomen, towards his groin. 'Where I come from, we have a saying,' she said, allowing her long dark hair to brush his skin sensuously.

'Which is?'

'A man shouldn't go into battle without one last fuck from his woman.'

Steve grinned. 'The tourist board should make that bit of information more widely available.'

Twelve

THE SMELL OF FRYING EGGS filled the kitchen of the villa when Steve walked in at just after eight in the morning. Jeff was leaning over the stove, flipping eggs over one by one, then putting them down next to the steaks he'd just fried. Most of the guys were already tucking into breakfast, all of it washed down with huge mugs of milky tea. Stevie Wonder's 'You Are The Sunshine Of My Life' was playing in the background on a pair of speakers Jeff had managed to fix up to his iPod. Maksim was there, sitting next to Ollie.

'Steve bloody West,' said Jeff, cracking another pair of eggs into the hot pan of fat spitting on the electric stove. 'The only bloke I know who couldn't pull to save his life down at the Liquid Heat nightclub in Bromley. But bring the sod out to Kabul, the bloody totty desert of the universe, and he gets lucky within ten minutes of tumbling off the plane. How can we explain that?'

Steve grinned, splashed some ketchup on to the steak and eggs, and started to eat. A night with Orlena had given him an appetite; the woman was ravenous, and not for food. Around him, the men seemed to have split into groups, but as far as he could tell, they were all getting along just fine. Ollie was chatting to Ian and David. Dan was chatting to Chris – he'd found a shortwave radio, and Australia, according to the BBC World Service bulletin, were now 482 for 3 in their second innings – while Ganju was impressing Nick with Gurkha techniques for slitting a man with a knife. Ollie was right, Steve reflected. If they were going to fight together, they had to get on, and to do that they had to start getting to know each other. Once you were out on the field of battle, you were fighting for the man standing next to you as much as anything else, and if you didn't rate him, then you weren't going to risk your life for his.

'So what's she like?' said Jeff.

It was typical of the man, thought Steve. He acted rough, but in truth Jeff was the gentlest guy he'd ever met. He made sure everyone else had something to eat before he even thought about making anything for himself. Now that everyone else had finished, he was finally sitting down to his own breakfast.

'You remember Alison?'

'That bird who used to work as a fitness trainer down in Lewisham?'

Steve nodded.

'Don't tell me, better looking than Alison.'

Again, Steve nodded.

'Lucky bastard.'

Steve mopped up the rest of his egg. 'I'll find out if she has a sister for you.'

'I don't think Russian birds go for us black dudes,' said Jeff. 'We stick to the Bromley bottle blondes. They like us OK.'

'Thanks for coming along, Jeff,' said Steve. 'It's good to have an old mate along on a gig like this.'

'Like I said, Steve West's big payday, I wouldn't miss it for the world.'

'It could be dangerous.'

'You should try nightclub bouncing, that's real danger for you,' said Jeff. 'Try telling some of those thirteen-year-old girls they're too young to get in. The little bitches try and bite you to death.'

'I mean it, Jeff, a lark's a lark, but . . .'

He paused, and took a swig of his tea. He loved Jeff like a brother but he had learned over the years that it was virtually impossible to have a serious conversation with the man. Sometimes Steve felt he'd have to slap him around the head to get him to listen properly; he'd try it, but the muscles from all that body building meant he didn't much feel like taking the inevitable response.

'Most of the guys are here because they need money real bad.'

'And who says I don't?'

'You? There's always work for a guy like you.'

Jeff swallowed hard on his steak, then picked up his mug of tea. 'It's my mum,' he said, his voice suddenly reflective.

'Estelle,' said Steve.

'She was seventeen when she had me,' said Jeff. 'Think about it, mate. Seventeen. My dad buggered off when I was six months old, so by the time she reached our age, thirty, she already had a thirteen-year-old kid. She got a job cleaning, doing the morning shift at the government offices down in Croydon, which meant getting the four fifty-five bus every morning so that she could be there by five thirty. And she's been doing that job for thirty years, since she was just seventeen, just so she could look after me properly, and keep the flat together. She spent so much of her life on that bloody bus, I think the driver proposed to her once. But she never looked at another man. Maybe she decided they were all trouble after my dad, and frankly, who could blame her.'

'So it's about her?'

'She's forty-seven now, and I'd like to give her something back before she's too old to enjoy it. One of those swank new apartments they're building even around Lewisham. Lovely new kitchen, close to all her old friends, but a nice place, and enough money in the bank so she can give up the cleaning.'

'We'll get there,' said Steve. 'We just need a few days, that's all.'

'I sodding hope so,' said Jeff. 'I haven't come here for the scenery or the local cooking, that's for sure.'

Ollie was introducing Maksim to the other members of the group. Steve noticed how each man winced when their hands were pressed into Maksim's car crusher of a handshake. Even Jeff seemed pleased to pull his hand away.

'So what unit did you say you were with?' asked Ian, sitting down with Ollie and Maksim.

'Third Guards,' said Maksim.

'You were the first guys into Prague, weren't you?'

'In sixty-eight, sure, that was us,' said Maksim. 'We went in as the first ground troops. There were tanks rolling through the streets, but they were for show mostly. It was the Spetsnaz that rounded up all the important people.'

'But not here,' said Ian. 'In nineteen seventy-nine, the Spetsnaz came in and assassinated President Hafizullah Amin and just about all the palace staff, then secured the airport, before the main invasion force came in. But, and correct me if I've got this wrong, that was the Twelfth and Sixteenth Brigades.'

'You know a lot about our history.'

Ian attempted a smile but there was no warmth in it. 'It pays to know your enemy.'

'We're all on the same side now,' said Ollie.

'Let's hope so,' muttered Ian.

Steve went to the door. Bruce Dudley had just arrived. He was accompanied by a tall man with dark brown hair, clear blue eyes, and a strong, muscular build. He didn't introduce himself, and Bruce did not say who he was. His eyes flicked over his surroundings like those of a man being shown round a place he's already decided not to buy.

'Ten men, all present and correct, just like you asked for,' said Steve.

'The desperate and the damned?'

'I don't know about the damned bit. But they are desperate all right.'

The kitchen where'd they'd been eating was a long, narrow room that opened on to a small patio yard in one direction and led through into the main sitting room in the other. Even with ten men sitting round the table, it didn't feel cramped. Steve introduced each man to Bruce in turn. As he did so, he could feel a sense of achievement. They might not look like much, but they were a good bunch of blokes, and if their backs were against the wall, they'd turn round and fight. He felt certain of that.

He noted Bruce's expression as he chatted briefly with each man. He could see that he rated them. Bruce could be a mean bastard but his judgement of soldiers was uncanny. If a man was going to bottle it, Bruce knew it long before the man himself did. In the end, soldiering wasn't about training or tactics or weapons, it was about the stuff you had inside you. And Bruce had some kind of eye, Steve felt certain. He could peer straight into a man, see what he was made of, and tell you whether he was going to be OK or not.

Steve clapped his hands, gaining everyone's attention. Stevie Wonder was halfway through the *Innervisions* album, and Jeff stood up to switch the volume down.

'Listen up, guys,' said Steve. 'We've come a long way, and we've got a big job ahead of us, and I'm sure we're all anxious to kick this thing off. This is Bruce Dudley, and he's going to tell us what the hell we're all doing here, because I don't think we've come all this way just to work on our tans.'

Bruce stood up. 'Thanks, Steve,' he said. His voice was stern, yet clear, the tone of a man who was used to telling men what to do, and expected to be obeyed. 'And thanks to all of you guys for coming out here. I hope we can make it worth your while.' He turned to the man he had come in with, who, up until now, had remained silent in the background, watching but not saying anything. 'This is Colonel Simon Lockhart, of the British base down in Helmand. And he's going to explain what we want doing.'

Steve had watched Lockhart while he made the round of introductions; he hadn't said anything, but he could see he was clocking each man, assessing his strengths and weaknesses. Now he cleared his throat and stepped forward. As soon as he opened his mouth, Steve could tell he was a typical public school Rupert.

'Welcome to Afghanistan, boys,' he said. 'As I'm sure you know, we've got ourselves into a rough fight out here, probably the roughest the British Army has been involved in since the Second World War. We're not bellyaching about that. Rough fights are what we do. But we would like to start winning it. And to do that, we need to forget about the rules the bloody social workers who've moved into the Ministry of Defence have drawn up, and begin to fight like soldiers instead. That means we go in hard and we give old Terry Taliban a solid beating before he gives us one.'

He laid a map out on the table. Steve recognised it at once. It was a long, boxy rectangle, with one big lake up to the north and not much in the way of roads or towns. Helmand Province, southern Afghanistan.

'The biggest man in this godforsaken corner of the world is a guy called Zabit Salangi,' Lockhart continued. 'I have a theory that Genghis Kahn must have shagged some of the local girls when he came through these parts and Salangi's one of his descendants. He's a rough, vicious bastard, and he controls most of the drugs trade in Helmand, which means that in effect he's the bloke in charge of the whole show. The farmers grow the poppies and they sell them to Salangi, and he provides them with all the protection they need. He supplies the poppies to the refiners, and once he's got it down to pure heroin, he arranges for it to be shipped out to the dealers in Europe and America. He's good at what he does, and he doesn't allow anyone to stand in his way.'

He paused, and Steve noticed that he was looking straight at him. 'Salangi has a personal army about a thousand strong, and within that there is an inner core of about a hundred men. He's formed an alliance with the Taliban. He supplies them with the money to buy weapons and munitions. In return, they give him protection throughout the region. The Taliban want to drive the British out, and Salangi's helping them every way he can. In return, once they are back in power here in Kabul, which will happen pretty bloody quickly if they manage to get us out of Helmand, then they'll allow Salangi to control the drugs business for the whole country.

'Salangi's taking a bet that right now we're losing this war, and if I'm being honest, I can't say I blame him. We're in a hell of a fight. We haven't got enough men, we haven't got enough kit, and we're fighting with one hand tied behind our backs, and as I'm sure you know, that isn't much of a combination. The Taliban are awash with money, and that means their supply of weapons is getting better, and they can recruit all the young men they want here in Afghanistan and across the border in Pakistan because, as I'm sure you've noticed, there aren't many alternative careers, and at least the Taliban pay wages. They look like winners as well.

'So here's what we propose to do,' continued Lockhart. 'We're fed up with sitting around on our arses all day getting shot at. The buggers back in Whitehall won't do anything about it because we're supposed to be fighting the "terrorists", whatever the hell that means, not the local warlords, and since none of the politicians have ever been anywhere near an army, they've no idea what we're up against. No one in Kabul is interested because Salangi has bribed everyone who matters, and anyway, most of them reckon the Taliban are going to be back in charge soon and don't want to rock the boat. We need to hit Salangi, hit him hard, and in the only place that really hurts – in his wallet. The man is a savage and he doesn't trust banks. He knows that even the Swiss would freeze his accounts in an instant if we asked them to. So he keeps his money in gold and diamonds. About fifty million dollars of the stuff in total, according to our intelligence.'

Lockhart leant over the table. His eyes scanned the map briefly, then he pressed his thumb down on a small smudge of darkness in the far right-hand corner. 'And the bastard keeps it right here, in a village called Kajaki.'

He removed his thumb so everyone could get a look at the map.

'All we want you boys to do is go and get it.'

Steve glanced around the room. He'd had some idea during the past week of what the job was going to be, although Dudley hadn't spelt out the details even to him, but none of the rest of them knew anything.

A robbery. Possibly the greatest robbery of all time. And with no possibility of any charges ever being pressed against them. There was no such thing as the perfect crime, he reflected. But this was about as close to it as they were ever going to get. And he could see the excitement on each of the faces around the room.

'Like I said, there's fifty million dollars in there, in gold and diamonds, stored in an old Soviet fortress that Salangi uses as his base,' said Lockhart. 'We'll give you maps, and intelligence, and any back-up you need. After that, you're on your own. And we'll turn a blind eye while you clear off out of the country with the stash. All we care about is that Salangi is bankrupted and stops bankrolling the Taliban.' Lockhart stood back from the table stiffly, and Bruce stepped forward.

'This is a deniable job,' he said, speaking clearly and slowly. 'You certainly aren't working for the British Army, and you're not going to be working for DEF either. You're on nobody's payroll except your own. So if you get into any trouble, you have to find your own way out of it. That's the bad news. The good news is that we'll arrange for all the support you need. It will be a tough, hard fight, I know that, but you're all bloody good soldiers, and you'll be up against gangsters and teenagers, so you should be OK. Once you get the stash, all you have to do is get down to the border with Pakistan. We'll arrange for it to be picked up, and then we'll fence the gold and diamonds. We'll probably take it across to Dubai, because that's one of the greatest gold and precious stones markets in the world and they don't ask too many questions over there. After it's all been taken care off, fifty million dollars should translate into thirty million to be divided equally between each man. That's three million each, just the way Steve said it would be.'

'And what kind of force can we use?' asked Steve.

'Anything you need to get the job done,' said Lockhart sternly. 'This is not some UN peacekeeping mission, this is real war, and that means you can hit them with anything that will do a lot of damage. We don't care if you kill Salangi, but remember, this isn't an assassination mission. If he's killed, then some other bugger will just take his place. What counts is that we take his money, because once that's gone, he's broken. And then we can have a shot at winning this war.'

Bruce looked at each man in turn. 'If any man doesn't want to do it, I've got a ticket home for him, and there's no shame in taking it. It's going to be sodding dangerous, so if anyone's not up for it, they should say so now.'

Steve's eyes moved from man to man. He could read their expressions: grim, determined and unyielding. They knew the task ahead would be tough. They would be staking their lives on a roulette wheel. But it wasn't impossible. And the prize was a large one, probably larger than they would ever be offered in their lives.

Each man remained silent. Nobody was going to quit now.

'Good fellows,' said Lockhart. 'If anyone asks you, you never saw me.'

Before he left the room, he said, 'And I expect one of you boys to buy me a glass of champagne at the bar of the Ritz when we're all back in London. The money you're about to make, you should be able to afford it.'

Thirteen

THE SILENCE AROUND THE TABLE stretched from thirty seconds into a minute. Each man was alone with his thoughts, pondering the task ahead, assessing the risks, and weighing the decision in his own mind.

Nobody was thinking about leaving.

And yet, thought Steve, you could see the questions lurking in the backs of their eyes.

The life of a mercenary was nothing like the life of an ordinary soldier, he reflected. In the regular army, you accepted your orders without questioning them. Out here in the PMCs, you weighed up the risks against the rewards. Every job was a shifting calculus: sometimes you'd do it, sometimes you wouldn't. It all depended on whether it was worth it.

'I'm bloody glad you all seem happy with the job,' said Steve, standing up and addressing the table. 'I'm sorry we couldn't tell you any more about it before we left Britain, but I think you can understand, this had to be top secret. If any word gets out about this, then Lockhart's going to be in deep trouble. The garrison can't go around authorising bands of mercenaries to start robbing the Afghans, at least not without getting their bollocks chopped off by the MoD when they get home. But we're all here now, and I reckon this could be sodding good for the lot of us. With a bit of guts and some determination, we can handle this job. We get to give some evil bastards a right good malleting, and we'll make ourselves a few quid in the process. I reckon you can't ask for much more out of day's work than that.'

A couple of feet away, Nick slammed his fist down on the table. He was about to say something, but the words got lost somewhere between his chest and his throat, and so he just looked up at Steve and grinned wildly. Steve recognised the expression. Nick was starting to look up to him as a mentor, the same way he himself had with some of the older soldiers when he'd first found himself at the army training base in Bassingbourn, near Royston in Cambridgeshire. That's OK, thought Steve to himself. Just so long as I don't ever let him down.

'But it's going to be bloody dangerous, isn't it?' said Ian. 'I mean, I come from Ulster, and over there we know what it's like for soldiers to operate on enemy territory.'

'You won't be too far from the British garrison,' said Bruce. 'Like Colonel Lockhart said, they'll give you all the logistical and intelligence back-up you need, and if you judge it necessary they'll launch some diversionary attacks to help you out. In a real emergency, they'll send in a chopper to evac anyone that gets wounded. In the end, that's all support really means, so you'll be no more on your own than any regular military force.'

Chris leant forwards on the table. 'I can see how we are going to get the stuff,' he started. 'So long as we hit them hard enough, and have the right kind of kit with us, that's not going to be too much of a problem . . .'

The man always launched into a sentence, then paused to think about it, noticed Steve. He was like a big bull: immense strength and perseverance, deadly when aroused to anger, but not very quick on his feet.

'What worries me,' he continued finally, 'is how the hell are we going to get out of there. We'll have half the bloody Taliban chasing us all the way to the border. And since they control the whole stretch of Pakistan on the other side as well, it's not going to be much easier when we get there either.'

'We just kill the bastards,' said Ian.

There was a silence around the table while the words sunk in.

'We're not butchers,' said Ollie sharply.

'Then maybe we need to learn,' said Ian, drilling the words home. 'We go into Salangi's fort, and we let all the bastards have it. Our best chance of success is to make it a massacre. If there's no one left alive, then there's no one to raise the alarm, or to say what happened. That leaves us at least a clear twelve hours, so we run like hell for the border and hope to be well away before anyone has any idea what happened or who did it.'

'He's right,' said Bruce. 'It's not pretty, but it's the best plan.'

'We did the same thing in Namibia,' said Chris. 'If you took on a village, you finished the lot of them, or there wasn't any point in bothering.'

'So we'd better take plenty of ammo,' said Dan. 'We don't want to stint on that if we're going to double tap everyone before we piss off.'

Steve glanced at Nick. He was listening intently, but also swallowing hard as he heard to the word 'massacre'. Welcome to soldiering, mate, he reflected. Most of the time you'd be better off working in an abattoir; at least there wouldn't be any pretence about what you do for a living.

'It's not just the Taliban we have to worry about,' said Dan. 'I've fought through this country, and there are at least three al-Queda training camps in precisely the territory we'll be moving through. Those bastards are always up for a bit of target practice, and they don't care whether they live or die. We need to know exactly where they are, because if they get hold of us, they'll slice our heads off and display them on Al-Jazeera in less time than it takes to open a copy of the Koran.'

'Lockhart will make sure you know where they are,' said Bruce. 'And you'll have maps so you can skirt around them. You're not here to fight al-Queda, so the main thing is to stay out of their way.'

'And the fencing?' said Jeff.

'I know a good man in Dubai,' said Bruce. 'Like I said, the souk there is the biggest gold market in the world. While you're on the mission, I'll open an account for each of you, and the money will be deposited there within ten days of the stash being handed over. You have my word on that.'

'And what happens if we die?' said Ian. He was leaning forward on the table as he spoke.

'Nobody's going to die,' said Ollie.

'We all know this is dangerous,' said David. 'It's a fair question.'

'If nine men come back, then we split the money nine ways,' said Bruce. 'If it's eight, then it's eight ways.'

Ian chuckled. 'I'm watching my back then.'

'What do you mean?' said Ollie.

'Do the maths,' said Ian. 'If one of us goes down, the share to the other men rises by three hundred and thirty-three thousand dollars. I've met a lot of men who wouldn't mind slotting a bullet into my back for a lot less than that.'

'None of us would do that,' snapped Nick. His face was suddenly bright red with anger.

'You've a lot to learn,' said Ian, an indulgent smile creasing his face.

'Calm it, boys,' said Bruce. He stood up. 'We run a tight ship, and this job might be off the books but that doesn't mean it's off the record. Anyone messes around, anyone plays any mind games, then they're going to have to answer to me when it's all over.'

He shot a sharp glance at each man, the same one Steve knew he'd used on the training grounds back in Hereford.

'So let's put our backs into this and try to make it happen. And I'll see you boys in Pakistan.'

He left the room and Steve followed him to the door. They shook hands briefly, and Bruce walked across to the taxi he'd kept waiting. The man didn't stick around, it wasn't his style; he gave you the job, sorted out the money, then left you to get on with it. Whether you made a go of it was up to you.

Except, reflected Steve, he wouldn't have picked you if he didn't think you could pull it off.

By the time he got back to the kitchen, Jeff and Dan and Ian were involved in a conversation about why Bruce was taking twenty million dollars. After all, it was them that were putting their lives on the line. 'When we hit the border, we could just split the loot up amongst ourselves,' said Dan. 'I mean, how hard is it to fence gold and diamonds? You just get a boat and sail it across to Dubai.'

'And have Bruce Dudley hunting you down to the ends of the earth,' said Steve, sitting down next to them. 'Just remember, he's Scottish, and he's Regiment, and that tells you that he's a mean fucker, in both senses of the word. You don't steal from the man because he'll kill you for certain.'

'Just seems like a lot for the middleman, that's all,' said Dan. 'Cut him out, and it's an extra two million for each man.'

'Listen up,' interrupted Jeff. 'If it wasn't for him, we wouldn't have this job. It's a lot of money, more than any of us are probably worth.'

'And we gave him our word,' said Ollie. 'The only way this job is going to work is if we all trust each other, and that means we trust Bruce as well. Anyone wants to start questioning that, we might as well pack up and bugger off home right now.'

Steve was looking hard at Dan. The man had been jailed for a year and they only had his side of the story about how that had happened. Now here he was talking about doing a runner with Bruce's money. Someone to keep an eye on? Maybe.

'In the meantime, we need to get organised,' said Ollie. He was leaning over the map, with David at his side, both of them studying it. 'We need to get down as close to Kajaki as possible, and find ourselves a safe house where we can lay up for a couple of days and start sorting out a plan. 'I reckon David and I should find ourselves a pair of Afghan scouts and get down there tonight if possible.'

Steve nodded. 'You take care of that, and we'll spend thirty-six hours here kitting ourselves out with everything we might need. As soon as you've found somewhere, we'll follow you straight down.'

'Right,' said Ollie. 'And then we can have a look at the whites of this Salangi fellow's eyes.'

Fourteen

THE JOURNEY WAS A LONG and hot and dusty one, with every crater and pothole in the road smashing into the tired suspension of the twelve-year-old Ford Transit van in which they were travelling. Ollie was fairly certain he'd been on more uncomfortable journeys, but right now, he reflected sourly, he was buggered if he could remember them.

David seemed to be sleeping soundly on the few planks of battered hardwood that lay across the floor of the van. It was just after four in the afternoon. Up front, the van was being driven by pair of Afghan scouts, Abdul and Haji, both of them in their mid-thirties, with close-cropped black beards, and a manner that suggested if you found them back in Britain they'd be selling dodgy DVDs at a car boot sale. They had found the scouts through a guy Dan had known last time he was fighting in Afghanistan and for a fee of five hundred dollars in cash up front they'd agreed to take Ollie and David to Gereshk, right in the heart of Helmand Province. When they arrived there, they'd introduce them to another scout who'd be able to start sorting them out with a safe house. That was the plan anyway. Until he saw it for himself, Ollie wasn't going to start believing anyone.

It had taken the best part of the morning to organise the journey. The Ford van needed an oil change, and a full set of spare tyres, since the state of the roads meant you were always at risk of a puncture. They slung six jerry cans of spare diesel in the back as well, since filling stations were rare in Afghanistan, and they were often staked out by robbers, which meant you might not want to stop at them anyway. Next, Abdul put in four crates of live chickens – if you were stopped, you could always claim you were in the poultry business – and two changes of number plates. They'd be travelling through Kandahar and Helmand Provinces in the lawless far south of the country, and one way of avoiding drawing any attention to yourself in both places was to stick local number plates on to your vehicle. Plenty of locals got robbed, but at least you had a chance of getting through; if they thought you were from Kabul, they'd rob you just for the fun of it.

The Kabul-Kandahar highway covered the three hundred miles that separated Afghanistan's two biggest cities. It had been rebuilt in 2003 by the Americans at a cost of three hundred million dollars, and although it was by far the best road in the country, cutting what used to be a two-day drive into a manageable six or seven hours, it was still a slow and tough journey. Ollie and David stayed in the back, keeping themselves out of view, but that only made the journey duller. You couldn't look out of the windows, and because you couldn't see the potholes coming, they hit you with added, unexpected force.

David stayed asleep for most of the journey, but Ollie found he was wide awake. Too much on my mind, he reflected. It had been a tough two years, bouncing from one failure to another ever since he had crashed out of the Blues, and it was probably only now, he realised, that he could see how low his life had sunk. This is my chance to climb back, he thought to himself, and this time I'm not going to blow it. With the money he'd make, he could buy that house Katie wanted so much for cash. And then? I can do whatever I want with my life.

At just after five, they turned east at Kandahar, on to Highway One, which would take them straight through to Helmand Province. Further on up this road, Ollie knew, the British were stationed at Camp Bastion, and from what he'd heard from the men who'd been out there, the fighting was rough and desperate. There were attacks each and every day, and you couldn't expect a week to go by without at least one of your mates being wounded or killed. If there was one thing he regretted about leaving the Blues, it was the fact he hadn't had a posting to Helmand. It was real, live soldiering, the sort of fighting that tests a man and puts some steel into his soul, and even though you knew it might kill you, most soldiers wouldn't miss it for the world. Doesn't matter, he told himself. We're here now, and we're taking on a fight that's even tougher than what the boys in the garrison are facing. They'd be proud of us if they knew.

David woke up as they skirted Kandahar, and they spent the last couple of hours of the drive chatting. At first, David had been disappointed not to have a chance to stop at Kandahar. The city had been founded by Alexander the Great, and the Battle of Kandahar in 1880 had been decisive in the Second Afghan War. It was a battle in which the British eventually prevailed, but only at the cost of horrendous losses to the 92nd Highlanders and 2nd Gurkhas who took the brunt of the fighting and the casualties. After the battle, the war wound down to an uneasy stalemate, and Afghanistan eventually went back to being a buffer state between British India and an expansionist Russia. 'Just like this time around,' said David. 'We'll go home eventually, and I reckon there will be no real victory. At best a buffer state between the modern world and the medieval nutters that make up the Taliban.'

It was just after seven when the van pulled up in a narrow street in Gereshk. By Afghan standards, which admittedly weren't very high, it was a relatively clean and civilised place. It had a population of fifty thousand, and a local hydroelectric plant meant there was plenty of electricity, and clean drinking water, both rarities once you got outside Kabul. The UN had a base there, and the British garrison had stationed a forward operating base there through much of 2006. Overlooking the main part of the town were the ruins of a British fort, left over from the First Afghan War, where the British troops had withstood a siege that lasted more than sixty days. Today the fort was reduced to dust, but as Ollie glanced at it from the side of the van, you could still see the formidable obstacles to an attacker it must have once presented. Along the centre of the town was a busy, bustling market, but the van drove past all that, ignoring the honking scooters all around it, until it pulled up outside a small cafe on one of the side streets.

Ollie waited in the back of the van. They knew they had to be careful over the next few minutes, and for a moment Ollie wished they'd taken the time to buy themselves some guns back in Kabul. They hadn't brought any with them because it was impossible to get them on a plane. Steve was planning to buy all the weapons they needed in Kabul, then bring them down. They hadn't wanted to delay heading south to find a safe house, and even in Kabul, getting hold of a weapon took a few hours if you didn't know your way around. Even so, a pistol would have been handy. They had no real idea whether they could trust their scouts. Plenty of them would take your money then hand you in to the Taliban for an extra fee; you'd be tortured to find out what you were doing in the country, then you'd have your throat cut.

'We should have a damned gun,' hissed David.

'I know,' agreed Ollie.

He was angry with himself for not having insisted to Steve that they arm themselves before they headed south. He knew the man's reputation: brave, clever, resourceful, but also slapdash, and sometimes careless. Like many of the Regiment boys, he wasn't a detail man. He just assumed that guts and determination would get you through. Well, sometimes it did. And sometimes it just got you a bullet in the face.

'Typical Dudley,' said David. 'They don't call his outfit Death Inc. for nothing.'

'We'll be fine,' said Ollie.

Haji opened the back of the van and motioned them inside the cafe. It was late dusk outside. A half moon was looming out of the blackish sky, and a few of the lights from the houses combined to fill the narrow street with a hazy, misty light. The cafe was just a small shop front with a couple of tables and chairs outside it, one of them filled by an elderly man sipping tea by himself. In the flat above, Ollie could hear a baby crying, but otherwise the street was mostly quiet. Haji motioned them to step inside. 'Quick, quick,' he muttered.

Ollie and David followed him into the cafe, then through an open door into what looked like a storeroom. Abdul was already inside, and closed the door behind them. Ollie was well aware that a couple of white men didn't want to be seen around town; even if these guys weren't going to turn them in to the Taliban, the place would be teeming with informers who would tip them off if anyone suspicious moved through. The Taliban didn't respect any rules of warfare, and they didn't expect their opponents to either. They expected covert operations and special forces attacks to be directed against them. If they heard of a couple of military-looking guys searching for a safe house anywhere in Helmand they'd make their own assumptions about what they were up to and deal with them accordingly.

Haji lit a candle, which filled the room with its soft light. Around them were rows of shelves holding packets of tea, cartons of juice, bread, tins of food, and everything else you needed to run a cafe. A man stepped out of the shadows. Ollie tensed instinctively. If it came to a fight, it was three against two. He didn't mind those odds, but the opposition was probably armed, and that made things tricky.

The man was in his fifties, with drooping, sad eyes, and a thick black moustache.

'Farooq,' said Haji, introducing the old man.

Ollie nodded curtly.

'You're British?' asked Farooq.

He spoke in heavily-accented English, but clearly, and with an ease that suggested he was an educated man. That reassured Ollie. Most of the middle-class Afghans, and particularly the older ones, hated the Taliban and had no problems working with the British.

'That's right,' said Ollie carefully.

'And what is it you want in Gereshk?'

'We are looking for a house where some guys can lay up

for a few days, a week at most,' said Ollie. 'Out in the countryside. Somewhere discreet.'

'And who are you working for?'

Ollie reached into his pocket. Dudley had left them twenty-five thousand dollars in fifty dollar bills. Steve had taken twenty of that to buy weapons, and Ollie had five to secure them a house. Three thousand was strapped to his calf with masking tape, next to a six-inch blade he'd borrowed from the kitchen in Kabul, but the other two thousand was in his pocket. He pulled out the wad of notes so they were clearly visible in his hand.

'Let's just say we are working for Mr Cash,' he said. 'You find us the house, we pay you, and nobody asks us any questions.'

Farooq nodded. 'I can find you a place,' he said.

Ollie glanced at David, then looked back at Farooq. 'Let's go then.'

He paid two hundred dollars to Abdul – they'd already paid three hundred before they left Kabul – and thanked them for the ride. Farooq asked them to wait for a moment, then returned with two flashlights. He led them out of the back of the cafe into a narrow maze of twisting side streets that led away from the centre of the town. There was no lighting, and even though the town had electricity, most of the ordinary houses weren't wired up to the grid, so there was only the light of the moon and the stars to guide them. They'd been walking for about ten minutes when they reached a lock-up with a corrugated metal gate. Farooq pushed it aside and opened the door on an elderly Suzuki Swift, one of the smallest and ugliest cars ever built. 'Here,' he said.

Ollie climbed into the front seat, David got into the back, and Farooq took the wheel. It clearly wasn't his car – he was looking around for the headlight switch. It started on the second attempt, and Farooq steered them out on to the main road. They were already on the outskirts of Gereshk, and he drove away from Highway One, north-west into the hills. Gereshk was sited on the Helmand River, a waterway that ran straight through the province, then twisted down into Pakistan. At its head was the Kajaki dam which provided power and irrigation for much of the region, and the valley through which the river ran was kept lush and green by its waters. It was, noted Ollie, a stunning landscape, even in the darkness: high, sweeping hills, interspersed with carefully cultivated fields, almost all of them now given over to growing poppies. The tarmac road ended a couple of miles outside Gereshk, and Farooq twisted the Suzuki on to tracks of baked mud, the surface pitted with pebbles and rocks. They passed a couple of tiny villages, little more than a collection of a dozen huts and a water well, and then started to climb a steep mountain. Ollie could feel the temperature dropping a couple of degrees as the altitude got up past a thousand feet. He remained on his guard. Farooq hadn't turned on them yet, but that didn't mean he wasn't driving them straight into a Taliban camp where they'd be handed over to the enemy.

The car laboured to get to the steep summit of the hill. Farooq took it down into second gear and slammed his foot hard on the accelerator, but the one-litre engine still struggled to make any progress. Eventually the reached the summit, the track turned, and then it started to fall away, twisting precipitously down the hillside. Farooq killed the engine, letting the Suzuki freewheel, just using the brake to control it. Ollie tried to make out the landscape ahead. They had passed through the valleys irrigated by the river now, and were out into the dusty stretches of scrubland beyond. There were no fields, just long, rolling vistas of desolate ground, broken by occasional clumps of wild irises.

The real Afghanistan, thought Ollie to himself. The hellhole of the universe.

They freewheeled for another twenty minutes, bouncing through the potholes, until Farooq turned the engine on again and steered the Suzuki on to a track that led along the side of the hills. They were about two-thirds of the way down to the valley below, but the hills were folding in on themselves, creating a valley within the hill, with steep ridges surrounding it. Farooq slowed the car and brought it to a stop outside a simple, two-roomed mud and brick hut, with a corrugated iron roof, and a water well outside it. It was completely dark now, and Ollie could only see by the headlamps of the Suzuki.

He climbed out carefully. If this was a trap, this would be the moment they would strike, but the place seemed abandoned. With David at his side, he walked carefully towards the building. It was simple, but not derelict. The walls were in a decent enough state, and the roof gave plenty of cover; it would make a hell of noise in the unlikely event of rain, but it would keep you dry. There was some straw covering the dusty floor, and a metal trough to one side, which you could use to either water your donkey or wash yourself. There were no lights, and no sign of any plumbing, but it was clean enough. Ollie walked across to the well. It was just a hole in the ground, with a brick surround, and a metal bucket on a piece of rope at its side. He tossed the bucket down, and from the time it took to drop, he reckoned it was forty feet down to the water. He pulled up the bucket and dipped his hands into the water, then pressed them to his lips. It seemed OK. He could taste no chemicals or human or animal waste in it. Looking up, he scanned the horizon. There were ridges all around them, which meant the building couldn't be seen from any of the surrounding valleys, and if you went inside, the building would give you plenty of cover to fight off any attackers coming over the hills. 'Drinking water, and cover,' said Ollie, glancing at David.

'That's all we need,' replied David. 'It'll do.'

'How much?' said Ollie, looking towards Farooq.

'For one week, two thousand dollars.'

'For this crap hole?'

Farooq shrugged.

'I can stay in the bloody Hilton for less money than that.'

Farooq opened the palms of his hands. 'Then go to the Hilton, my friend.'

Ollie grimaced. If there was one thing he hated it was being ripped off. Nobody ever messed with the British Army, but once you moved out to the PMCs there were always people who thought you were on some big, all-expenses paid contract, and they could charge you whatever they damned well liked. And sometimes they could. That didn't stop it from sticking in your throat.

'Ollie, we need this place,' whispered David. 'It's close to the target, it's got water, and it's secure. We're not going to find anything better.'

Ollie nodded. He knew David was right, he just couldn't stomach paying over the odds. 'We'll take it, on one condition,' he said, looking at Farooq.

Farooq nodded.

'You've got email?'

Farooq nodded again. 'There's a cafe in town with a computer.'

'Then send a message to SayeedSalem2261@hotmail.com, and give him the precise GPS co-ordinates of this place.'

'It will be done.'

Slowly Ollie counted out two thousand dollars in bills and handed them across. 'And make sure no one knows we're here.'

Farooq turned round and walked back to the waiting car. He started the engine.

Ollie remained silent as he watched the car chug its way back up the side of the hill. He glanced up at the stars, and took a moment to smell the scent of the wild irises drifting on the cold night air.

'We'd better start making ourselves at home,' he said. 'The rest of the lads should be here by tomorrow, or the next day at the latest.'

Fifteen

KABUL WAS SHORT OF JUST about everything that made up a civilised society, but there were two things it had in abundance: beggars and arms dealers. The country had been in a continuous state of war for the best part of thirty years, and two superpowers had poured every form of munitions and armament known to man into the nation. If it killed people, or blew them up, then you could get it in Kabul.

Steve ignored the beggars crowding the street corner and pushed on to the cafe. He had a rough list of dealers supplied by Bruce, a man who made it his business to know at least one decent weapons merchant in every city in the world. He'd chosen Amazai because he'd been told he had the best stocks, decent prices, and went out of his way to help his customers. And, at least the way Bruce told it, he didn't immediately sell on your details to the Taliban.

The cafe was located a third of the way along Chicken Street, the bustling market that lay at the centre of Kabul's life. In the 1960s, Chicken Street had been at the end of the hippie trail, the cheapest place to buy drugs in the world, and it still retained something of its bohemian, lawless character.

All along the street were dozens of shops selling antiques, rugs, swords, CDs, electronics and mobile phones, while the street itself was teeming with food stands, cafes, and clerks who helped the mostly illiterate Afghans fill in their visa applications and other forms. Judging by the amount of business they were doing, Steve reckoned that just about everyone in Kabul was trying to get a visa for somewhere else. And, looking around, who could blame them?

'So where the hell is it?' asked Chris.

Steve had brought Chris and Dan along to start scouting the weapons they'd need, Chris because of all of them he had the most experience of fighting in rough, hostile territory, and Dan because he was the most technically sophisticated of them. According to Bruce, Amazai would be meeting them at a cafe known only as Number 93, but all the shops were so cluttered with stuff for sale it was impossible to see any numbers even if they were there.

'Mr West?'

Steve looked across. The man was sitting outside a food stand, sipping a cup of Afghan green tea. He was small and wiry, with grey hair and a distinguished manner. He was wearing a dark suit instead of the robes that most of the Afghan traders wore.

'Amazai?'

He nodded, stood up and shook Steve by the hand.

'You come highly recommended,' said Steve.

'Then I hope I can justify your trust,' said Amazai.

Steve declined the offer of mint tea; the stuff was far too sweet for his taste. All three of them bought bottled water from the cafe – it was past midday now, and the clear blue skies meant the temperature was climbing steadily through the thirties – and followed Amazai as he walked steadily along Chicken Street, before turning sharply to the right into a narrow maze of side streets that led towards the city's main mosque. 'Here,' he said finally.

It didn't look like much, thought Steve. A long, thin building, shabbily constructed out of concrete and breeze blocks maybe twenty years ago, it now looked to be a mix of apartments and small offices. Stepping into the foyer, Amazai explained that it had been built by the Russians in the early 1980s as an apartment building for the KGB men stationed in the city, and as he retold the story, Steve had the strong suspicion that Amazai himself might well have worked for the KGB in those days. He certainly had the look of a man who could survive any regime, and most of the weapons for sale in Kabul were of Russian origin, so an arms dealer was certainly going to need contacts with that country's army.

'Downstairs,' said Amazai.

He pushed open a pair of metal doors to one side of the foyer and led them down a concrete staircase. In the basement, there were two rooms filled with fuse boxes and boilers for the block, but another set of doors led to more stairs, leading down to a lower level. 'This was built for the KGB,' explained Amazai. 'And they always knew they would be the main targets for any bombing raids on the city. So they built a deep bunker. It makes the perfect place to store our goods. Secure, and the rent is reasonable.'

He flicked a switch. The room was long and square, measuring eighty feet by thirty, and must have run under the street outside as well as the building itself. It had no windows, and only six low-wattage light bulbs, but it was decently constructed, dry, clean, and with no sign of the crumbling concrete you could see on the street outside.

Along its length were six rows of metal shelves. And each one of them was packed high with every weapon you could imagine.

It wasn't so much an arsenal as a trade show for the world arms industry, decided Steve.

'Great gear, mate,' said Dan, sounding impressed.

'If you tell me what you need, we should be able to find it for you,' said Amazai. His tone was stiff and polite, but he clearly appreciated the compliment. Everyone liked to get some satisfaction out of their work. Even arms dealers.

Steve had made a mental checklist of what they would need. They wouldn't know for certain until they scouted Salangi's fort and decided on a plan of attack, but they could take the basics with them. They'd need at least a dozen AK-47s, the sturdy, reliable, indestructible Russian assault rifle, one for each man, plus a couple of spares in case any of them got lost or damaged. They'd take along a couple of M-16s as well. The American-built weapon has been standard issue through NATO for years, which meant all the men were familiar with it. Anyone who'd been in the special forces would have had training with both weapons, and most of them preferred the AK to the M-16. It was a simpler, more reliable weapon, whereas not everyone trusted the M-16, particularly as sand could make it jam, and there'd be plenty of that where they were going. The locals would use AKs, which would make it easier to pick up extra ammunition locally if they needed it. Against that, the M-16 was more accurate over longer distances. Best to have both, decided Steve. When it came to weaponry, it was always better to be safe than sorry.

'Which country?' asked Chris, inspecting a row of AK-47s.

The AK was made not just in Russia, but in several of the

former Soviet bloc countries, and fakes were churned out all over the Middle East. The consensus among professional soldiers was that the Romanian guns were the best: they had the best build quality, they never jammed, and the spent case spat away efficiently from the mag, allowing a rapid rate of fire.

'Romanian,' answered Amazai.

Chris picked one off the shelf, assessed its feel and weight, then checked its proof mark. Every AK had one, to tell you which of the many factories had manufactured the weapon. This one was a Romanian WASR-10 model, and the proof mark showed an arrow shooting up inside a triangle: the mark belonged to the Romanian Cugir arsenal, the better of that country's two main armaments centres. To anyone else, the Cugir proof mark could easily be confused with the Russian Izhevsk arsenal, but that had a feather as well as an arrow inside a triangle. Everyone Chris had fought in southern Africa had carried Eastern bloc manufactured AK-47s, and he'd staged countless raids on rebel weapons dumps. He'd learned how to distinguish one from another: the better the gun your opponents were carrying, the better financed and organised you could assume they were. And the more dangerous.

'It looks OK,' he said to Steve.

He checked that the chamber was clear, then locked back the bolt and put his thumbnail in the chamber so that he could look down the bore. It looked clear as well. Next, he took off the top cover and checked all the working parts. Nothing wrong with those either. 'I don't suppose you have a firing range to check its accuracy,' said Chris.

Amazai laughed. 'Not unless you want to kill us all with the ricochets.'

Steve placed an order for twelve AKs, and three M-16s. They'd take ten thousand rounds of ammunition as well, plus four mags for each gun, so that each man would have plenty spare and wouldn't have to stop halfway through a battle to reload. The one thing he'd learned from the soldiers he'd spoken to who'd been out fighting in Helmand was that once the Taliban started coming at you, they didn't stop. They threw wave after wave of men into an attack. 'You need a lot of bullets because they've got a lot of mad bastards,' was the way one Regiment bloke had put it. And the last thing Steve wanted to do was find himself in a fire fight and running low on ammo.

Amazai stocked 7.62 × 39mm Kalashnikov rounds, enough to inflict serious damage on a vehicle, and to kill a man if you hit him in the right place. Steve inspected one of the bullets, and judged it acceptable. The bullets came in steel boxes, each one holding a thousand rounds. Ten of them were stacked up next to the door, along with the rifles.

Next, they inspected the RPGs. There were three models to choose from. The rocket-propelled grenade was originally developed by the Germans during the Second World War to counter Russian tanks. Steve wasn't reckoning to come up against any armoured vehicles – at least he hoped not to – but an RPG was still the most effective way of delivering a high-explosive charge over a thousand metres or so. It was accurate, simple to use, and packed a big punch. It consisted of nothing more than a simple metal tube, slung over the shoulder, and a series of bulb-shaped missiles. You could fire it directly into a wall, or a clump of trees, or whatever your opponents were using for cover. Alternatively, with the right training, you could use its self-destruct feature, then lob it into the sky to explode directly above the enemy, to create a nasty rain of fire and molten shrapnel. Not pretty, reflected Steve, but bloody effective.

Of all the models, the most famous was the Russian made RPG-7, first deployed in 1961. It was followed by the 16, 18, 22, 26, 27 and 29; the latest, the 29, had been deployed in 1989, and had been widely sold in the Middle East. In Iraq, the British Army had learned to be wary of them: a single missile could knock a nasty hole even in a heavily armoured Challenger tank. But Steve preferred the RPG-7, and so did Dan. Weapons were like cars, Steve reminded himself. The older, simpler versions were often the best. The engineers added on all kinds of bells and whistles, but usually you just wanted something you could point and fire, and the RPG-7 did that just fine.

Steve placed an order for three, with thirty missiles.

Next they needed at least a hundred hand grenades. Amazai had a stock of ARGES 84-P2A1, a small hand grenade made by Pakistan Ordnance Factories, the state-controlled arms manufacturer set up by the Pakistani government after partition from India. They were neat, and by reputation reliable: each one weighed only 480 grams, made from hardened plastic with a steel ball, and they had a good kick on them, creating an explosion that would hurt anyone within a twenty-metre radius of the detonation point. If they needed to finish off any stragglers at the fort, the grenades would be just what they needed.

'Handguns,' said Dan. 'We need at least one for each man.'

The pistols were laid out in open crates. Amazai had a selection of Berettas, Glocks and Colts, but it was the Makarov 9mm that captured Steve's interest. The Makarov was a Russian sidearm, developed along similar lines to the classic German Walther PP. Unlike the Walther, however, it was double-action, so that once you had a round in place, you could fire it just by pulling the trigger, rather than having to cock the weapon. What Steve liked about it, however, was the ammo. The Makarov used 9mm x 18mm rounds, but the Russian-designed bullets were actually slightly larger than a standard Western 9mm round. The result was that although it was a compact weapon, it packed a hefty punch, more than capable of killing a man at thirty yards if you knew what you were doing. It had a small mag, holding only eight bullets, but if they ran low on ammo they'd be able to steal or buy plenty down in Helmand. Steve placed an order for twelve, plus a thousand rounds of ammo.

On top of that, they needed all the basic kit. Steve scooted around the warehouse, buying up Kevlar body plates to strap round their chests – the lightweight body armour could stop anything up to a 9mm bullet – webbing and holsters to hold their weapons in place, helmets to put on their heads, ropes, plastic explosives and ten-inch hardened steel hunting knifes. They took rucksacks, water bottles, and American Army MREs, the meal-ready-to-eat sachets of food that the US soldiers carried, and which meant you could have a quick, hot, nutritious if not particularly tasty meal anywhere you went.

'Christ, is that an M2A1-7?' said Chris, pointing to a box in the corner.

Steve had heard of the M2A1-7, but he'd never actually seen one before. Consisting of two green cylinders, mounted on a metal frame, with a tube leading to a powerful metal nozzle, it didn't look like much but the American-designed flame-thrower was, by reputation anyway, one of the nastiest weapons ever produced. Flame-throwers were first developed by the Germans during the First World War and were widespread on both sides during the Second World War, but the M2A1-7 was by general consent the most lethal ever built. It was widely used in Vietnam, but the horrific casualties and burns it inflicted on civilians meant that by 1978 the US Army had bowed to public opinion and production of the M2A1-7 finally stopped, and the weapon was phased out of use. By the 1980s, all the major armies around the world had given up on flame-throwers. They weren't specifically banned, but using one could easily land you a war crimes charge.

'You ever used one?' said Steve, looking at Chris.

'Christ, yes, we used them all the time,' said Chris. 'I mean, I know we weren't meant to and all that crap, but out in the bush, a flame-thrower is a bloody effective weapon. There's something about flame that scares the shit out of a man.'

He picked up the nozzle of the M2A1-7. 'You get a thirty-metre stream of pure liquid flame jetting out of this bastard. It lands on a guy, it starts to cook him instantly. You should hear the sound, a kind of low, squealing noise as a man gets burned to death. Scares the fuck out of everyone that hears it, and most of them just start running away. I remember once we came across the river out in Namibia, and a group of Swapo boys, probably only fourteen or fifteen, but brutes, were getting some water, and we took a position behind them, and turned a couple of these bastards on them—'

'All right, all right, leave it out, we can imagine,' interrupted Steve.

'It'll be bloody hot and dry where we're fighting,' said Chris sharply.

'Meaning?'

'Meaning things will catch fire real easy.'

Steve looked at Amazai. 'We'll take it,' he said.

'How about a thermobaric?' said Dan, perking up. 'Any chance of one of those?'

Christ, thought Steve to himself. This is like taking a pair of six-year-olds to Toys'R'Us for the morning: a sodding expensive way to fill up the time.

Amazai nodded, a thin smile on his face. 'I believe so.'

If the M2A1-7 was an old and obsolete weapon, a thermobaric would bring their fighting capability bang into the twenty-first century. Thermobarics were the latest thing in military hardware, a fuel air weapon that produced an exploding cloud inside a building, sucking out the internal organs of its victims.

Amazai led them towards a thick steel chest, and opened up its lock. It was clear that this was where he kept the good stuff: the high-end weaponry that only well-trained, well-financed soldiers would be looking for. Dan peered inside like a kid looking into a sweet box. Laid out in the box were a pair of American-made SMAW-NE thermobarics.

The first part of the acronym stood for shoulder-mounted assault weapon, which was an accurate enough description of what it was, but that didn't distinguish it from a standard RPG, or dozens of other missiles on the market. The second part stood for novel explosive, which struck Steve as an excessively polite way of putting it. FDE – fucking deadly explosive – might have been more accurate. Manufactured by Talley Defence Systems, the shell literally ignited the air inside a building. The weapon fired a fine, flammable mist into the air and set fire to it, creating a massive fireball and sucking out all the oxygen over a wide area. Anyone in the vicinity would either burn or suffocate to death, while a building struck by a thermobaric missile would cave in on itself. The US Army had used them to devastating effect in the Battle of Fallujah in Iraq, where they allowed a single trooper to take out a whole building at a hundred yards or more with just one round.

Steve had two thoughts in mind. They might need one to attack the fort. Then again, thermobarics were also perfect for attacking caves, exactly the kind of place the Taliban and al-Queda holed up in Afghanistan. A single missile could rip through a network of caves, sucking out the oxygen, and killing everyone inside. That was why the American forces had brought plenty into the country; presumably these two had fallen off the back of a lorry somewhere.

'How much?' asked Steve.

'Five thousand dollars each,' replied Amazai.

'Bollocks,' snapped Steve. 'They are worth three, tops.'

Amazai remained totally impassive. 'Three Western soldiers looking to buy an SMAW-NE on the black market? I haven't asked what you're doing in this country, because I never ask any of my clients what they are doing. Their business is their business. But allow me to make this observation. If you need one of these weapons, it's worth any price.'

'Four thousand,' said Steve.

'Nine for the pair.'

'Done,' said Steve.

It was a lot of money. But Steve reckoned he knew of no other weapon that had such lethal power on the battlefield. And given the prize at stake, there wasn't much point haggling over a couple of grand here and there.

They quickly checked off the remaining items they needed. They collected two M24G machine guns, complete with ammo, and one M107 long-range sniper rifle (LRSR) that could take out a man at two thousand metres. They weren't planning on any sniper attacks but, same as always, it was better to be prepared. Finally, Dan insisted on buying an old Vickers aircraft gun, a piece of kit that looked as if it might have been slung on the underside of a Spitfire.

'What the hell is that for?' asked Chris.

'Just put it on the back of a jeep and see how much damage it can do,' said Dan.

In total the bill came to thirty-two thousand dollars, but Steve managed to haggle it down to thirty all in. It was more than they had planned, but he knew Bruce was good for another few thousand. He could be mean, and he'd want to know what you were spending it on, but in the end he wasn't going to send you into battle without anything to fight with.

'Get everything ready,' said Steve, counting out half the money, with the promise of the other half on collection, 'and we'll pick it up at dawn tomorrow.'

Jeff looked around the grimy garage. From their base, Jeff and Ian and Nick had taken a taxi up to the Bagrami industrial park on the outskirts of the city. The park had been built with aid money soon after the invasion, in the expectation that plenty of foreign investors would soon be building factories in the newly liberated country. So far, they had mostly stayed away. Funny that, thought Jeff wryly to himself as he looked around.

Most of the industrial units remained empty, and the few that were rented out were mostly used by the aid agencies to store food and medical supplies. But Mirwais Sadiq had managed to build a decent-sized business, supplying, renting and servicing trucks and SUVs to the aid agencies. Jeff was here as the logistics expert, he was in charge of getting the team and its kit down to Helmand. Ian was there because he wanted to pick up some kit he needed of his own, and Nick was there because he was desperate to get out of the house, and Jeff reckoned it would do him good.

'So why aren't you joining the regular army?' Jeff asked Nick as they rode in the taxi.

'And get my bollocks shot off for thirteen grand a year?' answered Nick. 'Fighting some stupid war out in some hellhole, which the rest of the country doesn't even know about, and then getting dumped in some crap hole of a hospital if I get my legs blown off or something? Why the hell should I want to do that?'

His voice was suddenly passionate, full of rage and aspiration.

'I want to do what you guys are doing,' he continued. 'Fighting, sure, I like the sound of that. But I want to do it for myself and my unit. Choose my own battles and my own pay packet.'

'There's easier ways of making money,' said Ian.

'There's no jobs around Swansea, none that I want anyway,' said Nick. 'It's just the bloody call centre. What kind of work is that for a man? Sitting in front of a crap screen all day, with a pair of headphones stuck over your head, saying "Thank you for calling us about your credit card today, I'm afraid we screwed up your bill, so piss off."' He snorted, and Jeff could see the anger in his eyes. 'It's not much of a job for anybody, is it? But what you boys are doing, now that's an adventure.'

Jeff shook his head. 'It's not the way you think it is,' he said flatly.

The garage wasn't neat, but it was well stocked. There was a selection of trucks, vans and SUVs out the front, and inside the workshop a well-equipped engineering crew who looked as if they knew how to get any vehicle into shape for a hazardous journey through Afghanistan.

'That beauty,' said Jeff, glancing towards Nick and Ian as they climbed out of the taxi, 'is exactly what I'm looking for.'

He was nodding towards a Volvo A30D dump truck, its front bright yellow, with a fat black metal grille, and a huge yellow dumpster stretching behind the cabin. With its big wheels, it was capable of a top speed of only 33 miles an hour, but this was a machine built for delivering cement or sand or steel to building sites in big loads, and it didn't usually matter much how long it took you to get there.

'We're going to a building site?' said Nick. 'I might as well have stayed in Swansea.'

'That is the ultimate close protection vehicle,' said Jeff. 'We get our men and kit into that vehicle. Some of us can kip down in the back if necessary. Then we fill her up with diesel, and drive south, making sure that we put about fifty sandbags in the back. Anyone tries to attack us, the bullets are just going to ping off that beast. If there's anything really nasty starting to blow up, then we just drive into a side street, pause, lift up the dump truck, and tip the sand bags on to the street. Hey presto, an instant roadblock, and the fuckers chasing you have to stop. After that, you just sail off into the sunset.'

'But it's slow,' said Ian.

'Thirty miles an hour is all you're going to make in Afghanistan most of the time as it is,' said Jeff. 'Anyway, five or six hours' driving doesn't make any difference. What counts is getting there in one piece.'

Ian shrugged. It sounded fair enough to him.

Jeff walked across to find Mirwais. He didn't look any

more than thirty, but he had a natural air of authority about him, and spoke good, if heavily accented, English. The Volvo was an expensive piece of kit: a new one would cost well over a hundred grand back in England, and they were built so sturdily they didn't depreciate very fast. The machine on the forecourt looked at least seven years old – Jeff could check its serial number if he needed to, although you couldn't trust Kabul dealers not to change them – so it could easily have a retail value of fifty grand. It took a few minutes to hammer out a deal. They would lease out the vehicle at a rate of two thousand dollars a week, on the condition that Dudley put down a deposit for a hundred thousand dollars to secure the Volvo's return. Jeff insisted the Volvo had a full service before it left the garage, and he wanted at least half an hour before they took it, to test it for any faults. Mirwais agreed; indeed, he agreed quickly enough for Jeff to feel reassured the machine was in good nick.

Next, explained Jeff, they'd need two SUVs. There were a dozen for sale on the forecourt: Toyotas, Nissans, Hyundais and two Land Rovers. After starting up all the engines and taking a look inside, Jeff chose two Toyota Land Cruisers. There were Toyotas all over the place in Afghanistan – at one point they were practically the official vehicle of the Taliban – so you wouldn't be drawing any attention to yourself. And with a 4.7 litre V8 engine that sent 275 horsepower through a five-speed automatic transmission and full-time four-wheel drive, it was a brutally rugged and powerful machine that could stand up to any kind of punishment you threw at it. Before he took them, however, Jeff wanted some modifications. Four-millimetre steel plating had to be riveted into the side panels and roof of the vehicles: that should be enough armour to protect it from light arms fire. It would slow them down from the Land Cruiser's usual top speed of around 85 miles per hour to more like 70 but, just as with the dump truck, it was safety that was important, not time. Ideally, Jeff would have liked bullet-proof glass as well, but Mirwais didn't stock any, and there wasn't time to start hunting around Kabul now. If they got into a rough fight, they'd just blow out the windscreen themselves to stop any glass shattering in their faces.

A full service before we take it out, insisted Jeff. And there was one more request as well. The steel plating should have a hole in its centre, measuring ten inches by three.

'What's that for?' said Nick.

'Wait and see,' said Jeff.

He looked up to see where Ian had got to. For a moment, he'd lost sight of the man, but he showed up a moment later carrying a pair of electronic garage-door openers he'd found at the back of the workshop, and had just bought them for thirty dollars each.

'OK,' said Jeff. 'We're sorted for transport. Let's go.'

'This isn't a beer I'd usually choose,' said Jeff. 'But sod it, we're in Kabul, it's our last night in anything that even starts to resemble civilisation, so I reckon we'd drink wallpaper stripper if that was all we could find.'

He put down two cases of Turkish Efes beer he'd managed to find in the market, along with some lamb, olives, and piles of rice and pitta bread. He and Nick had cooked up a stew and they put that down on the table as well.

'As the only Welshie on the crew, I designate you the resident pisshead,' said Jeff, handing Nick an open bottle.

Nick took a long hit of the cold beer and grinned. 'No worse than a pint of warm Stella anyway.'

Steve sat down at the table and helped himself to some food. He'd already been to an internet cafe close to Chicken Street, and a message had come through on the Hotmail address he'd set up to communicate with Ollie. They had a set of GPS co-ordinates, which was all they needed. It meant Ollie had found them a place. They'd head straight down there tomorrow morning, leaving Kabul at the crack of dawn.

'We eat, we have two beers each, and then we get a good night's kip,' said Steve. 'Because tomorrow morning, we stop faffing about and do some real soldiering.'

There was a good mood amongst the men, he decided. You could tell when a unit was coming together, and this one was doing fine. Even Maksim was slotting in OK, although the two-beer limit looked like it had hit him hard: most Russian soldiers got through a couple of bottles of beer before breakfast, and often washed it down with half a pint of vodka as well. He seemed particularly excited by the acquisition of the thermobarics, regaling them with stories of how the Spetsnaz had used them in Chechnya, attacking an old schoolhouse full of enemy fighters, lobbing a single thermobaric through an open window, then watching as the massive fireball ripped through it. 'The guys who weren't killed by the explosion died when the roof collapsed on top of them,' he said, chuckling to himself. 'Some of us reckoned those missiles were going to put the Spetsnaz out of business. They wouldn't need tough-guy special forces anymore. Just get some kid like Nick here to lob a thermobaric into the enemy and—'

'I'm not a kid,' snapped Nick.

'Enjoy it while you can,' said Chris. 'You'll grow up faster than any man really should once the fighting starts.'

Steve ran through the plan. They'd get up at four, collect the vehicles, then load them up with the weapons they'd bought, ready for the long drive south. The two Toyotas would go up front, driven by local drivers, with Jeff in one and Ganju in the other, while the rest of the men would follow on behind in the Volvo. If they got into any serious trouble, the Toyotas would steer into a side street, the Volvo would follow, and then dump its sandbags to create a roadblock. If it looked safe, they'd all drive off together. If not, Jeff and Ganju would bundle them all into the Toyotas and they'd drive like hell. Drill, drill and more drill, Steve reminded them all. Every man had to know exactly what he was doing, as well as what his mates were doing, in every conceivable circumstance. It was the only way they were going to stay alive.

'What's the chances of an attack?' said Ganju.

'Kabul is a gossipy city,' said Dan. 'And it's crawling with bandits. We've been out splashing a lot of cash around on weapons and kit and that means a fair few people know by now that we're up to something, and we've got stuff worth nicking. That means we're a target.'

'So we stay together and we stay careful,' said Steve.

He ran briefly through the weaponry, detailing what each man would be carrying, and what resources they'd have. Again, they had to know how to react, and with what weapons, otherwise it would be chaos, and when you got into a fire fight, it was usually the unit with the best organisation that prevailed.

'Sounds like we're ready to mallet the bastards,' said Jeff, when he'd finished. 'The only thing that puzzles me is what the Irishman wants a garage door opener for. What's that all about, Ian?'

Steve laughed. 'You're planning to build a patio?'

'We could get a barbecue set up as well,' said Jeff. 'Our own little bit of suburbia down in Helmand.'

'We could get Dave to bring his kids over,' said Steve.

'Get a Ford Focus,' said Jeff.

'I thought you wanted a bomb-maker,' said Ian.

Chris looked up from his beer. 'You're planning to use them to detonate a bomb, right?' he said. 'I've heard of garage door openers being used as low-cost, simple detonators. The IRA perfected that technique, they taught it to their mates in Hezbollah, and now it's used all the time in Iraq.'

Ian nodded. 'That's right.'

'The IRA?' said Steve suspiciously.

Ian looked at him. 'Yes, the IRA.'

'What regiment did you say you were with again?'

'I already told you, one of the Ulster ones.'

'I sodding know that. Which one?'

Ian remained silent.

'I said which fucking one,' snapped Steve.

Jeff was looking at him; his expression said he wanted Steve to cool it. But we need to know where these blokes come from, thought Steve. You can't fight with a man if you don't know who he is.

'So?'

'It wasn't a regiment exactly,' said Ian coldly. 'More like a cell.'

'A jail? You learnt how to detonate bombs inside . . .' He suddenly realised how stupid it sounded. Ian wasn't talking about that kind of cell. He was talking about the political kind.

'Jesus, you were IRA, weren't you?' he said. 'That's the kind of cell you mean, isn't it?'

Ian nodded curtly.

'You're a fucking Provo,' said Steve.

'Retired,' said Ian. 'I *was* a Provo. There's a difference.'

'Once you're a sodding terrorist, you stay one,' said Steve angrily. 'That's the way it is in my book anyway.'

'Let the man tell his story,' interjected Dan.

Ian took a hit of his beer. His face was creased, and for the first time Steve reckoned he looked worried. And rightly so. The men around this table were going to need a lot of convincing to work alongside a Provo.

'I spent ten years in the Provisional IRA as a bomb-maker,' said Ian. 'I signed up in nineteen eighty-five when I was just fifteen, and I was one of the best they had. In nineteen ninety-five I was arrested, tried, and given a life sentence. They pinned all sorts of bombs on me, and although I wasn't guilty of all of them, there wasn't much point in arguing about it since I was sure guilty enough to be banged up. I headed off to the Maze, and I reckoned that was it for me, I'd be there for the rest of my days. Then in two thousand and three I was released. It was part of the Good Friday Agreement. They were letting all us boys out, and there was worse than me in there, much worse. And I was bloody glad to be out of that crap hole, I can tell you that much. After that, I moved to London. I reckoned I needed a change of scene. The war was over, and there was no point sticking around on the field of battle. I wanted to put my technical skills towards some kind of a career. But it's been tough, I don't mind admitting that. Very tough.' He glanced around the table. 'After all, it's not much of a CV, is it?'

'So what the hell makes you think we should take you along?' said Steve.

'Simple, really,' said Ian quietly. 'You need a bomb-maker,

and I was one of the best men in the best bomb-making organisation that ever existed.' He looked Steve straight in the eye. 'You don't have to like me, and I don't have to like you, but if Gerry Adams and Ian Paisley can sit down together, than I reckon you and I can do one robbery.'

'Your boys killed a lot of our boys.'

'It was a war,' said Ian. 'What the hell do you expect?'

'Plenty of them were my regiment.'

'So what are you saying? That you'll never drive a BMW because the British once fought the Germans? Bollocks. It's over, and we're all moving on with what remains of our lives.'

Steve fell silent. The argument was solid enough, the war with the IRA was over, and there was no point in holding grudges. Even so, inside he felt uneasy. Ian might have the skills, and the IRA were good fighters, you couldn't take that away from them. But trust them? He didn't think so.

He looked round the table.

'A man needs a second chance,' said Dan.

'It was a war,' said Ganju. 'We don't hold it against a soldier for fighting. He's just doing his job.'

If that's the way they want it, then that's the way they can have it, thought Steve sourly.

'Then like I said, we should all get ourselves some kip,' he said, his tone curt.

He stood up and walked into the bedroom without another word.

Sixteen

THERE WAS JUST THE HINT of a soft, orange sunrise rising above the haze of the city as Steve signalled for the convoy to hit the highway and start rolling south. As he gave the command, he could feel the muscles in his stomach tensing. We're off. This is where it starts to get serious.

It was just after six in the morning. They had risen at four sharp, and stuffed as much breakfast down their throats as they could manage. With any luck, they should be able to rustle up some decent grub down at the safe house, but on a job like this you never knew where your next meal was coming from, and you didn't want to take any chances. Over breakfast, Steve had caught Ian's eye, and he could see the hostility there. Of all the men there, he seemed to be the only one who had reservations about working alongside an IRA man. There were reasons for that, but Steve wasn't about to discuss them with the others. Ian could see it, however, Steve felt sure of that, and it would be hard work to get any trust restored between them now.

Breakfast finished, they tidied the house, then headed to the garage to collect the vehicles, then to the apartment block to pick up their weapons. By six, they were all set, ready to climb up the slip road on to the highway that would take them due south, and into – well, God knows what, reflected Steve.

The garage had lent them three drivers, one for each vehicle. Once they got to the safe house, hopefully by nightfall, and hopefully in once piece, the drivers would take the tipper truck back to Kabul, leaving the two jeeps behind. It was better for the drivers to be local Afghans, they knew the roads, and they were less likely to draw attention to themselves. Just like Ollie and David, they carried extra sets of number plates, which they changed when they crossed provincial borders.

The two Toyotas were riding up front, with Jeff in one and Ganju in the other, along with their drivers. The Volvo was following behind, with one man riding in the cabin with the Afghan driver, but wearing a turban and a patoo, the traditional shawls that most Afghans wrapped themselves in, so as not to draw attention. The other men were hidden inside the truck. Any group of white guys riding this highway was inevitably going to be a target – if they didn't kill you for ideological reasons, they'd still rob you – so it was important to remain as inconspicuous as possible.

Steve looked up into the sky. It was a crystal sharp morning, without a hint of cloud anywhere to be seen. It would be baking hot by eleven, and they'd need to pull some kind of sheeting across the top of the truck to stop themselves frying to death in the midday sun, but at this time of the day the air was still clean and fresh. The men were sitting on the metal floor of the truck, with their backs up against the side, facing each other. At the back, the sandbags were piled one on top of the other. Next to those, their boxes of weaponry. Each of them had five bottles of water – they would need to drink at least three litres to survive the midday heat – and they'd stocked up on some fresh food to take down to the safe house. As he surveyed their faces, Steve could see the anticipation in their expressions. It was the look written into the bones and skin of men heading into battle over thousands of years, a grim, nervous concentration, mixed with a pepped up anticipation of the battles ahead. Steve could feel it himself: you longed for the battle to begin, and for the blood to start flowing from your enemies' open wounds, and yet at the same time you dreaded the heat, and noise, and pain that you knew inevitably lay ahead.

'So how many bombs did you let off exactly, mate?' said Steve, looking across at Ian.

'Leave it out,' snapped Dan.

'It's OK,' said Ian. 'It's a fair question. I'm not hiding anything.'

'But you weren't exactly rushing to tell us, were you?' said Chris.

'Like I said, it has a way of poisoning your CV. Mention it, and people don't want to know anymore. And believe me, I need this job.'

'Family?' asked Chris.

'No, nothing like that,' said Ian. 'When you're PIRA, they're your family. No one else is allowed to come between you and the organisation. It's worse than a bloody monastery. And when you're in the Maze, you don't get to meet any birds. But I was just kicking my heels in London, getting doors slammed in my face. There's only so many times a day you can be told to piss off before it starts getting on your nerves. So I need this to get my life back on track. With some money, I can start doing something again, maybe put a bit of meaning back into my life.'

'So how many was it?' said Steve.

'About thirty in total,' said Ian. He was looking straight at Steve as he spoke. 'Ten of those didn't go off, or the job got cancelled for one reason or another. The others? Well, there was a lot of dust and broken concrete, and people died as well. I never counted how many, that's not a calculation I'd care to make.'

'Because it means you're a sodding murderer.'

'Really? At least we always gave a warning, so as to avoid civilian casualties. I don't remember the British Army ever doing that.'

'But that's—'

'And I don't suppose this is going to be a peace mission. If there are casualties—'

'They're the bloody Taliban.'

'And to us you were the *bloody* British.'

'But they were civilians. It's different.'

Ian paused. 'If you've got a problem with me, we can pull up the truck, you can give me my ticket, and I'll walk back to the airport.'

'Nobody's got a problem with anyone,' said Dan fiercely. 'Let's just get on with the job.'

'If it's killing civilians you're worried about, maybe you should throw me out,' said Maksim with a broad grin. 'You should have seen the way the Spetsnaz took apart whole villages in Chechnya.'

'And I couldn't say we drew much of a distinction between military and non-military out in Namibia,' said Chris.

Steve stood up. Even standing, he could only just see over the side of the truck, but he needed to stretch his legs. He'd never enjoyed sitting down. It was just after nine now, and they were about forty miles due south of Kabul. There was a steady steam of traffic on the road, but nothing to delay them too much. The two Toyotas were making steady progress right in front of them, sticking to the slow lane of the two-lane highway. Normally, they'd drive on the outside lane; that way, if an assailant tried to pull up alongside you, they'd be level with the passenger, not the driver, and you'd have a chance to take them out. It was hard to drive and shoot at the same time – not impossible, but the chances were, either your shot or your steering would go haywire. But on this highway, it was impossible to drive all the way south in the fast lane at forty miles an hour. In Britain, you'd be hooted for lane-hogging. Out here, they'd probably shoot you.

As he looked at the outer lane, Steve saw a black Nissan with shaded windows overtake them.

Instinctively he felt uneasy. There was something about the vehicle he didn't like.

Jeff was riding in the first Toyota, sitting in the passenger seat next to Rahman, their driver. He was a silent, grey man, with only a few words of English, whose only form of conversation consisted of the phrase, 'Paris Hilton. Sexy. Yes,' followed by a long laugh. Jeff got bored with that after a few minutes, and contented himself with scanning the road. There were plenty of trucks and cars about, and his instincts told him to trust no one. The highway was full of robbers, and they'd make a tempting target. An attack could come from anywhere.

He had his AK-47 sitting on his lap. The mag was full, and he was holding his finger on the trigger, ready to fire at the slightest provocation. Trigger-happy doesn't begin to describe it, he thought. Trigger-sodding-ecstatic would be closer to the mark.

He noticed the vehicle first in the rear-view mirror. It was a black Nissan Pathfinder, one of the blocky, second-generation models. Jeff couldn't see the driver, or the number of passengers, and that made him instantly suspicious.

It was approaching them on the outside lane, but hardly accelerating. They were only doing just over thirty miles an hour, to allow the Volvo to keep pace with them, and the Nissan could easily have cruised past them at seventy or eighty. Instead, it was hovering just on the tail.

As if it's checking us out, decided Jeff. And if it looked that way, it probably was.

'What do you think?' he said, nodding towards Rahmen.

'Paris Hilton—'

'Not that,' snapped Jeff. 'The sodding Nissan.'

Rahmen glanced round. The unease on his face was clear.

Most professional drivers on this highway were used to bandits. They usually carried a wad of cash to buy them off – fifty dollars was enough to satisfy most of them. If necessary, they'd hand over the keys to their vehicle. The one thing they wouldn't do was stop and fight. It didn't make sense. You might win one or two or even three conflicts. But sooner or later you'd end up dead.

We can't stop, decided Jeff. If they find out who we are, and what kit we have on us, they'll kill us for sure. Or else sell us to the Taliban.

'Switch lanes,' he ordered.

Nothing happened.

Maybe Rahmen hadn't heard. Or maybe he was working with the bandits, thought Jeff, delivering us straight to them.

That was the trouble with the Afghans. You could never tell what side they were on.

'I said switch fucking lanes,' he shouted.

Using his left hand, while his right remained gripping the AK-47, Jeff pulled sharply on the wheel, sending the Toyota skidding into the outside lane. There was a blast of horns as the traffic all around them protested. Rahmen gripped the wheel harder, but the message had got through. Behind him, Jeff could see the Nissan pulling into the inside lane. The driver was starting to accelerate, pulling up level with them.

As it drew alongside, Jeff could see the passenger window slide down an inch, and the barrel of a gun poke through. He knew exactly what they were planning. It was standard tactics for highway bandits, and Jeff would do exactly the same if he were in their place. They'd blow out the tyres, wait for the vehicle to pull into the hard shoulder, then close in fast, robbing the victims of everything they had.

But not today, mate, decided Jeff. You chose the wrong victim. On the wrong highway.

He waited until the Nissan was level. Rahmen had steadied the Toyota in the outside lane, so the Nissan was inside them, putting Jeff on the same side as the pursuing vehicle.

'Hold us level,' he told Rahmen.

Jeff kept the AK-47 level on his lap. Its barrel was pointing straight at the ten-inch gap he'd told the garage to leave in the steel plating bolted to the frame of the Toyota. He could see the window of the Nissan edge down another few inches, and suddenly he could see the face of his assailant. A thin man, with dark brown eyes and a thick black beard. He was looking straight at Jeff, then he glanced down at the nearest tyre and pointed his gun at it. He shouted something in

Afghan, but Jeff couldn't understand. Don't need to, he told himself grimly.

He pressed his finger down hard on the trigger of the AK-47. Automatic fire slashed through the thin steel skin of the Toyota, puncturing a hole where it wasn't reinforced and slashing into the bodies of the men behind.

Jeff looked into his assailant's eyes.

And he permitted himself a brief, thin smile. You weren't expecting that, were you, you bastard.

The Nissan swerved violently, knocking into the bonnet of the Toyota, sending a nasty jolt running through the whole vehicle. Jeff felt the impact of the collision in his spine, but he ignored the pain, held himself steady, and lifted the AK-47 in his hand so that it was pointing out of the window. The Nissan had steadied itself, and was dropping behind them now, veering across into the hard shoulder. The driver was badly wounded, with blood pouring out of his eyes and mouth, blocking his vision and making it impossible for him to drive straight. The first gunman was wounded as well; Jeff could see he was clutching his leg in pain. Another man was leaning forward, an AK-47 in his fist, trying to aim at the Toyota. He steadied himself, then started firing. The first couple of rounds smashed into the tarmac, one of the bullets ricocheting upwards and hitting another vehicle. Then a bullet smashed into the back of the Toyota, chewing up part of the back panels. Jeff squeezed hard on his own gun, letting off another few rounds. At the same time, Ganju opened fire from the window of the Toyota he was controlling, while up in the Volvo, Steve was loosing off a few rounds from his vantage point on the top of the truck.

Suddenly, the Nissan was drowning amid a hailstorm of fire. The rounds were ripping through the vehicle, shredding it to pieces. Jeff could see the driver was dead, and the machine was sliding off the road into the scrubland that lay on either side of the highway. Fuel was leaking from its tank, and the windows had been shattered. Another round of bullets had pumped through both the other men, leaving them slumped and bleeding across the seats. Next, the Nissan hit a rock and turned on to its side with a vicious thud, blood leaking from inside the vehicle, mixing with oil and petrol from the broken engine to create small puddles of dark crimson.

Jeff folded his AK back on to his lap and took his finger off the trigger. 'Back to the slow lane, mate,' he said to Rahmen.

He looked back at Ganju, then up towards Steve in the Volvo and gave them the thumbs up. They had already agreed that, should they be attacked, they wouldn't stop. In Afghanistan, people didn't stop for shootings on the road; they drove by on the other side as fast as they could. Sometimes, the first attack was just a trick, to get you to slow down while a second attack was readied.

So the convoy kept rolling south. And within minutes they had left the Nissan a long way behind them.

Jeff plugged his iPod back into his ears, and flicked his playlist towards Springsteen, tapping his fingers against the dashboard as the rousing opening chords of 'Badlands' cranked at full volume through his brain. When you'd just killed a man, some Bruce was exactly what you needed. The Boss understood.

Twenty yards behind him in the Volvo, Steve put down his gun, and sat back down.

'First blood, for this unit at least,' he said.

*

Ollie paced around the perimeter of the dusty compound. It was late afternoon, and they'd already spent nearly twenty-four hours in the two-room shack. Through the morning, they had made the place ready, shoring up the outside walls so that they would have plenty of cover in the event of an attack, drawing up some water from the well, so that they had plenty of spare buckets to cook and wash with, cutting open a pair of old barrels and stashing them out the back, so that the guys would have something to use as a toilet. They could crap into the barrels, and then, in the evening, they could play a round of cards, with the loser getting the job of burning off the day's barrel load with some spare diesel fuel.

They had rested through most of the mid-afternoon, then as early evening approached they spent an hour or so scouting the surrounding territory. If there was a fight, the more you knew about your surroundings, the better your chances of survival. Ollie glanced out across the arid landscape. The hills rolled remorselessly south, desolate and empty, the surface pitted with rocks and boulders, a sprinkling of sand and dust covering everything. Armies have marched through this rathole for millennia, he reflected. What the hell they were looking for, it was impossible to tell.

Judging by the tracks, some of them fresh, the shack was being used regularly. But by whom? It wasn't much of a place, that was certain. Drug couriers maybe, making the run from the Helmand poppy fields, across into Pakistan. Bandits? The Taliban? Let's just hope to hell they don't stop by while we're here.

They hadn't brought a satellite phone with them, even though that had been Ollie's first instinct, but they'd be bringing one on the main convoy. Steve and Dan reckoned satellite phones weren't safe. The Taliban might be scanning the area for satphone signals. If they got a fix, they'd assume it was British special forces and prepare an attack, and then they'd be in trouble. This was the Taliban's territory, and they didn't like trespassers.

'What are you planning for the money?' asked David. He was kneeling on the bank of the ridge that led away from the shack and looked out on to the valley below, sifting clumps of sand through his hands.

'Getting married,' said Ollie. 'Katie's got her eye on a big house.'

'Sure you need the aggro?'

Ollie grinned. 'I know, I know. With any luck I'll get my bollocks shot off and won't have to worry about it anymore.'

'The kids are great, but it's a lot of pressure.'

'You going to be OK with twins?'

David grinned. 'So long as we get the three million at the end of this job.'

'We will.'

David's expression suddenly turned serious. 'In case it doesn't, I took out some insurance.'

'For a job like this? You're joking.'

None of the men in the PMCs were covered for anything. There wasn't an insurance company in the world that would touch them. They didn't understand the work. And if they did understand, they wouldn't like it. Getting shot at by a bunch of madmen who thought they were going to paradise if they died wasn't the kind of trade that came with life cover.

'I need it for the kids,' continued David. 'I have a policy for half a million. And as far as they know I work in management for my brother-in-law who runs a Skoda garage down in Guildford. The point is, I don't mind taking the risks. With that much money on the table, I reckon there will be a few, but I'll take my chances along with the rest of you. But I can't leave Sandy and Laura fighting it out over the pitiful few quid left in my bank account. So this is the way it has to work. If anything happens to me, then I want you to ship me down to Goa or one of the other tourist resorts and dump my body in the gutter somewhere the local police can find me and assume I've been murdered in a robbery or whatever. The insurance company will pay out on that. They just won't pay out if I'm off fighting with a PMC.'

It sounded bloody dangerous, thought Ollie. A thousand-mile drive through a couple of borders with a dead body in the back of your car? If the police or customs decided to take a look, that was going to take a lot of explaining. Not to mention the investigation by the insurance company.

'I need to know you'll do that for me.'

'It's guaranteed,' said Ollie firmly. 'Anything goes wrong, we'll make sure there's some money for your families. Even if I have to carry your corpse on my back.'

Somewhere in the distance, he could hear a noise. He stood up. It was the convoy. A cloud of dust was kicking up from the dirt track, the two Toyotas in front, while the big Volvo chewed up the dust behind them. Ollie waved his arms. The GPS satellite system would bring them to within a few feet of the shack, but it was hidden in the folds of the hills and they might struggle to find it without help.

The Toyotas steered right, following the track, and within a couple of minutes the convoy pulled up close to the shack. Steve jumped down from the side of the truck and looked up at the shack. 'Jesus, remind me not to ask you blokes to book my next hotel.'

'How much are we paying for this then?' said Jeff.

'Two grand, in dollars,' said Ollie.

Jeff whistled. 'I know some estate agents who would love to meet you.'

The rest of the men climbed out of the truck, unloaded their weaponry and their kit, and started to store it away inside the shack. Ganju used his limited knowledge of Pashto to pay off the drivers. He offered them the chance to stay overnight, eat some food, then drive back to Kabul at dawn, but they quickly declined. They'd seen enough of Jeff's firepower on the drive down to have a fair idea of what business their passengers were in, and they showed no inclination to stick around to see the rest of the show. As soon as they'd counted their cash, they kicked up the engines on the Volvo and started to haul the heavy beast back up the hillside. The sun was ebbing fast, slipping below the dusty horizon, streaking the sky with fierce blotches of crimson as it did so. Driving around Helmand was dangerous at night; even so, these guys clearly preferred it to kipping down with the unit.

'I can't say I blame them,' muttered Steve. 'I'm planning to make a fortune, but for ten Afghanis a day, I wouldn't be sticking around either.'

'I got the feeling they knew this place,' said Ganju.

'What do you mean?' asked Ollie.

Ganju watched the Volvo roll away. It was as if he was checking they couldn't hear him.

'I just sensed they knew something,' said Ganju, glancing around the shack, and the hills that rose up around it. 'Maybe this is bandit country. Maybe there's an al-Queda base nearby. I don't know, they were just a bit too eager to leave.'

'We haven't got time to worry about that now,' said Steve firmly. 'If there's any trouble, we've got the kit to defend ourselves. We need to get ourselves sorted, so that we can start cracking on with this job in the morning.'

'If Ganju's right, the sooner we get out of this bloody place the better,' said Ian.

For the next hour, as darkness fell over the hillside, they got their kit sorted. Ollie was organising them as they unpacked. Each man needed to be assigned a place to kip down, and they needed to know where the water and food was. They'd brought chlorine dioxide tablets to drop into the buckets of water from the well – it was important that each man drank only purified water. 'There's no way of knowing what kind of crap is inside that well,' said Ollie.

Next, they needed to test the weapons. Even if a gun was brand new, you didn't know if it worked until you tried it. Nick was given the job of unpacking each rifle, and zeroing it. It was basic drill. You 'zeroed' a new rifle by selecting a target, adjusting the sites, firing, then adjusting them again, until the weapon was a hundred per cent accurate. Not just each rifle, but every magazine had to be tested as well. If your rifle worked but your mag got jammed, you were still in big trouble.

'I don't know how you learned to shoot like that,' said Steve as he watched Nick.

'I had this guy who taught me in the Territorials,' said Nick. 'Big old bastard of a sergeant. But he gave me one piece of advice. Every time I pointed the gun, I used to mutter the word "aim". He suggested I replace that with "kill".' Nick flashed a big grin. 'After that, I hit the target every time.'

He levelled the rifle to his shoulder, fired, missed, then shifted the position of the sites again. 'Kill,' he muttered as he squeezed the trigger.

Steve walked away, shaking his head, staring at the

ground. Jesus, I thought Maksim was the only homicidal nutter around here. Now it looks like I'm surrounded by the bastards.

The kit and sleeping arrangements sorted, Jeff rustled up some food. They'd stocked up on American MREs – bags of pre-cooked pasta and stews that heated themselves by releasing some chemicals into a sachet. Out here, they'd be eating cockroaches and snakes in a couple of days if they didn't have those. But they'd also stocked up on some fresh food in Kabul, enough to see them through a couple of days, and Jeff had made a stew of lamb, beans, some spices and rice and flatbread, all of it cooked over an open fire scrambled together from the bits of broken brushwood they'd managed to collect from the hillside. Steve had no idea how the guy did it – he could stage a party on the moon if he needed to – but it tasted delicious. Maksim had scored some cheap Russian vodka back in Kabul, and that tasted pretty good as well. It scorched the back of the throat, but it also hammered your nerve endings like a mallet. If necessary, they could always pour what was left of it into the fuel tanks of the Toyotas. A litre of this, and the big, powerful SUVs would probably go over 200mph.

Looking around the fire, Steve felt proud of the unit he'd put together in such a short time. They were an ugly-looking bunch, and with no showers, and nowhere proper to kip down, they'd get a lot uglier over the next few days. But they were a unit, they worked together like the cogs of a machine, and he was starting to get an idea of how they'd fight together.

'Tomorrow we start work,' he said as they polished off the remains of the food.

Behind him, a half moon had risen in the cloudless sky,

sending a pale, silvery light skimming across the rocky landscape.

'We'll figure out a plan, and let everyone know the drill in the morning,' said Ollie.

Steve glanced sharply towards him. 'Regiment rules apply here, mate,' he said. 'That means everyone's voice is equal.'

'We need—'

'There are no Ruperts in this unit,' interrupted Steve. 'We take decisions together, and that way we're all signed up to them, and we stick to them.'

Ollie was about to argue but held himself back. OK, we'll do it your way, he said to himself. But sooner or later this unit will need someone in charge of it. And it might well be sooner than you think, Mr West.

'So,' he said, unable to keep the sarcasm out of his voice. 'What exactly is the plan, comrade?'

Steve ignored him. 'Dan, you know this territory better than anyone.'

'We need to scout out Salangi's fort, that's the first priority,' said Dan. 'Until we know where the bloke is hiding up, we don't have any clue how to hit him.'

'Who goes?' said Steve.

'Small unit,' said Dan. 'I reckon me, Steve, Ganju and David.'

All three men chosen nodded.

'And we need to talk to the British garrison,' said Ian. 'We need to get as much information from Lockhart's boys as we can.'

'I'll do that,' said Ollie. He looked at Steve. 'We Ruperts know how to talk to each other.'

'Ian will go with you,' said Steve.

Ollie nodded. 'Just don't mention the IRA thing, old boy,'

he said. 'I know we're meant to have buried the hatchet, but it doesn't go down that well with the British Army.'

'OK, c'mon, boys, let's all try to get along,' said Chris.

Maksim nodded his head enthusiastically and handed round his bottle of vodka. Each man drank from the bottle, letting it wash down the taste of the food. 'You British are all crazy,' he said, hitting the bottle with the side of his fist. 'I don't know how I ended up fighting with a bunch of crazy fuckers like you.'

'Crazy to be fighting the Afghans,' said Ganju. 'On their own territory as well.'

'How's that?' said Nick. 'They can't be any worse than anyone else, can they? From what I hear, they can't even shoot straight.'

Ganju laughed. 'They shoot like madmen,' he said. 'But they torture like experts.'

'Torture . . .'

'They'll pull your eyeball out, just one of them, then boil it in front of you, and feed it to one of their dogs.'

Nick looked visibly pale, noticed Steve. But Ganju was right. If the Taliban captured any of them alive, they wouldn't imprison them. They wouldn't even shoot them with a good clean bullet to the head. They'd torture them to death with exquisite cruelty. Worse, they might hand them over to al-Queda, and those sods would put the execution up on the internet.

There weren't many thoughts Steve couldn't live with but torture was one of them.

'I've got a suggestion,' he said, his tone turning serious. 'If anyone is about to capture me, then I want one of you blokes to put a bullet through my head pronto. I'm not being taken alive.'

'Me too,' said Dan.

'And me,' said Nick.

Maksim pulled the Makarov from his shoulder holster and shot a round into the hillside thirty yards away, kicking up a small cloud of dust. The sound of the bullet echoed around the empty valleys. 'Don't worry, Englishmen, we have the same rule in the Spetsnaz when we fight the Chechens. I shot two men, Grigor and Vladimir, good comrades of mine, but I shot them all the same, rather than see them taken alive by those animals.' He laughed. 'And you know what? The men died with smiles on their faces.'

'I believe you would and all,' said Steve.

'Christ,' muttered Chris, shaking his head, and taking a final swig of the vodka. 'What the hell happened to our lives that we ended up here in the middle of bloody nowhere promising to shoot one another rather than be tortured to death by the sodding Taliban.'

Seventeen

THE LAST DUSTY EMBERS OF the moonlight were fading in the distance as Ganju steered the Toyota through the peaceful, lush valleys that surrounded the Helmand River. Steve sat in the passenger seat, looking steadily out of the window, but after the first few miles there wasn't much to see any more. They had only the moonlight to steer by, it was too risky to put the headlamps on, so there wasn't much you could see. Just the hills in the distance, the broad river punching its way through the brutal landscape like a battering ram, and field after field of poppies.

They had been driving for more than an hour now, having left the shack at four in the morning after grabbing a few hours' sleep. It was just over twenty miles from the shack up to Kajaki, the small town where Salangi had his base. They wanted to cover most of the journey in darkness so as to draw as little attention as possible to themselves but it was slow going. The road was rugged, and in the darkness even a driver of Ganju's skill was struggling to make progress. A couple of times they hit big rocks, sending the Toyota bouncing up into the air. Steve winced as the shockwaves crashed through his muscles and cracked into his spine.

It was just before six when they pulled the Toyota to a halt. Ganju had steered them up into the hills that rose above the Kajaki valley. Dawn was breaking, sending shafts of light flooding out across the hills. To the west, they could see the massive Kajaki dam that blocked the Helmand River, creating a reservoir behind, which powered a hydroelectric station and kept the valleys to the south irrigated.

Steve climbed out of the Toyota. They had driven up high, taking them beyond the poppy fields, but you could still catch their delicate, sugary fragrance on the morning air. They had steered the Toyota into a gully to keep it hidden, and they would tab the rest of the way on foot. They spread out their map on the bonnet of the vehicle and Ganju located their position, then pointed to where Salangi's fort was. It was two miles away, and one mile from the village itself, and they could get there easily enough on foot.

'Let's get moving,' said Steve, 'before it gets too sodding hot.'

Ganju led the way, followed by David and Dan, with Steve bringing up the rear, marching in single file across a narrow track that sneaked its way through the hillside, then took them round the lake and down towards the fort. They were carrying water bottles, they had their AK-47s strapped to their chests, and their pistols strapped to the webbing. Each man was wearing light cargo pants and a grey sweatshirt; underneath, they had on Kevlar body armour to protect their chests. It would be hot once the midday sun started burning into the dry ground, but it was a lot better than the full body armour the regular army guys fighting in Helmand were wearing. And it meant that if anyone stumbled across them, they could stand and fight their ground with at least a decent chance of success.

'Looks like some other armies have been here before,' said David.

Steve could see what he meant. Ahead of them were the remnants of an old Soviet pillbox, a tough, concrete bunker, with space for three men and a machine gun, overlooking the high ground next to the dam. The ledge in front of it ended in a sheer drop of a hundred feet or more, and at the bottom the charred shell of a T-55, the standard Soviet battle tank, was slowly rusting away. From the look of it, it had taken an armour-piercing shell to the rear – always the most vulnerable point on a T-55 – and had blown up from inside.

'The Russians fought like hell over this piece of ground,' said Dan.

'And what happened?' asked Steve.

'They got beaten, the same way everyone does in the end.'

'Not us,' growled Steve.

Dan nodded. 'But we're just smash and grab boys, we're not trying to conquer the place.'

The ground was rocky, and the hills rose and fell all around the lake. They could have driven a lot closer, realised Steve, but a vehicle could always be heard, and if Salangi had any kind of warning that his fort was being staked out, that would make their job ten times harder. It was certainly possible for a small group of men to overwhelm a much larger force – indeed, most of the SAS training was designed to do precisely that – but you had to take your opponent by total surprise. If he was waiting for you, you were already dead.

It took them an hour to tab round the lake, and another hour to cross the hills that rose up above the village. From there, it was just another mile or so to get down close to the fort. From the hillside, Kajaki looked much like every other Afghan village. A main street with a few shops, and a market, a few dozen houses, and a police station. It was a nasty, brutal and remote place, about as far from civilised life as you could hope to get. They moved on, noticing more shattered Soviet military equipment along the way. As they walked, the sun rose steadily in the sky and the dry, thin air of the hillside rapidly warmed up.

The fort was a mile outside the town. It had been built by the Russians to station the garrison that battled for control of the dam and the valleys beyond it through much of the 1980s. It was set on the back of the plain, with hills around it, and with a tarmac road leading straight into the village and on to the dam. It was roughly made, with four concrete walls, about eight foot high, topped with barbed wire and broken glass. Each wall measured eighty yards, forming a big square block. Inside, there were three rows of steel barracks: semi-circular tubes of corrugated iron, their surfaces now rusted with age, on a wooden frame. That, no doubt, was where the men kipped down. To the back was a square, flat-roofed building, with a satellite dish on top: the admin building, Steve reckoned. And next to that, a small barracks made of breeze blocks. If Afghan drug lords have Ruperts, thought Steve, and let's face it most organisations have a few of the bastards, that's probably where they kip down.

'Shit,' muttered Dan.

'You don't fancy it,' said Steve, glancing at him.

They had nestled down into the rocks, in the high ground, a good half-mile distant from the fort, where they could observe it but feel confident they couldn't be spotted themselves.

'When he said fort, I didn't think he meant a whole bloody barracks.'

'The Aussies not up for a fight?'

'We'll see when the shooting starts. If you think we're good at cricket, wait until you see what we're like at malleting ragheads.'

Steve took out a pair of field binoculars and trained them on the fort. It was getting close to eleven in the morning, and the place was full of life. There were a pair of big steel gates at the entrance, and that was the only way in or out of the compound. The doors were open right now as a truck approached, but there were six sentry guards, three on the outside, three more on the inside, each man armed with an AK-47, checking anybody that came in. Inside, Steve could see ten men being put through a training drill, and at least six more men walking about. It was impossible to tell at this distance what they were doing but they looked well-organised, disciplined and focused.

'What do you reckon?' Steve hissed, looking at David.

'If we were expecting a few half-arsed tribesman with spears, then I think we've just been disappointed,' said David. 'But there's fifty million dollars in there, or so we're told, and you don't make that kind of cash without having some idea of the difference between your arse and your elbow, even in a rathole like Afghanistan.'

'Think we can take them?'

'You can take anything with the right men and the right kit,' said David.

Steve scanned the perimeter, using the binoculars to zoom in on the wall around the fort. To the left, closest to the hills where they were hiding, there was a strip of barren ground, with warning signs up. They were in Pashto, reckoned Steve, but you didn't need to have any grasp of the language to guess what they meant.

'Reckon those are landmines, Dan?' he asked, pointing to the site.

Dan nodded. 'The Soviets mined half the bloody country. That's why you see so many kids with one leg in this place. Start kicking a football around and you get blown up.'

Steve nodded. Landmines remained a threat years after they were laid. There were Second World War landmines that could still take your leg off. You could clear them if you needed to, but it would take a lot of time and work. And it would be dangerous. Very dangerous.

'There are warnings around that field, but that's probably just to let people know they mean business,' said Dan. 'I reckon they'll have landmined the whole area around the fort, to stop anyone even thinking about attacking the walls.'

'So that means we go in through the front door?' said Ganju.

Steve trained his binoculars on the gates. They were thick and tough, and heavily guarded, but that didn't mean you couldn't take them out. It was just a question of figuring out how.

'Maybe the flame-thrower would do it' said Dan.

'We don't make any decisions today,' said Steve. 'We watch, get an idea of what's going on, then we put together a plan.'

Ganju suggested that he head down into the village, and that made sense to Steve. He was the only one among them who could blend in with the locals; with the right clothes, which he'd stashed into a kitbag, Ganju could pass for an Afghan.

He tabbed his way down to Kajaki, promising to be back before nightfall, while David, Steve and Dan stayed in position, making careful notes of how many men were inside, what shifts they did, what weapons they carried, and the movements of everyone going into and out of the fort. And looking for the one thing they needed most – a possible point of weakness. Every fort has one, Steve reminded himself. You just have to find it. And then hit it hard.

By mid-afternoon, the sweat was pouring out of every part of his body. The sun was baking hot, touching forty degrees at one point, and there was no shade up in the hills. By the end of the afternoon, even the rocks they were leaning against were too hot to touch. But they were collecting the data they needed.

By the time the sun started to fade into the distance, and the first of the cool evening breezes started to blow gently across the hills, they had a decent idea of the strength and capabilities of the fort. Even if they didn't know how to crack them, at least they knew what the problems were.

Before the light had completely faded, they saw Ganju trudging up the hill towards them.

'What did you find out?' asked Steve.

'I'll tell you when we get back,' said Ganju quietly. 'First we should move. We don't want to spend the night out here.'

Eighteen

THE TOYOTA PULLED UP BENEATH the shadow of a big, dirty grey rock that looked as if it might have landed there from outer space a couple of thousand years ago and hadn't been disturbed since. Ollie climbed out and checked his watch. It was just before eleven. Yet as he looked around, there was no sign of anything on the hillside except more rocks, more dust, and more barren scrubland.

'Reckon he's coming?' said Ian.

'He's British Army,' said Ollie stiffly. 'Whatever else you might say about them, they are at least punctual.'

They had driven for an hour from the shack. Before they left Kabul, Bruce Dudley had been in touch with Lockhart, and, in response, he'd been given a set of GPS co-ordinates, and a time. That was all. Be there, in the right place, at the right time, and a guy from the British garrison will be out to meet you.

The journey had been quiet enough. Ollie and Ian had ridden up front in the Toyota, using a map to steer themselves along the dirt track and hill roads until they hit the rendezvous point. Over a distance of just under fifteen miles, they had seen few signs of life: a herd of goats clustered underneath one of the few trees; a shop on the closest thing to a proper road they'd driven on, with a single petrol pump, and a few groceries; and one tiny farming village consisting of no more than a dozen buildings. They were driving due east from the shack, and could only assume the British would be coming from Forward Operating Base Rob, or Fob Rob as it was known among the soldiers. It was a heavily fortified compound close to Sangin, from where British artillery pounded the Taliban positions, and patrols sneaked out on sorties into the surrounding hostile countryside.

By the time they arrived, they felt as if they'd driven a hundred miles or more.

Ollie scanned the horizon. They were halfway up a hill, and the giant rock soared forty feet into the air, making it the most recognisable landmark for miles around. As the clock ticked towards eleven, he saw a cloud of dust in the distance. Through the swirling sand, a pair of vehicles finally emerged, both of them the heavily armoured Land Rovers the army had been using to get around since they'd arrived in Helmand. The first vehicle contained just two men, a driver and a passenger, noted Ollie, but the second had four heavily armed soldiers and a manned machine gun on its rear. That tells you something about how much control the army has of this territory, Ollie thought. They can't travel except in a convoy and with enough firepower to blow away a small town.

A man stepped out of the Land Rover and walked across to where Ollie was standing. A major, according to the man's uniform, B Company, of the Light Dragoons. Based in Norfolk, they'd been out here for six months, and had probably learned by now not to trust a single inch of the country. That explained the firepower. Anyone came close, they'd machine-gun them and ask questions later. In the rough wastelands of Afghanistan, it was the only way to stay alive.

'Ollie Hall, I presume.'

Ollie nodded. 'And this is Ian,' he said, nodding towards him. 'He's part of the team.'

'My name's Angus Muirhead, from Fob Rob. I'm told you're doing a job for us on the quiet.'

'Salangi's fort,' said Ollie. 'We're taking it out for you.'

'Good show,' said Angus. 'The bastard's a right royal pain in the backside, and the sooner he gets a good bollocking the better.'

'We need to know everything we can about the fort before we go in.'

Angus glanced at his men, and told them to stand easy. Ian noticed the way three guys had climbed out of the Land Rover and cocked their rifles, holding them steady on their chests, ready to fire at any moment. He'd seen British soldiers go through the same drill in Londonderry in the 1980s, and he knew what it meant: they were alert to the danger of sniper attacks, and were constantly monitoring an environment of total hostility. Doesn't exactly fill you with much confidence about the safety of the place, he reflected.

'We'll fill you in on what we know.' Angus spread out a map on the bonnet of the Toyota. It was at least up to date, noted Ollie; there were plenty of times when the MoD desk monkeys had sent the army into a country without even managing to get a decent map of the place.

'The guy's fort is right here,' said Angus, pointing to the location of the stronghold outside Kajaki.

'We've already got guys scouting it,' said Ian tersely. 'We need to know what he's got inside.'

'Salangi has about a hundred men fighting for him in total, and he has the Taliban to call upon as well,' said Angus. 'But there are usually thirty guys in the fort at any one time. The rest of them are out dealing with the poppy farmers, or running the crops down to Pakistan, all of which needs armed protection. On any given day, about ten of those guys should be out on patrol, so if you go in, there should be about twenty men there.'

'Reinforcements?' said Ollie.

Angus pointed to the map again. 'There's a Taliban base camp right here,' he said. 'By road, that's about an hour away.'

'At full speed?' said Ian.

Angus paused. 'If you step on it, you could probably do it in forty minutes, but the road is crap, just like everything in this country.'

'And Salangi is close to them?' asked Ollie.

'Best of buddies,' said Angus. 'So once you get in there, you'd better assume he's going to be calling up his mates, and the Taliban boys are going to come down on you hard.'

'How many at their camp?'

'Jesus, you never know with those buggers. Too many, that's for sure. It's a training base, so a lot of the peasant boys they bring in from Uzbekistan and Kazakhstan and all those places will be there. They die like flies whenever they get into a fight with us, but there's always a fresh supply. So there could be a couple of hundred of them.'

'We don't want to find out . . .'

Angus nodded. 'I'd say you've got an hour,' he said. 'Get in there, hit them hard, and get the hell out before Terry Taliban and his merry men descend on you.'

'Do they have landlines or mobiles?' asked Ian.

'Landlines,' he said. 'There's no mobile reception out

here, and anyway the Taliban don't trust mobiles because they reckon the American satellites are intercepting all the calls, and they are absolutely right. But there's an old Soviet-era landline system they trust because the switchboard operators are all Afghans, and they are way too scared of the Taliban to betray them. So if you can sever the lines, there's a chance of stopping Salangi and his men making contact with anyone, but it's a risk. It's up to you.'

'And where inside his fort does Salangi keep his stash?' said Ollie.

Angus shrugged. 'How the hell should I know? The bugger hasn't exactly invited us boys in for tea.'

'We need to know,' said Ian. 'If we've only got an hour before reinforcements arrive, we need to get the loot out quick. We can't faff around looking for it.'

'I can't tell you because I don't know,' said Angus. 'But I can tell you that this is a good time for you boys to go in. The poppy crops are fresh, and that means half the drug dealers in Europe will have made upfront payments to secure their supplies. The place will be bursting with even more money than usual. And we're hearing on the ground that a convoy is due to go out to meet the Taliban leadership the day after tomorrow, which means the fort should be undermanned.'

'It also means we've got thirty-six hours to plan the hit,' said Ollie.

'It's your call,' said Angus, with a shrug. 'I'm just telling you the fort should be weak that day. And if you can't scratch together a job in thirty-six hours, well then . . .'

'We'll manage,' said Ollie.

'We need to know where the stash is,' pressed Ian.

'I already told you, we don't bloody well know.'

'Then it's madness,' said Ian. The anger was evident in his

voice. 'We can't go in cold. With twenty guys in there to deal with, and reinforcements close by, we won't have time to look around. Without any proper information, we'll just be target practice.'

Angus turned and talked briefly to one of the men sitting inside the Land Rover, then handed Ian a slip of paper. 'This guy lives in a nearby village,' he said. 'I've written down his name, and what we think is his address. The way I understand it, he works at Salangi's fort but he's home at the moment, seeing his wife and kids. If you can grab him, maybe slap him around a bit, perhaps he'll talk.'

Ian folded the slip of paper into the back pocket of his cargo pants. 'What about evacuation?' he said. 'If one of us gets hurt, can we call on you for support?'

'I thought this was a black op.'

'Lockhart said there would be medical back-up.'

'Right, well, he's the boss, so if he says so, there is,' said Angus. 'We've got a chopper on standby in Fob Rob, plus a couple of medics, and they can come out so long as you've secured a landing spot. It'll have to be on the quiet, though. They can patch you up, but if it's anything major we can't fly you out of the country. If it's nasty, then I'm afraid you've bought it. Understood?'

'Understood,' said Ollie crisply. 'We know the risks.'

'Then good luck,' said Angus. 'And give the bastard the kicking he deserves.'

'We'll try.'

Angus turned round and started walking back to the Land Rover, motioning to the men to climb back inside the vehicle. Then he glanced back at Ollie. 'So what regiment were you?'

'Blues.'

'Then how the hell . . .' He paused.

'Did I end up doing this?' Ollie finished for him.

Angus nodded.

'You don't want to know,' said Ollie.

'I—'

'I told you, you don't want to know,' repeated Ollie sharply.

He walked swiftly towards the Toyota. 'Let's get the hell out of here,' he said tersely to Ian and slammed the door shut.

Nineteen

DARKNESS HAD ALREADY FALLEN BY the time the Toyota carrying Steve, Dan, Ganju and David rolled down the side of the hill and pulled up outside the shack. Jeff had cooked up another stew and boiled some big bowls of rice, but the fresh food was starting to run low, and they only had stocks for another day before they were on to the American MREs. Nick and Maksim had spent the day on target practice, testing out all the weapons, while Chris had taken apart all the guns methodically, cleaned them, checked they were working fine, and put them back together.

'Any of that vodka left?' said Steve, climbing out of the Toyota and stepping across to where the rest of the unit were sitting.

'First we plan, then we drink, this is the rule in my army,' said Maksim.

Steve laughed. 'More of the drinking than the planning, the way I hear it,' he said.

'OK, OK, we plan quickly, so we can get on with the drinking,' said Maksim.

Steve sat down next to the fire. He spooned some big

helpings of rice on to a metal plate, stirred in some of the lamb stew, and grabbed a couple of the dry flatbreads. It tasted good, and he was hungrier than he'd expected. From here to Kajaki and back again had been a long drive, and they'd done it in darkness both ways, making the journey slow and hard. They'd spent the entire day in the baking sun, and Steve reckoned he'd sweated off at least five pounds today. His body felt drained. The more food he shovelled inside himself, the sooner he'd start getting his strength back. He knew guys in the Regiment who could last days without food, like camels, but Steve was not among them. He needed plenty of fuel to keep himself fighting fit.

'We should go in the day after tomorrow,' said Ollie.

'Christ, that's too soon,' said Steve. 'We need time to plan, or else we'll get a malleting.'

'There's reports of a convoy going out of the fort that day, some kind of big Taliban pow-wow,' said Ian. 'The fort should be under-strength.'

'Hit them when they are at their weakest,' said Chris. 'It's never a bad policy.'

'Only as long as you're prepared,' said Steve.

He chewed on his food. Go in when they were weak, or go in when you were ready? Maximum force, maximum aggression, that was always the way of the Regiment, and he believed in it.

'If there's a chance to catch them with their pants down, then we should take it,' he said. 'But if comes to it, we'll have a vote, and I'll accept whatever the verdict is. First we have to map out what we're going to do. Until we know how we're going to take the fort, we can't go in, no matter how depleted they are. One bloke with a machine gun can kill the lot of us in about thirty seconds, so we need a plan.'

For the next ten minutes, David sketched out everything they had discovered during the day observing Salangi's fort. It was yet another cloudless night, so the moonlight was mingling with the remnants of the fire to make a soft, comforting light. The temperature plunged in the evening, almost as dramatically as it rose in the late morning, and Steve was grateful for the cool breeze blowing through the compound. David drew a rough map in the dusty ground with a stick, pointing out all the landmarks, and the ridges and folds in the hills around the fort from which they could stage their attack. He detailed the defences, the number of men and their routines. As he spoke, Steve glanced around the faces of the men listening, and realised something immediately. With the exception of Nick, they were all hardened, experienced soldiers, that's why they were here. And their experience told them this was a tough fort to take: an entrenched, dug-in enemy, on his own turf, was always a lethal foe. Well, that's life, he told himself, and if it comes to it, death as well. Nobody should have imagined that fifty million dollars was just going to be left in the middle of nowhere for us boys to come and collect.

'So that's the challenge,' said David. 'The issue is how do we crack it?'

'The way I see it, the minefield is the real problem,' said Ollie. 'It stops us getting close to the walls.'

'So we come in through the main gate,' said Dan. 'Blow it up with the RPGs, then smash our way through.'

'Good to see the Aussies are living up to their reputation for subtlety,' said David.

Dan fell silent.

They all knew that a frontal assault was the worst of all possible options. It was what the enemy expected, and it was where he was best prepared. You couldn't guarantee that even accurate RPG rounds would kill all the guards. And you had no way of knowing what traps might have been laid around the main gate. There could be all kinds of tripwires and concealed snares around the main entrance. Unless you had someone on the inside to explain where they were, you could walk straight into any of them.

'We can destroy the minefield,' said Ian quietly.

Steve looked at him. 'You sure?'

'It's dangerous, but I don't think there are any safe options for this job,' said Ian. 'We get down into the minefield, and we wire it up, then we blast it, creating a massive series of explosions. That clears a channel we can get through. At the same time, the explosions should bring at least four or five guys running out to see what's happening. We're waiting for them, and gun them right down. It's a technique we perfected in the IRA, and it worked all the time. One explosion to bring the army rushing into the killing zone, then you ambush them.'

'That's British soldiers you're talking about,' snapped Steve.

'We're all on the same side now,' said Ollie sharply.

'The Brits wised up about it eventually,' said Ian. 'As soon as a bomb went off, they expected an ambush. But I reckon the Afghans won't be expecting it.'

'And you can set the minefield off?' asked Ollie.

Ian nodded. 'With a day to prepare, it should be OK.'

'That still leaves the problem of how we get into the fort,' said Steve.

'A ladder,' said Nick. 'We could scale it.'

Steve glanced across and grinned. 'Wait till you've grown up, Nick.'

'Hold on,' said Chris. 'We could scale it with ropes – if we've cleared a safe channel through the minefield.'

'They'll be waiting on the other side,' said Dan. 'We can't count on Salangi's men being that bloody stupid. They'll know the mines have been blown so they'll be expecting someone to come over right there, and they'll be waiting to cut us down.'

'Punch a hole in the wall, then,' said Chris.

'We don't know how thick it is,' said Ollie.

'About a metre,' said Dan. 'From our observations earlier today, that's my guess.'

'But we don't know what it's made from,' said David. 'If it's just breeze blocks, an RPG should take it down. If it's reinforced, then the missiles will just bounce off it. And they'll be able to see exactly where the RPG rounds have come from, and start picking us off.'

'It's a Soviet fort,' said Maksim. 'It will be made from horse crap.' He chuckled to himself. 'Soviet buildings fall down if you tap them. With an RPG, they turn to dust.'

'Salangi might have reinforced it,' said Chris. 'He's not short of money. If I was hiding fifty million in a place like that, I'd splash out on a few decent bricks.'

'Not with a Soviet building.'

'It's our lives on the line.'

True, thought Steve. The reality was they didn't know nearly enough about the fort or its defences to start planning an attack. Maybe they should delay for a few days until they knew more.

'We could tunnel in,' said Nick.

Ollie looked at him, and already Nick was regretting having spoken.

'Yes, thanks, Nick,' Ollie snapped. 'We'll come round to

your house one day to watch your collection of great Second World War movies. Until then, we're trying to have a serious discussion here.'

'No, he's on to something,' said Ganju. As usual, his voice was quiet.

'What do you mean?' asked Ian.

'Stealth, that's always the way.'

'You've got an idea?'

'I was scouting around the village earlier today, and I managed to get talking to people,' said Ganju. 'I didn't want to ask too many questions, because if word gets back to Salangi that someone has been asking questions about his fort, it will alert him to the fact an attack is imminent. But I did pick up one piece of information that might be useful.'

'Which is?' said Ollie.

'The fort has no fresh water,' said Ganju. 'There was a well there when it was built but the Soviets experimented with biological weapons, and the underground stream that fed it was contaminated. Nobody can drink the water. So once a day a truck drives up from the village with barrels of fresh water to supply the men in the fort.'

'Maybe we could contaminate it,' said David. 'Poison the bastards.'

'With the biological weapons we just happen to have at hand,' said Ian sarcastically.

'Cyanide,' said David.

'Tastes like crap,' said Ian. 'The Afghans would spot it.'

Ganju raised a hand to quieten them. 'We take the truck,' he said quietly. 'I've marked out the route, and it only has a driver on board, with maybe one man riding shotgun. We hijack the truck on its journey, then I drive it in, made up to look like an Afghan. Three more of us are hiding in the back . . .'

'Then we take the bastards from the inside,' said Steve. He slammed his fists together. Already, he was excited by the plan.

'Like a Trojan horse,' said Ollie.

'Precisely,' said Ganju.

'So here's the plan,' said Steve, looking at each man in turn. 'Ian and three other guys lay up close to the fort, and blow the minefields. They draw as many men out as possible, and deal with them. Four of us go in on the truck. Once we're inside, we let them have it hard from the inside. When Ian's blown the minefield and dealt with anyone who comes out, those four guys can blow a hole in the wall and come in from another angle. We'll squeeze them in a classic pincer. It'll be short and nasty but we'll get the job done.'

'That makes eight guys,' said Ian.

'Two of us will hold the RV point,' said Steve. 'We'll choose one about half a mile away, up in the hills. I reckon it's bloody important we get out of the area as fast as possible, and that means we can't afford any fuck-ups with the transport.'

'Why not send all the guys in?' said Dan.

Steve knew what he was thinking. They were up against twenty or thirty guys and they needed all the firepower they could muster. He had a point.

'If you'd ever spoken to a bank robber, then you'd know what Steve is saying,' said Jeff. 'The getaway driver is the most important man on the job. Doesn't matter how clean the job is done, if you can't get out then it doesn't mean sod all.'

'So,' said Steve, 'if that's the plan, are we going in the day after tomorrow, when Salangi and his boys are at their weakest?'

He looked round at them all and couldn't see a flicker of hesitation or doubt in any of their faces as each of them raised a hand in agreement.

'Then I reckon we all have a drink and get some kip,' said Steve.

'Make that two drinks,' said Maksim. He unscrewed the top of a vodka bottle with his teeth and started to pass it round.

'The stuff you're serving, mate, one glass is a binge-drinking session all in itself,' said Steve. He laughed, took the bottle from Nick, and took a hit of vodka, letting the cool, rugged alcohol thump into his bloodstream.

Twenty

STEVE KNELT DOWN NEXT TO the fire, where Jeff was stirring some coffee into a pot slung over the burning embers. He poured a generous helping of the strong, black liquid into a tin cup, and drank. Dawn was just breaking over the rough, scrubby hills, and the cool night air was blowing across them. Somewhere in the distance he could hear the rumble of a fighter jet blasting through the morning sky. One of the Yanks coming to give some air support to the British boys who've got themselves in a spot of bother, decided Steve. They'll probably bomb the hell out of the opposition – and maybe our side as well.

'We're a long way from home,' said Jeff, looking across at Steve.

'What you mean?'

'It's in the morning that it strikes you,' said Jeff. 'You wake up thinking, Christ, what the hell are we doing here?'

'This is home,' said Steve. 'A dusty battlefield, in the middle of God knows where. It's where men like us feel comfortable.'

'You maybe,' said Jeff. 'This is my last job. Get that money banked, then I'm out of this game.'

Steve nodded curtly. 'That's what we're all doing.'

'Not you, mate, you can't give this up. Like you just said, it's in your blood.'

'Just watch me.'

'I already have, Steve.'

Over the next ten minutes, as dawn broke over the horizon, the rest of the unit roused itself. They'd been sleeping five men to a room, stretched out on the floor with a bit of straw beneath them, and their kitbags under their heads. The place didn't amount to much but it hadn't taken long for it to start to feel like home. Chris had lost at cards last night, so it was his job to burn off the crap stacking up in the sawn-off diesel tanks. Nick hauled up some fresh water from the well, disinfecting it so everyone could splash some water across their face and have a shave. As they assembled, Jeff handed around tin cups of steaming coffee and dried flatbread and dates that they had brought with them from Kabul.

'Nice beard, mate,' said Jeff to Dan.

Alone among the men, Dan hadn't shaved for the last couple of days, and the growth was starting to show.

'Yeah, nice bit of stubble, very George Michael,' said Steve. 'I know some wine bars down Orpington way where the birds really go for that look. Even an ugly bastard like you might get lucky.'

'It's an SASR tradition,' said Dan. 'We don't shave when we're out on patrol. I'll take this off when I'm having a nice hot bath in the Dubai Hilton. Maybe get one of the Thai girls to do it for me.' He chuckled to himself. 'And get her sister to help her . . .'

'Ah, well, it's better than Taffy over here,' said Steve, grinning. 'Apparently he doesn't wash . . .'

Nick punched Steve in the ribs. 'Piss off.'

'Got to learn to take a joke, boyo,' said Steve.

But Nick just scowled.

Ollie and David took control of planning the morning, and that was just fine with Steve. They were the two best organisational men on the team. They had to assign each man his role so he knew exactly where he fitted in and what was expected of him. There was only one problem, reflected Steve. They wouldn't really know how they fitted together until the shooting kicked off. And by then it would be too late to fix anything that wasn't working.

'We know what Ian and Ganju are going to do,' said Ollie. He was drawing a map in the sand again, using a stick he'd just sharpened with his field knife. 'Ian is going to handle the minefields, because that's his box of tricks. And Ganju is going to drive the truck into the fort because he's the only one of us who's the right . . . er . . . shade to blend in.' He paused, looking around at the men. 'I'm going to nominate the rest of the roles, but if anyone doesn't like their job, just shout.'

'I'll stay back here and prepare the cocktails, if it's all the same to you,' muttered Jeff.

Ollie smiled but ignored him.

'I reckon Ian and I should lead the assault through the minefields with Jeff and Chris as back-up,' said Ollie. 'We're going to need a lot of wallop to punch our way through there, and we'll need boys who don't mind a few loud bangs going off around them. Ganju drives the truck in, with Steve in operational charge, and with Maksim and Dan riding along with them. It's going to be bloody dangerous, and you'll need to keep damned calm. David and Nick should be in charge of the RV. With any luck, the water truck should survive the initial onslaught, so we'll load the loot on to that, then drive like hell to the RV point. You two boys will keep the Toyotas ready, armed to the teeth, and as soon as we show up, we transfer the stash, blow the truck up, then scarper for the border.'

'I want to be in the thick of things,' said Nick. There was a quiet determination to his voice. Despite his youth, there was some steel in there somewhere, thought Steve.

'Then you're a bloody idiot,' said Ollie. 'You've never heard a shot fired in anger in your life, and if you had any sense you wouldn't want to either. So you'll help David keep the getaway vehicles warm.'

'But—'

'He's right,' said Steve. 'We can't risk it.'

Nick fell silent, but the disappointment was clear in his face.

'I'd trade with you if I could, Nick,' said Jeff. 'But trust us, getaway is a bloody important job.'

'Everyone else happy with their jobs?' asked Ollie.

There was a silence that signalled assent.

'Then let's get started,' said Ollie. 'We've a long day ahead of us.'

The team split into groups, dividing up the tasks ahead. Ian was adamant that they had to go down to the village to snatch the local that Muirhead had told them about, and Steve agreed. Without some knowledge of where the gold and diamonds and banknotes were stashed, they couldn't get out fast enough. And if the loot was locked up, which it almost certainly was, Ian would need to know what kind of explosives he needed to blow it out. None of that was going to be possible without a man on the inside.

Ollie and Dan volunteered for that job. They decided to

take one of the Toyotas, sneak down to the village to collect the guy, and bring him back to the shack. They'd wait until it got dark, however; that way, there was a lot less chance of them getting caught.

Meanwhile, Steve, David and Ganju would travel back to the fort. They needed three more pieces of information before they went in for the kill tomorrow. They needed to study the precise route of the truck into the fort, so that they could work out the best place to hijack it. They had to find a place where they could sever the landline running into the fort before the attack started. The timing had to be right. If they cut it too early, it would alert Salangi that something was up; too late, and he'd have time to contact his Taliban mates. Lastly, they needed to choose the RV point where Nick and David could lay up in the Toyotas, and map out a route that would take them to the border in the shortest possible time, with the least possible chance of running into any al-Queda camps.

While that was happening, Ian would prepare the explosives, and Chris would stay with the rest of the men, running through the drills for the attack itself. They would all meet up at the shack by nightfall.

Ollie moved quietly across the dusty ground.

Dusk had just fallen. This was the quietest time of the day, between the sun setting and the moon rising fully in the clear sky. The village was six miles from the shack, and another seven miles short of Salangi's fort. It nestled beside a small tributary of Helmand River, irrigating a dozen fields that were planted with corn and poppies. In total the village consisted of eight houses, strung out along a dirt track. Each one was no more than a couple of rooms and a flat roof, with no electricity or phone lines. There was a well at the centre of the community. It can't have changed much since Alexander's time, decided Ollie. Who knows, maybe it had even gone backwards.

They left the Toyota five hundred yards back, pulled into the side of the road, and tabbed the rest of the way in on foot. They had the name of the man from Muirhead: Jamal. And he lived in the third house into the village as you approached it on the road running in from the east. Let's just hope we get the right man, thought Ollie.

As they approached the main street, a woman was walking towards the well, carrying a thick, earthenware jar. She was dressed in a full black burqa, covering her entire face. To Ollie, that meant this was a Taliban village. He'd heard that if guys were wearing black turbans, that also meant they were Taliban. He wasn't certain this was true but a full burqa was a sure sign. Tread carefully, he warned himself. If we're spotted here, we'll bring the whole damned lot of them down on us.

They were standing right on the very edge of the village, taking cover behind a barn that was used to store grain. There was no lighting anywhere, but the moon was coming up in the sky, and smoke was rising gently from most of the shabby buildings. Ollie waited patiently as the woman filled her jar with water, then turned and started to walk back towards the last house in the village.

'OK, let's move,' he hissed.

Dan had a strip of cloth twisted tightly into his fist. The plan was to sneak into the village, put a gun to the man's head, gag him, and take him straight back to the shack for interrogation.

They started to move.

The dirt track was eight feet wide, with houses on only one side of it. They had already established which building they were hitting. As they approached it, they ducked into the space alongside it, so they could come round from the back. It was just after eight in the evening. The back of the building was a wall of breeze blocks, whitewashed, with a pile of rubbish stacked up outside it, and a hole in the ground, which, from the smell, was used as a toilet. There was a gap in the wall which led into a small, dusty backyard, and beyond that was a door that led into the second of the two rooms in the building. Ollie drew his Makarov pistol and checked that the clip was in place.

'Ready,' he whispered.

Dan nodded.

Ollie went first, with Dan following close behind. They moved swiftly up to the door, paused for a moment to co-ordinate their actions, then Ollie gave the door a light tap with his foot. It swung gently open on its hinge. 'Go,' he snapped suddenly.

He burst through the door and pushed on into the main room. The pistol was out in front of him, gripped hard between his hands. Behind him, Dan completed precisely the same manoeuvre. In the blink of an eye, both men were pointing their guns straight at the heads of the Afghan couple.

Jamal was a man of twenty-five, maybe twenty-six, with close-cropped hair, a thin, wiry build, and dark, suspicious eyes. His wife was younger, no more than twenty, but with a face that told you she'd grown up fast. In the other room, two children were sleeping and instinctively the woman started to rush towards them. Dan grabbed hold of her and yanked her back, jabbing his gun up into her throat.

'Just keep fucking quiet,' hissed Ollie, keeping the barrel of the Makarov trained tightly on Jamal's forehead.

The man was about to speak.

'I said quiet,' hissed Ollie.

How much English the man spoke, Ollie had no idea. A few words, probably – most Afghans did, Ollie reminded himself. Particularly if you shouted loudly enough and held a gun on them.

'You're coming with us,' he said. He was straining to keep his tone level. There were houses on either side just a few yards from them. A raised voice could bring the whole village down on top of them. And this was a Taliban village.

'Do exactly as we say, and you'll be back here by the morning, unharmed,' hissed Ollie.

'I . . .'

The man was breathless, still straining to speak.

Suddenly, the woman threw herself forward and clawed at Ollie's cheeks with sharp fingernails, drawing a smear of blood.

Dan grabbed her and with one massive blow from the curled fist of his right hand struck her across the face. She reeled backwards, thrown across the floor, banging her head against its dusty surface, a trickle of blood running from her open mouth. Dan checked her pulse quickly, then pulled himself up. 'She's out cold, but she'll be all right by the morning.'

The man started to wriggle furiously. Ollie twisted the barrel of his gun tighter into the man's throat. 'She'll be OK,' he said. 'Just so long as you behave.' He looked at Dan. That was a hell of punch to put into the jaw of a defenceless woman, he told himself. It reminded him that they'd only heard his side of the story of how he'd ended up in jail for brutality towards the Afghans.

'I'll come,' whimpered the man. 'Just don't hurt my family . . .'

Ollie grabbed the strip of cloth from Dan and, keeping his pistol trained steadily on the man's throat, tied it round his mouth, taking care that the knot would make it impossible for him to speak. Next, he slipped a pair of plasti-cuffs round his wrists and secured them behind his back.

Dan had slipped into the other room. Both the children had started screaming when they heard their mother being punched to the floor.

Ollie went to check what Dan was doing in there.

As he moved towards the dark room, he felt nervous. He'd just seen Dan punch out a woman, and the sight had sickened him. Dan had been imprisoned for allegedly killing two children in Afghanistan.

The kids had suddenly turned quiet.

Christ, he wouldn't . . . would he?

Ollie turned on his flashlight. The room measured just eight feet by five, with a straw bed where the parents slept in one corner, and a couple of mats laid out for the children. Dan was keeling down, stroking the head of a small boy and cradling the baby in his arms. The boy had gone back to sleep, and the baby was nodding gently as Dan rocked it from side to side. The massive palms of his hands made a natural cradle, and the warmth of his chest made a warm and snug pillow.

'They OK?' hissed Ollie.

'I'll just get the baby off to sleep,' said Dan. 'They'll be as quiet as lambs until the morning.'

Ollie felt ashamed of what he'd just suspected.

'I'll get you over for some babysitting if I ever get around to knocking out a sprog,' said Ollie.

'Seven quid an hour, mate, and I get to drink all your booze,' said Dan.

'Let's get the hell out of here,' said Ollie. 'Before we get into any more trouble.'

Ian handed across mugs of hot black tea to both Chris and Nick. They'd spent the last five hours cleaning all the weapons, filling all the mags, and making sure all the kit was assembled for tomorrow morning. Jeff had finished the last of the fresh food but had lined up some MREs, and Nick had scrambled together enough brushwood to start a fire. The fierce heat of the day was starting to ebb, but there was still a dry humidity to the air that would take hours to cool down. The tea would help. A bit.

'The two of us have something in common,' said Ian, glancing across at Chris. 'We're on history's losing side. We were both on the wrong side of the wrong wars, and that's something none of the rest of these blokes know about.'

'That's certainly true,' said Chris. There was a note of bitterness in his voice.

Ian took a hit of the tea. 'So what happened to you?'

'I left the army seven years ago, back in South Africa,' said Chris. 'I've nothing much against black guys, at least no more than the average South African soldier, and I don't mind a few of them being in charge of the government, but when they put some monkey who can't tell one end of a rifle from another in charge of your platoon then it's just bloody dangerous. So I quit. The bloody country isn't worth fighting for anymore anyway. I'd stashed away a bit of cash while I was doing my time, and I used some of it to buy a farm up Mpumalanga Highveld, growing maize mostly, some sunflowers. Cash crops, things I could sell, and where I could work the fields by myself if I had to. I didn't pay too much for it, because nobody wants those farms anymore. Too many attacks, and too much interference from the government. They think you're some sort of class enemy just for trying to make a living. But I was still mortgaged for ninety per cent of it, and I had to borrow even more money just to make sure I had enough seed.' Chris fell suddenly silent.

There were soldiers like that, thought Ian. They'd say nothing for months, then the stories would come tumbling out of them, but you had to let them go at their own pace.

'I lasted for three years,' continued Chris eventually. 'Then the bank foreclosed on me. I paid nine hundred thousand rand for the farm, and borrowed another hundred and fifty thousand to try and keep it afloat. They took the whole thing off me, and they sold it at auction for four hundred and eighty thousand, which means that I don't have the bloody farm anymore and I still owe them five hundred and seventy thousand rand. That's forty grand in British money. Where the hell am I going to get that kind of money?'

'Right here,' said Ian.

'You reckon?'

Ian's face twisted away to the horizon. 'I don't know,' he said flatly. 'Three million dollars? As they say, if it sounds too good to be true, it probably is.'

Steve took a final measure of the dirt track.

It was twelve feet across, wide enough to carry a truck but not enough to allow another vehicle to pass.

He looked at David, then at Ganju. 'We could bring one of the Toyotas sharply round this corner,' he said. 'That should stop them.'

It had been a long day, and night was starting to fall. The

three of them had driven through the hard, dusty terrain up towards Salangi's fortress, then stashed the vehicle and completed the rest of the recce on foot. First, they'd found a point where the phone line out of the fort could be cut with relative ease. They'd marked its position on the map. One of Jeff's jobs would be to cut the wires just a few minutes before the attack was scheduled to kick off. Next, they'd chosen the RV point. It was a side track, leading away from the main road, half a mile from the fort. The track led up to an abandoned well, and there might have been a house there once but it had long since fallen down. The track was overshadowed by high rocks, hiding it from view. They should be safe enough there, reckoned Steve, and there would be enough time to reload the loot from the truck on to the Toyotas. Finally, they needed to study the route taken by the truck that carried the water up from the village. And they had to find somewhere they could stage the ambush.

'Too risky,' said Ganju, examining the road. 'The truck won't necessarily stop. It's a big, powerful Tata machine made in India, and its got reinforced fenders. It will just tear a strip of the Toyota, then crush it and move straight on.'

'We need a roadblock,' said David.

'And a turn,' said Ganju, 'so the truck can't see it coming. If the driver sees a roadblock, he'll turn round and head back to the village.'

They walked on another few hundred yards. The road was empty at this time of night – no one drove around in Helmand after the sun went down if they could help it – but they still walked through the scrubby hillside twenty yards parallel to the road to make sure they weren't spotted. A twist in the road loomed up ahead of them. Steve and Ganju dropped down to examine it, leaving David on lookout. The road turned into a channel cut into the rock, rising to about ten feet on either side. It narrowed to a single lane as you approached the bend. Steve stood still for a moment to examine it. Anyone approaching in a truck, he decided, would inevitably slow right down. Ten miles an hour was the fastest you could take this turn. He took a few paces along the road as it turned. As it completed ninety degrees, it opened out again.

'We can put a roadblock right here,' said Steve, kicking a line in the dust. 'That should stop it.'

Ganju was digging his fingers into the rock face. There were no trees in sight, but a few boulders should come loose, making a simple but effective barrier. 'And if one man stays up on the hillside, he can use a rifle to sort out any trouble,' he said.

We're sorted, thought Steve.

They collected David, and started to tab their way back towards the RV point. They'd made a mental note of everything they needed so they could run through the drill with the boys when they got back to base camp. Already Steve was feeling more confident. Tomorrow was going to be a tough, hard fight, with no certainty of coming out alive on the other side. Of that, there was no doubt. But they'd made their plan. They had the right kit. And the men were blokes you could trust to fight to the last bullet. A soldier couldn't ask for much more than that.

'Stop,' hissed David.

He was tabbing a few yards ahead of them, making sure the way was clear, and from his position Steve guessed he already had a clear view of the RV point.

David had obviously seen something.

It was a cold, dark evening, with only the moonlight

filtering across the desolate countryside. David was scuttling back towards them. He stopped a couple of feet short of where Steve was standing. 'There's a guy messing with the Toyota,' he muttered.

Steve's eyes darted forward. He pricked his ears but could hear nothing.

With Ganju at his side, he started to edge forward, careful not to make a single sound. As he approached the side of the hill where it dropped down into the gully, he paused. He looked ahead. The figure was no more than a shadow, moving silently along the length of the vehicle. It looked to Steve as if he was searching for a way to get inside, hot-wire its engine, and drive off. Whether he was or not, this was not the time to start asking questions.

Steve scanned the horizon, looking to see if there was anyone else with him. In the darkness, it was impossible to say; a camouflaged man could remain invisible even if he was only a few feet away.

But probably not, Steve decided. If he had any mates, he'd have called them by now. He'd want their help nicking the Toyota.

'Cover me,' he whispered to Ganju. He pointed left. 'You as well,' he said to David, pointing right.

Both men fanned out, taking up position in the hills overlooking the gully on either side of the approach. They had already drawn their handguns, and readied their fingers on the triggers. They knew the drill; it had been drummed into them on parade grounds by sergeant majors with ears that glowed red in the cold like diseased tomatoes and they weren't about to forget it now. One man would go forward to test the enemy, two men would watch over him, ready to start shooting at the first sign of trouble.

Steve took two more steps forward.

The man was tapping a rock against the window of the Toyota. To Steve it looked as if he was testing its strength, judging the size and weight of rock needed to break through it.

He drew the Makarov from its shoulder holster hidden beneath his sweatshirt.

'Stand back,' he barked.

The man looked up. Wild fury filled his eyes. His hand started to slip inside his robe.

Wrong move, pal, Steve thought grimly.

He squeezed hard on the trigger. The bullet smashed into the man's shoulder, sending him spinning to the side.

Rubbish shot, thought Steve. But it doesn't matter. There's a whole mag full of bullets in this gun, and they've all got your name on them. He squeezed again, then again, the bullets punching gaping wounds in the man's chest as he fell to the ground. From the hills, both David and Ganju loosed off couple of rounds, the bullets crashing mercilessly into the man's body from opposite ends of the gully.

Steve ran forward, scanning the hillside as he did so.

If there was anyone else out there, the gunfire would have bought them out, but there was just an eerie silence.

He knelt down, and placed one clean bullet through the centre of the man's forehead, to make certain he was never getting up again. 'The Taliban would have done worse to you for nicking a car,' he muttered to the corpse.

'We better bury the body right here,' said Ganju. 'This is Afghanistan. If anyone finds out we killed him, we'll bring down a whole clan war on our heads.'

Twenty-One

STEVE COULD STILL SMELL THE blood on his hands as he stopped the Toyota outside the shack.

He tossed the keys into his pocket and walked across to the fire Jeff had lit. Some tea was still hot in an open pan and there was a selection of American MREs and some water Nick had pulled out of the well and disinfected. Steve took a tin cup of water and splashed it across his face and hands. It washed away only a fraction of the grime and blood, but it felt better all the same.

He glanced around the flickering flames. Everyone was back.

'How'd you get the scratch?' asked Jeff, nodding at Ollie's cheek.

'Down in the village,' said Dan when Ollie remained silent. 'The guy's wife had a go at him.'

'Makes a change from scratches on the back,' joked Jeff.

'That girl of yours a scratcher?' asked Dan.

'Last time I shagged her she was,' said Jeff.

Steve ignored the banter, his eyes looking straight ahead of him. Between Ollie and Dan was a bound and gagged man. An Afghan.

'Is that our pal?'

'He's called Jamal,' said Ollie. 'We just got back from the village where we picked him up.'

'Has he squawked?'

Ollie shook his head.

'He needs to,' said Ian roughly.

He stood up and walked across to Jamal. The man was kneeling on the ground, his eyes bulging with terror, his hands shaking inside the tough plasti-cuffs. Ian took his knife from his pocket, slashed the blade through the air so that the firelight glimmered off its hardened steel surface, then grabbed hold of the gag and cut it. The blade lingered on Jamal's cheek for a fraction of a second longer than necessary before he split it open – just enough for him to get a feel of its sharpness.

'We need to know the layout of Salangi's fort,' he growled. 'And we need you to tell us.'

Silence. Saliva was running down the front of the man's face but his lips weren't moving.

With the blade still in his fist, Ian leant forward so he was less than an inch away from the man's eyes. 'Like, right now.'

Silence.

All you could hear was the crackling of the dried-out bush that Jeff had used to make the fire.

'Right now,' said Ian, louder this time.

'I can't,' spat Jamal suddenly. His English was heavily accented but the words were clear enough all the same.

'You bloody will.'

'I can't.' His voice was wild with terror now. 'He'll kill me . . . Salangi kills all his enemies.'

'*I'll* sodding kill you.'

'I can't tell you anything . . . I'll die.'

Ian slashed the blade menacingly through the air, missing the side of Jamal's cheek by just a fraction of an inch. 'You'll die tonight if you don't talk.'

'Then kill me,' spat Jamal. 'Do you know what Salangi does to traitors? He nails them to a cross, and leaves them out in the midday sun. Your skin burns, and you die a slow, suffocating death. I've seen it happen.'

'Talk to us,' demanded Ian.

'They grab your wife and children,' he screamed. 'They hack them apart then roast them alive in front of you while you die on the cross. I've seen it happen. I'd rather die here tonight than face his fury . . .'

Ian leant forward again, the blade close to Jamal's throat. 'I said bloody talk.'

Jamal screamed.

Steve stood up. He could see the terror on the face of the Afghan, and he could see as well the unsettling impact it was having on the rest of the men. An enemy in a fire fight was one thing. A monster who tortured woman and children was another.

'We just need to know the layout of the fort,' said Steve.

Ian glowered at him but Steve ignored him.

'Tell us, that's all, and we'll take you back to your wife and children, and no one need ever know you were here.'

'They'll find me . . . they'll kill me.'

'Let me handle this,' snapped Ian. He pushed Steve aside. 'You talk, or you'll die tonight.'

'Then kill me . . .'

Ian spun round to face Chris. 'What would the Recces do with the bastard?'

'Water-boarding, maybe,' said Chris, with a casual shrug. 'Duck the man's head under water until he thinks he's drowning. Pull him up when he's already accepted he's dead, then put him under again after he's filled his lungs with air. Another one we used a lot was wrapping a sack over a guy's head, then pushing him downstairs. There's something really terrifying about falling when you can't see anything and you've no idea how bad the drop is. What about the IRA? They knew how to rattle a bloke's nerves.'

Ian grinned roughly. 'There was always knee-capping,' he said. 'Take one knee out with a hammer, and they usually talked before you started smashing the second one to pieces.'

'Sod it,' barked Steve. 'Can't you see the man's scared out of his wits?'

'That's the way we want the bastard.'

'It's torture.'

'It's bloody necessary, that's what it is.'

'We'll shoot our way in there, then we'll find the stuff,' said Steve.

'In half a sodding hour? If the loot is all in safes, we can't blow them open without preparation. For that, we have to make the bastard talk.'

'Not by torturing him.'

'If we have to, we will.'

'Then we're no better than they are,' said Steve.

'Spare us the fucking morality tutorial.'

'We're soldiers, not torturers.'

'One kills a man fast, the other slowly – big fucking difference.'

Steve pushed Ian on the shoulder, sending him back a couple of yards. His face was red with anger. 'Jesus, I knew we shouldn't have brought a bloody Provo with us. You're fucking psychos, the lot of you.'

'I'm just getting the job done.'

Ollie jumped to his feet. 'Bloody cool it, both of you,' he barked.

Steve stepped away. Maybe Ollie was right, maybe it was getting out of hand. But I'm not about to stand back and watch a guy be tortured. We're not animals.

Ollie looked at Steve. 'We need to make him talk if we can,' he said.

'Not this way,' said Steve.

Ollie thought for a moment. 'How much of Bruce's cash have we got left?'

'A thousand bucks,' answered Steve.

Ollie turned round and looked Jamal straight in the face. 'Here's the deal,' he said, a line of steel threaded through his voice. 'We'll give you a thousand dollars and drive you back to your village and drop you off in the darkness tonight. No one saw us leave, and they won't see you come in again. In return, you draw us a map of the fort, showing where Salangi keeps his gold and diamonds. Otherwise, I'll turn you over to these two bastards. And trust me, they don't fool around.'

Jamal looked at the ground in silence.

Ollie walked to the Toyota, opened up Steve's kitbag and took out the crisp roll of notes. He held them close to Jamal's face – straight from the bank, you could still smell the ink on them.

'It's a bloody good offer.'

'Get me a piece of a paper and a pen, then,' said Jamal. 'And untie my hands.'

Steve sat down, and ripped open one of the MREs.

For the next twenty minutes, Ian sat in front of Jamal while he drew a map of the interior of the fort. At first, it didn't tell them very much they hadn't been able to work out from their own observation: the barracks, the sentry points, and the gun placements were all as they had seen them from the hillside. Then Jamal added two important details: there was a row of concealed landmines along the back wall, stretching ten yards into the compound, that would blow to pieces anyone who set foot on that piece of ground; and the money was all stashed in a set of vaults that could be accessed only via a concealed entrance within the officers' quarters. The Soviets must have built a bunker down there to protect their weapons, and now Salangi was using it to protect his gold and diamonds. The officers' building was always guarded by two men, Jamal explained to them, and there were four men who were permanently billeted there, in addition to Salangi himself, plus usually some young boys they brought in for their entertainment, but there were no additional guards at the entrance. Once you went down into the bunker, there were three safes made of reinforced steel encased in toughened concrete. How thick? Ian kept demanding. Jamal just shrugged. He had never been senior enough to be shown inside, but at a guess he reckoned four or five inches.

'You reckon you can handle it?' asked Ollie.

Ian nodded. 'You can blow anything with the right amount of explosive, but four inches is tough. The problem isn't getting the door open. It's getting it open without blowing up everything inside.'

'Combination locks or keys?' Ollie asked Jamal.

'Combination,' said Jamal. 'Only Salangi himself knows the code.'

'We could torture it out of him,' said Chris.

Steve had finished his food and was standing next to them. 'I reckon a bastard like that has a pretty high pain threshold when there's fifty million dollars at stake,' he said.

Ian nodded. 'We'll only have a few minutes, and we can't break him in that time, even if we catch him alive. We have to blow the safes.'

The issue was settled, and there was no further use for Jamal. Ollie and Dan counted out his money, warning him that if he raised any kind of alarm he'd be dead before the day was over, along with his wife and children, then drove him back to the village.

While they were gone, Steve checked that every man knew his drill. The truck was scheduled to drive the water supplies into the fort between nine and nine thirty in the morning – this was Afghanistan, and time-keeping wasn't what they did best – which meant they'd be attacking the fort between ninety forty-five and ten the next morning. Jeff had mapped out a route through the southern half of the country that avoided the two known al-Queda bases along the escape route and should get them safely to the border. It would be a rough journey but, with luck, they should make it with two days' hard driving. He'd checked the tyres, serviced the engines, and made sure the Toyotas were kitted out with enough food, water, fuel and ammunition for the journey. All they had to do now was get started.

They'd been assigned their roles, and they memorised each task, but they also knew that chaos was the only god the battlefield respected, and once the shooting started, they could forget about plans, they'd be fighting for their lives, and the only thing they could expect was the unexpected. There was a mood of sombre reflection among the men, a tension that was always there on the night before a battle. The conversation dropped, until everyone was silent, and Steve knew he had to get them talking again. Left to themselves, alone with their thoughts, men turned in on themselves, and that was when the fear would get to them. And fear was the only real enemy they had. Compared to that, a few Afghan hotheads were nothing.

'More vodka, Maksim,' barked Steve.

Maksim had only one bottle left, but he handed it round, pouring a mean shot of the pale liquid into each man's cup.

Steve raised his cup. 'Two days' drive, that's all,' he said. 'And a couple of days after that, we'll be rich men.' He poured the vodka down his throat. 'So, have you got a girlfriend then, Nick?'

Nick hesitated. He wasn't exactly blushing, but there was a slight, unmistakable reddening of the cheeks. 'Tons, mate. I'm fighting them off.'

'What's her name then?' said Chris.

Again, Nick paused. 'Danielle.'

'Danielle,' said Steve. He chuckled. 'French bird, eh. Don't meet many of those in Swansea.'

'You get some,' said Nick.

'Well, tell you what, when I get my hands on the dealership I'm planning on buying with my share of the loot, I'll lend you an Aston Martin DB5 to take her away for the weekend.'

'Really?'

'Just bring her in, that's all.'

Around the campfire, everyone laughed. Jeff proposed another toast, then another. After a lot of fiddling around, Dan managed to tune his shortwave radio to the World Service and discovered that Australia had beaten England in the Test match by an innings and seventy-eight runs.

'You can toast that one all by your sodding self,' said Steve.

'Just wait until you play the South Africans,' said Chris,

looking at Dan. 'Then you'll start seeing what's it like to start losing.'

'Which means it's time to get some kip,' announced Steve. 'We're getting up at four sharp so we can do our driving at night.'

Within a few minutes, the fire had been put out, the vodka stashed away, and most of the unit was asleep. They had set up a rota for keeping watch. Nick had volunteered to take the first couple of hours, followed by Chris, followed by David. Steve put his head down on his kitbag and rolled over on to his side. He lay still for a moment, thinking first about Orlena, then about a DB5, and then about Orlena in a DB5, and finally with a grin to himself he closed his eyes and went to sleep.

When he woke up, it was one in the morning. He sat bolt upright, grabbed his watch and checked the time.

He'd heard voices. He was sure of it. But there shouldn't be anyone talking at this time of night.

He stood up and walked outside, taking care to glance around the dusty hillside before stepping out. He'd slipped a pistol into his right hand. Outside the shack, there were still a few embers burning in the fire, and three men were sitting round it. Steve recognised them at once: Nick, Ollie and Maksim. He stood in the doorway, observing them quietly. There was a pack of playing cards. And a bottle of vodka. Both of them were open.

Nick was laughing, his voice carried on the gentle night breeze.

'Shit, I'm down how much?' he said.

'Thirty grand,' said Ollie, his voice slightly slurred.

Maksim laughed. 'But you'll make that money back from our Afghan friends,' he said. 'You'll still be a rich man.'

'I sodding hope so.'

'Those Swansea girls, they'll be all over you, you see,' said Maksim, still laughing.

Steve walked quickly across the dusty ground. 'What the fuck are you doing?' he snapped.

Nick stood up, his expression embarrassed, and backed away a couple of feet.

'What the hell does it look like?' growled Ollie. 'We're having a game of cards.'

The bottle of vodka was almost empty, on the ground next to the fire. Steve kicked it over, spilling the remaining liquid into the ground.

'This boy's supposed to be on watch,' he said, nodding towards Nick.

'We're all on watch,' said Ollie. He was standing up now, looking straight at Steve.

'You're sodding drunk,' he snapped.

'If you think this is drunk, then you don't know what the bloody word means,' said Ollie.

'I know what it means all right,' snarled Steve. 'L-O-S-E-R – is that clear enough for you?'

Ollie's right hand jabbed upwards and grabbed hold of Steve's sweatshirt. His face was so close, you could smell the scab on his cheek, and the vodka on his breath.

'Fuck off,' he spat. 'Stop being such a miserable chippy tosser. We're risking our bloody lives in the morning, and if that doesn't earn us the right to a drink—'

Steve pushed his hand away before he could finish the sentence and stepped back.

'We need to be fighting fit,' he said angrily. 'I couldn't give a fuck how you screw up your own life, but you're not wasting mine because you're too sodding pissed to shoot straight.'

Ollie whipped his pistol out of its chest holster and pointed it straight at Steve. 'I shoot just fine, drunk or sober,' he said coldly. 'And if you want, I can prove that right now.' He took a step closer. Steve was standing rock steady, with not so much as a bead of sweat on his face. He ignored the barrel of the Makarov and looked straight into Ollie's eyes.

'We're walking into the fire tomorrow morning,' said Ollie. 'I don't know where you get your courage from, Steve West. Some men get it from a flag, a few men get it from a dream, or a cause. But most of the soldiers I've known got theirs from a bottle, and I wouldn't ever think less of a man for that.'

'It's true,' said Maksim. 'A soldier can drink. Russian soldiers don't even think about fighting sober. They wouldn't know how.' The man was grinning. He reeked of vodka, and the high-strength 'Brilliant' brand of Russian disinfectant that he splashed on to his skin every day.

'It's your choice,' said Steve quietly. He looked at Nick. 'Don't listen to this wanker. A Rupert might be able to get away with being a drunk, but ordinary men can't.'

Nick grinned sheepishly at Ollie and Maksim, then walked back to his watch position. There was still another hour to go before the shift changed.

Steve kicked the embers of the fire angrily away and stalked back into the shack.

Twenty-Two

THE MOON WAS STILL SLIPPING down towards the horizon as the convoy kicked up sand and dust and started its climb up the track that ran into the hills. Steve glanced back just once. The fire was out, the crap in the oil drums had been burnt off, and all traces of their stay had been eradicated. With any luck they wouldn't be coming back.

They'd packed five men into each Toyota: Steve, Dan, Chris, Nick, plus Ganju at the wheel in one. Ollie, Ian, David, Maksim, plus Jeff at the wheel in the other. Before they left, they'd run through their roles one more time. They knew the drill.

'Right then,' muttered Steve tersely. 'Let's go and mallet some ragheads.'

As soon as he'd got up, Steve had prepared his weapons. Each man had his own kit he liked to take into battle, and his own way of arranging it. Steve always put his Kevlar body armour on first, and his webbing over that. Inside, there were two pouches for maps, in case they got lost. There were two grenade pouches, both filled, and four long thin pouches for rifle magazines. Next to those were the field dressings; if you went down, you weren't going to be in any fit state to fix yourself, so you put those on the outside so one of your mates could rip them off and patch you up. Steve always carried at least two. One bandage would hold in about a pint of blood, but if you took a nasty hit, you were going to need at least two. He stuffed in enough food and water to last twenty-four hours. If you couldn't feed and water yourself, you were no use to anyone. Finally, he packed in a knife and a compass, and round his neck he clipped into place an old army dog tag, plus a vial of morphine. At his side, he had a hard hat; it wouldn't stop a high-velocity bullet, but it would deal with shrapnel, and any glancing rounds. Finally, he stripped down his AK-47, cleaned and oiled it, dusted away any muck, and reassembled it. It was a routine, one he didn't even need to think about. But it made him feel prepared for what lay ahead.

The drive took just under two hours. Again, no headlights. By the time they arrived at the RV point, Steve felt that he knew every bump in the road. He told Ganju to pull up a hundred yards short, and then tabbed across the open county, checking the hollow in the hillside before signalling to the Toyotas to follow. They'd been compromised here yesterday, and he wasn't about to take the chance of finding there were fifty Afghans waiting to greet them. As far as he could tell, the coast was clear, and within another minute the two Toyotas had pulled up. The men climbed out. They checked their weapons. Each man was carrying an AK-47, a Makarov handgun, two grenades, and a hunting knife. In the back of the Toyotas they had the RPGs, plus the bombs Ian had devised for detonating the landmines and breaking open the safes. Everything else they'd leave here at the RV point. There was a limit to how much they could carry; the attack would depend on speed and manoeuvrability, and they didn't want anything that would weigh them down.

Steve looked at Ollie. 'Sobered up?'

'I'll be fine,' snapped Ollie. 'Never felt better.'

'Then let's crack on.'

They split into two teams, leaving Nick and David to guard the RV point. Nick made a last-ditch attempt to join Steve's assault on the water truck, but Steve was adamant. They needed two men at the RV, and Nick was one of them.

Steve, Ganju, Maksim and Dan started to march through the arid landscape. It was the best part of a mile down towards the twist in the road they had chosen for the attack, but they crossed the ground in just over twenty minutes. The sun was starting to break through the horizon, and for a moment Steve glanced into its brilliant orange rays. He'd always enjoyed a sunrise on the morning he was going into battle. You could feel the adrenaline juicing through your veins, making all your senses come alive. Sometimes you could even feel death lurking on your shoulder, close, but not so close that you couldn't brush it away.

'We'll stay right here,' said Steve.

The four men crouched down in a hollow in the hillside. They were thirty feet above the road, and twenty feet back, with a clear view of the track as it led up to the twist, and, at a stretch, a view into the bend as well. Ganju went ahead and prepared three sizeable boulders, rolling them into position just above the road, from where they could be pushed down with a single shove. By the time he rejoined the rest of the unit, it was just after seven in the morning. The truck was expected some time between nine and nine thirty.

Traffic on the road was sparse. One vehicle every ten minutes, Steve reckoned. They saw a couple of trucks, but mostly just battered old SUVs. One of them looked as if it was taking a couple of guys into the fort. But otherwise they were just farmers and traders. Steve glanced at his watch every few minutes, but mostly he just lay back and watched the sun arc through the clear blue morning sky. Most soldiers hated the waiting more than anything; they were all right once the shooting started and they got themselves into the thick of the battle, but the hanging around drove them insane. The fear started to creep into their souls. But he didn't mind it. The time gave you a chance to relax, to compose yourself, to sort out your priorities. And once you'd done that, the battle wouldn't be nearly so hard.

Any moment now, he told himself, as his watch slowly started to tick towards nine.

Ollie led the way through the hillside towards the fort, followed by Ian, Chris and Jeff. The ground was rough as they made their way to the back of the lake, and twice they had to duck down to make sure they weren't spotted by farmers crossing the countryside with their mules. But by eight o'clock in the morning, they'd got themselves into position. They were two hundred yards away from the fort, and fifty feet above it, nestling behind a dusty, jagged set of rocks jutting out of a crack in the land.

'Enjoy your breakfast, boys,' said Ian with a rough smile as he opened up his field glasses and looked down on the fort. 'It's going to be your last one.'

Ollie looked through his own field glasses. The guards were all on duty, and there were at least ten men visible on the parade ground. Smoke was rising from the officers' quarters as they cooked food, and men were heading in and out of the main barracks. Ollie smiled briefly to himself.

Everything was just as they expected. Sooner or later, the job would start going pear-shaped – every assault always did – but for the moment the mission looked about as smooth as a lake on a summer's day.

'You ready?' he muttered.

Ian nodded.

'Then let's go.'

They had an hour and half at least before they could expect to see the truck approaching the fort. During that time, Ian would wire up the minefield, while Ollie and Chris lay in wait to provide covering fire if necessary. At nine fifteen, Jeff would slip away to sever the phone line, making sure he was back in position by nine thirty. They'd wait until the gates had opened and the truck was inside the fort. Then they would turn on the fireworks.

Should be some show, Ollie thought grimly. The buggers won't know what's hit them.

Ian started to scramble down the side of the hill. Lying flat on the ground, Ollie and Chris unhooked their AK-47s from their chests and positioned the weapons so that they were pointing straight at the wall. If Ian was spotted, they'd lay down enough covering fire on to the wall to give him a chance to scramble back up the hill. But their cover would be blown. Salangi and his men would know they were under attack, the element of surprise would be lost, and they'd have to retreat and decide whether to press on with the assault today, or try another day.

Either way they'd have lost their main advantage.

Time to hold our breath, decided Ollie. And keep our fingers crossed.

He could see Ian approaching the minefield. He was lying flat on the dusty ground, pulling himself along by his elbows, no more visible than a snake. He was getting closer to the minefield. Ollie glanced up at the sentry posts. None of them directly overlooked the minefield. They probably figured no one would be mad enough to attack from there. Obviously they'd never met any Provos.

Ian paused as he reached the perimeter of the field. He glanced back at Ollie, nodded, then pressed on. He was inching forwards, and Ollie could feel his heart thumping in his chest as he did so. One wrong move, and he'd blow one of the mines. Lying right on top of it, he'd take the force of the blast either in the face or the chest. Either way, he'd be a dead man. The Kevlar wouldn't protect him against a landmine. Ian would be dead, and Salangi's men would be pouring out of the fort, hunting down their attackers.

Inch by inch, Ian edged forward. At ground level, you could see a mine by the small mound it made in the ground. That was why soldiers always crawled through them. There were three main types of mine: blast mines, that sent an explosion straight upwards, injuring both troops and vehicles; fragmentation mines, which had a metal casing that would splinter and explode on detonation, sending vicious shards of shrapnel to cut down any soldiers in the area; and bounding mines, which contained a small charge that shot them into the air before exploding, wounding every man in the vicinity and not just the bloke unlucky enough to step on one. They had no way of knowing what mines were laid here, but Ian reckoned they were probably fragmentation mines, designed to protect the fort from an assault by ground forces.

He kept on moving forwards. Dogs were often trained to clear minefields, and although he had nothing like an animal's sense of smell, there was a rusty, metallic odour to a mine, particularly if it had lain in the ground for years. He paused and glanced up at the fort to check he hadn't been seen, then started to scratch the surface of the ground. A lump, plus the smell of metal, made him certain there was a mine. He scratched away the surface soil to a depth of one centimetre, until a round plate of grey metal was clearly visible. Ian recognised it at once. A Soviet-era TM-46, a mixed-use anti-tank and anti-infantry mine. Basically, the bastard would blow the legs or the wheels off anything that came near it. It weighed 8.6 kilograms, and would detonate under twenty-one kilos, or about forty-five pounds, of pressure. A dog or a snake wouldn't set it off, but a man or a vehicle certainly would. Ian carefully placed a small Semtex charge, with a radio receiver attached, to the mine, then dusted a few scrapings of earth back on top of it. He started to crawl forwards again. His task was to clear a channel that they could run through to storm the fortress wall. In total, he reckoned the minefield covered about twenty yards around the perimeter of the fort. If he could find two more, that should clear a way through. With any luck, the blast from the TM-46s would detonate the other mines in the field, creating a rolling wave of explosions that would shake the bastards inside the fort.

It took another ten minutes. Dust from the bone-dry earth was filling his lungs by the time the job was done, but Ian reckoned he had done enough to punch their way through. Three mines, three explosions. That should spoil their breakfast. He glanced once at the wall, now just a few feet in front of him, then looked back towards Ollie and Chris. He could just see the barrels of their AK-47s nudging out of the rock, all but invisible unless you knew precisely where to look. And then he turned and started crawling and sliding his way back to their position.

'Job done,' he muttered as he finished scrambling up the

hillside and fell back, leaning against the jagged rock. He grabbed a bottle of water and drank a couple of mouthfuls. The sun was already rising fiercely in the sky, and the dust had parched his throat.

'Good man,' said Ollie.

Ian picked up the garage door opener he'd bought in Kabul. It was a standard radio-operated device, the kind you'd find in any DIY shop. It transmitted a highly-focused radio signal, and worked over a radius of a hundred yards. Press it, and it would pulse an electrical signal into the Semtex, exploding the mines.

'We're all set?' said Ollie.

'Set,' replied Ian.

Ollie looked at Jeff. 'You know where the phone line is?'

Jeff nodded.

It was just after nine in the morning. Any minute now, and the show would start.

Steve checked his watch. Just after nine.

He could feel the minutes ticking away as he looked down the road. I don't mind the waiting, he reminded himself. Except for the last few minutes. Then you just want to crack on.

Ganju pointed.

Steve looked up. He could see the cloud of dust that accompanied every vehicle along this stretch of highway, and for a moment he could feel his pulse accelerating. Then he looked closer into the cloud. It was a local SUV, pulling a trailer.

Still no sign of the water truck.

He relaxed slightly, loosening his grip just a fraction on the trigger of his AK-47. Dan was directly to his right, with

Maksim to his left, and Ganju just a few yards away, ready to roll the rocks into place. The SUV, a fairly new Kia Sorrento, kicked past them, braking hard into the turn, and then accelerated past the bend. Come on, muttered Steve, under his breath. Let's see the truck.

He heard it first. Somewhere in the distance, the low grumble of a rough, overworked diesel engine shattered the peace lying over the valley. Steve glanced up. There was no mistaking it. He looked through the dust and could see the vehicle moving steadily down the road, running at no more than forty miles an hour. He nodded towards Ganju. 'That our boy?'

Ganju stuck a single thumb into the air.

Steve tightened his grip on his gun, and could feel the muscles tightening within him. 'Let's go, lads.'

Ganju was already heaving the rocks with his shoulder.

The truck was eight hundred yards away, and Steve reckoned they had at least thirty seconds before it slowed down into the bend.

One rock fell, crashing down across the road. A few chips splintered into the road, but the bulk of the boulder was lying right in the centre of the tarmac.

Steve glanced along the highway.

Six hundred yards.

Another boulder. Then another.

The rocks were now spread across the road.

Three hundred yards. You could hear the engine loud and clear now.

'Move down, boys,' barked Steve.

The AKs were gripped tightly in position as the four men moved steadily down the hillside and took up their positions along the side of the road.

The plan was simple enough.

As the truck turned into the bend, Ganju would step on to the road and flag it down, pointing to the fallen rocks across the road a few yards ahead. When the driver stepped out to see what the problem was, the four of them would step out, surrounding him. If he caused any trouble, they'd kill him. If he co-operated, they'd tie him up, knock him out cold, then leave him on the side of the road for someone else to rescue when he came round. Steve wasn't much bothered which route they took. He didn't enjoy killing men who hadn't caused him any trouble, but nothing was going to stop him getting his hands on that truck.

A hundred yards.

Steve nodded to Ganju.

He stepped on to the side of the road. Steve could hear the truck drop down a gear, and the engine spluttered as it turned into the bend. Suddenly it lurched into view. Steve glanced at the driver – a man of about thirty, with dark, sunburnt eyes, and thick shoulder muscles from hauling a truck across difficult terrain.

Ganju was waving, pointing at the rocks across the road.

Steve readied himself, his finger tight on the trigger. He could hear the screech of a brake. And then the roar of an engine. The brake was being released and the truck was accelerating hard.

Ganju threw himself to the side of the road as the truck swerved towards him. It was bouncing across the scrubland, the driver determined not to slow down.

Steve could see Ganju rolling on his back, unhooking his AK-47 and taking aim at the driver.

'Don't bloody shoot,' shouted Steve. He ran forward to grab hold of Ganju. Blow the windscreen and the truck would be useless. It would never be allowed inside the fort.

But the truck was starting to move away from them. It had swerved ten feet out into the scrubland to get past the fallen rocks. Its wheels were skidding on the dry, caked earth of the ground, but there was enough tread on the tyres to maintain a grip. The driver was shuttling through the gears, desperate to power the machine forwards and back on to the road.

Steve began to run, with Maksim pounding furiously at his side. Then he accelerated past Steve, hitting the tarmac. Sweat was pouring off his face. The truck was swerving violently back towards the road, swaying as it struggled to keep a grip on the churned-up earth, fumes spitting out of the exhaust pipe as the engine roared and spluttered.

'Jesus, man, don't fucking kill yourself,' shouted Steve, his lungs straining.

He could see what Maksim was doing. He was heading straight for the point where the truck was going to hit the road again. And the chances were it was going to hit him, too.

'Don't bloody try it, you fucking madman,' shouted Steve.

The truck skidded and stalled as the tyres collided with the tarmac edging to the road. It bounced into the air, and Maksim had to skid to a halt to stop the two tons of heavy machinery brushing him aside. The truck was slowing as the driver struggled to bring it back under control, then steer it on to the tarmac.

With one leap, Maksim jumped for the back of the truck. His fingers gripped its bumper.

'Jesus,' muttered Steve out loud.

There was a crunching of gears, then a roaring of the engine as the driver settled the truck back on to the road, and slammed his foot hard on the accelerator. Its speed started to climb, from ten miles an hour, to fifteen, up to twenty. Maksim was clinging to the bumper, his feet dragging behind him along the tarmac. He levered himself upwards, so that his feet were clear of the ground, then grabbed hold of the canvas that covered the back of the truck. Using the material as a rope, he climbed up it and flung himself inside.

The truck was disappearing along the road.

'Run,' shouted Steve. 'Run like hell.'

The truck was two hundred yards ahead of them, and accelerating. Another ten or fifteen seconds and it would be completely out of reach. Steve took a lungful of air, and pushed hard, his feet pummelling against the tarmac. He could see the truck swerve, then heard the sound of gunfire. Go, you mad bastard, he muttered to himself. Don't sell them your life cheaply . . .

The truck turned off the tarmac and slowed dramatically as it skidded across the scrubland. There was a huge cloud of dust around it and the sound of another gunshot echoed in the still, empty landscape. Steve was running harder, with Ganju and Dan at his side. He reckoned Maksim must be putting up a fight in there, and for a brief moment he almost felt sorry for the Afghans – nobody would want that mad Russian sod going crazy in the back of their truck.

They were closing fast, and the truck had slowed to a virtual halt. A hundred yards, then fifty. Steve heard a scream, the eerie, strangulated howl of a man having his windpipe severed. Whether it was Maksim or one of the Afghans, it was impossible to tell.

He grabbed hold of the back of the truck. It was shaking violently, its engine still running, but the gears must have been disengaged because it was no longer moving. With Dan at his side, he levered himself upwards, pushing aside the canvas flap. In the same swift movement, he unhooked his AK-47 and flicked the rifle into position, ready to shoot anything that moved.

Maksim was lying flat on his back, his rifle knocked clean out of his hands, and an Afghan was leaning over him. His knee was pressed down on Maksim's chest, and there was a knife in his right hand. He was pushing down hard, trying to stab it into Maksim's throat, aiming straight for the windpipe, but Maksim had grabbed his wrist and was just managing to hold him back. There was a corpse to one side of him, blood trickling out it, and the driver was slumped over the wheel of the truck. It was impossible to tell whether he was alive or dead. The Afghan was grunting, putting all his strength into hammering the knife down into Maksim.

Suddenly his eyes flicked up. He was looking straight at Steve.

And you could see in his face that he knew he was a dead man.

Steve squeezed the trigger of the AK-47, loosing off three rounds in quick succession. The bullets shattered the man's face, breaking open his mouth, taking out an eye, then slicing clean through his forehead to chew up what remained of the brain still left inside his skull.

He slumped forward across Maksim's chest. Blood was pouring out of his head, soaking into Maksim's tunic.

Steve glanced at the driver.

Not dead. He could tell. The man had been wounded, and was slumped forward on the wheel, but you could see the veins in the back of his neck quiver with fear.

He raised his AK-47 to put a bullet through the man.

'No,' shouted Maksim. 'You'll crack the windscreen.'

With one massive heave, Maksim tossed the dead Afghan

off his chest. He lunged towards the driver, yanking back his head with one brutal twist of his blood-soaked arms.

The man grunted, then squealed, like a pig in an abattoir.

Maksim twisted again, unscrewing his head as if it was the cap on a bottle of vodka. You could hear the bone and the veins snapping, and then, when he was satisfied the last breath had left the man's chest, he dropped him, letting his corpse slump.

Dan levered himself up into the truck. 'Fuck me, that wasn't exactly Plan A, was it?' he muttered.

Steve looked at Maksim, then Dan, then Ganju, checking that each man was OK. Then he looked out into the road. They'd been lucky. The fight had only lasted a minute – time always stretched when you were in combat, Steve reminded himself – and no one else had come along the road. If they had, they'd have been done for.

Sometimes you just needed some luck on your side.

Steve checked his watch. Nine twenty-five, and it was at least another ten-minute drive to the fort.

They were running late already.

'We'll get rid of these bodies and try and stop this place smelling like a slaughterhouse,' said Steve. 'And then we need to get a sodding move on.' He looked at Maksim. 'Good work, mate,' he said.

The Russian's cargo pants and sweatshirt were soaked with blood, and it was still dripping from his hands and face. But there was hardly a scratch on him, and he wasn't even out of breath.

'That was nothing,' he said, casually flicking away a chip of skull and lump of soggy grey brain that had got stuck to his cheek. 'Now I'm in the mood for a real fight.'

Nutter, thought Steve. But at least he's our nutter.

Twenty-Three

T HE FORT LOOMED UP IN the distance, its grey, concrete walls rising up out of the scrubland, threatening, impregnable.

Steve glanced at it just once. Then he ducked down into the back of the truck.

He took a deep breath of air to ventilate his lungs, and steeled himself. Then he relaxed. There might be a lot of them but they are just ragheads, he reminded himself.

They'll go to pieces once they see some proper soldiers.

They had cleared the three bodies out of the truck and dumped them behind a rock for the vultures to pick at. Maksim had splashed some diesel over the cabin to disguise the smell of the blood. It still stank, but there was nothing suspicious about a truck smelling of fuel. The truck was filled with five big steel drums of water, and another thirty plastic jerry cans. One of them had been split open during the exchange of fire, splashing water everywhere, but the rest of them were OK. Steve, Dan and Maksim lay down flat between the water drums, their rifles unhooked, ready for action.

*

Two hundred and fifty yards away, on the ridge of the hill, Ollie was holding his field glasses to his eyes. He was looking straight at the truck as it slowly approached the gates.

'They're here,' he muttered.

Jeff had already severed the phone line, returning ten minutes ago. 'Job done,' he'd said tersely as he crouched down next to them. The line had been cut, but as far as Ollie could tell, no one inside the fort yet knew. They wouldn't find out until they tried to make a call. And by then it would be too late.

The truck was just fifty yards from the gates now, slowing to a crawl.

Ollie trained his glasses on the driver, but the man behind the wheel was covered in a black robe. He had Ganju's build, however.

Ian had the garage opener in his hands.

'Ready?' asked Ollie.

Ian nodded.

Jeff and Chris both had their RPGs in position, ready to blow a hole in the wall.

'Wait for the signal,' said Ollie.

Steve could feel a bead of sweat on his brow but ignored it.

It was baking in the back of the truck. The sun was rising in temperature by the minute, and the diesel engine was hot and furious, sending fumes up into the cabin. He could feel the truck slowing, its brakes creaking as Ganju applied pressure to them, and soon it came to a complete halt.

Ganju had picked up the driver's packet of Morven Gold, a Pakistani brand of cigarette, and flipped one into his mouth. He wasn't a smoker, but a cigarette and a small cloud of tobacco smoke would help to obscure his face.

The gates swung open, the same way they did every morning to take in the day's supply of water. The sentry muttered a couple of words, and Ganju just shrugged and puffed on his cigarette. He kept his body language relaxed.

With a small tap on the accelerator, he pushed the truck into first gear and drove inside.

'OK, boys,' said Steve, a note of quiet determination in his voice. 'Let's give them hell.'

Ollie tracked the truck, following every inch of its progress into the centre of the compound.

It was doing no more than ten miles an hour, and as soon as it had cleared the gates, the sentries swung them shut behind it. The truck came to a gentle halt about twenty yards inside the main compound.

'Go,' said Ollie quietly.

Ian leant forward. He was holding the garage opener in his right hand. He checked that it was pointing straight at the minefield.

Ollie started to scramble down the hillside. He wanted to be far enough away not to be injured in the blast but close enough to mow down anyone who came out to see what had happened.

Ian pressed the button.

It took just a fraction of a second for the radio transmitter to power a signal into the detonating charges strapped to the side of the landmines. Then there was a creaking sound, as if an axe was opening up the ground itself. The hard, baked earth vibrated, shuddered and groaned, then there was a deafening roar as the mines exploded. Dirt and dust hurtled up into the air, and the noise of the explosions crashed into the thick concrete walls of the fort, then echoed off the hillside. As the three mines rigged up by Ian exploded, the scattered debris ignited another two, then the debris from those sparked more detonations. Within less than five seconds, the entire stretch of ground was popping and fizzing, the ground itself heaving upwards. Ollie could feel wave after wave of heat and noise wash over him.

'Bloody carnage,' he muttered to himself. 'Just exactly what the doctor ordered.'

Steve listened for the first explosion.

Outside, he could hear some men shouting, then the sound of boots tramping across the baked earth. Men coming to unload the water, he reckoned.

Just hold it right here, he told himself. Let them get closer. Let them hear that minefield exploding.

Within seconds of the truck stopping, he heard it blasting. It roared, shaking the ground, rattling the suspension of the truck.

Steve rolled on to his side, hit the ground with his shoulder, and sprayed a round of automatic fire, all in one swift movement. He had no idea who or what the bullets were hitting, and just at this moment he didn't care. The body count, that was all that mattered. There were twenty to thirty men inside the fort, and when they'd killed most of them, they'd won.

'Go, go, go!' he shouted.

He slammed the AK-47 hard into his shoulder. Five men dressed in black jeans and sweatshirts were approaching the back of the truck. Dan and Maksim rolled from the vehicle and the three of them formed a tight line, their rifles jammed into position. As their fingers locked on to the triggers, a murderous barrage of fire sliced through the men approaching them. All five dropped to the ground, one man still groaning pitifully as he clutched his stomach, trying to stop his intestines falling out on to the ground. Steve put a single bullet neatly though his head to finish him off. Next, he ran round to the cab and flung open the door. Ganju jumped out. Beyond the far wall, there were multiple explosions from the minefield, which sent plumes of smoke and fire straight up into the sky. There was shouting everywhere, but Steve had no idea what was being said. And then he heard the slow, cold chatter of a machine gun kicking into action.

'Pull the truck, pull the truck,' he shouted.

They were close to the front of the compound. Ahead of them were the three barracks blocks and the officers' compound, and behind them, the parade ground and a firing range. Dan had just spun round and put two bullets into a man who was running towards them from behind. Christ, I didn't even hear that one, thought Steve. And it was my back he was aiming for. He turned round, but as far as he could see, it was clear all the way to the wall. If they could get the truck on its side, that would give them some cover, and they could move forward from there.

Maksim was already scaling the side of the truck.

The Russian hung on grimly to the metal frame of the vehicle. From his webbing, he pulled out a hand grenade, then lobbed it towards the barracks. Still holding on to the truck's canvas canopy, like a pirate holding on to the rigging of his vessel, he threw himself towards the ground. Dan grabbed the side of the truck, and so did Ganju. It was wobbling on its wheels. Steve got hold of it and started to climb the side, then flung himself on to Maksim. Their combined weight brought the truck crashing on to its side.

Its exposed underbelly would make a wall that would protect them. There was another vehicle parked at the back of the barracks and they could use that to drive them out of this madhouse – with any luck.

Cautiously, Steve peered round the edge of the truck.

And then retreated from a hailstorm of bullets.

'Jesus fucking hell,' he roared as he looked into the wave of men running towards them. 'There's fucking dozens of the bastards . . .'

Ollie trained the man in his sights. He'd jumped up on to the wall of the fort, shielding his face from the mines still exploding across the broken ground.

The noise was deafening, crashing into Ollie's eardrums in deep, heavy waves, and the stink of sulphur and gunpowder was filling the air, stinging his eyes, and choking his lungs.

One squeeze of the trigger, thought Ollie, bringing his finger down into position.

And he was dead.

He waved towards Jeff, Chris and Ian. They were scaling down the side of the hills, their RPGs on their shoulders. The closer they got, the more chance of an accurate shot, and amid the smoke from the explosions, they had all the cover they needed.

'Fire, fire,' shouted Ollie.

Chris fired his RPG. It kicked back as it exploded into life, but Chris was expecting that and absorbed the blow in his neck and spine muscles, and held the device steady. The grenade whizzed through the air, screeching like a mangled cat, and leaving a bright, electric-blue trail of tracer fire in its wake. In the same instant, Jeff knelt down beside him, his own RPG held easily on his broad shoulder. He was humming a few bars of 'Born To Run', noticed Ollie, and there was a broad grin on his face. He loosed off a round from his RPG, sending another grenade fizzing through the air. The wall was thirty yards away. From the hillside, it had looked at least a foot thick to Ollie, but they had no way of knowing how well built it was. If the concrete was reinforced with steel, it could take a hell of a battering and stay standing; if he'd been building it, that was what he'd have insisted on. But as Maksim had pointed out to them, this was a Soviet fort, at least twenty years old, and the Russians had never been known for the quality of their building materials. With any luck, it would crumble like a stale biscuit.

Ollie tried to focus on the wall. A couple more mines had blown, sending showers of earth up into the sky, and lumps of hot, baked mud were falling on them like hailstones. Ollie shrugged those aside; it was the shrapnel from the mine casings he was worried about. Razor-sharp slices of metal exploding away from the mines could slice out an eye or open up an artery in an instant. Through the chaos, it was difficult to see anything, but as he squinted, he saw the first grenade going into the wall, then the second. Both grenades exploded on impact, chewing up the concrete and sending huge clouds of dust up into the air.

'Again, again,' Ollie shouted, straining to make himself heard above the din of the explosions.

Chris and Jeff put in another round, then another. Through the clouds of dust, Ollie was straining to see what had happened. He wished for a moment that they had some full-scale artillery, then they could take down the walls in a matter of minutes. But there was no way they could have hauled that kind of kit up here without somebody seeing them. Instead, they had to pound away with grenades, the same way a medieval siege unit would pound away at a fortress with slings and stones. It wasn't pretty, but you got there in the end. There was only so much pressure any wall could take.

'To the left,' Chris told Jeff. 'That's the weakest point.'

He pounded another round in, while Jeff adjusted his line of fire to smash his own grenade into precisely the same point. At his side, Ian had spotted an Afghan on the fortress wall, climbing up to try to see what was happening. Ian put a shot through his chest. The man fell forward, tumbling down just as an RPG round detonated. The grenade struck his body, sending blood and guts flying everywhere. Ollie could see what looked like a human hand landing just a few feet away from him, and swallowed hard to suppress the lump of vomit rising up his throat.

'Another, just there,' Chris told Jeff.

There was a creaking as the next two rounds went in, then a crash. Ollie leant forward. He could see a pile of broken concrete, and a huge crack in the wall. Another crash and a section of wall collapsed in on itself.

'We're through,' said Ollie.

Half a dozen men moved instantly towards the breach in the wall. They were advancing in a tightly formed unit, with their AK-47s held firmly in their hands. They fired round after round through the hole in the wall. It was loose, undisciplined fire. If they hit anything, it was going to be pure luck. But that didn't mean they wouldn't get any breaks, Ollie reminded himself.

Chris put another RPG round straight into them.

The grenade exploded just inches in front of them. Two of them were torn in half, dying instantly. One man was kneeling down, blinded, his face a messy pulp of blood and bone. Another was reaching for his gun – but his hands had been blown off. Two more had run back inside screaming.

'Cover me,' shouted Ollie. 'I'm going in.'

'We're fucking fucked,' bellowed Dan.

'How many?' yelled Steve.

Dan shrugged. 'Too fucking many.'

Jesus, thought Steve to himself. Who the hell said there were only twenty blokes in here? It looks more like forty.

Bullets were smashing into the side of the truck. The fire was wild, and not many of the rounds were hitting their target, but they were deadly all the same. Across by the barracks, a line of men had formed up. Their fire was more focused. Behind them, RPG rounds smashed into the wall, but so far there was no sign of Ollie and the boys making a break-through. So much for the sodding cavalry, thought Steve.

'We're bloody pinned down,' he said.

'So break out,' snapped Dan.

Steve was trying desperately to get a grip on the challenge they were facing.

There were at least a dozen men directly opposite them, lined up alongside the main barracks, laying down fire in close formation. Much longer, and the bullets were going to shatter the base of the truck to shreds, leaving them totally exposed. Another small unit was advancing around the side; it looked as if they were planning to come round the back. Inside the officers' mess there were yet more men, their rifles sticking out of the window, taking pot shots at anything that moved. Those bastards aren't even trying, decided Steve. They think the lads on the front line can finish us off. And, hell, they might well be right. This is tougher than any of us imagined.

'Shit, grenade!' Maksim was shouting at the top of his lungs.

A lethal two-pound lump of certain death was fizzing over the top of the truck.

In a single deft movement, Ganju ran out, caught the grenade in his right hand, and lobbed it underarm towards the line of men firing into the truck.

'Christ, if this was cricket, I'd pick you,' said Dan, grinning.

Steve saw his chance. The grenade was going to explode in mid-air. It would be loud enough and nasty enough to stun their attackers.

'Cover me,' he shouted. 'Get another bloody grenade ready . . .'

He started to run.

His legs were kicking up against the dusty ground. He could feel the adrenaline coursing viciously through his veins, and his heart thumping in his chest. He veered hard to the right, taking him away from the overturned truck and towards the main gates. One second passed, then two. In the next instant, there was a riotous explosion as the grenade detonated a foot or so above ground level. A brilliant orange light flashed through the parade ground, and then, a split second later, a thunderclap swept across it. For a brief second, it was impossible to see or hear anything. Steve steadied himself. He paused, turned left, then knelt down. He could feel himself growing calmer, more confident by the second. He raised his AK-47 to his shoulder, pressed the trigger and started to lay down a rapid burst of fire. Amid the smoke and the exploding light from the grenade, it was impossible to see the target, but that didn't matter. He knew where they were. And he knew as well that, from here, they had no cover from his fire.

He heard a scream. Then another. Then another . . .

Steve permitted himself a brief, tense smile. It was the sound of the enemy having the life shot out of it.

Another grenade had just exploded, this one tossed into the air by Ganju. As it detonated, another flash of brilliant orange light blinded the whole square and kicked up a cloud of dust.

Steve ignored it. He kept firing.

Another scream. Then another – two more bastards down.

Finish the mag, he told himself. With any luck we can rip the balls off this defence.

Thump.

Steve keeled over. He could taste dirt on his lips. For a moment his head spun. As he'd fallen forward, his mouth had opened up, and he'd taken a deep lungful of air, and now his chest was wrecked. He was coughing and spluttering, trying to get a steady focus again. 'What the fuck . . .'

The smell of the corpses was horrible as Ollie stepped over the rubble.

Through the smoke and dust, he could see at least three men lying dead on the ground. They had crapped themselves as they fell, the excrement running into pools of blood. Two more men were lying wounded beside them. Ollie raised his AK-47, and slotted a pair of bullets into each man's lungs. One of them died instantly. The other was clinging on but didn't look as if he would make it past the next minute. No point in wasting another bullet on that one.

Ollie waved back towards Ian, Chris and Jeff. The three of them had to get inside fast. The gap in the wall had been blown, but he could see that Steve's guys were pinned behind the upturned truck. They'd cleared out one line of attack but another group of men was delivering heavy fire from the main barracks building.

Ollie knelt down. With enough covering fire, they could at least get the other three guys inside. They just had to work out what to do once they were all behind the truck.

'Run, run,' shouted Ollie.

He could see the three of them charging across the minefield. The ground was broken up as if an earthquake had struck it, potholes everywhere, and it was impossible to know how many mines were left unexploded. But all three of them were running hard. Ollie slammed his finger on his trigger, emptying out the remains of his magazine, spraying bullets in a semi-circle to cover the guys as they came in.

Chris came through the wall.

'Get behind that truck,' yelled Ollie.

Ian was running hard after him. Followed by Jeff.

Ollie was still firing, pinning down a pair of snipers shooting at them from the barracks building. But his magazine was empty. He tossed it aside and started to reach inside his webbing for a fresh one.

Jeff was punching his shoulder. 'There's no bloody time to reload,' he shouted. 'Run like fuck, I'll cover you.'

Kneeling down, Jeff put round after round into the sniper's position.

Ollie started to run, his feet skidding across the dusty surface of the ground. His heart was pounding and his eardrums exploding with the brutal sound of shouting and gunfire all around him. He threw himself behind the truck. As he did so, Maksim grabbed hold of him, pulling him back.

All around him he could hear the relentless chatter of bullet after bullet. He glanced back towards the wall. For a moment, his blood froze, and it seemed as if the world around him had fallen silent.

Jeff was lying on the ground, clutching his right leg. Blood was seeping out of him.

'Man down, man down,' shouted Ollie.

Steve spat the dirt out of his mouth. Dan had already hauled him back up on to his feet. He was dizzy and dazed, but he knew he was all right. A bullet had struck him in the back, but the Kevlar underneath his sweatshirt had held the bullet. He'd taken a knock, and had the wind thumped out of him – Kevlar only protected you from the bullet, not the impact of the blow. But he'd be OK. He looked around and saw the sniper who'd shot him was lying dead on the ground. Half his face had been blown away when Dan had put two bullets straight through him.

'Man down, man down,' he heard Ollie shouting.

Through the smoke, Steve could see they'd cleared the first unit. Eight men were lying dead on the ground, another couple were wounded. But the rest of them had retreated inside the barracks and were laying down fire from its windows.

'Jeff's down,' Ollie shouted.

Steve turned back towards the truck. 'Cover us.'

With Dan at his side, he started to run towards Jeff. A blizzard of bullets was streaming towards the barracks, peppering its surface with metal. The fire was directed at the windows, and for a few seconds there was a lull in the enemy response as it was impossible to get a gun out of the building. Steve took hold of Jeff's head and told Dan to grab his legs, and with one clean jerk the man was clear off the ground. They started running back towards the truck, Steve going backwards. Jeff was moaning gently, drifting in and out of consciousness, and there was blood gushing from where a bullet had opened up an artery in his leg.

'Steady, mate, steady,' muttered Steve.

They dropped Jeff on the ground as they arrived back at the truck.

'Water,' snapped Steve.

Ganju was at Jeff's side, pouring a bottle of water down his throat. Steve ripped out a bandage from his medi-pack, and strapped a tourniquet round the wound. If nothing else, we can try and stop the bleeding, he thought. At least until we can get on top of this situation. We're under heavy fire, and if we can't break out soon, they're going to shoot us to pieces.

'Thermobaric?' he said, looking at Ollie.

'Let the fuckers have it.'

Maksim had already unpacked the weapon. It was no bigger than an ordinary RPG round. Just a lot more deadly.

Chris lifted the RPG to his shoulder, while Maksim readied the missile.

'The barracks,' said Steve. 'Let's take them down in one hit.'

Chris was going to need space to put a clear shot into the barracks building, and that meant stepping out from behind the truck. Ollie and Dan led the line, slipping out from behind the truck, and put down a barrage of deadly accurate fire into the barracks. Steve, Ganju, and Ian followed them, putting round after round into the building. The windows were peppered with bullets, making it impossible for any of their attackers to go anywhere near them. They had a brief respite, but Steve was well aware that they could only hold this rate of fire for a few seconds at most. Once their magazines were empty, they would be forced to fall back.

'Bloody give it to them,' he yelled.

Chris held the RPG steady on his shoulder. The missile blasted out of the barrel. The range was only twenty yards, and it would have been hard to miss anything at that distance. A building was no problem.

The hardened steel tip of the missile drilled through the corrugated iron roof of the barracks like an arrow puncturing a lung.

'Back, back,' shouted Ollie as soon as Chris had fired the missile.

There was a momentary pause. And then a blinding flash of white light lit up the fort, like a torch being shone into a dark cellar. A second of stillness followed: the eerie, ghostly silence of a funeral parlour. All of the men had fallen back behind the truck and were reloading their magazines. As the white light faded, there was a sucking sound, like a sudden gust of wind blowing out of nowhere. Steve could feel his lungs suddenly aching as the oxygen appeared to have been emptied out of the fort. Then a huge fireball exploded out of the barracks, ripping the iron roof clean off. Shards of molten hot metal flew in every direction, many of them smashing into the underside of the truck but many more falling inside the building, creating a lethal rain of red shrapnel that could melt straight into a man's brain. The flames licked up high in the sky, sending wave after wave of intense heat rolling across the fort, singeing everything it touched. Then the wind started to whistle again, and suddenly there was a crashing sound as the breeze-block walls fell in on themselves. Clouds of dust rose into the sky, instantly ignited by the flames, creating a brief but deadly display of pyrotechnics. Underneath it all, you could just hear the groans of dying men. But not for much longer. No man could survive that inferno for more than an instant. The barracks looked like a burning, smouldering tin can.

Dan was grinning maliciously. 'Fucking A, mate,' he growled. 'Toasted bloody Afghan – best ten grand we'll ever spend.'

The parade ground was suddenly gripped by a deathly silence. The fires were spluttering but fading fast, and wherever Steve looked, nothing was moving. He glanced towards the officers' mess. There are still men in there. We're not done yet.

He heard an engine start and a Land Rover Discovery suddenly appeared from behind the mess building. It was heading straight for the exit. Through its blacked-out windows it was impossible to see anything, but Steve reckoned he had a good idea who was inside. Salangi.

'The fucker's getting away,' he snapped.

Standing away from the truck, he slammed his fist on to the trigger of the AK-47, peppering the Discovery with bullets. But they were bouncing off the skin of the vehicle scratching up its dirty black paintwork but not doing any significant damage. It must have armour plating. They could shoot at it all day, but unless they could blow up at least two of the tyres, they weren't going to have any chance of stopping it.

'Put a grenade into the bastard,' yelled Steve.

Behind him, Dan pulled the pin from a grenade and lobbed it high into the air. Steve could see immediately where he was aiming for. The exit. If they could blow up the vehicle on the way out, or bring down enough rubble to make the exit impassable, there was still a chance of stopping them.

'There,' shouted Ollie.

Two men had stepped out from behind the officers' mess and were running towards them, their guns blazing on automatic. It was a suicide mission, but that didn't mean it wasn't effective. Steve started to blast on automatic. He could feel the bullets whizzing past his head, but remained calm, as did Ollie. One man fell, then the second, both of them ten yards short of their target, both of them ripped apart by the high-calibre munitions smashing into them. But that didn't mean they hadn't accomplished their mission. They'd distracted the unit while the Land Rover made its escape.

Steve heard a blast behind him. He turned to look at the exit.

Dan's grenade had exploded right underneath the gates. Dust and smoke were flying everywhere. But the Land Rover was punching its way through. Steve started firing, with Ollie, Chris and Dan doing the same. Then Steve raised his hand. 'We're just wasting rounds.'

Their guns fell silent. The Land Rover was disappearing in to the distance, leaving a trail of dust in its wake. One man down. One man – at least – escaped.

'Sod it,' muttered Steve.

He looked around. There were smouldering fires, piles of rubble, and the stink of corpses everywhere.

'Let's get the hell out of here,' he said. 'If that bastard's escaped, we haven't got much time before half the sodding Taliban descend on us.'

Twenty-Four

J EFF WAS LYING PROPPED UP against the wall. His leg was bandaged up, and Steve had shot some morphine into him. But he'd lost consciousness. Christ, thought Steve as he stood up. The man needs proper medical attention, and he needs it fast.

He glanced at Ollie. 'Let's get ourselves sorted,' he said.

You could see the strain on the faces of all the men. The battle had been a lot harder than anyone had expected, and it wasn't likely to be over yet. They still had to get out of there, and if Salangi had escaped to rally his Taliban mates, then the journey into Pakistan would be a long and dangerous one.

'Ian, you're in charge of getting the loot out, with Steve alongside you,' said Ollie briskly. He pointed to the truck at the back of the barracks. 'Maksim and Dan, I want you two guys to get that truck over there and make sure the bastard will drive us out of here. Ganju, you get up on that pile of rubble, make sure there's enough clear space to get the truck through, and keep an eye on the road. Chris and I will make sure none of the stragglers are left alive. OK, let's move.'

Each man snapped into action.

We just crack on, reflected Steve.

Ollie and Chris stepped up towards the barracks building. There were bodies everywhere. Ollie reckoned there had been at least forty blokes inside the fort; when Muirhead had told them it should be below strength, he'd been talking bollocks. Men were lying dead on the ground where they'd been shot. As they walked past them, either Chris or Ollie put an extra bullet through their heads. No point in taking any chances, Ollie told himself. The bastards were dead or dying anyway.

The barracks had been reduced to a wreck of smouldering rubble. The roof had melted and the walls had collapsed. Most of the corpses weren't even recognisably human. There were legs, arms, torsos lying around like the rubbish at a municipal dump. Ollie swallowed hard to stop himself throwing up as he saw a severed head, with one eyeball left in its socket, looking straight up at him. The body had been burned away from the neck down.

'Remind me never to be on the receiving end of a thermobaric,' he said tersely.

Suddenly a hand reached out and brushed against his legs. Ollie jumped.

'Steady, mate,' said Chris.

Ollie recovered himself. Looking down, he could see a man, his body crushed by the weight of the rocks on top of him. One arm was pinned down, and there was blood all over him, but miraculously there was still breath in his lungs. 'Please . . .' he cried. He was looking straight up at Ollie. 'Please . . . English.'

Chris knelt down at his side. There was a kindly expression on his face. The man tried to smile, but winced with pain. Chris took his Makarov out, pressed it into the man's cheek, and pulled the trigger. 'South Africans, mate,' he said quietly. 'We don't do the mercy thing.'

Twenty yards to the left, Ian and Steve walked towards the officers' quarters, the only building left standing in the compound.

There was damage to every wall and window, and the front door was blown out. Ian paused directly outside. 'It could be an ambush,' he said quietly. 'If this was the Provos, we'd leave one bloke behind, ready to take out anyone who tried to nick our stuff.'

'Or else booby-trap the bloody place.'

Ian nodded. 'That and all.'

The two men stepped carefully into the building. It was spartan. Whatever Salangi was spending his opium cash on, it wasn't the living quarters for either himself or his men There was an iron stove, a map hanging loose from the wall, and some filing cabinets. In the next couple of rooms, there were some metal frame beds, all of them now empty. It looked like six guys lived here most of the time.

'There should be a staircase,' said Ian.

Steve tapped his foot against the floorboards of the second dormitory room until he found one that sounded hollow. He knelt down and lifted a trapdoor. A wooden ladder led straight down. He took his torch from his webbing and shone it down. The drop was about eight feet, leading to what looked like a concrete bunker.

'Looks safe enough,' said Steve. He started to lever himself down.

'No, me,' snapped Ian. He grabbed hold of Steve's shoulder.

Steve shrugged, then stood aside.

Ian gripped his Makarov in his right hand, then dropped

down the ladder in a single sliding movement. As he did so, he fired his handgun. Once, then twice. The shots echoed around the bunker. Steve slid down the ladder, his own gun in his hand. An Afghan was lying slumped against the wall. He didn't look more than sixteen – there was some wispy hair on his cheeks where he'd been trying to grow a beard. Ian had put one bullet through his chest, and another into his face.

To the right were three big metal doors. Each safe measured ten foot by five, made to a Soviet design. They had combination locks on the front.

Ian was unpacking his bombs. 'We'll just have to hope they haven't put any more guys inside these safes.'

'Just get a move on.'

'This is delicate work,' snapped Ian.

He leaned close to one of the doors and tapped the metal with his fingers, trying to get a fix on how thick it was. He was touching it the same way you might touch a woman, noticed Steve; caressing the steel, finding out where its weak spots were. Too much explosive and he'd destroy everything inside. Too little, and he'd just singe the door.

He carefully adjusted the amount of Semtex inside the bomb, then used some masking tape to attach its frame. There was nothing fancy about it: just plastic explosive, wrapped round a tiny electric detonator. The trick was to put precisely the right amount of pressure on the lock to break it open.

'Get the hell out of here,' he muttered to Steve.

Steve scrambled up the ladder. Ian followed close behind him.

'Back,' he muttered. 'Get out of the building.'

'I thought we were just blowing the door.'

'There's no such thing as a safe explosion,' said Ian.

Steve retreated a few more yards to the doorway. He looked round the shattered compound. Dan and Maksim had driven the truck from the back of the barracks out to the centre of the compound. One tyre had been blown in the fire fight and they were already changing that. The truck they had ridden in on was blown to pieces; they couldn't drive out in that. Ganju had cleared the exit and was keeping his eyes on the road. Judging by his calm expression, it was empty out there. Ollie and Chris were working their way methodically through the dead, putting bullets into anyone left alive. Steve paused for a moment to catch his breath. The air smelt of cordite and blood, he could feel it clinging to his lungs. One payday, he reminded himself, as he watched Chris put another bullet through a badly wounded man. Then I'm done.

A loud, throaty explosion rumbled up from the cellars. Steve could feel the ground tremble beneath him. What the hell's happening now?

Ollie and Chris were running fast towards him. Maksim and Dan had stopped working. Steve rushed inside the building. There was smoke everywhere, thick, angry clouds rolling up from the cellars. Ian was bent down, hacking his guts out. Steve grabbed hold of his arm. 'Jesus, what happened?'

Ian brushed him away angrily. He dropped down into the cellar, shielding his face and eyes from the smoke.

'What the hell's he done?' asked Ollie as he reached the officers' quarters.

'Looks like the sodding Irishman's just blown up half the building,' said Steve.

'No bloody way,' said Ollie. His face was red with anger as

he rushed towards the trapdoor. Steve pulled him back. The smoke was still billowing out.

'Fuck it,' he heard Ian swear.

Steve shone his torch down into cellar, but the smoke was still so thick it was impossible to see anything.

Ian emerged, his face blackened by tar. 'Stand back,' he muttered tersely.

Steve was trying to judge his expression. But Ian was inscrutable at the best of times. With his face blacked out you could no more read him than you could a stretch of tarmac on the road.

'What happened?'

'Stand back,' repeated Ian. 'We're going to blow the next one.'

Ollie grabbed hold of his sweatshirt, curling his fists round it, leaning into Ian's face. 'What's bloody happened to our money?'

Ian looked at his garage door opener, then down at the trapdoor. 'Your man Salangi, he's a slippery little fucker.'

'What happened?'

'He booby-trapped the door,' said Ian. 'Blow it, and there's an explosive device inside. That gets triggered and it blows the stuff inside.'

Ollie's face drained of colour. 'You're bloody kidding, right?'

'Do I look like a man who has time to kid around?'

Steve felt as if he'd just taken a blow straight to the stomach. 'So the loot – it's destroyed?'

Ian shrugged. 'The diamonds might be OK. You need a couple of million degrees to melt those, and I don't think the blast had anything like that impact.'

'Our money . . .'

'There's two more safes,' said Ian. 'I'm using a much lower density explosion for the second one. With any luck, it won't trigger the device.'

'And if it does?'

'Then we won't be any poorer than when we came in, will we?'

'Bloody Irishman,' snapped Steve. 'The only reason I let you come on this job was because you said you knew about bombs.'

'I bloody do and all,' said Ian. 'How the hell am I meant to know it was booby-trapped?' He looked sharply at Steve. 'Did you know?' His eyes swivelled to Ollie. 'Did you?'

'We can't risk another bomb,' said Ollie. 'There must be another way.'

'Can you think of one?'

'We could shoot our way through.'

'It's four inches of sodding hardened steel,' said Ian. 'It would take a couple of days.'

'We can't bloody risk it.'

'We have to.' Ollie reached for the detonator but Steve grabbed hold of his wrist.

'Are you sure this will work?' he asked Ian.

'It's my money as well, and I need it as much as anyone,' said Ian.

'Then blow it,' said Steve.

He and Ollie moved away across the room, and Ian took five paces backwards, then pressed the detonator. A blast rumbled a few feet below them. Some smoke and sparks were visible from the trapdoor. Ian waited for a moment, letting the aftershock of the explosion rumble through the cellar, then dropped down through the trapdoor. Steve wasn't sure how long he was down there. It seemed like an eternity, though in reality it was no more than a few seconds. Eventually, Ian climbed back out. His face was even dirtier and so were his hands, but his expression had relaxed; it wasn't a grin exactly, but there was a tune in his eyes, one that meant money.

He rolled a diamond across the floor, then tossed a gold ingot.

'Payday, boys,' he said. 'The big one.'

Steve reached down and picked up the single bar of metal.

It weighed precisely one kilogram, and had been minted by the Union Bank of Switzerland. A kilo was slightly over 32 ounces, so at the current market prize, the brick he was holding in his hand was worth around twenty-five thousand dollars. And there were dozens of them down there. Serious money.

'Stand back further,' said Ian and once again disappeared beneath the trapdoor.

Steve and Ollie took another few paces back and waited in the doorway. Ian detonated the third and final safe.

'Let's move it,' said Steve as soon as Ian had re-emerged and they knew that the third of the safes was now open. 'The sooner we get away, the better.'

Maksim had already driven the truck up to the back of the officers' quarters, and Ollie organised the men into a file. Ian hauled the crates out of the safes, then passed them back along the line to Dan who put them on the back of the truck. It was just after ten fifteen in the morning now, and the sun was beating down. All of them were sweating furiously, but they were working hard, desperate to get as much as the gear out as fast as possible. They'd shot some more morphine into Jeff and lifted him up into the back of the truck. In total, Ian reckoned there were forty boxes to lift out. They had lost a lot of gold in the first safe but there was still a decent haul. From the looks of it, Salangi had stashed more money inside this fort than Lockhart and the British garrison realised.

'He's going to do his nut when he finds it's all gone,' remarked Steve.

There was a shout from the fort's gates. Ganju was waving at them. And yelling.

Each man in the line was immediately alert.

Steve stashed the box he was holding into the back of truck and ran across the parade ground to see what was happening.

But he didn't need to ask. He could see it clearly enough for himself. Some kind of armed vehicle was approaching the fort along the main road. Through the cloud of dust it was kicking up, it was impossible to see what it was or how many men might be on board. It was hostile, however. You could tell that right away.

'Move out, move out,' he shouted to Ollie, running back towards him.

Ollie started bundling the men on to the back of the truck.

'How many more boxes?' Steve shouted down to Ian.

'Maybe twenty,' replied Ian.

Steve didn't need a moment to think about it. He didn't know precisely how much money was in each box, but they'd already loaded twenty of them on to the truck, and it looked like a good haul. This fort had already proved much harder to take than any of them had expected. They were a man down, and in no state for another fight. The truck approaching them might just be the first of a dozen or more. Better to cut and run with what they had than die here a few gold bars richer.

'We're moving out right now,' shouted Steve.

Maksim objected. 'We stand and fight.'

'Get in the truck, you mad fucker,' yelled Steve.

Ian ran out of the building with one box weighing him down. He managed to sling it in the back of the truck, then bundled in himself. Chris and Dan had laid Jeff down flat on the truck's hard wooden surface. There was more blood seeping out of his wounded leg but there was no time to deal with that now.

'Go, go, go,' yelled Steve, his face red and sweaty.

'We stand and fight,' growled Maksim.

'Just bloody move,' snapped Ollie.

'There's money down there, I'm not leaving it behind.'

Steve tossed a grenade into the air towards Maksim. The pin wasn't released, but he couldn't see that. Maksim's hands reached out into the air to catch it.

'Then you're fighting alone, mate,' Steve said. 'Do us all a favour and hold the fuckers up for a few minutes before they kill you.'

Dan was in the driver's seat and the engine rumbled into life. Steam rose from the bonnet and oil was leaking from the undercarriage; even though it had been stashed at the back of the barracks, it had taken some damage in the fire fight. But it was powered up and ready to move.

'Go, man, just bloody go,' Steve yelled, climbing into the back of the truck.

He glanced behind him. Maksim had disappeared inside the building. It's his funeral, reflected Steve. We haven't got time to worry about a guy with a death wish.

Dan slammed his foot on the accelerator and the truck

lurched across the parade ground. At the exit it stopped to enable Ganju to climb aboard. Steve looked back again and saw Maksim running hard towards them. He threw himself on to the back of the truck just as it pulled out of the rubble that surrounded the gates. He grinned. 'I changed my mind.'

Steve shuttled towards the front and looked through the grimy windscreen. They were out on the main road now, and the other vehicle was driving straight towards them in the opposite direction. You could see it clearly now. A big, heavy Hyundai Tuscon, it had blacked-out windows, making it impossible to tell how many men were inside, or what kind of weapons they might have.

'Everybody down,' barked Steve. 'We could be about to take some fire.'

They had no way of knowing who was in the armoured vehicle. It wasn't the Land Rover that had escaped. It could just be carrying some of Salangi's men returning from a job; they weren't necessarily the first wave of a counter-attack. But if they didn't already know what had happened to their fort, they would in a few seconds, and then they would come after the truck.

Steve looked at Dan. 'Stay on the tarmac as long as you can, then swerve to avoid the bastard.'

They were closing in on them fast. A hundred yards, fifty . . .

The road had two lanes, blending into the rocky, dusty scrubland on either side. There was space for both vehicles to pass, but only if they slowed and took it carefully. Dan's foot was pressed down hard on the accelerator, but the engine was spluttering badly. The weight of the men and the gold was making the axles sag and it was struggling to get much above thirty miles an hour. The Hyundai was bearing down on them fast, not giving an inch of room. Dan slammed his left fist on the horn, and used his right hand to steer the truck off the road. A blast of raw noise screeched through the air, followed by a crunching of the gears as Dan slipped the truck down into second. It hit a rock, and bounced nastily as it slid out into the scrubland. Steve was thrown sideways and landed on top of Chris, who was knocked on to Ollie. Jeff was jerked up into the air, and as he landed, the bandage took a knock, sending blood squirting out of his wound, dyeing the base of the truck a deep crimson. A howl of pain erupted from Jeff's lips and his eyes opened wide, then shut again.

'Jesus,' muttered Steve. He grabbed his own medi-kit from his webbing, and tried to steady his hands to get a bandage out, but the truck was swaying violently from side to side.

They were on the open scrubland now, while the Hyundai kept moving at full throttle towards the gates of the fort.

Another crash, and the truck lifted almost a foot in the air. Dan struggled to hold the wheel steady as he pushed the truck back on the tarmac. Oil was leaking hard from the engine, and there was more steam rising from the bonnet. Steve was struggling with the bandage. Ollie was doing his best to hold Jeff still while Steve put the dressing in place. It wasn't going to stop all of the bleeding, maybe not even half of it, but it was the best he could do while they were escaping.

'We'll get you evacuated to a hospital in a few minutes, mate,' he muttered.

He looked back. The Hyundai had turned round, and was screeching back along the tarmac. Straight towards them.

'Bloody step on it,' said Steve.

But even empty, with a freshly tuned engine, the truck

wasn't capable of more than sixty. In its current state, it wasn't going to do any more than fifty. The Hyundai could cruise at eighty, and you'd still hardly hear the engine. We're not going to outrun it, Steve realised. No sodding way.

A bullet smashed into the tarmac, a few feet short of the truck. A man was leaning out of the side of the Hyundai, firing an AK-47.

'Chris, we'll drop off and take the bastards from behind,' said Steve.

Chris nodded.

'Dan, slow down,' said Ollie.

'Make it to the RV point,' said Steve. 'We'll catch up with you there.'

The truck dawdled, and slowed as it went into a bend. Steve waited until it was down to about fifteen miles an hour, then threw himself out into the scrubland. He hit the ground hard, but he had rolled himself into a ball, with his knees bent, the same way you would on a hard parachute landing. There were a couple of rocks directly beneath him, and he could feel one of them snagging on his sweatshirt. He pulled it free, and crouched down at the side of the road. Chris knelt right next to him. The truck continued on down the road. Steve calculated they were about half a mile from the RV point. Finish off the Hyundai, and they could tab the rest of the way on foot. With any luck, the rest of the boys would have already lifted the heavy boxes and have a nice cup of tea waiting for them.

'Wait until he's level, then let him have it,' said Steve.

The Hyundai was two hundred yards away, accelerating all the time.

Steve and Chris were kneeling next to a rock; if it turned into a fire fight, they could slip behind that for cover.

A hundred yards.

Steve checked his mag was full, and steadied his hand on his trigger.

Fifty yards.

'Go for the tyres first, then the fuel tank,' he said tersely.

The Hyundai was approaching at speed. One window was down, with an Afghan hanging out of it, brandishing his AK-47. It looked as if there were two more guys, plus the driver. The gunman was loosing off a few rounds, but he wasn't a good enough shot to hit anything from a moving vehicle except tarmac. Not many men were, reflected Steve. Their plan looked to be to catch up with the truck, then fire as they overtook it. It would probably work. In any battle between two vehicles, the fastest usually won – unless some guys on the ground intervened.

'Go,' snapped Steve.

The Hyundai was twenty yards away, but at the speed it was travelling they would have only a brief few seconds when it would be within their arc of fire.

Bullets sprayed out of the barrel of Steve's AK-47 and empty cases slipped out of the side of the gun and fell to the dusty ground. The 7.62 calibre ammo packed plenty of punch but was mainly designed for accuracy and lightness on the battlefield, not for the weight of damage it could inflict on its victim. The Hyundai was armour-plated and anything hitting the side panels or glass was bouncing straight off; you'd need a tank cannon to bring it down in one hit. Steve twisted his body on his ankles to keep the moving vehicle in his sights and lowered his line of fire a fraction. You couldn't armour-plate a tyre. He squeezed hard on the trigger, permitting himself a smile of satisfaction as he heard the front right tyre blow. The Hyundai swerved, twisting over the scrubland, as the driver tried to escape from the attack. It rose up into the air as it hit a rock, and both Chris and Steve adjusted their fire again, this time peppering its undercarriage with bullets, splintering the metal, and sending a dozen rounds up through the underside of the vehicle, and into the engine. It stalled and, smoke rose from within it.

'Circle them,' shouted Steve. He didn't want whoever was inside to have a chance to get out. Not alive anyway. If they dug in behind their vehicle, it could turn into a long and hard fire fight.

Steve ran across the road to the right, Chris to the left, attacking from both flanks.

The Hyundai had stalled but they could hear the driver struggling desperately to turn the ignition. The back door flew open and an Afghan tumbled out, an AK-47 rammed into his hip, spraying bullets Rambo-style. Wrong movie, mate, thought Steve. You're not going to hit anything like that. Calmly, he raised his own rifle to his shoulder, slowed his run, took aim, and slotted a pair of bullets into the man's chest. He fell screaming to the ground. Chris was slamming the windscreen with his rifle butt, until eventually it cracked open, sending shards of glass in every direction. As he heard it crack, Steve raced forward, lining up the driver in the sights of his rifle. He fired a bullet into the man's forehead, sending splinters of skull and brain shooting backwards, then turned his gun on the man in the passenger seat. He had thrown up his hands and was immobilised with fear, unable to think about anything other than protecting himself. But Steve felt not a moment's pity as he put one bullet, then another, into him. The metal sliced through the bones of his hands, and chewed up his face, sending it back against the seat.

A silence fell over the road.

Steve took a deep breath, then turned away, trying to shield himself from the noxious smell of blood and oil rising up from the Hyundai.

'It's half a mile to the RV,' he said to Chris. 'Let's get out of here before any more of the bastards start to descend on us.'

Twenty-Five

NICK WAS STANDING SLUMPED against a rock. Alone.

Ollie climbed out of the truck and walked towards him. The two jeeps were standing in the dust, their engines switched off.

'Where's David?' said Ollie.

Nick remained silent.

Dan climbed out of the truck and joined them.

'He asked you where David was,' he said.

Nick looked up. You could see the fear in his eyes. 'They took him,' he said flatly. His lip was trembling as he delivered the sentence.

'What the hell do you mean, they took him?' snapped Ollie.

Nick tried to take a step backwards, but he was already up against the rock and there was nowhere for him to go.

'Just tell us what bloody happened,' growled Dan.

'The Taliban came,' said Nick, his eyes darting from man to man. 'At least I think they were Taliban. I don't really know who the hell they were. They were Afghans, I could see that much. There were at least five of them. They crept up on us, coming out of the hills. We didn't hear so much as a whisper. I was out scouting the hills, trying to see if anyone was out there, and looking for you guys on the road, then I looked down and David was surrounded by five men with guns. They were shouting at him, then they started to march him down the track towards a vehicle they had waiting. There wasn't anything I could—'

'Why the fuck didn't you shoot them?' shouted Dan.

Ollie was looking at Nick fiercely.

'I . . . I . . .'

'You've got a bloody gun, haven't you, man?' Dan's face was red with anger. He walked up to Nick, grabbed hold of his AK-47 and ripped it off his chest.

'I don't know,' stuttered Nick. 'There were five . . . I mean I wasn't . . .'

'This is a fucking war, mate,' shouted Dan. 'When you get attacked, you bloody dig in and defend yourself.'

'But I—'

'But you bloody bottled it,' said Ollie.

Dan was leaning into Nick, his fist raised.

'Drop it,' snapped Steve.

He was walking across the ridge of the hill, with Chris at his side. From where they'd taken out the Hyundai, it was less than half a mile to the RV point, and they had covered the ground at a fast clip. He hadn't heard the whole conversation but enough to get an idea of what had happened. And he knew they were in enough trouble without starting to fight among themselves.

'He's a fucking coward,' said Dan, looking at Steve.

Steve marched straight up to him. 'He's just a kid. You weren't there, so you don't know what the sodding hell happened.'

'I know when a man's bloody bottled it.'

'I didn't bottle it,' yelled Nick. 'I was—'

Steve put a hand on Nick's shoulder. He looked sharply at Ollie and Dan. 'He's just a kid. If anyone's to blame, it's us for bringing him along.'

Dan walked off towards the truck without saying a word.

Nick was still looking at Steve. 'I didn't—'

'We know. Now, where did they take him?'

'Due east,' said Nick. 'They had an SUV, and they drove back in that direction. I reckon that was where they came from.'

'And they were Taliban.'

'I don't know,' said Nick. 'They could be Taliban, or they could be some local boys out doing some robbing.'

'They didn't take the Toyotas,' said Ian, gesturing towards the two vehicles.

Nick shook his head.

'Then they aren't just robbers,' said Ian. 'Those two are worth a lot more than some English bloke. They were looking for something.'

'We'll worry about that later,' said Steve. 'We've got Jeff to deal with, and a man to find. Let's get the loot transferred on to the Toyotas, then we need to get some medical help for Jeff.'

Ian took charge of the transfer. There were twenty-two crates in total, each of them heavy. While Chris and Dan and Ganju and Nick were loading the boxes, eleven in the back of each Toyota, Steve and Ollie got out the one satellite phone they had brought with them, an Iridium 9505A. It was much bigger than a normal mobile, and they'd kept it switched off until now in case the signal was detected. It was for emergencies only. Like now.

Steve punched a call through to Angus Muirhead at the British base in Helmand. The call was routed via London through to Kabul, then back to the southern province. It only took a couple of seconds.

'Muirhead here,' said a stiff-sounding voice.

'Steve West here. We've got a man down. He needs a medi-vac right away.'

There was a pause on the line. One that made Steve worry.

'We'll need an RV point.'

'We're a mile from the fort,' said Steve. 'I can give you the co-ordinates.'

'Too close,' said Muirhead. 'We can't be seen to be giving your little operation any official support. If we send a chopper in there now, it'll look like we're helping out. Get yourself a safe distance away, and we'll see what we can do.'

Steve could feel the anger welling up inside his chest. 'The guy's badly hurt.'

'Well, I'm sorry about that, but—'

'He's a bloody British citizen.'

'He's a mercenary,' snapped Muirhead. 'You boys knew the rules. You were hitting that fort on your own, and we told you we couldn't have any British Army fingerprints anywhere on the operation. So there's no point in bloody well crying about it now. Get yourself a safe distance away, and when we can agree a discreet RV point, we'll bring your man out and get him to a hospital.'

Steve summoned up every curse he could think of, but the line had gone dead.

'Wanker,' spluttered Steve.

Ollie glanced at him. Steve didn't need to explain. One half of the conversation was enough to get a fair idea of what had been said. They were on their own.

Steve walked across to the back of the truck. Ganju was wiping Jeff's brow, trying to put some water down him. He'd removed the bandage, and replaced it with a thicker and stronger dressing. With Maksim's help, they rubbed down the wound with some raw alcohol, and pumped some morphine and antibiotics into him. But he'd lost a lot of blood. There was a bad entry wound where the bullet had torn into his thigh, but no sign of an exit wound, which meant the metal was still in there somewhere. They had no idea what kind of ammo Salangi's men were using, or what kind of damage it was meant to inflict. But from the look of the wound, it was already infected. He needed a doctor to get the bullet out of him, and he needed more blood as well. Otherwise, he could lose his leg. And that's if he's lucky.

'Hang in there, mate,' said Steve, resting a hand on Jeff's shoulder.

'I'll be OK,' said Jeff.

His voice was weak, noted Steve. He'd known the man for years, and although there was plenty of determination there, there wasn't much to back it up.

Christ, he muttered, under his breath this time. That Muirhead bastard has to send a chopper in soon. Or else we have to get Jeff across the border, and into a hospital in Pakistan. Because I'm certainly not going to be the bloke who has to tell his mum we've lost him.

'We're packed up and ready to go,' said Ian. 'I reckon we destroy the truck and get the hell out of here.'

'We need to get David back first,' said Ollie.

'We need to get out of here,' said Ian sharply.

Steve frowned. 'What the hell are you talking about?'

'Jesus Christ, man,' growled Ian, the exasperation evident in his voice. 'We know Salangi escaped, and he's bringing the

Taliban down on our heads. And we know some bandits, or maybe the Taliban, have already been here. So I suggest we get our sodding skates on and get the fuck out of here before the whole of Afghanistan comes down to kill us.'

'One of our men has been taken,' said Ollie.

'He knew what the job was just like the rest of us,' said Ian. 'It didn't work out for the man, and I'm sorry about that, but those are the breaks of war, and if you aren't willing to take the odds, then you've got no business sitting down at the table.'

'Are you seriously saying we don't try and rescue him?' said Steve.

Ian took a step closer to him. 'Are you seriously suggesting we piss around here for a day or more with half the Taliban coming down to mallet us.'

'Too right we bloody are,' said Ollie. 'Jesus, I can't believe I'm listening to this.'

'You're just looking to get your hands on more money,' snarled Steve. 'The more of us go down, the more there is for you.'

'He's talking good sense,' interrupted Maksim.

Steve turned to look at the Russian.

'In the Red Army, we don't stop to rescue prisoners. If a man gets taken by the enemy, that's his lookout. He should have carried on fighting.'

'For Christ's sake,' snapped Steve.

Ollie grabbed hold of Steve's arm. He could see he was close to losing it.

'SAS rules, remember,' said Ian, looking at Steve. 'You're not here to give orders, and neither is Ollie. We make our decisions together.'

'Then what does everyone think?' asked Ollie. 'We know

where Steve and I stand, and I think we know what Ian and Maksim think.' He looked at the rest of the men. 'Chris, what about you?'

'It's a tough one, mate,' said Chris. 'In the Recces, we reckoned once Swapo got hold of you, they'd pop you in the pot, mix in a few herbs, and make a nice stew out of you, so there wasn't much point in trying to rescue a bloke.' He laughed roughly. 'I'm not bloody kidding either, it happened to a mate of mine. I reckon it's the same out in this hellhole. Bandits or Taliban, it doesn't matter. They don't look like Geneva Convention boys to me, and that means David's probably already a goner.'

'The longer we hang around, the less chance we have of getting Jeff to a hospital,' said Dan. 'So we could lose Jeff, and put our own lives at risk, just to go after one man who is probably dead already.'

'So you're saying we piss off,' said Ollie.

'I'm not going that far,' said Dan. 'I'm just not sure.'

'He's a family man,' said Ganju. As always, his voice was quiet and certain. 'He's the only one of us here who's got kids to support. His wife is pregnant with twins, for God's sake. We can't just leave him.'

'Then we go and get him,' said Nick firmly.

'That's because you feel guilty,' said Dan.

'There's worse reasons for going into battle,' said Steve.

He looked at each man in turn. If it came to a vote, he reckoned they'd decide to go and have a crack at getting David back, but that wasn't the right way to make a decision.

'Here's what we're going to do,' he said. 'We need to get Jeff to some medics and we need to do that fast, and the truth is that right now he's got more chance of surviving this job than David has. So that's the first priority. I reckon that

Nick, Ganju and I should go and see if we can find out what's happened to David. Ollie and the rest of you should take Jeff, plus all the gear, and get the hell down to the border. We'll meet you there in three days.' He paused. 'Agreed?'

No one spoke.

'Right then, let's crack on. It's all been a sodding mess so far, it's time to start sorting it out.'

Twenty-Six

STEVE WOKE WITH A START.

He grabbed his AK-47 and looked instinctively for a target. But all he could see was Nick standing twenty yards away, kicking stones into the distance.

Steve checked his watch. It was just after seven in the evening. He picked up a water bottle and drank. They had driven for five miles from the RV point, taking the beaten-up truck while the rest of the unit took the Toyotas towards the border. They'd stopped just after two, when the heat of the mid-afternoon made it impossible to move around the country, and grabbed some kip under the shade of the truck's canopy. They needed rest. They'd been through a long, hard battle, much tougher than any of them had psyched themselves up for, and they needed to loosen up and wind down.

Except that it didn't look like Nick was able to.

How long he'd been standing there, kicking stones into the dust, Steve couldn't tell. He'd been too busy getting his head down and keeping his eyes shut. It didn't matter. However long it was, it was too long.

'You OK?' he said.

Nick just shrugged.

'Try talking about it.'

'I'm crap, aren't I?' said Nick. 'There's sod all else to say.'

Steve glanced into the sunset. It was melting away in the distance, merging into the arid, orange landscape. 'Because of what happened to David?'

'I should have bloody done something about it,' said Nick. 'Now all the blokes think I'm crap, and they're bloody right as well. Even you didn't want me to come along on the main assault. You left me minding the garage, and I couldn't even get that right.'

'Don't listen to the hotheads,' Steve replied quietly. 'You did the right thing. There's no way one man can take out five Afghans and rescue his mate. That kind of rubbish only happens in films. All that would have happened is you'd both have got shot, and that's not soldiering, that's just getting tooled up in the pub and getting into a ruck. If there's one thing you need to learn about this business, it's that it's about winning battles. Any idiot can start a fight but it takes a man to win one.'

Nick shook his head.

He's going to take some convincing, thought Steve. And only time is going to do that, which is the one thing we don't have.

'Now stop bloody moping around, because we've got work to do.'

He walked to the truck, woke up Ganju, and within minutes they were back on the road. They were heading towards Barikju, a small village due east of Kajaki. They'd debriefed Nick a dozen times, but all he could tell them was that David had been snatched by five guys, all of them Afghans, and driven east. That limited the search to about ten million people and a few hundred square miles. They didn't want to go anywhere near Kajaki because the truck would certainly be recognised. Instead, they headed for the next village along. If they were going to pick up any kind of lead, that was the place to start. If they couldn't find anything there, maybe it was futile. They owed David a search party, but not their lives.

They pulled off the road half a mile from the village. Steve and Nick laid up in the back of the truck while Ganju went into the village to scout the situation. It was an hour before he returned, a slow and tense sixty minutes, most of which Steve spent twitching his finger on the trigger of his AK-47. Every time a vehicle passed them on the road, he could feel his pulse racing. By now Salangi would have alerted the whole territory to the fact that he'd been robbed by a gang of British mercenaries, and he'd have described the truck they'd used to make their escape. No doubt there was a substantial reward on their heads already. Not that it would make much difference. Out here, most of the locals would slit their throats for nothing. Salangi controlled the local drugs economy, and that meant he controlled the lives of every man, woman and child in Helmand. Even the dogs would be turning on us if they knew we were here, reflected Steve, as he cautiously watched another truck go by on the road.

At last Ganju climbed back into the truck and downed half a pint of water in one gulp. Even though it was close to nine now, the air was still humid, and a man sweated buckets walking half a mile and back in this heat.

'He's alive,' he said.

'Who took him?' said Steve.

'I was just asking for rumours in the one cafe in town, and I didn't want to say too much in case they got suspicious,' said Ganju. 'It's a small town, and they don't get many strangers. Just Pakistani truck drivers on their way up to Kabul, so I passed myself off as a trucker from Faisalabad, and managed to talk to some Iranians who do the same run. Everyone already knows about the hit on Salangi's fort. They reckon it was forty or fifty guys who overran the place, foreign mercenaries, or a British armoured division, depending on who you want to believe.'

'And David?' asked Nick.

'He's been taken by a guy called Karmal Masood,' said Ganju. 'The gossip is that he's taken a British hostage, and that it's related to the assault on Salangi's fort.'

'Who the hell's he?' asked Steve.

'Local warlord,' said Ganju. 'Not one of the drug dealers, but a bandit who robs the locals, forces them to pay him protection money, and hires out his men to anyone who wants them for some rough stuff. You get guys like that all over this part of the world. It's what passes for law and order around here.'

'So why's he snatched David?' asked Nick.

'Like Ian said, I think those robbers around the RV point knew what they were looking for,' said Steve. 'And I reckon they were working for this Masood bastard. They knew something was going down, and they wanted a part of it.'

'They'll have already figured out that David was part of the assault on the fort,' said Ganju.

'Which means they'll want the loot.' Steve rubbed his face with his hands. 'We're right in it now, boys. Where does this Masood hide out?'

'About ten miles due east of here,' said Ganju, 'in the cave system up in the mountains.'

'Then that's where we're going next.'

Twenty-Seven

OLLIE CHECKED THE TYRES ON the Toyota, then the water levels inside the engine.

The vehicle was weighed down by the boxes it was carrying, plus the men on board; it was a big sturdy machine, but it wasn't built to haul four soldiers and half a ton of gold. And there were at least another eighty miles to the border.

'Ready?' he said, looking across at Ian.

'I reckon,' said Ian.

They had driven ten miles the night before. They stuck to the mountain tracks, using their maps to make sure they didn't go anywhere near a main road or any kind of settlement. They knew that Salangi's men would be fanning out through the countryside looking for them; any sign of either vehicle would instantly bring a massive attack. The tracks were used for herding goats, or for donkey trails, and consisted of packed, cracked mud, with some rocks at the side to indicate where the trail went next. It was hard, difficult driving, and impossible at night. They quickly decided the best bet was to camp out until dawn, then try to make as much progress as they could in the few hours between sunrise and the blazing heat of midday.

Dan was fixing the dressing on Jeff's leg. He'd given him more water and tried to get him to eat some dried biscuits, but he was weakening all the time.

'You all right, mate?' said Ollie, walking across to where Jeff was lying on the ground.

His eyes flashed open. He was drifting in and out of consciousness, they way men will when they've been badly wounded, but he wasn't making the kind of recovery Ollie was looking for. It was getting on for twenty-four hours since he'd been hit, and by then you'd expect him to be getting stronger again. If it was just a flesh wound, his system would be starting to deal with it.

But not Jeff. Maybe the bullet had chewed up his bone. Or delivered an infection. Either way, he needed a doctor, and fast.

Before the convoy kicked off, all the men drank some water and ate dried dates and biscuits for breakfast. Then they cleared up their mess so as not to leave any kind of trail. They were in good spirits when they climbed on board the two Toyotas. The fighting yesterday had shaken all of them up, and when a man went down the way Jeff had, there was always a hit on morale. But they'd got a good night's kip and they had some grub inside them, and they reckoned that with a couple of days' hard driving, they'd be out of here and on their way home again. They were all professional fighters, and their determination was evident in their faces.

Dan took the wheel of the first Toyota, with Ollie squeezed up next to him in the cabin, and Jeff laid out on the back seat. Chris was driving close behind, with Ian at his side, and Maksim in the back. They hit the road just as dawn was starting to break over the horizon. The engines of the two

SUVs growled as they pulled up the steep, rugged incline of the mountains.

Jeff had mapped out a route for them while they were still back at the shack, and Ollie was doing his best to stick to it. It would take them due south, hitting the Pakistani border at the small town of Bahram Chah. To get there, they had to cross two mountain systems, and a pair of valleys. The ground would get more and more rugged the closer to the border they got; the highlands between Pakistan and Afghanistan were some of the roughest, wildest country in the world, one reason why, for more than a thousand years, the territory had never been decisively controlled by any army.

The Toyotas made good enough progress for the first ten miles or so. Ollie was hoping to cover at least forty miles today, then rest up for the afternoon and night, then cross down to Bahram tomorrow morning. But that schedule was flexible. They had to make sure no one saw them. It was better to arrive a couple of days late than find themselves in a major face-off with the Taliban.

It was just after ten when Dan brought the lead Toyota to a stop.

'What is it?' asked Ollie.

'Listen,' said Dan. He turned the engine off.

Close behind, Chris killed his engine, and the three men in his vehicle climbed out to see what was happening.

'Stopping for a piss, are we?' said Ian.

Ollie ignored him. He took a couple of steps away from where the Toyotas had pulled up. They were high on a ridge of hills, about twenty miles south of Kajaki, and close to the Helmand valley. According to the route Jeff had mapped for them, they should be dropping out of the hills right here, crossing the Helmand River at a ford used by farmers, then climbing again into the mountains on the far side of the valley to continue their journey south.

But Dan was right. Ollie could hear something.

Gunfire.

'It's a cannon,' said Dan.

Ollie knew he was right. He'd listened to it often enough. A Warrior tank was fitted with a 30mm Rarden cannon, a piece of kit that made an unmistakable spitting sound as it punched its shells into the enemy. Ollie had trained on those cannons plenty of times. As well as Warrior tanks, they were fitted to Fox armoured cars and the Scimitar tracked reconnaissance vehicle, and Ollie was certain that was the echo of a distant Rarden he could hear right now.

But what the hell was it doing out here?

'We'll check it out on foot,' he said. 'Ian and I will get up on that ridge and survey the lie of the land. The rest of you guys keep guard on the vehicles.'

With Ian at his side, he tabbed his way up the hill. There were another twenty yards to climb to the peak of the ridge, but Ollie judged it was too risky to go any closer in the Toyotas. If there was any fighting going on, they needed to keep the gold and diamonds as far away from it as possible.

He dropped down to the ground and took out his field glasses. The Helmand valley stretched out before them. Right at the centre, the river twisted its way through the knotted landscape, narrowing as it came through a steep canyon, then broadening out as it spread through a fertile plain. It was close to midsummer now, and the river was at one of its lowest points of the year; there were long stretches of baked mud, some of them fifty yards or more, on both of its banks. Ollie could see the ford they were meant to be crossing. A pair of wooden pillars marked the spot, and there was a track on each side so the local farmers could get across the river.

But not today.

'Christ,' muttered Ollie.

He could see at once what Dan had heard, and Ollie felt immediately grateful for the Australian's razor-sharp hearing. If they'd driven over this ridge, they'd have dropped down straight into a vicious fire fight. Five British Warrior tanks were pounding what looked to be a well dug-in Taliban position. They were punching round after round of shells from their powerful Rarden cannons, while behind them a platoon of what looked to be about fifty British soldiers were laying down a solid barrage of mortar fire. Even up here, three hundred or more yards from the action, the noise was terrifying, and Ollie could well imagine what the racket was like for the men in the thick of the action. They were hitting a defensive encampment of what looked to be about three hundred Taliban fighters. Their positions were protected by sandbags and barbed wire, and for now it looked to Ollie as if they had decided to dig in and see how much punishment they could endure. They had dug themselves trenches and covered the tops with sandbags. The experience of being inside a trench under sustained mortar and cannon fire was absolutely terrifying. Ollie had done it once in training, when it was just blanks being fired, and hoped to hell he never had to do it in real life. But as long as you didn't die of fright – and there were always a few guys who did – you were likely to pull through. The British looked to be planning a long pounding, followed by an infantry and tank assault on the Taliban position, but if the boys on the other side hadn't been turned to jelly by the cannon fire, they could still rise up out of their positions and give a good account of themselves. It looked as if it was going to get very nasty down there before the night was done.

And we don't want to be any part of it, thought Ollie.

He scanned the hillsides. There was almost certainly a British reconnaissance unit up here somewhere. And probably a Taliban one as well. This ridge was the best place from which to get a sense of the ebb and flow of the battle, and Ollie felt certain that the commanders on both sides would have got some guys up here to report back.

He didn't want to meet the bastards. Not from either side.

'Christ,' he muttered again.

'So you keep saying,' said Ian.

'There's a full-scale frigging battle going on down there.'

Ian took out his own field glasses and surveyed the scene. The Warrior tanks were loosing off round after round, subjecting the Taliban position to a furious barrage. Some shells were landing directly on their positions, others were drifting right, landing in the river, throwing up huge waves. Curls of smoke, and the unmistakable smell of gunpowder were drifting up the hillside. To his right, Ian could see some snakes taking refuge from the battle by crawling up the hills. We've a good idea how you feel, boys, he thought bitterly.

'The Taliban must need to hold that river crossing,' said Ian. 'If the bridges are down further up, then this crossing may well control access to the whole of the southern half of the province, and they aren't about to let go of it without a fight.'

'Jesus,' muttered Ollie. 'On the one bloody day we need to get across it.'

Ian laughed.

'I don't see what's so bloody funny.'

'You really don't see it, do you?'

'See what?'

Ian pointed to the battle raging below them. 'We were just a diversionary tactic,' he said, a thread of bitterness running through his voice. 'The British don't give a toss about Salangi or his money, and never have done. They wanted us to stage a hit on the fort to distract those bastards' attention while they geared up for a strike on the Taliban. They deceived us right from the start.'

'It's the British Army,' snapped Ollie. 'They wouldn't—'

'They've been bloody doing it for centuries,' growled Ian.

Ollie was about to reply but he heard a shot close by. His head spun round.

Dan had just hit an Afghan soldier in the chest. There was still smoke drifting from the barrel of his AK-47. The man was lying dead on the ground, the blood seeping out of the five wounds Dan had inflicted. Maksim walked across to the corpse, gave it a hefty kick with the side of his boot, and pronounced the man dead. He bent down to take the magazine out of the man's AK-47, adding it to his own ammo belt, then looked up at Dan, grinned, and gave him the thumbs up.

'Scouts,' said Ian, climbing back down the side of the mountain to join the two Toyotas. 'The whole mountain range is going to be crawling with them. It's not safe to stick around here.'

'We need to get across the river,' said Ollie.

'We can't,' said Ian. He pulled out Jeff's map and laid it on the bonnet of the Toyota. All the men gathered round.

'There's no way we're going to get across that valley, not with the battle that's raging down there,' said Ian. 'We'll get shot to pieces by one side or the other, and very probably both of them.'

'We'll go further south,' suggested Ollie.

Ian ran his finger across the map. 'It's impassable,' he said. 'That's why the ford they're fighting over is so strategically important. It's the last crossing point for at least fifty miles.'

Ollie was looking at the map, studying the contour of the mountain ranges that ran from here to the Pakistani border. Ian was right, he conceded reluctantly to himself. They couldn't stay here. And they couldn't go further south either. That left them with only one option.

'We'll have to go back, pick up Steve, and map out a fresh route south,' he said.

'Then let's get a bloody move on,' said Chris. 'Before the Taliban start sending some more boys up here to find out what the hell happened to their mate.'

Twenty-Eight

THE CLIMB WAS A STEEP ONE, over rocks that felt as if they'd been carved out of razor blades.

Steve was treading carefully. The mountain was ten miles to the east of the village, remote even by Afghan standards. There were no tracks nearby, and the last signs of vegetation were at least five hundred feet beneath them. All you could see was mile after mile of pale grey rock covered in a film of sand and dust. The moon probably has more life on its surface, thought Steve as he pulled himself forwards.

He looked ahead. Ganju was a few yards further up, scrambling towards a ledge on the mountain that looked as if it led into a cave system. Nick was a few yards behind, climbing steadily, and with little sign of tiredness.

Ganju waved. Found it, he was saying.

Thank Christ for that, thought Steve.

The night before, they had driven the truck through the darkness, pulling up as close to Masood's base camp as the road would allow them. They kipped down in the back of the truck for the night, the three of them taking it in turns to keep watch. They'd been lucky: the road was virtually empty after dark, and the couple of vehicles that did pass paid no attention to what looked like a trucker grabbing a few hours' sleep on the side of the road.

This morning they'd used the directions Ganju had picked up in the village to get a lead on Masood. They found the mountain he was holed up in marked on the map, and drove as close as they could in the truck, stashed the vehicle in a gully of rocks away from the road, then completed the rest of the journey on foot. It was a mile to the base of the mountains, then another mile up the steep hills before you got close to the cave system where Masood had his lair.

You needed a mule, thought Steve, as they tabbed through the early morning. Not three blokes with heavy packs on their backs. He'd done long marches over the Brecon Beacons when he was training for the Regiment: long, two-day walks through the pouring Welsh rain, with five hundred pounds of kit strapped to his back, and nothing to eat. That had been tough; by the end of it you felt as if every muscle in your body had been beaten and drowned. But at least nobody was shooting at us.

Steve looked up.

Ganju was tumbling down the side of the mountain. And the echo of a gunshot was bouncing off the acres of granite.

Ganju grabbed his arm, pushing him away from the track. 'Cover,' he hissed.

Steve didn't even look around. A rock, ten yards to his left, formed a natural wall. He scrambled across the dusty ground and threw himself behind it. He heard a couple of bullets strike the ground behind him, the echoes ringing around the hillside.

'Nick, move your arse up here.'

It was only when all three of them were safely behind the rock that Steve took a moment to assess the situation.

Two men were standing on the ledge that led up to the entrance to the cave system. They were both carrying AK-47s, had short black beards, and were wearing robes and turbans round their heads. As soon as Ganju had climbed up on to the ledge, they must have heard something, and started firing from inside the cave. As he'd scrambled down the mountain, they'd opened up with a burst of rapid fire, kicking up a lot of dust and pebbles but narrowly missing all three men. Both of them had their rifles trained on their position. They weren't wasting any more ammunition firing into the rock but they were going to keep them pinned down. More than an inch in either direction, and a hailstorm of ordnance would lash into them.

'We can't stay here,' said Ganju.

Steve nodded. 'They're going to keep us pinned down, then they'll send someone round the back to finish us off.' It was exactly what he'd do if he were in Masood's position. Keep the enemy in a tight corner, then sneak around the side, and put a bullet or a hand grenade right into their backs.

'We should get back to the truck and find another way in,' said Ganju.

Steve glanced down the mountainside. It was a mile and a half back to the truck, across open, exposed country. In truth, he didn't rate their chances. Masood might have men anywhere who could pick them off. But now they'd been spotted, it was probably their best chance.

'I can take them,' said Nick.

'It's five hundred yards,' Steve pointed out.

'Just give me the chance,' said Nick.

From his backpack, Nick took out the M107 long-range

sniper rifle they'd bought back in Kabul. He'd stripped it right down to its component parts, the largest of which was its twenty-nine-inch barrel. Expertly, he reassembled the gun, slotting its parts into place, finishing with the Leupold scope that fitted on to the firing muzzle right above the magazine. The M107 was an American-made rifle. In theory, it was accurate at up to seven thousand yards, but it took years of training to achieve that kind of accuracy. The weapon was designed to kill. It fired a heavy-duty 0.5 calibre bullet, able to punch its way through anything other than full body armour.

'You've got two minutes,' said Steve. 'Then we're getting the hell out of here.'

Nick wedged the spiked feet of the bipod that supported the barrel of the weapon into the rock. He slammed the magazine into place and pushed the gun deep into his shoulder to steady it. He put his right eye to its scope. Up on the ledge, the pair of Afghans had retreated into the entrance to the cave. In their black robes, they were just shadows within shadows, scarcely visible. Nick paused for just a fraction of a second, adjusted the position of the rifle less than a millimetre. Then, so quietly it was barely above a whisper, he muttered the word, 'Kill . . .'

The explosion as the bullet fired kicked the gun back against Nick's shoulder, but he instantly steadied himself, adjusted the rifle another fraction of a millimetre, and fired again. 'They're dead,' he said, looking up.

'You saw them go down?'

'They're bloody dead,' said Nick angrily.

At his side, Ganju nodded to Steve and started scrambling up the side of the hill. Steve followed hard behind. If Nick said they were dead, they were dead, he told himself. There was something about the boy's expression that told you once he put a man down, he wasn't going to stand up and start shooting at you again.

Within seconds, they were standing on the ledge that led into the caves. Two corpses were lying on the ground.

Steve was about to put a bullet into them. Regiment training was always to put an extra couple of rounds into your enemy – there were too many good men lying in military cemeteries because they'd decided a bloke was too dead to do them any harm. But with these guys, it was a waste of perfectly good ammo. Nick had slotted the M107 bullets straight into the men's necks, severing their windpipes, and then cutting through the carotid artery that ran through the neck and delivered oxygen to the brain. No man could survive a 0.5 calibre lump of hardened steel ammunition smashing into them there, and these two had gone down like grass being cut by a lawnmower.

Steve punched Nick on the shoulder. 'Good shooting, mate.'

'Thanks,' said Nick, with a rough grin.

Steve took a torch from his backpack and flashed it into the darkness. The cave was about ten feet high where it opened up to the side of the mountain but it quickly narrowed to about four feet. It was carved out of twisted, jagged rock, with a dry, dusty smell, stretching inwards for twenty yards, then twisting round a corner.

'Let's move,' hissed Steve.

He switched off the torch. Carrying any kind of a light in here just made you a target – shoot straight at the light, and you could be certain of hitting your enemy. Steve led the way, followed by Nick and Ganju. For the first twenty yards they could see by the light filtering through from the entrance to the cave, but as they approached the corner the light faded and when they turned they were plunged into near total darkness. Steve cursed himself for not buying some night vision goggles, standard kit for most soldiers these days. He felt certain he could have found some in Kabul. Edging along the side of the wall, he used his hands to feel his way through the blackness. It was slow, uncomfortable work, particularly for the man in front; the other two could make out his body and follow him. The walls were jagged and sharp, with flinty fragments of rock jutting out, digging some scratches into Steve's hand.

They had covered forty or fifty yards into the interior of the mountain when the roof dipped abruptly, and they had to crawl several yards through a space that was only three feet high, until they hit an opening where a partial crack in the mountain, just a few centimetres wide, allowed some pale light to filter through. It came down in a single shaft and bounced off the grey stone walls, but it was enough to see by. Steve looked around the cave. It contained the remains of human habitation: a burnt-out fire, probably left over from the winter judging by how old the ashes looked, a ditch which, from the smell of it, was where some guys had had a crap. Alongside it were a few empty tins and plastic water bottles. Leading off the cave were three separate tunnels, all of them pitch black.

'Where the hell do we go now?' hissed Steve.

Ganju was down on his knees, using the pale light to examine the rock. 'This one,' he said, pointing to the first of the three tunnels. 'There are some scuff marks. This is the tunnel that has been used most recently.'

Steve edged his way forward. There was some light from the opening for the first ten yards, then darkness again. He used the walls to guide him, stretching out his hands to follow it, inching forward. At one point he discovered a ravine that dropped down five hundred feet or more, and all three of them needed to step carefully across it before continuing. It was slow, hard work, every yard a hard-won victory over the darkness.

'Look,' hissed Steve.

About thirty yards ahead of them a glow of light was visible, its source round a corner.

Probably some kind of bottled gas lamp, judged Steve. As he inched closer along the wall, it grew in intensity. 'Careful,' he whispered.

All three of them came to a halt, their backs pressed against the side of the wall.

Voices.

Steve listened carefully.

Inside the tunnel, sounds were echoed and amplified, making it hard to tell whether there were a couple of men there or twenty. Focus on the sounds, Steve told himself. They were talking fast in Pashto. Steve couldn't follow the language, and certainly not at these speeds. But he reckoned there were three guys there. He held up three fingers to Ganju, who nodded back. That was the way he calculated it as well. Steve drew out his knife from his chest webbing.

'We rush at them, and cut their throats with these, but try and leave Masood alive,' he said quietly. 'And have your pistols ready in case anything goes wrong.'

Both Ganju and Nick nodded, their own knives at the ready.

Steve looked at Nick. 'You ever stabbed a man?'

'Have you ever gone drinking in Swansea on a Saturday

night?' Nick replied with a grin. 'Stabbing's what we do, and that's just our mates.'

'Good lad,' said Steve.

He started to run, kicking back hard against the stone surface of the tunnel. He turned the corner, running hard, adjusting his eyes to the sudden light as he did so. It took a fraction of a second to assess the situation. Two men were standing around a gas lamp, looking down at a map spread out before them. They had kitbags next to them, and some matted straw they were using as beds. Next to those was a small gas camping stove, attached to the same canister as the lamp, a few bottles of water, some flatbreads and water jugs. At their side were AK-47s, pistols, and knives. In an instant, Steve guessed the man standing was Masood. He was by far the oldest of the three men, approaching forty, with no beard, but a thick, bushy, Saddam Hussein moustache, thinning hair, and a nasty, curled scar running down the length of his right cheek. Steve closed in on him fast. Ten yards, then five separated him from the man. He could see him kneeling down, reaching for his gun. His body was lowering, and his grip opening. Three yards . . .

Steve slotted his knife into his mouth and launched himself into the air. Back at school, he'd been taught the move as a rugby tackle. Steve hated the game – the way he saw it, if you wanted pointless violence, you might as well join the army – but he was grateful for the memory right now. Once you knew how to bring down a hefty-looking prop from the school down the road, the knowledge never left you. His shoulders collided with Masood's midriff with a sickening, bone-crunching thud. The weight of the impact sent the man staggering backwards. His legs were strong and his balance was good, but no one could have stood up against the blow crashing into him. He fell backwards, cracking his head against the stone wall, crying out in pain. Steve could feel warm blood trickling down his hands. He punched the man hard around the face, once, twice, three times, smashing into his jaw with cruel ferocity. Blood ran down the side of his face, and the man was left just on the edge of consciousness. Steve squatted across his chest, dropped the knife from his mouth, then wedged the gleaming steel blade tight into the man's throat. He nicked the skin, letting loose a thin trail of blood – nothing fatal, but enough to let the guy know he meant business.

'One move and you're a sodding corpse,' he growled into Masood's face.

He looked round.

Ganju had gripped one of the younger guys from behind. Although Ganju was a small man, at least fifty pounds lighter than the Afghan, he had the deceptive, subtle strength of the Gurkha. His right hand was lashed round the man's chest, holding him in a vice-like grip, while with his left hand he'd grabbed hold of the man's hair, yanking his neck back, so that his throat was exposed. The man's eyes were wild with anger and fear, and he was struggling to scream, but his throat was so stretched it was impossible for him to utter a sound. Still holding his hair, Ganju released his chest, and in the same swift movement stuck the blade of his knife into the man's throat. It went in smoothly enough, slicing through the soft tissue, and cutting into an artery. Ganju yanked the knife forward, so that his throat was as neatly sliced as that of any farm animal in an abattoir. The man fell forward, blood gurgling from his open wound, but with the dead, glazed expression of a corpse already in his eyes. Ganju pushed him aside.

Nick was still struggling with the third guard. He was the

biggest of the three Afghans, about six feet two, and weighing more than two hundred pounds, with a brutish, twisted face, and eyes so dark they were almost black. Nick had crashed into his stomach, sending the man flying backwards, but he'd recovered his balance quickly, delivering a crushing blow to Nick's chest that briefly emptied all the air out of his lungs. Nick recovered his ground, head-butting the Afghan with a bull-like ferocity. Steve watched with wry amusement as Nick used his head like a battering ram, hammering the man's chest, ribs, then smashing upwards, so that his crown crashed right into the bone of his jaw. It was British pub fighting at its worst, and it took the Afghan completely by surprise, leaving him lying sprawled on the floor, gasping for air. In the next instant, Ganju, his bloody knife in his mouth, leaped on top of the Afghan, pinning down his chest and arms. Ganju let the knife drop from his mouth and gripped it in his right hand. The man was breathless but screaming for mercy. Ganju nicked his throat with his knife, tearing out a chunk of skin.

'No, let Nick finish him,' said Steve.

Nick walked across to the man. Ganju was still sitting on his chest, making it impossible for him to do any more than wriggle impotently.

Nick knelt down and thrust his knife into the side of the Afghan's throat, sliced upwards, then stepped back as a couple of pints of hot blood spilled out on to the rock. The man was pissing himself as he died, creating a nasty stagnant smell around his corpse.

'Good lad,' said Steve tersely.

In the last five minutes Nick had killed three men. He had the makings of a fighter within him, decided Steve with grim satisfaction.

Steve grabbed Masood's knife and his AK-47 and got off his chest. The man got unsteadily to his feet, looking nervously at the three men who had just attacked him.

Steve glanced around the cave. In front of him was a brutal array of torture equipment.

A wooden frame had been constructed where you could hang a man from a pair of manacles attached to his arms. Below it were a pair of gas canisters. Steve could see what it was for. A man would be hung by the hands, then the flames would be turned on, slowly burning his feet until he did precisely what you wanted.

Next to that was a petrol chainsaw. The teeth and blade were stained crimson, and there were specks of human skin and bone stuck to it, from the hacked-off limbs of Masood's victims.

It didn't take much to figure out the man's business. He was kidnapping Western aid workers, or any other profitable victims he could get his hands on, torturing them and holding them to ransom.

Scum.

'Where's the Englishman?' snapped Steve, looking straight at Masood.

'Who?'

He obviously spoke English well enough. Useful for making ransom demands, Steve figured. The man's hands were shaking, but he was holding himself steady.

'Bloke called David, but I suppose you don't bother with names much around here,' said Steve. 'Your bastards snatched him yesterday.'

'I know nothing . . .'

Steve picked up the chainsaw, a Ryobi with an eighteen-inch blade. He yanked hard on the chain, and the machine roared into life. Steve held it in his right hand, hovering just a few yards from Masood's face. He stepped back nervously.

Steve looked at Nick. 'Hold the bastard down while I take his knee off.'

'We took him, we took him,' shouted Masood.

Steve switched off the chainsaw. 'Then where the hell is he?'

'We sold him,' said Masood. He laughed, although whether it was from nerves or cruelty Steve found it difficult to judge. 'We got a good price for him as well, for an old man like that.'

'Who to?'

'Salangi.'

Steve started up the chainsaw again. 'Hold him, Nick. This time I really am taking the bastard's knees off.'

'No, no,' shouted Masood. He was backing away nervously, but Nick had already grabbed him from behind.

The noise of the chainsaw was echoing through the cave, doubling back on itself, creating a terrible racket that made it almost impossible to hear what Masood was saying.

'Listen to me,' he was shouting.

Steve killed the chainsaw again. 'You've got five seconds.'

'As soon as we discovered who he was, and what he was involved with, we took him to the one man who wanted him most, and that was Salangi,' said Masood, talking with the speed of a man who has only seconds to prevent his limbs being hacked off with a chainsaw. 'Salangi wants to exchange him for his gold. Let me go, and I'll arrange the transfer.'

Steve thought for a moment. He was remembering Ken, a guy he'd been on a smash and grab raid with across the border into Iraq in the run-up to the 2003 invasion. They'd been bringing out an Iraqi general who wanted to defect and was promising to reveal everything he knew about Iraqi troop deployments and defences. They'd dropped into Basra to pick him up, but there had been a fire fight on the border and Ken hadn't made it back. Soon afterwards, Steve had had to go to talk to Michelle, his wife, and Rory, his two-year-old son. He could still feel Michelle's hot tears on his cheeks as he talked to her about Ken's last mission, and it wasn't an experience he cared to repeat. He certainly didn't want to have to tell Sandy why the father of her twins wasn't going to be taking her to the hospital when they were due. There were expressions on a woman's face that could break your heart; and Steve had no desire to see one of those again. If that meant doing business with a piece of scum like Masood, then so be it.

He put the chainsaw down. 'You're on.'

Masood visibly relaxed.

'You go and tell your mate Salangi we have a deal,' said Steve. He could see both Nick and Ganju looking at him intently but he ignored both of them. 'Organise a time and a place for tonight, and we'll arrange a transfer.'

'I'll need to contact you,' said Masood.

Steve glanced at his watch. It was just after ten in the morning, and it would take a few hours to set anything up.

'Leave a note at the entrance to this cave system by five o'clock, telling us the time and place for the swap,' he said. 'Make sure no one is watching the cave because if there is we'll kill them, and we'll make sure it hurts while we're about it.'

Masood nodded.

'Now piss off and arrange the deal,' growled Steve.

Masood started to run. His feet clattered against the

stone as he dashed through the tunnels that would lead him out to the open countryside.

'You're going to swap the money for David?' asked Ganju.

Steve shook his head. 'I'm just telling them that. Once the swap is agreed, we'll find a way of breaking David out.'

'There's three of us,' said Nick. 'And there could be dozens of men with Salangi.'

'I know,' said Steve flatly. 'But I've got a plan.'

'Which is?'

'The oldest plan known to the British Army and usually the best as well.'

Nick looked at him, a question hanging on his lips.

'Something will turn up,' said Steve with a broad grin. 'Just don't press me on the details of what it might be.'

Twenty-Nine

'**W**HAT THE HELL ARE YOU doing here?' said Steve.

Ollie was hunched down in the back of the truck, examining a map. The two Toyotas were parked alongside, partially obscured by a wall of rock. Ian and Chris were looking at the map with Ollie, their faces dusty and their expressions tired.

'We missed your lovely face,' said Ollie. 'And we thought you boys were probably lost by now so we'd better come and help you out.'

Steve grinned. The truth was, there was no one he'd rather see right now than the rest of his unit.

In the last half hour, as he, Nick and Ganju had tabbed their way back down the mountainside to where they'd stashed the truck, he'd been thinking over the bargain he'd struck with Masood. He didn't care whether the man lived or died, it meant nothing to him. But if he was going to get David back, he would have to overcome Salangi and the dozens of men he might bring with him. And that was going to be tough. Maybe, if he was honest with himself, impossible. In which case, he'd have to walk away and leave

David to his fate. He didn't want to, but there was no point in committing suicide.

So he was bloody glad to see Ollie and the rest of the boys. With the whole unit, they'd have a chance of hitting Salangi – and finishing him off this time.

'So why the hell aren't you in Pakistan?' said Steve. 'I figured you guys would be halfway to Dubai by now, planning how you were going to spend the money.'

Ollie explained how the route to the border had been made impassable by the British assault on the Taliban positions. So they'd tabbed back, planning on making contact with Steve. When they'd seen the truck partially hidden off road, they figured he couldn't be far away.

'We've been studying the maps,' said Ollie. 'We reckon the main roads are all going to be impassable for the next few days. But we can unload all the kit and tab our way through the mountains on foot.'

'With twenty-two boxes of stuff?'

'You not up to it, mate?' said Ian.

'It's a long way.'

'I thought you SAS boys knew a bit about tabbing with heavy loads,' said Ollie.

Steve looked down at the map. Ollie had drawn a red line down towards the border that ran through the old mountain passes, all of them impassable to a vehicle, even a rugged SUV. It would be a long and wild journey, a total of nearly sixty miles, in baking heat, with a wounded man to carry as well. It would test the endurance of each of them to its limit, and quite possibly beyond. But if that was the only way home . . .

He looked at Ollie and nodded his agreement. 'But first we have to get David back.'

'Where is he?'

'Salangi has him.'

'Christ.'

'We're supposed to be making an exchange tonight.'

Steve had seen many different expressions on Ollie's face in the couple of weeks they'd been working together – amused, detached, bored, aggressive. But he hadn't seen him stunned before. His eyes stared and his mouth was half open. Steve explained how they'd tracked Masood down, how he'd offered to arrange a swap of the money for David, and how the exchange was scheduled to take place some time tonight.

'You're not swapping my money,' growled Ian. 'You can do what the hell you like with your own stash, but mine is staying right here.'

Steve took a step forward, his expression angry. 'Then maybe you should just take your share and piss off right now, because I'm not sure anyone wants to listen to any more of your bloody moaning.'

'Cool it,' growled Ollie.

'No one's giving Salangi the money anyway,' continued Steve. 'We're not that sodding stupid. He doesn't sound like the kind of guy who is just going to peacefully hand David over, take his cash back, and shake hands while we all agree it was a terrible misunderstanding. He'll take the money, kill David, then the rest of us, probably one by one, and probably very slowly.'

'So what's the plan?' said Ian.

'We set up the RV with Salangi, then we kick the shit out of the bastard and get our man back.'

'Right,' sneered Ian. 'Glad to see the subtle tactician is back in charge.'

'You don't have to come if you don't want to,' said Steve. 'I already said you could piss off. The same goes for anyone else who wants to bottle out.'

'No one's bottling out, Steve,' said Ollie. 'We just need a plan, that's all.'

It was nearly midday, and the sun was approaching its fiercest – more than forty degrees, enough to start burning your skin the moment you exposed yourself to it. The unit hunkered down under the canopy of the truck, drinking lukewarm bottled water to try and stay hydrated. They wouldn't have any idea where the exchange was until the note was dropped off at five. Until then, all they could do was rest up and get themselves in shape for the fight ahead.

Jeff was lying still in the back of one of the Toyotas. One of the men took it in turns to stay with him, making sure he was getting enough water inside him. The Toyotas didn't come with any air-con, and the temperature inside the vehicles rose to more than fifty degrees by the middle of the afternoon. But there was nothing they could do about that.

At one point, Jeff briefly snapped into consciousness. He was drowsy and his lips and eyes were swollen, but for a moment the pain appeared to have abated, and he was able to speak.

'Where the hell are we?' he asked Steve as soon as he opened his eyes.

Steve started to explain. But even as he talked, he wasn't sure how much Jeff was taking in. The man was fading. Once again, Steve cursed Muirhead for not sending a chopper out to collect him. And now they were going to have to carry him out of the country across the mountains.

'Christ,' muttered Steve to himself.

He started to tell Jeff about David, and about the assault they were planning on Salangi.

'We don't have to, mate,' he said. 'We could just drive you into Helmand, drop you off at the British base, and then try and make a break from there . . .'

Jeff lifted himself up and grabbed Steve's hand. Steve was struck by how cold Jeff felt, even though it was baking inside the Toyota.

'No,' he said, a sudden blast of strength surging through him. 'David's still OK. And the man's got kids. You boys try and break him out . . .'

'But—'

'No buts, man,' said Jeff. 'I'll be all right.' He put his head back down and closed his eyes again.

Steve shook his head. This isn't working out, he told himself. Not the way we planned, anyway.

At half past four, Steve and Ganju tabbed their way back up the hill towards the cave. Steve had thought about placing a spy to watch for Salangi or Masood, then following them after they collected the note. He decided against it. They could easily be spotted, and if that happened, David would be killed on the spot.

They approached the entrance to the cave slowly, scanning the scabby hillside for anyone positioned to observe them. They saw nothing but that didn't mean anything. An Afghan could melt into these hills as easily as a rattlesnake.

Steve spotted a single sheet of paper taped to a rock. He walked up and pulled it loose. 'Nine. One man. Here,' was all it said.

Clearly, Salangi wasn't a man who bothered with small talk.

They tabbed back down the mountainside and Steve showed the note to the rest of the unit.

'So what's the plan?' said Ollie.

Steve had been thinking about that as he walked back down the mountain, and although he had plenty of ideas, he hadn't settled on anything yet. Maximum speed, maximum aggression, those were the only two phrases that ran through his head.

'Take the loot and piss off, that's my plan,' said Ian.

'You'll have to get past me first,' said Nick.

'Cool it, boys,' said Ollie firmly. 'No one's going to go anywhere without David.' He looked at Steve. 'You're going to be at the cave at nine, right?'

Steve nodded.

'Then our first task is to get the boxes of gear hidden,' said Ollie. 'We choose one of the caves and we stash it away nice and safe. That way, at least we remain in control of events.'

'I'll meet up with whoever Salangi sends to meet me,' said Steve. 'I'll tell him I can take him to where the loot is stashed but only after I've seen David and seen that he's OK.'

'They'll take you to meet Salangi,' said Ollie.

'I think so,' said Steve. 'I want Chris and Ollie and Maksim to follow me from a safe distance and get a fix on where Salangi and his men are.'

'Then we launch a massive attack,' said Dan with a broad grin.

'We give them everything we've got,' said Chris.

'It's going to be bloody dangerous for you, Steve,' said Ollie. 'You're going to be right in the thick of it.'

'They'll be tooled up,' said Ganju. 'Men like Salangi, they feed their men on opiates, the same stuff they grow around here. It twists their mind. Some of them are so high they think they're invisible. Others think the bullets just bounce off them.'

'What he's saying is, they're nutters,' said Chris.

'And you're going to be handing yourself straight over to them,' said Dan.

Steve shrugged. He knew that already. He'd be walking straight into the enemy camp and the odds of coming out again alive weren't the kind that any sane man would accept. But a man from his unit was there, and he couldn't walk away without trying to break him out. This was the only plan they had.

'I know, I know,' said Steve. 'Don't bloody do my head in. I've made my decision, and that's final. We're going in and we're getting our bloke out, and this is the way we're going to do it.'

Ollie nodded. 'All right, boys, if we're doing this, then let's get a move on. We've got twenty-two boxes and one wounded soldier to move.'

Thirty

STEVE CHECKED HIS WATCH. EIGHT forty-five.

Night had already fallen but it was a clear evening and a three-quarter moon was casting a pale light across the freckled granite of the hillside, turning the whole landscape a pale silver.

Time to make my move, he told himself. There's no point in telling myself I'm not afraid. I'm bloody afraid. Every nerve in my body is on edge. My guts are churning, and my stomach has gone to pieces. But you just have to harness the fear, get it working for you. Do that, and you'll be all right.

He took a deep breath, then began to walk across the rough, broken stones of the track that led up towards the cave. He was starting to know each twist and gully.

For the last three hours, they'd been humping boxes into the hills. They'd chosen a remote cave, a mile to the west of where they'd stashed the truck. It was halfway up the side of the mountain and, as far as they could tell, hadn't ever been used by any of the bandits who hid themselves away in these hills. They'd broken out the planks that made the base of the truck, and turned them into rough stretchers. You could fit five boxes on each one, with two men carrying each load.

Walking steadily, they humped them up the side of the hill. Next, they carried Jeff up on a stretcher; he was still unconscious, and they pumped some more painkillers into him to try and keep him that way while they moved him. Later on, once they had David back, they'd head south towards the Pakistani border, using the wooden stretchers to carry their kit.

Ollie, Chris and Maksim set off a few minutes after Steve, following him at a discreet distance. Nick, Dan, Ganju and Ian stayed behind in the cave, taking care of both Jeff and the loot. They'd spend the next hour checking their weapons for the battle ahead.

Steve picked up his pace as he approached the cave. He had his Makarov inside his webbing, and his knife, but he'd dropped the AK-47 off at the cave along with the boxes. Salangi would just take it off him, and there was no point in wasting a perfectly good gun. He could feel the sweat and the grime of the last few days clinging to his skin. Just a few more days, he told himself. Then you'll be sitting by a luxurious pool, counting your money.

A man was standing alone on the ledge that led into the cave.

Steve kept on walking steadily towards him.

He was young, maybe twenty, with a thick, strong body, but one he hadn't fully grown into yet. He was dressed in black jeans and a sweatshirt, with a stubby beard, and an AK-47 hanging from his chest.

'I'm looking for Salangi,' said Steve.

The boy took a step backwards but there was no trace of fear in his expression.

'First, you show me where the money is.'

His English was clear, the words delivered without

hesitation. He'd been taught the language well, thought Steve. The boy was both brave and smart, and that was going to make him a formidable opponent.

'First you show me my mate,' said Steve.

'We need to see the gold.'

'I'll speak to Salangi, and no one else.'

The boy nodded. He wasn't going to argue, he was just the delivery guy; as long as he brought Steve down to wherever they'd set up camp, then he'd have done his job.

'This way,' he said.

Steve started walking.

A track twisted away from the cave, just wide enough for a man to walk along. It turned through a canyon that stretched for a hundred yards, then dropped down steeply, curling back in on itself as it fell away. Steve kept up an even, steady pace, but he could feel his pulse quickening with every yard that passed.

A hundred yards back, Ollie, Chris and Maksim were following the path. They kept well out of sight crouched down low as they moved forwards, making sure each leg of the journey was clear before they moved forward. It wasn't hard. Regular rockslides meant the tracks around the hills were covered with tiny pebbles, and as anyone walked through them they left a trail that was simple enough to follow. All you needed to do was make sure you were quiet.

Steve followed the boy through a final turn in the track before it opened up into a plain on the other side of the mountain. The flat land stretched for a mile, before a fresh set of mountains rose up on its far side, but there was no river running through the valley, so the ground was arid. Salangi and his men were stationed five hundred yards ahead of them. Steve could see a campfire, and he could smell roasting lamb.

'Good of them to make us some grub,' he said to the boy. 'Very hospitable.'

The boy remained silent. He walked, with his head held high, looking straight forward, ignoring Steve.

Even from a distance, Steve could see there were at least forty men in the camp. There was one tent, a collection of five SUVs, mostly Toyotas and Hondas, all of them arranged in a rough circle around the fire. Most of the guys, he reckoned, would be sleeping on the ground, probably with their weapons at their sides. This was their country. Like the boy, they weren't afraid of anyone.

The boy raised a hand, telling Steve to stop.

'Wait,' he said.

Two hundred yards back, Ollie had seen enough. Maksim and Chris were beside him. They could see down into the plain, and they could see the campfire burning where Salangi had taken up position.

'You get the others,' Ollie whispered to Maksim. 'We'll stay here.'

Maksim slipped away into the night.

Ollie reckoned they'd been walking for about twenty minutes. That meant it would be twenty minutes at least before the rest of the men got here. Hopefully, Steve could stall the bastards until then.

Steve waited while the boy walked into the camp. He stood outside a green canvas tent until a man stepped out. He exchanged a few words, and then the man started to walk out towards where Steve was standing. He looked, Steve reckoned, about forty. He was short, no more than five feet five, with a stocky, muscular build, and a thin, cruel mouth beneath a thick black moustache. He was almost bald and he wasn't much to look at, nothing of Genghis Kahn about him. But it wasn't the way a man looked that counted, it was the way he acted. And this guy had a rock-like obstinacy to him, apparent in the way he held himself as he walked, and in the quiet deference with which he was treated by everyone around him. Even a dozen or more yards away, Steve could feel the determination and inner strength of the man.

Steve stood his ground.

'You Salangi?' he said.

The man kept walking. He didn't reply, just kept advancing. Five yards behind him were two big guys, both over six feet, with two-hundred-pound builds. Both of them were carrying AK-47s in their hands. But they maintained a respectful distance, never getting too close to the boss.

'I have a question for you,' said Salangi.

Steve nodded.

'How do you want to die?'

'I'm here to swap my man for your treasure.'

'I don't negotiate with robbers,' said Salangi.

'And I don't negotiate with drug dealers.'

Salangi took a step closer, examining Steve dispassionately, as if he was already a corpse.

'Where's my gold?' he said.

'I'll tell you once I know my man is alive.'

Salangi turned round abruptly and started walking back towards the fire. The sound of a light breeze rustled through the night. Steve walked a couple of paces behind, avoiding the stares of the men all around him. He could feel the heat of the fire on his skin. As he passed the row of vehicles he glanced down and saw David.

Poor bastard, he thought to himself. These people are worse than animals. Much worse.

David was lying on the ground, his hands and feet tied to a stake behind him, and his face pushed down into the dirt, so that he looked like a chicken about to be put on to a spit. A gag had been stuffed into his mouth, taped into place, and a blindfold had been strapped across his eyes. The shirt had been torn off his back, and his boots and socks removed. Across his back, there were welts and cuts that Steve knew could only have come from a whip. His body was smeared with dirt and sweat.

And they've had the man less than a day, thought Steve. What in Christ's name would he look like by the end of the week?

Two guards stepped forward, jabbing the butts of their rifles into Steve's ribs.

He took a step back, pushing them away angrily.

'So let's cut a deal,' said Steve to Salangi.

Hidden in the mountains, Ollie was monitoring the scene through his field glasses. He could see that Steve had walked straight into Salangi's camp, and he admired the man's guts. Ollie turned and saw that Maksim was scrambling down the side of the hill, with Ian, Ganju and the rest of the unit following on behind them. They were carrying some heavy kit: the Vickers aircraft gun that had been loaded on to the Toyota; the M2A1-7 flame-thrower; and the M107 sniper rifle.

'He's inside,' said Ollie.

Dan took the glasses, then Ian, then Ganju, and finally Chris. Each man took just a couple of seconds to assess the situation. Steve was playing for time, but he wasn't going to be able to survive in there much longer. They had to decide how to hit Salangi and his men. And decide fast.

They could see the five vehicles, and counted somewhere between thirty and forty men, all of them heavily armed, standing in a rough circle, the oldest, most natural defensive formation known to man.

'We faced a couple of situations like this in the Recces,' said Chris.

'And?' said Ollie.

'The trick is to confuse them. A circle is fine, but when you get multiple attacks, it can get shaken up.'

'We should attack from three different places at the same time,' said Dan.

'Maybe more,' said Chris.

'Like a *matryoshka*,' said Maksim.

'A what?' said Ollie.

'In the Spetsnaz, we have a formation we call the *matryoshka*,' explained Maksim. 'After the Russian doll. You know, the ones that fit inside each other. What it means is that to defeat an enemy circle, you create a bigger circle round it and then squeeze in on it.'

'Like you did to General Paulus at Stalingrad,' said Ian.

'Exactly.'

Ollie nodded. 'Save the history lessons for later, boys,' he said, his voice calm and decisive. 'Here's the drill. Nick, you get up high with that sniper rifle. You're the best shot in this unit, and when I give the signal I want you to put a bullet straight through Salangi's head. Make sure you don't miss, because we aren't going to get any second chances, and make sure you kill the bastard. Steve will know what's happening. Dan and Ganju, I want you to tab three hundred yards to the right, with that aircraft gun. Same signal, open up on the bastards. Chris, since you wanted it so much, you can use the flame-thrower. Go two hundred yards further round from

Dan, then turn the heat on to the buggers. Ian and Maksim and I are going to tab to the right, fifty, one hundred, and one fifty yards, then open fire. We'll put our weapons on automatic, and move in closer and closer as we get the chance.' He glanced at each man in turn. 'Any questions?'

No one spoke.

'It's not exactly subtle, but we'll hit them bloody hard and, in the chaos, let's just hope we hurt them more than they hurt us,' said Ollie. He grabbed his AK-47, and started to crawl away. 'Right, let's bloody do this.'

Ian looked at Nick. 'You sure you're going to make that shot?'

Nick nodded.

'I'll do it if you like. I know a bit about sniping.'

'I can do it.'

'Good lad. Now move.'

Thirty-One

STEVE LOOKED STRAIGHT INTO SALANGI'S eyes. They were hard, unyielding, stealthy and cunning – the eyes of a snake.

Steve was listening to the night air. For a brief second he caught what sounded like the whisper of a voice. Ollie. No, he told himself. It was just one of the cockroaches scuttling across the dust. He could hear nothing, and that meant they couldn't either. There was an assault being prepared out there somewhere, he felt certain of it, but when it came, it would take this lot totally by surprise.

'I said, let's cut a deal,' repeated Steve.

'I don't think you're in any position to negotiate,' said Salangi.

'I know where your gold is.' He kept his voice even and calm, betraying neither emotion nor fear. Although Christ knows, I've got plenty of both, he thought to himself. 'It could be hidden anywhere in these mountains. It could take you weeks to find it. And, you never know, someone else might find it before you.'

Salangi chuckled. 'First, I'll torture your friend, then I'll torture you,' he said. 'You'll speak soon enough.'

'It would be quicker to negotiate,' said Steve. He nodded towards David. 'Let that man go, and I'll take you to the gold. Then, when you have it, turn us free.'

'Men speak quickly enough once my torturers get to work,' said Salangi. He took a step closer to Steve, so he was standing just a yard from him. 'As I said, the only thing you need to tell me is how you want to die.'

Four hundred yards away, Nick had tabbed high into the mountains. He was now two hundred feet above the plain, settling down behind a rock, with enough moonlight behind him to give him a clear view of the target. The M107 was a heavy piece of kit, but he could carry it easily enough. He pushed its supports into place, then opened up the barrel, and gripped it tight into his shoulder. The shot was about five hundred yards, well within range, and he would be shooting downhill so he wouldn't have to worry about tracking the trajectory of the bullet. The magazine on the M107 was meant to take ten rounds but usually was loaded with just nine to reduce the risk of jamming. Nick had already used a couple, which meant he had seven left. Doesn't matter, he told himself. I've got another mag in my webbing. And I'm only going to need one.

He checked the scope. Through the cross-hairs, he could see Salangi's head.

He'd put the bullet downwards, entering the skull just above the ear, so that it could then drill its way right through the centre of the man's brain. The 0.5 calibre bullet fired by the M107 packed more than enough punch to take him straight down. No one could survive a shot like that straight to the head.

He held the gun steady. Just wait for the signal, he told himself.

To the left, Dan and Ganju were putting the Vickers into position.

It, too, was a monster. Dan carried the gun itself on his shoulder, while Ganju followed behind with the ammo. The Vickers K machine gun had first been developed before the Second World War for the big bombers of the era, the Bristol Blenheim and the Armstrong Whitworth Whitley. The ammo slotted into big circular drums that snapped on to the top of the gun. It was the round drum, rather than a more conventional belt-feed, that gave the Vickers its extremely rapid rate of fire, up to a thousand rounds a minute when it got up to speed. Its .303 calibre ammunition could shred any opponent within seconds. The gunners manning the turrets on Second World War bombers had such a small window of time to attack a fighter coming towards them that a rapid rate of fire was crucial to survival. You had only two or three seconds to put enough lead into your enemy to bring him down. But the Vickers had really come into its own when the first SAS squadrons formed in the North African desert in 1942 had stolen them from stricken aircraft and put them on to the back of their jeeps for their raiding parties. The machines were highly unstable; the weight and kickback from the Vickers was designed for a big, heavy aircraft, not a jeep, and the vehicle was liable to tip over as soon you started firing unless the driver was extremely skilled. But they were lethal. The punch on the weapon could rip the heart out of your enemy before they knew what was happening. A fair few had made their way to Australia after the war, and the SASR, whose inspiration came largely from the desert SAS of the Second World War, had trained on them and used them a few times when they were fighting in Vietnam. Dan was well aware of the power of the weapon. In the right hands, it could be devastating.

He snapped the tripod into position and set up the Vickers so that it was pointing straight down at Salangi's men.

Dan was holding the metal butt of the gun. Each drum of ammo contained a thousand rounds, and they had twenty drums in a wooden box. Ganju was kneeling down next to him, ready to snap a new drum into place as soon as an old one was used up. He could complete the manoeuvre in less than two seconds.

'Ready?' hissed Dan.

'Ready,' whispered Ganju.

To their left, Chris was lining up the M2A1-7. He'd last used one in the bushlands of Namibia, using vicious jets of flame to clear out some grasslands where Swapo guerrillas were preparing an ambush. The soldiers would lie in the long, twisted grasses, with their sniper rifles, opening up lethal barrages of fire on passing convoys, but the flame-thrower would burn off their cover, and even if it didn't kill them directly, once they were exposed, it was easy for the man coming in behind you to pick them off one by one. The canisters sat on your back, slotted into a metal frame, held in place by leather straps, then connected to a four-foot metal tube you could point at anyone you wanted to burn out. The flames would shoot about thirty metres forwards. Chris reckoned the best tactic was just to march straight into your enemy. Humans, just like any animal, had an instinctive fear of fire, and the heat and light thrown up by the machine blinded them. They'd start running as soon as the M2A1-7 got anywhere close to them. In fact, back in the Recces, the drill was that if a man was advancing on you with a flame-thrower, the best response was to run straight towards him and shoot the bastard; the flames would take a while to burn you, and if you fired straight into their source, you'd bring the man down. But that took a lot of experience, a lot of training, and a lot of guts. Chris reckoned Salangi's men might have the guts, but not the experience or the training. And that meant they were burnt toast.

He ran through a quick check of the M2A1-7, making sure the valves on the canisters were open and the fuel was flowing freely into the muzzle. If a gun jammed, it just stopped you from firing, but if a flame-thrower jammed, it blew your back off. Chris positioned himself behind a rock, two hundred yards from where Salangi's men were stationed. The parked vehicles, he decided, would be his first target; one lick of flame, and they'd turn into an exploding minefield. Let's get started, he muttered to himself.

To the right, Ollie was tabbing into position, with Ian and Maksim at his side.

Looking back, he could see that Nick had taken up position, with the rifle trained on the camp. He'd need to maintain eye contact with Nick so that he could give the signal for the attack to start. Ollie shuffled along the ground, bent double so that he wouldn't be visible from behind the rocks. When he was satisfied he had a decent line of fire on the men in front of them, he signalled to Ian and Maksim to take up positions a hundred and two hundred yards distant.

They'd have Salangi squeezed in a circle. He wouldn't know what hit him.

Ollie grabbed his field glasses and trained them on Steve. He couldn't hear what he was saying but he could see his lips moving. Well done, pal, he muttered to himself. You played the bastard for time. And now his time is up.

He looked towards Nick, and waved his hand.

*

Steve was still looking straight at Salangi. He could feel a bead of cold sweat dripping down the back of his spine. But his expression remained calm.

'Do you want a bullet in the head or the chest?' he growled.

'Enough of these games,' snapped Salangi.

He turned to his men and barked a series of commands in his own language then looked back at Steve.

'We're about to put your friend on the fire,' he said. 'If you've never heard the cries of a man roasting to death then you've never really lived.' He threw back his head and laughed.

Two men had already picked up either end of the stake to which David was strapped, while a third had used his knife to cut loose his gag. It was done roughly, nicking his skin with the blade, so that blood was dripping from his cheek as he was lifted into the air. He remained grimly silent, despite the evident pain. He could guess what they were about to do. And the cries of agony as the flames started to lick into his body would be enough to break Steve's will, to force him to reveal where the treasure was hidden . . .

Steve listened carefully to the night air, straining to hear the thud of a boot against the rocks or the click of a gun being snapped into position. Where the hell are they? We haven't much time.

Four hundred yards away, Nick watched as Ollie stuck a single thumb into the air.

We're on.

He pressed his right eye hard into the scope of the M107. It was level with Salangi's head, just above the ear.

Don't even think about it, he reminded himself. If you think about it, you'll miss.

'Kill,' muttered Nick. And squeezed softly on the trigger.

The first Steve knew about it was when a splatter of blood flicked across his face.

The bullet had crunched into the side of Salangi's skull, splitting it open the way a chisel opens up a rock. The bone cleaved apart, splinters flew everywhere, and the bullet drilled its way into the man's brain, chewing it up into a grey messy pulp as it went. It stopped with a vicious thump when it was caught by the hard bone on the back of the jaw.

'Looks like you chose a bullet,' muttered Steve.

He leapt forward, catching hold of Salangi's body before it hit the ground. He grabbed the man's chest in both arms, using the momentum of his own fall to drag him towards David. As gunfire started to echo all around them, the men carrying David dropped him roughly to the ground, smashing his back into the hard ground, while they grabbed their guns and ran to take up their positions. Steve rolled, curling up his body, and turned Salangi's corpse upside down. He collided into David's side and quickly pulled Salangi's body on top of both of them, so that it created a natural shield. Blood was dripping from the open head wound, and the heat from the fire just a few feet away from them was intense, but for the next few minutes at least they should be safe – as long as there was enough bone and muscle in Salangi to stop any bullets or shrapnel that flew in their direction.

'Just stay still,' he told David. 'It's going to be like the fucking Somme here for the next few minutes.'

Four hundred yards away, Nick slammed his fist into the rock. 'Fuckin' A,' he muttered. Then he pulled away his bruised knuckles and lined up the scope of the M107 to take out one of the guards.

'Kill,' he muttered again.

To his right, Dan slammed his fist on to the trigger of the Vickers. It was a big, greasy machine, and you could feel how old the steel was, but when it kicked into life it was still capable of unleashing a terrifying burst of force. He turned it on a group of men dashing into position three hundred yards ahead of him. There were at least ten of them, their rifles cocked, trying to figure out where the shot that had just taken out Salangi might have come from. There was a lot of shouting but not much sign of anyone taking command. Dan held the Vickers rock steady as the bullets poured out of its barrel in a blast of fire and metal. The gun was kicking back so hard, it felt like a jackhammer was trying to break open his shoulder but Dan had the strength in his muscles to just about hold the beast under control. It was vibrating wildly, and the barrel was starting to turn red-hot, but the ordnance was still flying through the air with deadly accuracy. The men still trying to get into position were being scythed down, the bullets peppering the front line, ripping open faces and lungs until there was only a row of fresh corpses to trip and terrify the men who remained standing.

'Another drum, man,' he shouted to Ganju. 'We're bloody getting them on the run.'

Ganju slammed the drum into position.

Dan waited just a second to let the drum settle and to allow the barrel to cool a fraction, then squeezed the trigger and let rip with another thousand rounds.

To his left, Chris had taken his cue.

He started to march steadily forward, across the open ground, straight into the row of five parked SUVs.

Three hundred yards separated him from the fight.

He could see a row of men going down where Chris had turned the Vickers on them. Another five men, each of them armed with an AK-47, some of them firing rounds wildly into the air, were diving behind the vehicles in an attempt to take cover from the barrage of gunfire from the Vickers. They'd been taken by surprise, and for the moment they were outgunned, but they still heavily outnumbered their opposition, and that meant that in a fair fight they had the upper hand.

Just have to make sure it's not a fair fight, Chris said to himself.

He marched steadily forwards.

Two hundred yards.

His finger was pressed on the muzzle of the flame-thrower.

There was no point in firing too close, the flame wouldn't reach its target and he'd just be wasting valuable fuel. The trigger that released the fuel from the hose was held in a handle in his right hand, while his left was poised on the igniter's safety catch close to the tip of the muzzle. The hot gas would come steaming through the muzzle, then be ignited just as it escaped into the open air, creating a huge wall of flame. A hundred yards, decided Chris, as he walked into the wall of noise. Close enough so they'll know what's coming for them.

One of the five men had spotted him walking towards them. He was leaning out of the side of a Hyundai, crouching down, his AK-47 raised to his shoulder. Not a typical Afghan, noted Chris. Most of them just started firing wildly, not caring whether they were likely to hit anything. This bloke was taking his time.

He released the trigger on the flame-thrower, and kicked the safety catch off the igniter. He felt a whoosh as the gasoline in his backpack vaporised then rushed down the hose, before being set alight. The blowback was terrifying: a wave of heat that struck you in the face like a fist. Chris circled his wrist slowly, like a spin bowler preparing to toss the ball. The motion created a huge circle of solid flame, totally obliterating his view of anything in front of him. And all the time he kept marching steadily forwards.

A shot.

He heard the blast of the AK-47, then the recoil as the weapon was reloaded. But the bullet wasn't striking home.

The guy was randomly firing into the fireball, hoping to hit the man at its centre, but it would be impossible to see anything through the flames, and there was no way of making an accurate shot.

The guy's going to have to get very lucky to hit me, decided Chris grimly, and kept on walking. And he's only got a few seconds before he gets burnt alive.

To the left, Ollie had his finger hard on the trigger of his AK-47. Ian and Maksim were doing the same, creating a barrage of lethal fire that was shredding through Salangi's camp. Slamming a fresh mag into his rifle, Ollie took a moment to survey the battlefield. If there were forty men in Salangi's camp when they started, he reckoned at least twenty of them were now down. The rattle of the machine gun had taken out maybe a dozen, Nick was picking them off one by one with the sniper rifle, and Chris had just turned the flame-thrower on the line of parked vehicles, igniting their fuel tanks and sending plumes of back oily smoke high into the air. A series of five explosions rocked through the night air, and the sky was suddenly brilliantly illuminated by the burning diesel. You could hear the screams of the men taking cover behind the SUVs being burnt alive. A few were starting to run, their clothes and hair alight, but they were running straight into Chris. His wall of flame just consumed them, scorching the air out of their lungs and pushing them dying, back on to the ground.

We've got them on the run, thought Ollie. But they still outnumber us by two to one. And that means they are still a threat.

He looked across to Ian and Maksim. 'Press forward,' he shouted, struggling to make himself heard above the roar of the fighting.

In any battle, Ollie reminded himself, all that mattered was momentum. Once you had the upper hand, you had to press on and finish your enemy off. Otherwise, you just gave them time to regroup.

They weren't beaten until they were all dead.

Salangi's men were bewildered by the suddenness and ferocity of the attack. They rushed to meet the oncoming fire but as soon as they reacted to it, they were under attack from another angle, making it hard for them to regroup and start fighting back. Ollie wanted to keep it that way. If the three of them could move right into the centre of the camp, they could finish them off. It was exactly the same tactics deployed in a cavalry charge: smash right into the centre of an infantry unit, then cut them to ribbons from the inside.

He started to move across the open ground, with Ian and Maksim at his side. There were fifty yards to cover to take them into the thick of the action. He could see ten men rushing to confront Chris and the flame-thrower, while another ten were forming themselves into a column to the rear of the camp. Somewhere inside the chaos of the battle, the enemy was starting to form a semblance of order and discipline, starting to work together, and that would make them more dangerous.

Thirty yards.

The three men moved forward in a tight unit. Ollie could feel a thump in his chest, the same heady mixture of adrenaline and suppressed panic he felt every time he went into combat.

Twenty yards. Fifteen.

Two men were straight in front of them, one holding an RPG, the other a box of ammo, trying to line up a shot. They were trying to take out the Vickers.

Maksim opened fire with a rapid burst from his AK-47. The bullets crashed into the two men. Maksim held his rifle steady, pumping round after round of ordnance into them. Bullets were ripping into their necks and lungs, pushing them to the ground. But as they went down, the RPG was fired.

Ollie watched in horror as the missile fizzed through the air.

Fifty yards away, Dan heard the RPG blast. From the flash of tracer fire, he guessed exactly where it was going. I don't even need to look, he told himself with a grimace. That's exactly what I'd do if I was in those bastards' boots – put an RPG round into the machine-gunner.

'Bloody dive,' he yelled to Ganju. In the same instant, he threw himself into the air and landed hard on the open ground straight in front of him.

The RPG wasn't accurately fired. It landed ten yards to the right of the Vickers. The missile exploded as it impacted on the rock, sending out shards of shrapnel and rock as it burnt up the surrounding air. Ten yards was close enough, though. The Vickers was shattered, and two remaining crates of ammo caught fire, fizzing and popping in a series of minor explosions like a box of firecrackers.

Dan lay still on the ground, his hands over his head, waiting for the shrapnel to settle.

'Jesus,' he muttered to himself. 'Too bloody close . . .'

He looked around. Ganju was lying flat on the ground.

'Christ, mate,' shouted Dan. He picked himself up and ran towards him. He grabbed Ganju by the shoulders and started dragging him to safety.

Shots were hurtling passed him. Somewhere inside the camp, one of Salangi's men had picked him out and was putting down round after round of AK-47 fire. The bullets were missing, but getting closer all the time.

Dan danced backwards, dragging Ganju as he went. As he fell behind the rock, bullets continued to spit all around him. He leant down to check Ganju's pulse. OK. It looked as if a splinter of rock had hit his helmet, briefly knocking him out. His eyes were already starting to open.

'Pull out of it, mate,' shouted Dan.

Fifty yards ahead, Ollie had spotted the man firing at Dan. He was kneeling down, next to the burning remnants of an SUV.

Ollie nodded to Ian and the two men turned their fire towards him. They let rip with their rifles, putting six rounds into his back, puncturing his lungs, and ripping open his heart. The man fell forward in a pool of blood.

But twenty yards behind them, Salangi's men were starting to move. A column of ten men had formed themselves into a tight square. They were retreating, walking backwards, letting off round after round from their AK-47s to stop anyone getting close to them.

Ollie and Ian dived behind a rock to take cover, kicking

away a bleeding, wounded Afghan as they did so. Ian had already taken out his Makarov and put a bullet into the wounded man's mouth to finish him off. The man had been screaming something in his own language but Ian neither cared nor understood what he was saying. The bullet silenced him. Then he looked forward. 'The bastards are trying to escape,' he muttered.

Ollie was concentrating hard. The column was heading steadily backwards, a fighting retreat that would take them into the hills fifty yards behind them. Once they were in there, they could lose themselves amidst the rocks and gullies, buying themselves precious time to regroup and prepare to strike back.

'We need to cut them off,' said Ian.

Ollie glanced towards Maksim. 'Here, here,' he shouted.

Maksim dived behind the rock and Ollie pulled him closer for more protection. There were still bullets flying everywhere.

'Hold these bastards,' shouted Ollie, his voice raw and hoarse. 'I'm going to get Nick, get in the hills behind them, put some grenades down, and drive them straight into your line of fire.'

'Like cattle,' said Maksim with a broad, mocking grin. 'Rat-a-tat-tat . . .'

'Christ,' muttered Ollie to himself, with a shake of his head. The man's actually enjoying this.

'Move, move,' Ian was shouting to Ollie.

He started to run, his feet pounding against the hard ground. He covered the fifty yards back to the rocks in a matter of seconds. He could see the smouldering, charred remains of the Vickers. Close by, Dan was bringing Ganju round.

'Get up to support Ian,' yelled Ollie, pointing forwards. 'We'll bring the rest of the bastards on to your guns.'

Dan and a revived Ganju ran hard towards the centre of the battlefield as Ollie scrambled up the hill. Nick was another hundred yards up and to the right, dug in with his M107, his scope scanning the battlefield for fresh targets.

'Bloody good job, Nick,' shouted Ollie as he arrived next to him.

Nick looked up, grinning broadly.

Not a trace of fear was evident on his face, noted Ollie. There was a real warrior in there somewhere.

'Now let's move our arses this way,' said Ollie, pointing straight ahead. 'They're not done for yet.'

'The gun . . .'

'Leave the sodding gun.'

Both men started running hard. They skipped across the crags and rocks of the hillside like mountain goats, then skimmed across the plain before climbing again into the hills on the other side.

Ollie could see Salangi's men retreating all the time. They were close to the hills but moving slowly because they were moving in formation, throwing off barrages of fire in every direction to protect themselves.

'Climb here,' he yelled to Nick. There wasn't much time. Another ten seconds and Salangi's forces would be protected by the hills.

He scrambled upwards, blistering the skin on his hands as he dug his fingers into the rocks, dragging himself forward. When they reached a height of thirty feet, some fifty yards away from the retreating column of Afghans, Ollie ripped a grenade from his webbing, pulled the pin, and lobbed the missile high into the sky. At his side, Nick did the same. Ollie pulled out the second of the three grenades he was carrying in his chest pack as he watched the first one arc through the air. It landed some ten yards from the column, exploding a fraction of a second before impact, kicking up a cloud of dust, and sending lethal shards of shrapnel flying everywhere. Nick's landed much closer, he noted. That boy can aim anything. His grenade had come down right at the head of the column, killing at least one man on impact and putting the rest into a panic.

Ollie lobbed his second grenade, then his third, while Nick did the same. The explosions were popping right at the head of the column, one after another, creating a terrifying fog of noise, shrapnel and smoke. Two more men fell, one with a leg blown clean off – the limb was lying yards from its owner. The remaining seven were shouting, some men clearly wounded by hot shrapnel, their discipline broken. Instinctively, they were running away from the grenades, but that meant running straight back into the murderous barrage of fire now being laid down by Dan and Ian and the rest of the unit. They probably knew it was a mistake, thought Ollie. But they couldn't stop themselves. It was just human nature to turn and run from an explosion, even if you know that behind you there is only certain death.

At his side, Nick raised his AK-47 to his shoulder and began putting rounds into the fleeing group of men. 'Kill, kill,' he was muttering softly.

'Down,' shouted Ollie. 'We'll never finish them off at this range.'

Below them, Ian, Ganju, Dan and Maksim were picking off the Afghans one by one. The slaughter was slow and deliberate, delivered without remorse or hesitation. A few rounds were being returned by the Afghans, but they had neither the ability nor the composure to retaliate. They were dropping, one after the other. One man veered off to the left, running wildly, but that just took him straight towards Chris and his flame-thrower, closing in from the flank. A blast of gasoline, and the man collapsed in a heap of charred flesh, a rotten, putrid smell drifting across the battlefield as his guts spilled out on to the ground and were instantly incinerated.

By the time Ollie and Nick closed in from behind, there was nothing left to shoot at. They were all dead. Forty of them at least, decided Ollie, looking around at all the corpses. He wasn't going to bother counting them. They were lying everywhere, with the pitiful, frightened expressions of men who knew they'd lost the battle, and that their time had come. There was a beastly smell of blood and guts and crap everywhere, mingled with the sulphurous remnants of the vast quantities of ordnance that had been punched into these few square yards of land over the past few moments. But despite the horror and devastation of the scene, he was still aware of the kick of adrenaline running through him, and the sense of triumph, of elation that came from knowing that your enemy was dead instead of you.

We've proved ourselves in battle once again. And isn't that what being a soldier is all about?

'Where the hell is Steve?' he shouted as he ran towards Ian and the rest of the men.

Nick pointed towards where he'd put the first bullet through Salangi. The corpse was still lying on the ground, close to the campfire.

Ollie started to walk towards it. As he did so, an Afghan groaned pitifully close by, and without missing a step Ollie pulled out his pistol and shot the man clean through the head.

Sarangi's body was literally riddled with bullets. The one that killed him had gone in cleanly enough, but since then he'd been peppered by stray bullets and flying shards of shrapnel, leaving his body one messy, bloody pulp.

Ollie bent down and got hold of the man's shoulder, ignoring the blood, and wrenched him aside.

Underneath, Steve and David had taken cover, using Salangi as a shield.

Steve stood up slowly. He was dripping in Salangi's blood. With his hand, he wiped it out of his eyes and face, then glanced around at the battlefield.

'Christ, boys, you're not really going easy on the sodding ammo, are you?' he said. 'That stuff costs money, you know . . .'

Thirty-Two

STEVE BENT DOWN TO DAVID and cut the ropes that were still binding him. He stood up uneasily, shaking, trying to find his balance. He'd been strapped up for more than twelve hours and his limbs ached and his muscles had lost their shape.

'You OK?' said Steve.

David nodded. 'I'll be all right.'

Steve surveyed the scene. The last time he'd been standing up he'd been surrounded by armed men, all of whom looked ready to kill him. Now they were all dead.

In total the battle had lasted only seven or eight minutes, but there was no more intense experience than a fire fight. Seconds dragged out into minutes, and minutes into hours. The noise had been deafening as the battle raged above and around Steve. There were moments when he'd reckoned the end might be close, and he didn't mind admitting he'd found the experience terrifying. He'd been in combat plenty of times, but always as a fighter, so pumped up with adrenaline that he couldn't think about anything except destroying the enemy, but this was the first time he'd experienced it the way a civilian might, as a bystander, keeping his head down, hoping not to get hit. It wasn't something he'd care to repeat. It had been impossible to tell how the battle was going; he knew men were going down, but since one dying bloke sounded much like another, he couldn't tell who was winning. All he could do was lie still beneath Salangi's body, and pray. To get up would be madness, though he'd been tempted. Anything would have been better than just waiting. But he kept reminding himself to stay where he was. Plenty of men had survived on a battlefield by hiding beneath dead guys, and there was no reason he shouldn't join them.

As he looked around, he could see how fierce the fighting had been. The vehicles had been reduced to lumps of twisted steel, still burning, throwing off a fierce heat, with bodies lying beneath them. There were corpses everywhere, some with limbs blown off, others with just a neat hole where a single bullet had cut through their brains, killing them instantly. There were discarded weapons, dropped as men went down, and there were craters where the high explosives had detonated.

He looked at Ollie. Steve wasn't a man who found it easy to admit mistakes. He'd rather dip his balls into burning oil than own up to getting something wrong. But maybe Bruce Dudley had been right about Ollie. There had been a fine soldier in him once. And you could bring that man back if you found the right key.

'Well done, mate. Thanks,' he said tersely.

Ollie nodded. 'It was you who put your life on the line coming in here,' he said quickly.

'That's bloody true,' said Steve. He grinned, wiping more blood off his face.

Next to him, David looked around at the men in the unit. A few days ago, he had never met any of them apart from

Ollie. Now he owed them his life. 'Good one, boys,' he said. 'I owe you.'

'Make that a beer back in London,' said Ian, grinning.

'And a double vodka,' said Maksim.

'Done,' said David.

'What the hell happened?' asked Ollie.

'The bastards came and took me while I was guarding the vehicles,' said David. 'It wasn't anyone's fault. They crept up on the position, not making a sound, and before I could react they had me completely surrounded. I reckon they must have known we were there, and had an idea of what we were up to, and so that's why they came to get me.' He paused and picked up a flask of water left by the fireside by Salangi's men. He drank a pint, then another, pouring the water down his parched throat.

'They strung me up in their bloody cave, and put a couple of lashes of the whip on to my back, but I think that was just to loosen me up, and make me frightened.' He laughed roughly. 'I don't mind admitting it bloody worked, as well. Then they untied me and sold me to our pal Salangi. He knew exactly what he wanted. He trussed me up like a damned chicken and then he told me he was going to use me to get his gold back.' He glanced at Steve. 'So I figured we must have hit his fort and got his loot . . .?'

'Most of it,' said Steve.

'Then we should get the hell out of here.'

'Are there any more of these bastards?' said Ollie.

'Salangi's dead, so that's the main threat out of the way,' answered David. 'But plenty of people in this province know he had a lot of money stashed away, and they know it's been nicked, so I don't believe anywhere is safe until we get ourselves across the border.'

Steve nodded. He checked his watch. It was just after ten at night. 'We'll pick up Jeff, and the loot, then I reckon we need to get ourselves at least ten miles south before we try and kip down for the night.'

Ollie organised the unit into a disciplined convoy. It was a twenty-minute hike back to where they had stashed the gold and diamonds, but they covered the ground easily enough. Everyone was up, Steve noted, the way men always were after a battle, but they'd been fighting at an intense pitch, and men couldn't keep that up for long without exhausting themselves. Ganju led the way, as the most surefooted of the unit, with Maksim bringing up the rear. All the time they were looking for scouts that Salangi might have sent up into the hills earlier in the day. It would only take one hidden sniper to lose a couple of men. But as they moved forward, the hills appeared to be completely deserted, and there was nothing to disturb them apart from the rustling of a light breeze through the quiet night air.

None of the gold had been touched, and Steve immediately checked on Jeff. He was on his side, groaning softly. He seemed in worse shape than ever. He looked up at Steve as he rolled him over to check he was OK, and he tried to smile, but it was clear the strength was ebbing away from him fast.

'You got David?' he asked.

Steve nodded. 'And we're going to get you a doctor.'

Jeff gripped Steve's hand but his touch felt cold and lifeless. 'I'm all right, mate,' he hissed. 'Get the money to safety. The big payday, that's what this is all about.'

'Not if you're sodding dead.' Steve turned to Ollie. 'We need to use the sat-phone to get hold of that bastard Muirhead again.'

It took a moment to patch the call through. A sat-phone was only a fraction of a second slower than a normal mobile and it located the number soon enough.

'I need to speak to Angus Muirhead,' said Ollie sharply. 'My name's Ollie Hall. It's urgent.'

There was a pause on the line. A woman had answered, probably one of the secretaries.

Ollie paced around, the phone clasped to his ear, casting nervous glances towards Steve.

'I'm afraid Major Muirhead is not available right now,' said the woman.

'I need to speak to the man right now,' snapped Ollie.

Another pause.

'I'm afraid he's not here.'

'Listen, there's a wounded man right here and he needs to be evacuated immediately.'

'I'm sorry, which regiment are you calling from?'

'Just put me through to Muirhead.'

'I'm sorry, he's not here.'

Steve grabbed the phone from Ollie. His hand was shaking with rage.

'Just sodding listen,' he shouted. 'There's a British soldier who's badly wounded and if he doesn't get a chopper right now he might not bloody pull through.'

'I'm sorry, sir, but unless I know what regiment or what patrol he's—'

'It's a bloody black op.'

'It should still be recorded,' said the woman stiffly.

'Fuck, this is worse than talking to the bloody call centre at the bank,' yelled Steve. 'Are you going to help us or not?'

'I'll leave a message for Major Muirhead to call you back when he has a moment.'

Steve was about to shout something, his face had gone even redder, but the line had gone dead.

Furiously, he hurled the phone against a rock. Ian scurried across to retrieve it.

'Don't break the bloody phone,' he muttered. 'We might still need it.'

'It's no sodding good to us,' snapped Steve. 'The bastards aren't planning to come to help us.'

'The British Army,' said Ian, with a dry chuckle. 'You should have asked me what that organisation's really like.'

'Just leave it,' barked Steve angrily. He took a deep breath and tried to compose himself.

'We'll move out by ourselves,' said Ollie. He looked at Jeff. 'Don't worry, we'll get you out of here.'

For the next ten minutes, the unit prepared the convoy. They had studied the map and marked out a route that would take them straight down towards the border. It was a journey of more than fifty miles, through the mountains, and it would be tough going, bad enough for men on foot but even worse with a heavy load and a wounded soldier to carry as well. But they'd make it. It was two days' walk, at most. And the country they were passing through was so wild and abandoned, there was relatively little chance of meeting any more bandits or Taliban units along the way.

At least that was the theory, Steve said to himself. But so far nothing had worked out the way it was meant to.

They advanced in a well-organised convoy. The crates were loaded on to the stretchers, and each stretcher was carried by two men. Ganju led the way, carrying his stretcher with Nick. At the rear, Jeff was on his feet. He had enough water and painkillers in him to try to walk. He was hobbling along, using a stick in one hand, and holding on to David with the other. The moon cast a pale light over the rugged mountain, so they had enough light to see, and the night air was clean and cool with a light breeze, refreshing them as they ploughed forward. For the first five miles, which took them an hour and a half, they were mostly heading downhill, following a track that wound its way to the foot of the hills. Then there was another mile across an open plain, again easy enough. Then they started climbing upwards, and that was harder going. The track that led up into the mountain was scarcely visible and was pitted with rocks and scrubby bushes as it twisted and turned. The air was draining out of their lungs; loads that were light when you were going downhill suddenly became a terrible burden as you headed upwards. But each man pressed on. There was no moaning, no complaining. They all knew they were carrying a fortune in each box. And that was enough to keep them going.

It was two in the morning by the time Steve decided they'd had enough. There was no point in pushing themselves too hard. Exhaust yourself to the point of collapse and you weren't helping anybody.

'We'll kip here for a bit,' he said.

They had reached a piece of flat ground. They were a thousand feet up, and according to the map they had another thousand feet to go before they were through this mountain and could crack on to the next. The ground was dusty, dotted with vegetation, mostly irises judging by the musty perfume in the air, and somewhere in the distance Steve could hear the howl of an animal. A wolf, probably. He'd heard stories about wild, starving wolves eating men out in this country. And there were snow leopards as well that patrolled the border country. Steve just shrugged to himself and put down his stretcher and its boxes, relieved to be dropping the weight from his arms and shoulders. We've got enough ammo to sort out any wolves that want a bite out of us. That's the least of our problems.

Nick and Ganju foraged enough scraps of wood and dried grass to get a fire going. They laid Jeff down next to it, and pumped a bit more morphine into him. He was shivering badly, and hadn't managed to hold down any of the dried biscuits they'd given him. He'd walked for the first couple of miles, but for the rest of the time Dan had been virtually carrying him. Steve couldn't help but admire the punishment Dan had put himself through to help Jeff. Dan was a strong guy, but Jeff was a heavy bloke, and it took determination to drag him up the mountain. Dan might have his ups and downs, and his temper was maybe shorter than it should have been, but it was very hard to believe he had harmed a couple of kids last time he was in Afghanistan. It just wasn't in his nature.

From their backpacks, each man broke open one of the American MREs. The food wasn't to Steve's taste, but when you'd been fighting and then trekking your way through the mountains for hours, it was just good to have something nutritious to eat. Steve's meal was a chicken and pasta bake. He used the metal spoon from his backpack to shovel the grub into his mouth, savouring every bland mouthful. He washed it down with a bottle of water, still lukewarm from the heat of the day but refreshing all the same. They'd need to conserve their food from now on; the supplies they'd brought with them would only last for another day. And they'd have to refill their water bottles as soon as they could find a source of clean water. It was going to be a long, hard trek down to the border. But for tonight, they just needed to get grub inside them, and rest.

'I want each man to think about what his first meal is going to be when we check into that five-star hotel in Dubai,' said Ollie, tucking into his own MRE and glancing around at the men leaning against their rucksacks around the campfire.

'I could bloody murder a Big Mac,' said Nick.

Steve laughed. 'You're going to be a millionaire, Nick.'

'Make it Burger King at least,' chipped in Dan. 'Treat yourself.'

'Yeah, maybe,' said Nick.

'Depends on the free toy, I suppose,' said Ian.

'Bloody leave it out,' said Nick crossly.

'What about you, Ian?' said Ollie.

'I'll make it a Chinese,' said Ian. 'Steamed fish, and lots of vegetables. Maybe some lobster on the side.'

'And Dan? Fried kangaroo?'

'A bloody barbie, mate,' said Dan, laughing. 'Burger, shrimp, chicken wings, and a fair few tins of the amber nectar.'

'Chris?'

Chris chewed on his food thoughtfully. 'I was about to suggest a lasagne, but now I'm thinking steak and chips, maybe with some salad on the side, and a whole bottle of South African red.'

'And you, mate,' he said to Ganju. 'Something Nepalese?'

Ganju shook his head. 'A whole plate of the finest smoked salmon,' he said. 'Followed by a rack of lamb encrusted in herbs.'

'Don't,' laughed Ollie. 'You're making me too hungry.'

Next, he looked towards Maksim.

'Who cares about the food?' grunted Maksim. 'I'd lick frozen vodka from a whore's belly button.'

'Don't stint yourself, Maksie,' laughed Steve. Then he looked at Ollie. 'And how about you, big man?'

Ollie polished off the last of his MRE, took a swig of water and stifled a burp. 'I reckon it would be a full English,' he said with a grin. 'Sausage, bacon, fried eggs, black pudding, mushrooms, toast, baked beans, a nice hot cup of tea, and the sports section of the *Daily Telegraph* to read.' He smiled to himself, as if in quiet contemplation. 'It's not much for a man to ask, is it?'

'Well, my idea of the best meal when we check into that hotel would be a bloody hot curry,' said Steve. 'A chicken tikka masala, maybe a lamb vindaloo as well, and one of those veggie things with the spuds, a big naan bread, some rice, and a big bottle of Tiger beer to wash the whole thing down with.' He stood up. 'And with those pleasant dreams, lads, I reckon we all need to get some kip. The sooner we get our heads down, the sooner we'll be tucking into all that grub.'

Thirty-Three

ALL THE MEN WERE PRACTISED enough at soldiering to get to sleep instantly. Ollie did an hour on guard duty, then handed over to Steve while he got an hour's sleep for himself. It wasn't much, reflected Steve as he lay down for the sixty minutes before he needed to start waking all the men. But they had to move out by four at the latest to get in six or seven hours' marching before the heat of the day became too punishing. All that stuff about needing eight hours' sleep was for civilians, he reminded himself. One of the first lessons he'd learned in the Regiment was that an hour was plenty of time for the body to recharge itself. Anything more was just a luxury, and they couldn't afford any of that right now.

Steve roused everybody just before 4 a.m.

It took just a few minutes to wash some water down their throats, munch a few dried biscuits, then load up the stretchers and get themselves moving. Jeff had slept a few hours and insisted he could hobble onwards. Dan would walk with him for the first couple of hours, then Steve would take over. It was still dark as they set off, but in another hour the first rays of the dawn would start breaking through. The loads were heavy, but for the moment they were bearable. At least they were going home, Steve told himself. And that made it all worthwhile.

For the first hour they climbed steadily along a narrow track, before reaching a twisting plateau and then starting the descent down into the narrow plain on the other side. The second hour of the trek was interrupted by Nick piping up, 'On second thoughts, maybe I'll make that a meal at TGI Friday's.'

Ollie laughed. 'We'll have you booking into the Savoy Grill before this job is finished.'

It was past six in the morning now, and the sun was already up. A hazy early-morning glow was settling over the country. Steve took over from Dan, helping Jeff to get down the side of the mountain. The peaks were casting long shadows, at moments plunging the unit back into something close to darkness before they emerged again into brilliant light. Steve kept a tight grip on Jeff's torso, steering him carefully down, painfully aware of the way his own muscles were being stretched as Jeff stumbled forwards, and it became harder to stop him falling down the track.

A fall that would almost certainly kill him, realised Steve.

'I'm not going to make it, Steve,' mumbled Jeff suddenly.

Steve gripped him tighter. 'Don't be bloody stupid.'

He was burning hot now. Even though the morning air all around them was cool, Jeff was sweating like a man in a sauna, and you could feel the fever that was gripping his chest as soon as you laid your hands on his skin. He was drifting in and out of consciousness, the way sick men sometimes will. At moments, he'd be calm and lucid; a few seconds later, his eyes would start to close and there would be dribble all down his chin.

Jeff was shaking his head. 'I'm just holding you guys up.'

Steve held him closer. 'We're fine, all right? There will be a hospital when we get to the border.'

'Just make sure my mum gets my share of the money, that's all.'

'You'll be giving it to her yourself,' said Steve. 'And the pair of you will be checking into the Ritz to try and count it all.'

Jeff tried to smile, but the moment of lucidity was gone. He'd closed his eyes again.

If it wasn't for the fact that they were going downhill, Steve was no longer sure how they'd transport him.

An hour went by, then another one, and before long it was after ten in the morning. Ollie called a ten-minute rest so that all the men could catch their breath, while he consulted the map with Ganju. There was no protection on the plain, no shade, just the hot, dusty, pebbled ground. Another couple of miles and they should get to a stream, where they could refill their water bottles, now getting dangerously low.

'We'll hit that by eleven,' said Ollie. 'Get ourselves some water, then maybe rest until this bloody heat passes.'

There was less energy to their step as they pulled themselves back up again, heaved their stretchers into the air once more and started to march into the hills. At this time of the morning, the sun was already fierce.

Chris volunteered to help Jeff for the next hour, and Steve was grateful to exchange the load. The boxes on his stretcher weighed at least six hundred pounds, the weight of three fully grown men, but it was shared between two blokes and felt light compared to looking after Jeff. They had covered ten miles so far this morning, reckoned Steve from the calculations they'd made on the map. They had another forty left to go, two of them up to the waterhole. How hard it was going to get, there was no way of knowing. From the map, they could see they had three more mountain ranges to pass through, and yet until they were on the trail itself, they could only guess how hard the journey would be. Pretty sodding hard, decided Steve. We're about to find out what kind of stuff each man in this unit is really made of.

By eleven, the sun was close to its fiercest. By mid-afternoon a sultry, suffocating haze of heat would settle over the land. It was already at least forty degrees, reckoned Steve. It would hit forty-five later on today, perhaps even fifty down on the plain. Hot enough for men to get heatstroke. Hot enough for them to keel over and die from exhaustion.

It was ten past eleven, only a few minutes behind schedule, when Steve looked up towards the head of the convoy and saw Ganju standing next to a dusty, rocky pool. He was mopping the sweat off his brow. And looking worried.

Steve put down his stretcher and ran towards him.

'Christ,' he muttered out loud.

The pool was empty. Just dried, cracked mud. Not so much as a trickle of water.

'Bugger it,' snapped Ollie, standing at Steve's side.

Ganju was looking up to where the spring was meant to foam out of the mountain and tumble down into this pool. It had dwindled to just a trickle. Close to the pool, there were some animal droppings. Ganju picked one up, smelt it, and tossed it aside.

'Donkey crap,' he said. 'There's been a convoy through these hills, and I reckon the animals and the men must have drunk the pool dry. At this point in the summer, there would only be a couple of inches left in it anyway.'

'How long ago?' asked Steve.

Ganju shrugged. 'From the smell of the droppings, I'd say twenty-four to thirty-six hours ago.'

Ian was glancing around the hills but, for as far as the eye could see, they were completely empty.

'How many men?' asked Steve.

'It looks like there were three animals,' said Ganju. 'Typically, that could mean a convoy of ten to twenty men. The animals carry the kit, the men follow on behind.'

'We could use some animals,' said Chris. 'If we could find them, we could kill the blokes then nick the donkeys.'

Ganju shook his head. 'We'll never catch them,' he said. 'With animals, they'll be moving a lot faster than we will with all this gear to hump.'

'And we haven't much water,' said Ollie.

'How much?' asked Steve.

Each man checked his kitbag. They'd started out with a couple of litres each when they'd hit the fort and most of them had already drunk it. They had expected to be motoring towards the border in the Toyotas, not walking through the mountains, and the supplies they had brought with them weren't going to be nearly enough.

'How far to the next waterhole?' asked Steve. Ganju and Ollie were already studying the map.

'About thirty miles,' said Ollie.

'That's another day's march,' said Steve.

With about half a litre of water per man, he thought to himself.

'We'll just have to go easy, and we'll have to make sure Jeff gets all the water he needs,' said Ollie. 'Everyone else should get as much rest as they can. There's no point in trying to walk through the midday heat. We'll only get even more dehydrated. We set off again at six.'

Steve did his best to make Jeff as comfortable as possible. He had lost consciousness again. Steve propped up his backpack against a rock, laid Jeff up against it, and, with Ganju's help, tried to pour some water down his throat. But his tongue was so badly swollen, nothing was getting through, and the water just ran down the side of his face and into his sweat-soaked shirt.

'You think he can make it?' Steve asked Ganju.

Ganju shook his head from side to side, a motion that meant he was undecided. 'If we can get him to a hospital in forty-eight hours, maybe,' he said quietly. 'I've seen men in this state hold on for days. And I've seen them die within minutes.'

Steve propped himself under a shaded rock. The ground was dry and hard, and there were a few insects crawling over the cracked ground. He shut his eyes. He knew he had to try to get as much rest as possible. They had a long march ahead of them still, and the faster they moved, the more chance there was of saving Jeff. Ganju was right, he could hang on for days, or die this afternoon. It depended on his determination – and at least Jeff had plenty of that.

The heat was intense, dry and dusty, and by noon the breeze had dropped completely. Even in the shade you could feel the sun burning everything around you, toasting the land, the rock, and anyone foolish enough to set out into the mountains without any protection. The sky was a dazzling yellow, the ferocity of the sun blocking out the blue, and Steve could feel the sweat pouring off him. He tried to stay as still as possible, conserving as much fluid as he could, but he knew he might easily sweat off a litre or more just getting through the afternoon – which was more than he had in his canister.

Steve thought for a moment about Orlena, wondering what she might be doing. He thought about the way her hair tumbled across his torso when they were in bed together, the way her lips ran down his chest, and the way her red fingernails dug hard into his ribs as he pressed his body close to hers. He permitted himself a brief smile, then closed his eyes again, and tried to sleep. A man needs something to march home for. And once he's found it, he just needs to keep on walking until his journey is completed.

'Let's move,' called Ollie.

Steve pulled himself sharply upwards and checked his watch. It was six exactly. The back of his throat felt like sandpaper, but what little water he had he would preserve for later. Immediately, he went to check Jeff. His eyes were still closed, and for a moment Steve feared the worst, but as he picked up his wrist and pressed his finger into his vein, he could feel there was a still a weak pulse in him. With Ganju taking the other side, Steve tried to lift him to his feet. 'Come on, mate, it's getting cooler.'

Jeff hardly budged. His limbs were lifeless, and there was a dry sweat running off his face. Steve tried to lift him again. But it was useless. The strength just wasn't there.

'Sod it,' muttered Steve.

'We're not going to be able to walk him, are we?' said Ollie, looking across.

'What the hell are we going to do then?' said Steve.

Ollie thought for a moment. 'We've got two options,' he said. 'We leave him here, along with one guy to look after him, while the rest of us dash for the border. When we're across into Pakistan, we'll find a chopper somehow, and come back to lift him out.'

'There's not enough water,' said Ian. 'It could be three days before we get back. In this heat, no one's going to last that long without anything to drink.'

'Then we take option two.'

'Which is?'

'We ditch five of the boxes and carry Jeff on one of the stretchers.'

Steve glanced at Ian and Maksim. He suspected both men would rather have the treasure than carry Jeff down to the border. They hadn't had a chance to count the money yet, and even if they did, they didn't have the kit to weigh gold or value diamonds. But each stretcher load was probably worth a million or more. Men had been left to die for a lot less money.

'Then we bury the boxes right here,' said Ian, meeting Steve's glance. He tapped Maksim on the shoulder. 'You help me.'

Maksim simply nodded.

Ian used a slab of broken rock as a makeshift pickaxe to break open the hard ground, while Maksim scooped up the earth with a fold-up spade from his backpack. Within minutes they'd created a hole deep enough to slot the five boxes into. Nick, Chris and Dan collected stones to put on top of it.

'We'll mark the spot on the map,' said Ian when they had finished. 'If any of us want to, we can always come back and collect the treasure another time.'

'I'll need to be pretty bloody broke to come back to this place,' said Ollie.

'The way your bird spends money, I reckon you'll be back here by Christmas,' said Steve.

They laid Jeff on the spare stretcher. Steve took one end, Dan the other, and then the convoy started its climb up the track that would take them along the side of the mountain, and then down into the next plain. The sun was starting to set, and the heat of the day had lost its ferocity. Jeff was a heavy load, but no worse than the boxes. As they pounded forward, Steve could feel himself starting to get into his stride. One hour passed, then another. By eight, they had done another six miles, through one plain, across a plateau, then up into the mountains beyond. The last embers of sunlight were disappearing now, and a sinister darkness was starting to fall over the mountains. In the fading light, long shadows were cast over their path and the twisted shapes of jagged rocks loomed over them like demons. Steve kept his head down and kept on walking, focusing only on each step. Keep going, he said to himself again and again. You'll be home soon enough.

At ten, they stopped for a half-hour rest.

Each man allowed himself a couple of sips of water, just enough to wet their tongues and bring a moment of relief from the thirst. As he put Jeff down, Steve could feel the soreness rippling through his muscles. While you were walking you didn't notice it so much, but the second you put the weight down, the aches started to hit you. Jeff was still alive, but only just. His pulse was growing weaker and weaker, and his eyes were closed. His tongue was so swollen it was getting hard for him to breathe. On his leg, the bandage was sodden with fresh blood, and there was a nasty smell of rotting, putrid flesh from the wound. Steve thought briefly about changing the dressing, but decided against it. Right now, the bandage was probably all that was holding the blood in. Take it off, and the man could lose another pint before they managed to staunch it. And, the state he was in, there was no way he could survive that now.

We just have to pray, and walk, Steve told himself.

Only the moon and the bright stars were providing any illumination, but they could see well enough. Ganju had already spread the map out on the ground. They used their GPS to fix their position: still another thirty-five miles from the border, but getting closer all the time. Only twenty-five miles until they hit the waterhole but there would be a couple of steep climbs before then, and they'd have to preserve all their strength.

'We'll do another five miles tonight, lads,' said Ollie. 'Then make a dash for the border tomorrow.'

Ian grinned. 'So how about starters, guys?' he said. 'We sit down for a slap-up meal, we know what we're having for a main course. But starters? Let's decide what we'll all order. Except for Nick here, because he likes to play with the free toy before he moves on to his main course.'

'I'm going to TGI,' said Nick.

'I'll have a plate of smoked salmon, with plenty of lemon and pepper, and some thin slices of toast,' said Ollie.

'Half a dozen poppadoms for me, and some chutney to dip them into,' said Steve. 'And I'll get started on the beer.'

'Some bloody hot soup,' said David. 'With good, hot crusty bread and lashings of butter on it, all melting down the sides.'

'Stop it, stop it,' growled Steve. 'My rumbling stomach will wake up the rattlesnakes.'

'How about you, boys?' said Ian, looking towards Chris and Dan.

'A nice piece of grilled tuna, I reckon,' said Dan. 'From the barbie, of course. And a pasting for the poms at the cricket. That always works up my appetite.'

'I'll have some nice grilled prawns,' said Chris. 'Big fat ones, dripping in garlic.'

'I want to know what the hell we're having to drink' said Maksim. 'Sod the food.'

'We'll sort out the cocktails tomorrow, Maksie,' said Ian. 'There's still a lot of hungry miles between us and that feast.'

The men stood up, stretched their aching muscles, took another precious sip of water, then lifted their stretchers into the air, and started walking. There was still a long hike ahead of them before they could rest for the night. The path wound along the side of the mountain, then climbed sharply, up to a high plateau, then tracked along the edge of a gorge that plunged down a thousand feet or more into an empty, wild ravine. In the night you could hear the distant sound of wild animals: like men, in the heat of the summer they only came out at night. Steve ploughed steadily forwards, ignoring everything apart from keeping his back straight and his load steady. But even though the temperature was starting to drop fast, and he was grateful for the first blasts of cool air on his face, the sweat was still dripping down his back and into his clothes.

When they stopped to make a camp, it was two o'clock in the morning. Light from the moon and stars was blocked out by the high ridges of the cliff face, and the path was treacherous when you couldn't see anything. Dan had already slipped, tipping his boxes on to the side, and one of them had broken open, spilling diamonds over the path. It took ten minutes to collect them all and put the box back together, and even then Steve reckoned a few had got lost down the side of the mountain. Some lucky bastard might find them one day, but not us, and not tonight. After that, he'd taken care, looking carefully for rocks and potholes before each step. There wasn't much chance that Jeff would survive a crash to the ground.

Nick and Chris scraped together some brush, made a small fire, and the men opened up their MREs. They had one more in each pack; apart from some dried biscuits, that was all the food they had until they broke through to the other side. Steve's was beef and rice, but he could hardly taste it, his throat was so parched. Dan was trying to kick-start a conversation about the cricket, and Nick was still trying to figure out what kind of starter he might have. He was wondering whether chips counted, but when Ian began to explain to him about side dishes, Nick just got fed up and decided he'd go for a thick crust pizza from Pizza Hut with cheese inside. The rest of the unit were too exhausted to talk. Their muscles ached, and the blisters were starting to break open on their worn-out feet. They just wanted to put their heads down and get some sleep. Kick into tomorrow, thought Steve to himself. And make that the last day of this march.

'We'll sleep through until six,' said Ollie. 'Then try to do another twelve to fifteen miles before the sun gets too hot for us to walk any further. With any luck, we might even be home and dry and drinking toasts to a successful mission by this time tomorrow.'

Maksim nodded. 'Make mine—'

'We know, Maksie,' said Ollie, grinning. 'We'll make yours a double.'

'A bottle . . .'

Steve put his head down and tried to sleep. For a few moments, he felt restless. The sweat was clinging to every part of his body, he could feel the dirt and dust clogging every pore in his skin. He was worried about Jeff. He was worried about how they were going to make it through the next twenty-five miles with hardly anything left to eat or drink. But within seconds, his training had kicked in. He'd pushed all of that aside, and was thinking just about the DB5 with Orlena in the passenger seat. She was running her hand along the smooth chrome and dark leather of the gear stick, and they were both listening to the throaty grumble of the car's magnificent four litre, straight six engine. And with a brief smile to himself, he was asleep.

'Wake up, Steve,' hissed Ganju.

Steve opened his eyes. He looked first at the stars. They were bright and clear, though the moon had all but disappeared from the sky. He glanced at his watch. Just after three in the morning. He'd only been asleep one hour, but Ganju wouldn't wake him without good reason. His expression was sombre.

'Come,' he whispered.

Steve stood up, shaking the sleep from his bones. He followed Ganju to where Jeff was propped up against a rock. Ganju knelt down and lifted Jeff's left wrist. He handed it to Steve.

For a brief second, Steve hesitated. Part of him wanted to postpone the moment, to make it go away. Then he took the cold flesh in his hand, and pressed down into the vein, feeling for a pulse.

It wasn't there.

Steve looked up into the night sky. He took a lungful of cold night air, struggling to compose himself.

'People think the word Gurkha comes from the Gorkha region of Nepal, but it's much older than that,' said Ganju quietly. 'The Gurkha people settled in the region in the fifteenth century, but our tribe was founded by a man called

Bappe Rawal, who was a disciple of the great Hindu Guru Gorkhanath, who, like all the scholars of those times, taught the creed of reincarnation.'

Steve was silent.

'According to my beliefs, Jeff's soul has left this body, but he will come back soon in some other form. He hasn't died, just moved on to some other place.'

'Better than this one?'

'Couldn't be much worse, could it?'

'You're right about that, mate,' said Steve.

'You going to be OK?' asked Ganju.

Steve nodded. 'We'll sit here by ourselves for a minute, thanks,' he said. 'Just me and Jeff.'

Thirty-Four

I T WAS A SHALLOW, DUSTY grave.

The earth was so hard it had been a struggle to dig down more than a couple of feet. Maksim used his knife to break open the clods of earth, and Nick scooped up armfuls of cracked, dried-out mud. Ian, Chris and Dan scoured the hillside for rocks to lay over the mound. And Steve used his knife to strip the bark from a piece of wood so that at least they would have something to mark Jeff's final resting place.

When they were done, they stripped Jeff of his weapons and supplies. And then they laid his body down in the earth. One by one, each man laid rocks on top of his corpse, until there was a mound that would at least shield him from the sun and the vultures. It was just after five in the morning, and the first glimmers of dawn were starting to rise over the distant horizon, sending shafts of weak, orange light shimmering across the hills.

As Steve hammered the plain wooden stick into the ground with the butt of his AK-47, Ollie stood at the head of the simple grave.

'Ashes to ashes, dust to dust . . .' He paused. Christ, I can't even remember how it goes. Bunked off too many RE lessons.

Ian stepped forward. '*Memento homo quia pulvis es et in pulverem reverteris,*' he said solemnly. 'Remember that you are dust, and that to dust you shall return.' He looked around at each man in turn, then crossed himself, before stepping back.

Next, David took a step forward. 'I think Rudyard Kipling wrote a poem about the soldiers in one of the Afghan wars, probably fought not very far from here,' he said. 'I had to learn it at school, and I can't remember it very well. But I think the last couple of verses went like this.' He coughed to clear his throat.

> *If your officer's dead and the sergeants look white,*
> *Remember it's ruin to run from a fight:*
> *So take open order, lie down, and sit tight,*
> *And wait for supports like a soldier.*
> *Wait, wait, wait like a soldier . . .*
>
> *When you're wounded and left on Afghanistan's plains,*
> *And the women come out to cut up what remains,*
> *Jest roll to your rifle and blow out your brains*
> *An' go to your Gawd like a soldier.*

As he finished, Maksim raised his AK-47 into the air and fired a single shot skywards. The noise of the bullet echoed through the mountains until finally it faded into silence.

Steve bent down and placed the last rock into position to secure the single strip of wood that would have to serve as a tombstone. 'Step lightly, old pal,' he said quietly. 'And stay free.'

He turned round, glanced into the rising sun, and went to collect his stretcher. While the grave was being dug, David had rearranged the boxes so that they could use Jeff's stretcher. He'd placed Jeff's weapons and supplies with the rest of the kit. The load would now be lighter for each man as they completed the journey.

'You did what you could for him,' said Ollie.

Steve shook his head. 'I could have left him back in South London, doing his weights, taking birds called Kylie and Megan to the nightclubs, and going round to his mum's for a roast on Sunday. That's what I could have done for him.'

It was well past five when they resumed their march. Ganju and Nick led the way, the two most agile men in the unit, and probably the fittest as well. Without Jeff, they were now travelling in four stretcher-bearing units, so there was always one spare man. They took it in turns to march alone, relieved to be spared the weight of the boxes. But the mood was sombre. As in any fighting unit, when a man died, the morale of the whole force went down with him. Soldiers always thought they were going to be OK, that they'd come through alive. That was the only way they could keep going. When you'd just seen a mate die, it was hard to maintain the illusion. Right now, each man was wondering which of them would make it home, and that was never a comfortable thought.

The heat was intense, burning into their skin like a scalding iron. Hot swirls of air rose around them, dry and dusty, and at times it seemed as if the wood of the stretchers would catch fire in their hands.

They stopped for a rest at eleven thirty. When they looked at the map, Ganju reckoned they'd done ten miles that morning. Only another fifteen to go, noted each man with evident relief. Only ten more to the waterhole, then another five to the border.

We can hold out until then, Steve told himself. One more

push and we're home. He emptied the last of his water down his throat. It was warm, probably more than twenty degrees, and the metal of the canister was burning his fingertips, but the moisture still soaked into him.

At his side, Nick was drinking the last of his water, and starting to unlace his boots. 'I don't think I've ever felt this bloody knackered,' he muttered.

'Keep your boots on,' growled Steve.

'My feet are killing me.'

'Just keep them on.'

Dan leant across from where he was lying propped up against a rock. 'On a march like this, Nick, if you take your boots off you'll never get them on again. Right now, your socks are probably the only thing holding your feet together. There will be blisters, and blood, and the cotton has probably started to merge into the worn-out skin. Take them off, and the blood and pus will be oozing all over the place, and your feet will swell up, and then we'll be carrying you on one of these stretchers.'

Steve chuckled to himself as he watched Nick's face turn pale. His face had been scorched fire engine red in the sun but somehow, despite that, his skin still managed to turn white. 'Not like a PlayStation game, is it?'

Steve closed his eyes. The sun was baking into him, but he was starting to grow used to the searing heat of the day. As long as you didn't try to move, it wasn't so bad. Another forty-eight hours maximum, he told himself, and he'd be sitting in a bath in a five-star hotel, wondering how much money he needed to spend every day to get through a million, or two million, or however much money turned out to be in those boxes. At least ten grand a day, he decided. And that included weekends.

By six, they were on the move again. They were aiming to cover at least fifteen miles so they could get some water, then finish the last five miles down into Pakistan before dawn, if they were strong enough. They were heading into the most treacherous part of the journey, the high ravines and steep crevices of the Chagai Hills. Once they were through those, they would drop down to the border village of Bahram Chah in Pakistan. After that, they would be home.

The first seven or eight miles were easy enough. The men were rested, and although they were hungry, thirsty and shaken by losing Jeff, they were close enough to the end of the journey for their spirits to be good. By midnight, they had covered another ten miles, and, quickening the pace, they reckoned they could do at least another five before it became too dark to continue any further.

'We're close,' said Ollie, at just after one in the morning.

Together with Ganju, he was studying the map. The Chagai Hills were among the most remote areas of the border region, so sparsely populated that the Pakistani Army tested its nuclear weapons on their side of the border. The track twisted through the mountains, rising and falling, but rarely did they come across any sign that anyone had used this route for years. There were rivers running through the rocks, but only for a few weeks after it rained, and that was many months ago. Sometimes water collected in deep basins, however, and if there was enough of it, it could stay there through the scorching summer. It was one of those that was marked on the map. Let's just hope to God there's something left, thought Steve. We're too dehydrated to carry on much longer.

It was another mile to the watering hole.

'Stop right here,' said Ganju from the head of the convoy.

He was flashing his torch straight ahead. For the whole of the journey so far, they'd used only the moonlight to guide them as they walked. The risk of a torch being spotted was too high; on these bleak mountains, an electric light could be seen for miles. But Ganju must have seen something. Steve put down the stretcher he was carrying with Chris and stepped up to take a look.

A bridge.

'Shut that off,' hissed Ollie.

Ganju flicked off the torch. In the moonlight, Steve could see a narrow rope bridge crossing a steep ravine. He looked down. In the murky, pale light, it was impossible to see to the bottom. At his side, Ganju flicked a stone down, then waited. At least five seconds passed before they heard the faint echo of it striking something down below.

'Christ, that must be hundreds of feet,' said Steve.

He felt the rope. It was old and frayed, made out of hemp rather than one of the newer high-strength nylons. Ganju was holding the other side.

'Is it going to hold a man?' asked Steve.

Ganju thought for a moment. 'A man, yes,' he replied. Then he nodded towards the boxes. 'But that lot? I don't know, they're bloody heavy.'

'We should take them across one by one,' said Ollie.

He reached into his kitbag and pulled out a length of strong nylon rope. 'One man goes across first, then we tie a rope around the boxes, and around a man, and we bring them across one by one.'

Steve nodded. 'I'll go . . .'

Nick stepped forward. 'I'm the lightest of us,' he said. 'I'll do it.'

Steve patted his shoulder. 'Good lad.'

Nick tied one end of the rope round his waist. Ollie and Maxim took hold of the other end. Nick glanced downwards, but it was so dark, he couldn't see the bottom of the ravine, and he hardly felt afraid at all. The rope bridge consisted of some webbing and planking between two ropes on either side, and Nick could feel the bridge swaying as he stepped on it. It was like walking on jelly. The tighter you tried to hold on, the wobblier it got.

'Go,' hissed Ollie from behind. 'The faster you are, the lighter you are.'

Nick accelerated, taking five big steps, bouncing forward like a cat, and within seconds he was on the other side. He took the rope from round his waist and tied it to a rock stump, then waved to the other side.

'We're moving across one by one, with every other bloke taking a stretcher with him,' said Ollie. 'Maksie, you're the strongest, so once we're across, you're bringing the boxes over.'

Each man crossed the bridge in turn, until they were all safely across. Steve could feel it swaying as he went across, and he could hear the old ropes straining under his weight but he'd always had a good head for heights and he wasn't going to let it bother him. By the time they were on the other side, Maksim had undone his own chest webbing, plus taken a spare web from his kitbag, and knitted them together to make a huge rope bag into which the boxes could be fastened: that would catch the boxes if they fell. He placed the first box inside, then tied a rope round himself, and started to walk across the bridge. The planks sweated under the weight, but Maksim ignored the creaking, and walked fearlessly forward. He tossed the box to the other side, waited a moment while Dan and Chris unstrapped it, then hurried back to the other side. The plan was to bring the boxes across one by one; when the last one was across, Maksim would bring himself over.

Maksim was working quickly, steadily. The temperature had dropped, and although he was tired and thirsty, his spirits were intact. One box came across, then another, then another. Within a few minutes, fifteen of them had come across, with only five left to shift.

We're almost there, thought Steve.

A cracking sound splintered the night air.

Chris and Dan were straining to hold on to the rope attached to Maksim. But he was already tumbling down into the ravine.

'Hold it, hold it,' shouted Ollie, a tone of desperation in his voice.

There was a wailing sound as Maksim vanished into the ravine.

The ropes on the bridge had snapped in two. First the left-hand side when Maksim was halfway across, then the right-hand side. The box tumbled out of his arms, spilling out of its webbing and crashing into the rocks far below.

Ollie grabbed hold of Dan, then placed his own hands on the rope, while Nick got hold of Chris. All four of them just about managed to stop Maksim from falling.

'Pull, pull,' said Ollie.

Steve grabbed the rope as well. All five of them were pulling hard, and slowly they managed to lever a sweating and swearing Maksim back up to ground level. Ian and David reached down with their hands, grabbed his arms and yanked him upwards. There were cuts on his arms and face where he'd collided with the rocks, but otherwise he seemed OK.

'You all right?' asked Steve.

'We're losing our money,' growled Maksim.

Steve looked first into the ravine, then across to the other side.

There was no way they could retrieve anything from down there, and the boxes on the other side looked out of reach too.

'Forget it,' said Steve. 'We press on for home with what we have.'

'I'm not leaving without the money,' said Maksim flatly. There was an edge of steel in his voice, the tone of a man on the brink of a fight.

'And how exactly are you planning to get across?' asked Ollie. 'Fly?'

Ian stepped forward, tugging on the rope that Nick had originally taken across the ravine. It was still intact, stretching from one side to the other.

'Neither Nick nor Ganju weigh much. They could probably get across on this.'

'Leave it,' growled Steve. 'There's plenty enough in these fifteen boxes for all of us.'

'We're leaving money everywhere,' shouted Maksim, suddenly flashing with anger. 'In the fort, when Jeff couldn't walk, more and more boxes get lost.'

'We're down to less than half of Salangi's loot,' said Ian. 'At least.'

'It's still millions,' said Steve. 'It's enough. We're not losing any more lives.'

Ian was about to speak again when Maksim put an arm on his shoulder.

'Just mark the spot,' he said. 'Maybe the two of us will come back for it.'

'You'll never find it,' snapped Steve. 'It's pitch black out here, and fuck knows where we are anyway.'

'I'll find it all right,' growled Maksim.

'You know what, I think he might,' said Ian. He was looking at Maksim, with the air of a man who was thinking something but wasn't about to say what it was.

'Let's get the hell out of here,' said Ollie.

'Listen,' said Dan urgently.

All the men stood perfectly still while Dan cupped an ear to the wind. For ten seconds, he held the position, then shook his head. 'I'm sure I heard something. A man . . .'

'You sure?' asked Steve.

Dan shook his head. 'No, not sure, but there was a movement. And there are at least three al-Queda camps in this area. We've been making a bloody great racket for the last ten minutes. Maybe someone has come out to see who's waking up the whole neighbourhood.'

'There are gazelles in these hills,' said Ganju. 'Could be that.'

Dan shrugged. 'Could be. It was just a movement of feet somewhere above us.' He pointed into the hills but in the darkness it was impossible to see anything apart from the brooding shapes of the rocks towering all around them.

'Then let's damn well move,' said Ollie. 'Get to the watering hole and rest. We'll keep a man on watch. The less time we spend hanging around here, the better.'

Within minutes, they'd reloaded the five stretchers. With only fifteen boxes left, there were only three boxes per team, and the load was lighter. But the men were shaken up by the ravine crossing, and by the loss of the money, and Steve was grateful there was only a mile to the watering hole. They needed some time to recharge themselves for the final leg of the journey. Nothing had gone right since they'd hit Salangi's fort, he reflected. *The sooner we're out of this sodding country the better.*

The last mile was tabbed mostly in silence. Ganju walked twenty yards ahead of the main convoy, his rifle cocked and ready to fire, keeping a constant lookout for an enemy that might be observing them. But the last leg passed without incident. If someone had been watching them, as Dan reckoned, they'd disappeared into the shadows. Even so, it didn't mean they weren't there, thought Steve grimly. No one would start a fight at this time of night. They'd watch and wait and pick their moment in the morning. *If the bullets are going to start flying again, it will be just before dawn. We're not out of this yet.*

For the last two hundred yards they climbed steeply on a path cut into the rocks by an ancient stream. In the monsoon, water would be gushing down this channel, and the grooves it had cut into the stone over thousands of years were visible. Tonight it was bone dry. The surface was smooth, polished by the winter water, and it was tough for boots to get a grip on its surface, but eventually they scrambled their way up on to the plateau. The waterhole was a bore sunk into the mountain, framed by a circle of rocks thrown up by an ancient earthquake. Ganju tossed a pebble into the hole, and you could hear the sound of each thirsty man holding his breath.

Christ, we need something to drink, thought Steve.

Splash.

Water.

Dan opened up his canister, tied it to the spare rope, and dropped it down into the waterhole. Within seconds, he was pulling up tin after tin of fresh, cold water.

Water flowed into the borehole during the rainy season, it was like a giant drain, and because it was sheltered, the water only slowly evaporated during the hot summer months.

The men drank lustily, spilling it down their throats, then washing their grimy faces and hands. Steve could feel the water flooding through him. It had a slightly coppery taste, from the trace metals in the mountains, but seemed clean enough. When he was finished, he sat back against the boxes on his stretcher and belched contentedly.

'You should have brought some mixers, Maksie,' he said, glancing towards the Russian. 'We could have set up a cocktail bar.'

Maksim grinned, and carried on pouring water down his throat.

'There's food out there,' said Dan. He was scanning the dark hills on the horizon. 'When we were fighting in these hills we lived on gazelle for days at a time. Fast little buggers, like deer but even quicker, and they're bloody hard to kill, even with a machine gun, but if you get one they taste good. Roast them on a fire and pretty soon you've got a bloody good barbie going.'

'Get a satellite dish and you could be on Bondi,' said Ollie.

Steve checked his watch. It was already two thirty in the morning. They needed rest and they needed to get home a lot more than they needed a barbecue.

'We'll eat when we get home,' said Steve.

'One and a half hours to rest, with two men on constant watch,' said Ollie. 'Then we tab down the five miles to the border at four. It shouldn't take us more than a couple of hours, so we'll be there before dawn. With any luck, we'll be having lunch in the Hilton.'

'I need a gazelle,' snapped Dan. 'I haven't eaten for twenty-four hours. I'm bloody starving.'

'A man can survive without food for at least a week,' said Ian. 'Even an Australian, according to the latest science.'

'Well, not this Aussie.'

'In the Recces, we went a week without food as part of the selection process,' said Chris. 'No sleep either. After that, everything else seems easy.'

'Well, not in the bloody SASR,' said Dan. 'In the Aussie Army, we eat. And when we don't eat, we fucking kill something and eat that.' He unclipped his AK-47 and stalked off into the mountain.

'Bloody hell,' muttered David, watching him march into the darkness. 'It's like having sodding Desperate Dan along for the trip.'

'Someone needs to follow him,' said Ollie. 'The man's a liability out there by himself.' He looked around the unit. His finger started to point towards David.

Steve got reluctantly to his feet. 'I'll go.'

Ollie shook his head. 'We need you—'

'I said I'd sodding well go,' snapped Steve.

He took one more hit of water and started to walk after Dan. The light was murky, and there were rocks all around them, making it hard to see anything. His legs were tired from the trek, but someone had to keep an eye on Dan, and all the other men were just as tired as he was so it might as well be him. Dan was about thirty yards ahead of him, no more than a silhouette in the darkness, striding forward, his rifle ready and cocked for action. He was following a twisting path that led down from the plateau into a section of scrubland covered in a few gnarled trees that somehow managed to grow in the thin soil. Some of the highest mountains in the range soared away in the distance. There was a night chill in the air, and a breeze was starting to blow off the mountain, whistling softly as it curled its way through the rocks and crevices. Away to the left, due south, Steve could just see the plains of Pakistan over a ridge of hills, and he was sure he could see a few lights that he assumed must come from the village of Bahram Chah. It was the first sign of civilisation – or at least as close an approximation to it as you got around here – that he had seen for days and for a brief moment Steve allowed himself to believe that the journey really was almost over.

A shot.

Dan was crouching low, his AK-47 jammed into his shoulder, pointing forward.

Then another shot. The gunfire echoed through the mountains like a clap of sudden, unexpected thunder.

Steve started running, arriving breathless at Dan's side.

'Got something for the barbie, mate?' he said.

Dan looked sullen, worried.

Steve glanced upwards. He could see nothing apart from the stony side of the mountain.

'There was a man up there,' said Dan.

Thirty-Five

Back at the waterhole, Steve looked at each of the men in turn.

'We have to move fast,' he said. 'The chances are al-Queda are on to us, and things could be about to turn very nasty.'

'You sure?' asked Ollie.

'I saw one of them,' said Dan. 'I think they've been tracking us since the ravine. This is their territory. Anyone sets foot on what they regard as their land, they kill them instantly. It's the only way they've survived up here for so long.'

'We need to hide the treasure, then disappear on foot,' said Ian. 'There's no way we can move fast enough with all this kit.'

'No sodding way,' said Steve. 'We tab down to the border with our money.'

'And make ourselves an easy target?' said Ian. 'This is their country. A nine-man unit with four stretchers. We might as well put up a big bloody target with the words "shoot us" written all over it.'

'Bloody hell, Steve, he's right,' said Ollie.

'I'm not heading out of here without my money,' insisted Steve.

'We stash the loot, then get down to the border,' said David. 'We'll come back for it when the coast is clear.'

Steve shook his head. 'I'm not leaving without my money.'

'Then you walk out with one box on your back,' said Ollie.

Steve bit down on the rage that had welled up inside him. He could see that Ollie was right. There could be thirty or forty al-Queda warriors on them at any moment. They were trained fighters, some of the toughest in the world, and a scrap with them would be a nasty old fight. They had to be able to move fast.

'OK,' he said eventually. 'We stash the loot. Ian and Nick can look after it, and the rest of us will head down to the border.' He looked at Ian, a flash of bitterness in his eyes. 'That OK with you?'

'Just so long as you come back,' said Ian.

'And just so long as you don't piss off with our money,' retorted Steve.

There was a cave eight hundreds yards down the hill due south from the waterhole. Ian had already scouted it out, one of a series of cuttings into the rock along the side of a track which led down into the border country. There were a dozen of them in all, and they chose the third one along. They dragged the boxes deep into the cave and stacked them in a pile, five along and three high, then covered them with scrub and brush and handfuls of cracked mud. The whole job was finished in ten minutes. When they were done, Ian and Nick hid themselves in the entrance to the cave, their rifles at the ready.

'Stay right here,' said Ollie sharply. 'We'll be back when we've dealt with this situation. We might even be able to get a vehicle and get it up this track.'

Ian nodded. 'I'll be waiting for you.'

The seven remaining men started to move swiftly down the track. As they got closer to the border, the wilderness through which they had been trekking for the last two days was left behind. They were close to a village now, and close to some al-Queda camps as well, and the tracks were getting solid enough for a vehicle. Men could pass across them easily. The first light of dawn was starting to break, the rays of sunshine rising to the west, and Steve felt certain he could see the border ahead. It was still four miles off, unmarked by anything, but just beyond, there was a road that travelled from east to west across a long, fertile valley, and since they knew the road was in Pakistan, then the border must be slightly before that. There were no crossing points, and no guards; the border was just a line on a map, argued over inside embassies and army HQs but with very little meaning to any of the people who actually lived here. Not that crossing the border made them any safer, Steve decided grimly. Al-Queda controlled both sides, and if they are onto us, they aren't going to let a border crossing stop them going about their business.

The track rose and fell, widening out then narrowing again as it cut a path towards the plain. Steve reckoned they were three miles from the border, with two more miles of mountainous country to trek through, when the first bullet struck. It came out of nowhere. Dan was walking at a fast clip, just below a jog, one of a line of seven men, when suddenly there was a crack that lashed through the air, and he was spinning round, grasping his left shoulder, his hand covered in blood. In the next instant, he dropped to his knees.

'Fucking hit, fucking hit,' he screamed.

Steve looked up. The bastard was a good shot. He was standing eight maybe nine hundred yards above them, on a ridge of high ground, dressed in a black robe, with a short, black beard, and a sniper rifle pointing straight down at the track.

He was lining up another shot, Steve realised. And he was the target.

'Take cover,' he yelled.

He spun round, unclipped his AK-47, and slammed his finger hard on the trigger. The gun spluttered into life, loosing off round after round. It was wild, poorly directed fire, with not much chance of doing any more damage than leaving a few chips in the rocks, but it was enough to put the marksman off his shot. He fired, but once a sniper has lost his concentration, he's never going to hit his target, and the bullet pinged harmlessly in the dirt five yards away from where Steve was standing.

The marksman was stepping back, but behind him five more men had stood up, all of them with AK-47s in their hands, and they were laying down a murderous barrage of fire.

'Christ,' muttered Steve.

Ollie and the rest of the unit had fallen back. Right behind them was a narrow ridge of rocks hiding a small plateau and the entrance to a cave. Steve retreated steadily, until the six of them were behind the rocks. But Dan was still exposed, the bullets raking the ground around him, the rounds kicking up small clouds of dust. At the range they were firing their AKs, there was not much chance of putting an accurate round into Dan. But they were going to hit someone eventually.

Steve grabbed Maksim by the arm.

Of all the men on the unit, it was the Russian's bravery and courage he'd learned to respect the most. If you were about to march into near certain death, Maksie was the man you wanted at your side.

'Cover us,' he told Ollie.

'You're not going to bloody make it,' snapped Ollie. His face was tense and drawn, sweat pouring off his skin.

Steve looked up towards the five al-Queda men. He could see one of them setting up the sniper rifle again, preparing the accurate shot that would blow Dan's brains out. Then he looked at Dan, still crouched in pain, clutching his shoulder. Dawn was breaking now, sending dazzling beams of light shooting across the mountains and straight into his eyes, making it hard to focus. Steve tugged Maksim's arm.

'We're bloody going,' he said. 'I'll cover, you bring Dan in.'

Without hesitation, the Russian started to run. Steve was at his side.

Dan was only five yards away but it felt like fifty. Steve's legs were kicking hard into the earth. His boots were clinging to his feet, and he could feel each blister as he pushed himself forward. The bullets were smattering on either side of him, like tiny lumps of metal rain. Behind him, he could hear Ollie shouting, then a volley of raking fire as the five men behind the rock opened up, their rifles smashing round after round into the high rocks where the al-Queda men were. The wild, chaotic riot of gunfire was all around Steve, and the smoky smell of spent cartridges. He put his head down, blocked the noise out, and kept running until he reached Dan.

'You're going to be all right, mate, we've got you.'

Steve raised his AK-47 and fired into the hills in a tight circle that would be impossible to aim into without getting your face blown off. Maksim yanked Dan up by the shoulders and pulled him backwards. Steve retreated step by step, firing off round after round. The volley of fire Ollie was laying down had subdued the al-Queda men temporarily, blunting the edge of their attack, reducing it to a few pot shots.

Within seconds, Dan had been dragged behind the cover of the rocks. David knelt over him with a medi-pack. He ripped open Dan's shirt, revealing a nasty mess of bloody, bruised flesh where the bullet had gone in. He took a canister and started to pour water down Dan's throat. It splashed over his face, most of it spilling into the dirt, but at least some of it was getting down his throat. He was grimacing in pain, his face contorted, but he was still conscious. Ian rolled him over and tore Dan's shirt to get to his back.

'Shit,' muttered David. 'The bullet hasn't gone clean through, it's still in there somewhere.' He looked up at Chris and Ganju. 'Hold the bastard,' he muttered.

Immediately, Chris and Ganju grabbed hold of Dan's shoulders. By the rocks, Ollie and Nick were putting round after round into the al-Queda position. They weren't likely to hit much, not unless they got very lucky, but they were at least letting them know their hold-out was still defended.

Ian took a bottle of pure alcohol from his backpack. He splashed it over his grimy, sweaty hands, rubbed them together, then jabbed an index finger into the wound. Dan screamed out in pain. His body bucked, the massive strength of the man evident. Chris and Ganju struggled to hold him down, using all the power in their muscles to try and keep him in position.

'Bloody hold him,' yelled David.

He pushed his finger harder into the swelling flesh, grunted, then yanked it swiftly out. In his hand was a tiny lump of twisted metal, barely visible amid the mess of blood and flesh he'd brought out with it. He tossed it contemptuously aside, then poured what looked like half a bottle of alcohol into the wound. Dan bucked even harder, his lungs bursting as he roared with pain. Ganju lost his grip, thrown sideways, but quickly recovered and slammed Dan down again. Next, David poured water over the wound and cleaned away the muck, leaving a nasty-looking wound, a square inch of exposed, raw flesh. Then he wrapped a bandage round it. He took one end, Chris the other, and they tightened it over the hole in the shoulder, staunching the bleeding that had already put at least a pint of fresh blood into the dusty ground.

Steve took a capsule of methadone from his own medi-pack, filled the syringe, and jabbed the needle into a vein in Dan's arm, as close to the wound as possible. He pushed hard, pumping the liquid into the man, before his violent shaking made it impossible to hold the needle in place anymore. He yanked the syringe out.

'You're going to be OK, mate, just hold it steady,' he said. 'Well done,' he said to David.

'Is he going to be OK?' Ollie asked. 'Because we're under bloody heavy attack here and I need all the help I can get.'

Steve grabbed his AK-47 and positioned himself up against the rocks. The al-Queda unit was still putting round after round down into their position but they were well dug in. The bullets were smashing into the stone, sometimes into the dirt behind them, but as long as they hugged close to the rocks they were safe enough. Chris and Ollie put occasional rounds into the opposition, just to stop them getting too cocky.

'I don't sodding like it,' said Steve.

'Not one bloody bit,' chimed Ollie.

Steve glanced around. It was the first moment he'd had since they'd come under attack to assess their position. They were holed up behind the line of rocks. Dan didn't look as if he was nearly as badly hurt as Jeff had been but he wasn't going to be back in action anytime soon. They had their AKs, their Makarovs, and about half a dozen hand grenades, but they'd left all the heavy fighting kit on the other side of the mountains. They were still a mile away from the border, and the track down to it was only a narrow strip of land. Staging an ambush along there would be no trouble; there was probably a team of al-Queda boys already lying in wait for them. I don't like it, he repeated silently to himself.

'How many rounds have we got?' asked Ollie.

Every man did a quick check.

In total, they had about six hundred for the AKs, plus three hundred rounds for the Makarovs.

'Christ,' Ollie muttered.

'How long can we hold out?' asked Ian.

David made the calculations. 'They're trying to wear us down with constant fire right now. We can hold them off just by firing three or five times a minute, and at that rate we can last here for several days.'

'There are going to be more of the bastards soon,' said Ollie. 'They've got camps near here. They don't call this bit of country al-Quedistan for nothing. These bastards are just keeping us pinned down until the big boys arrive.'

'At which point we're sodding dead men,' said Steve.

'We can try a break-out,' said Ollie.

'Down that track?' said David. 'Impossible.'

Steve looked up towards the al-Queda fighters. Ollie was right. They weren't trying to move forward, nor were they trying to manoeuvre themselves into a better position. They were clearly experienced, well-drilled soldiers, and they knew precisely what they were doing – keeping the opposition penned up like animals until the men with the RPGs turned up to blow them to pieces.

'Two men,' Steve said, his voice strained and tense. 'We'll get down to the road, find ourselves a vehicle, and go and get that treasure. You boys hold this position as long as you can. Once the treasure is safe, we'll slip you out one by one. It's the only way. If we stand and fight, they are going to sodding massacre us.'

'I'll come,' said Ollie.

Steve shook his head. 'We need you to take charge here.'

'I'll come with you,' grunted Maksim.

Steve nodded. If necessary, the Russian would stop a vehicle on the road with his bare hands.

'Right,' said Ollie. 'Good luck.'

'We'll need it.'

With the Russian at his side, Steve waited until he heard a volley of covering fire from the AK-47s then started to steal away across the rocks. He was flat on the ground, his gun slung over his back, using his elbows and knees to propel himself forward.

The surface of the ground was pitted with rough edges, and Steve could feel the rocks snagging on his clothes and scratching at his skin like a blunt razor blade, but he ignored the discomfort and pulled himself steadily forwards. The first fifty yards were the worst. He was wriggling flat against the rock, half expecting a sniper's bullet to split open his spine at any moment. He crawled over two ridges of rock, then the ground dropped sharply into a small plateau. Steve flung himself down, landing hard on the dusty ground, then looked at Maksim who had just landed with a thud at his side.

'OK?' he muttered.

Maksim grunted.

Steve glanced back. They were out of sight of the al-Queda boys now and at this distance they were unlikely to be shot at anyway. He could hear the exchange of gunfire as the two units probed and challenged each other's positions.

'Let's go.'

There was a track leading down from the plateau. Steve reckoned it was a dried-out stream. In the rainy season, water would be cascading down here, but in the summer it was dry, leaving a narrow channel through the mountain. Water always found the quickest way down any mountain. Follow the channel and they'd get to the bottom soon enough.

Steve remained on the lookout for any spotters; he kept his AK-47 ready and his Makarov pistol gripped in his right hand even as he slipped and slid over the polished surface of the channel. Al-Queda had been alerted to an enemy force on their territory and they might well have sent men fanning out in all directions to search for more incursions. For all the boys in the turbans knew, this could be the start of a major special forces push on their territory. They were going to use everything they had to make sure no one got out alive.

Steve and Maksim kept going as fast as they could. The sun was rising steadily, and as the clock passed six in the morning the valley was flooded with light. They dropped down through the mountainside, and then suddenly they were on the open plain that stretched towards Bahram Chah. The road was a mile distant. The first half mile was just scrubland, but closer to the road and the village were cultivated fields, planted with maize. Steve and Maksim strode through them, advancing steadily on the road. It took them fifteen minutes before they were standing on the edge of the two-lane highway.

'Ready?' said Steve.

Maksim nodded.

He looked nervous, thought Steve. The first time I've seen Maksie look afraid of anything.

Steve had packed three gold coins in his kitbag, with a total value of a thousand dollars. The plan was to flag down the first suitable vehicle that passed, preferably one of the sturdy Korean or Japanese SUVs that most people in the border lands drove if they could afford any kind of motorised transport, and swap the machine for the money. Whether the owner of the vehicle would agree, Steve didn't know, and didn't much care either. If they wanted to haggle, he had the barrel of an AK-47 to negotiate with. If that didn't work, they could talk to Maksie. He'd frighten anyone.

One lorry drove past, but Steve ignored it. Then another. He ignored that as well. A lorry wasn't what they needed.

Another five minutes ticked by before he saw a vehicle that looked right. A black Toytota Highlander, still some five hundred yards up the road but advancing steadily towards them.

Steve stepped into the road, preparing to flag it down.

Three hundred yards.

If it didn't stop, Maksim would blow out a back tyre. That should stop it, and there would be a spare on the back.

Two hundred yards.

Steve could see two people in the front of the vehicle, both of them dressed in military uniforms. 'Shit,' he muttered under his breath. He hadn't reckoned on seeing any soldiers along this road. The Pakistani Army had long since abandoned the area to al-Queda, and they didn't wear uniforms. The Toyota was advancing fast. Steve took a step back but the driver was already slowing and pulling to the side of the road. Too late to back away now, decided Steve. Maybe it was just some locals wearing army surplus kit.

The Toyota pulled up, kicking up a cloud of dust from its big wheels.

Steve stepped forward as the driver rolled down the window. He took his hands from the wheel, picked up a British-made SA-80 assault rifle and pointed it straight at Steve's face.

'Good to see you again, Mr West,' he said, a slow smile spreading across his lips.

Steve recognized him at once. Colonel Simon Lockhart, commander of the British garrison in Helmand. The man who had originally sent them to take out Salangi.

What the hell was he doing here? Pointing a gun at us?

'Put your hands in the air, take a step back, and throw down your weapon.'

Steve stayed as steady as a rock. I'm not putting up my hands for this bastard.

The door swung open and Lockhart stepped down on to the roadside. The barrel of the SA-80 was thrust so close Steve's face, he could smell the grease on it.

'Damn well do what you're told, man.'

Steve looked at Maksim. He was expecting the Russian to jump on Lockhart any second now. It would be dangerous, possibly suicidal, but there was a chance they could overpower the man and suffer nothing more than a flesh wound. But instead Maksim had meekly raised his hands.

The second soldier climbed out of the Toyota. Dressed in a generic military uniform, olive green with a thick leather belt, he had a black beret pulled over his face, dark glasses and a scarf, so that you could see nothing of what he looked like. As Maksim tossed his AK-47 and his Makarov to the ground, the soldier stooped down to pick them up, placing them carefully in the back of the Toyota. He motioned to Maksim to turn round, and snapped a pair of plasti-cuffs, the cheap plastic handcuffs the British Army used for prisoners of war, on to his hands, securing them behind his back.

Steve tried to look at him, but the Russian just stared at the ground.

'I said drop your bloody weapon,' barked Lockhart.

Steve dropped his AK-47.

With the gun still pointed into Steve's face, Lockhart reached inside his tunic and grabbed the Makarov.

'Turn round,' he ordered. 'With your hands behind your back.'

Reluctantly Steve did as he was told.

The second soldier snapped plasti-cuffs on to his wrists.

'Now, take us to the treasure and maybe we'll let you live.'

'What the fuck is going on?' growled Steve.

'We're taking the money, of course,' said Lockhart, a sneer in his voice. 'That was the plan all along. You boys kindly went in and dealt with Salangi, and brought all his loot out into Pakistan for us. Now I'm going to collect it.'

'Then you're no better than a bloody thief,' spat Steve.

Lockhart glanced at him contemptuously. 'I'm not planning to take any lessons in moral integrity from a damned mercenary.'

'How'd the hell did you find us?'

'I got lucky,' said Lockhart.

'Bollocks,' growled Steve. 'There was no way of finding us on this road. We weren't planning to be here ourselves. It's too much of a coincidence. There must be a traitor in the group. Someone must have tipped you off where to find us.'

Lockhart nodded, then a thin smile creased his lips. 'It's you.'

'What the hell do you mean?'

As he spoke, the second soldier unwrapped the scarf and pushed the dark glasses up.

Steve took a moment to recover from the shock.

Orlena.

A mane of black hair tumbled down her neck as she took off the beret and tucked it into her tunic. She walked up close to Steve, looked him coldly in the eye, then nodded towards the rabbit's foot round his neck.

'It's a tracking device,' she said. 'I gave it to you in Kabul so that we would know precisely where you were at all times.'

Lockhart jabbed Steve's ribs with the SA-80. 'Now get in the back of that vehicle and take us to the damned treasure.'

Thirty-Six

THE BULLETS WERE CHIPPING AWAY relentlessly at the rock in front of them.

Ollie glanced up into the hills, then immediately ducked as another round of bullets smashed into their cover. He checked his watch. It was getting close to nine in the morning, and they'd been under continuous bombardment for more than two hours now. The force ranged against them had been strengthened in the last hour. As far as he could tell, there were now at least twenty al-Queda fighters against them, armed with AK-47s, sniper rifles, and at least one automatic machine gun. They faced a terrifying barrage of fire, a relentless and brutal assault which, over the course of the next few hours, was going to take a dreadful toll on their ability to defend themselves.

He looked at David. 'How long do you think we can hold out?'

'Until lunchtime at most, I reckon.'

Ollie reviewed their position. Of the original unit of ten, one man was dead, two men were guarding the treasure, and another two had gone off to get them a vehicle. Dan was wounded. It looked as if he'd be OK; the morphine had put him to sleep and it was only a flesh wound, the bullet had been dug out, and he'd kept most of his blood inside him. But it was going to be a while before he was fighting anything apart from the pain. That left Ganju, Chris, David and himself against about twenty al-Queda.

Military units have overcome worse odds, Ollie reminded himself. But not often. And not for very long.

'We've got enough for six or seven hours, so long as we're just defending ourselves,' said David. 'But Dan's taken a lot of our water, and once the heat of the day gets up, we're going to get bloody thirsty bloody quickly.'

Chris let off a couple of shots from his AK-47. Each of them was firing a couple of rounds a minute from a tight semi-circle. They were spaced three yards apart, making it hard for the opposition to concentrate their fire, and they were laying down enough ammunition to make the al-Queda boys nervous about putting their heads up for long enough to take a proper shot. There was always a chance one of the enemy might get lucky, but for now they could hold the position. Just.

'They're going to try and break us,' said Chris.

Behind them, there was a ridge of high mountains leading up towards the cave where the treasure was stashed. To the side was a jumble of rocks over which Steve and Maksim had scrambled down to the plain. The al-Queda unit could keep them pinned down all day, but if they were to break them, they had to find a way of hardening their attack.

'How?' said Ollie. 'Artillery? RPGs?'

Chris nodded. 'Either would do the job, I reckon. If they have any.'

And if they don't have any, thought Ollie, they could try and find a way of coming round the back and take us out while we're facing the wrong way. We don't have enough men to defend ourselves from an attack in two directions.

'They've got RPGs,' said Dan. He rose to his feet. He was wobbly, and he was clutching his shoulder, but his eyes were clear and alert. 'They've got artillery as well.'

He picked up his AK-47 and walked unsteadily towards them. Ollie opened his mouth to say something. It was madness for the man to think he could get up again so soon after taking a bullet to the shoulder. But Dan carried on talking.

'The al-Queda camps in this area are where their most experienced military units are based. We're talking about men who fought the Soviets for ten years in the Mujahedin. These guys know what they're doing, and they don't plan on throwing their lives away carelessly.'

'So . . .'

'They'll shell us,' said Dan.

'Christ,' muttered Ollie.

'We could break out right now,' said Chris. 'Scuttle down the mountainside and try and link up with Steve. In a fighting retreat, we should be OK – at least while we have enough ammo.'

Ollie shook his head. 'We'll give him another hour,' he said. 'If we start changing the plan now, we'll never link up with him again, and then we'll never get the treasure out of this bloody country.'

'And if they shell us?'

Ollie shook his head. 'We'll just have to hope Steve has got a vehicle, and got that treasure to safety. If he can do that, then Steve, Maksie, Ian and Nick can attack those bastards from above and take the pressure off us.'

'And if not?'

'We'll need some other plan.'

*

Steve had never felt so certain he was about to die as he felt at this precise moment. He could feel his life hanging by the thinnest of threads. And he was angry and bitter at having walked into such an obvious trap.

He was sitting handcuffed in the back of the Toyota. Maksim was in front of him, his expression defeated, staring straight at the floor of the SUV. Lockhart was driving, with Orlena at his side. Steve felt certain he was going to be executed. He'd already told Lockhart where the treasure was stashed. Once he'd got his hands on it, he fully expected a couple of rounds to be slotted into his brain. Lockhart wouldn't want nine mercenaries on the loose knowing exactly what he'd done and determined on revenge. He'd do exactly what any man would do in his position. A bullet to the back of the head. Problem solved.

Steve glanced out of the window. The Toyota was climbing up the narrow track that led towards the cave. Its rugged tyres were gripping firmly to the dried-out dirt, pulling them steadily upwards. The distance was no more than five miles, and even over the rough terrain they were travelling at a steady fifteen miles an hour, and had been for the last ten minutes. Another few minutes and they'd be there. Somewhere in the distance, Steve felt certain he could hear the rumbling echo of gunfire. Ollie must still be holding out against al-Queda. But there was no chance of them coming to the rescue. They were pinned down where they were. Indeed, unless they could manage to break out, they'd be dead within a couple of hours. The only hope was that Ian and Nick could bring Lockhart down. But they'd be taken completely by surprise.

In war, no position was ever completely hopeless. But this was about as close as it ever got.

'How many men are looking after the treasure?' barked Lockhart from the front seat.

Steve remained silent.

'Two,' said Maksim sullenly.

Steve shot him a glance, but the Russian avoided his gaze.

Thanks for sodding nothing, thought Steve. You've been acting strangely since we came down to the road. Maybe you've been planning to betray us from the start.

Lockhart nodded, and steered the Toyota up through the ravine that would lead them towards the cave. He slowed the vehicle down to a crawl as he negotiated the rocks and boulders littering the dirt track, then killed the engine. He jumped out of the driver's seat, opened up the back door, and jabbed his rifle towards Steve. 'Get the hell out,' he barked.

As Steve climbed from the back of the Toyota, Lockhart grabbed his handcuffs roughly, pushing him forwards, and jabbing his SA-80 into his back. Orlena pointed her gun towards Maksim, forcing him reluctantly out of the vehicle and on to the ground.

Steve scanned the row of caves where they had stashed the treasure. Then he looked upwards, at the rocks above. He could feel his heart thumping inside his chest. He was hoping Ian and Nick had spotted the Toyota, realised he wasn't at the wheel, and guessed something was up. In which case, Nick would be hidden somewhere up in these rocks, ready to blast Lockhart's brains out of his head.

Let's hope, Steve told himself through gritted teeth. Because right now, there isn't a Plan B.

Lockhart was holding him roughly by the handcuffs, and he could feel the tepid steel of the SA-80 pressing into his sweat-soaked back.

'We've got Steve West here,' shouted Lockhart towards

the caves. 'If any of you bastards are here, I want you to come out with your hands up.'

The sound of his voice echoed around the rocky mountains. Then faded.

No reply.

Then there was a shot. The blast ripped through Steve's eardrums, making him shudder. Lockhart had just fired once into the air.

'There's another of those bullets ready to be slotted into Mr West's back,' shouted Lockhart. 'So damn well show yourself.'

Silence.

'You're talking to a brick wall, mate,' muttered Steve.

'Address me as sir,' snarled Lockhart.

Steve shrugged. 'You're talking to a brick wall, sir.'

'Where the hell are they?'

Steve shrugged again. I've no more idea than you have, he thought, but I'm not about to admit that.

'Just take us to the treasure then.'

Steve started to walk to the third cave where they had stacked the boxes. His mind was working furiously. If Ian and Nick were hiding in the hills somewhere, why hadn't they already taken a shot at Lockhart? Maybe because his gun is still pointed at my back. They know I'll be killed in an attack, so they're just waiting for the right moment. Let's keep hoping.

He stepped into the cave, its entrance shrouded in shadow. 'Here.'

Lockhart looked around. 'Where?'

Good question, Steve said to himself. Where was the treasure?

He counted the caves again, making sure he'd got the

right one. But he was certain. He could see the scuff marks where they'd hidden the boxes. But there was no sign of the loot. Where the hell had it gone?

He started to laugh, the sound echoing off the low roof of the cave.

'What's so damned funny?' demanded Lockhart.

'You double-crossed us,' said Steve, suddenly serious. 'And now the Irishman's gone and double-crossed the lot of us.' He pointed to the scuff marks in the dust. 'He's pissed off with all the money. I always reckoned we shouldn't have trusted a sodding Provo.'

'What do you mean?'

Steve looked at Lockhart, his eyes narrowing. 'We left the boxes with Salangi's money in them right here because some al-Queda bastards were on our trail. Ian and Nick were supposed to guard them while we went off to grab a vehicle. Now it looks like Ian's decided to take off with the lot.'

Steve suddenly doubled over in pain. Lockhart had just slammed the butt of his SA-80 into his back, crunching into the bone of his spine, sending shockwaves of pain rippling through him.

'It's a damn trick.'

'No trick.'

'Call me sir.'

'No trick, sir,' spat Steve. 'The treasure was right there. You can see for yourself, something's been moved.'

Lockhart was staring at the ground. There was a trail in the dust where the boxes had clearly been dragged across it, and the imprint of two pairs of boots in the dust as well. If you followed the signs closely, you could see that the boxes had been dragged out of the cave and back up the hill.

To where? wondered Steve. There was no way of knowing.

I've been double-crossed twice this morning. And I wouldn't be surprised if I get double-crossed again.

'We can follow them,' snapped Lockhart. He gestured towards the Toyota with his gun. 'Get in the back. I'm not letting that money get away from me now.'

Ollie checked his watch. It was just after ten in the morning, and they'd survived another hour under fire. He scanned the horizon, noted the position of the al-Queda forces ranged against them, then looked down the side of the mountain.

Where the hell is Steve? he asked himself for the tenth time this morning.

'We've got to break out,' said Chris.

At his side, Dan was nodding. 'If they bring in artillery, we're done for.'

Ollie made a quick mental calculation. Steve and Maksie couldn't have spent more than half an hour racing down to the roadside. It shouldn't have taken long to get hold of a vehicle. By now they should have shifted the treasure out of the cave and made their way back here to relieve them.

There was only one conclusion. Something must have gone wrong.

'Ganju and I will check if there's a way out,' he said, his tone harsh and tense. 'Give us five minutes, then follow on behind.'

Chris, David, and Dan laid down a barrage of fire while Ollie and Ganju headed for the same escape route that Steve and Maksim had taken earlier. Ollie pushed himself down as flat as possible on to the harsh surface of the rock and slung his AK-47 over his back. The sun was beating down as he levered himself forward yard by painful yard, using his elbows and knees. The sweat poured off him, and even the rock was getting uncomfortably hot to the touch. Ganju was a few yards ahead of him; with his wiry, slim build, he was able to drag himself a lot faster over the terrain, while still keeping himself completely flat against the surface of the rock. Ahead, Ollie could see the narrow channel through the rocks that Steve and Maksim must have used to make their escape.

Suddenly Ganju leapt into the air as a bullet ricocheted across the rock.

'Move back, move back,' he shouted.

Ollie took just a fraction of a second to assess the situation. Stay calm, he reminded himself. That's how you survive any fire fight. There must be some men ahead of them, and they must have spotted Ganju.

'Bugger it,' he muttered as leaped to his feet and started running back towards the safety of the small dip in the ground where they had been holed up for the last few hours. Behind him, gunfire was blasting, bullet after bullet smashing into the rocks. From the sound, he reckoned there were three men back there armed with assault rifles, probably AKs.

He got back at the same time as Ganju who immediately held his AK-47 to his shoulder and fired in the direction of their attackers.

Chris and David looked anxiously towards them.

'We're bloody surrounded,' shouted Ollie. He grabbed his own AK-47 and started firing at their attackers.

'What the fuck do we do now?' said Chris.

'Start digging trenches,' said Dan, his tone determined. 'They'll be shelling our position soon and they won't stop until we're all dead.'

Ollie nodded. Dan was right. If he was in their position,

he'd do exactly the same thing. So would any military commander. Why risk your own men's lives when you could finish the enemy off with some light artillery?

Steve leaned into the back of the Toyota. Opposite, Maksim was sitting quietly, his head bowed, staring morosely at the floor of the vehicle. Lockhart was driving, while Orlena kept a weapon trained on the two men in the back.

They were climbing into the mountains, along a track that twisted east, not the one they'd used in the middle of the night. Steve could see the tracks in the dust where Ian and Nick must have hauled the treasure away. The plan was clear. Hide the loot somewhere else, then make a dash for the border. With any luck, the rest of the unit would be finished off by al-Queda. With the team dead, Ian could come back in a few days when the dust had settled and collect the loot for himself.

I'm not surprised Ian betrayed us, Steve thought bitterly. But Nick? I'd expected better of him. But maybe Ian put a bullet into the boy's back. I wouldn't put anything past a sodding Provo.

They were turning into a bend now, the sun blazing in front of them, making it virtually impossible to see anything in the glare.

Suddenly there was loud explosion and a cloud of dust spat straight up into the sky. The Toyota rocked violently from side to side, blasted by waves of hot air. It was like being on an aircraft in heavy turbulence; the machine shook, every bolt rattling. Next, Steve felt it tipping on to its side. He tried desperately to grab hold of something to steady himself, but with his hands held behind his back by the plastic-cuffs, it was impossible. The Toyota approached a ninety-degree angle. Two wheels only were on the ground, the tyres crunching the dirt on the track. The Toyota wobbled, tipped another degree, and crashed to the ground on its side. It landed with a sickening thud. Steve fell on to his side, and Maksim was thrown against him. The Russian's knee landed in his chest, briefly winding him, before he tumbled off him.

There was a moment of silence as the explosion subsided and the Toyota's engine stalled.

Steve glanced anxiously forward. He could see that Lockhart and Orlena had both been stunned as the Toyota tipped over. They were lying together in a jumble. The windscreen had shattered and blood was trickling down the side of Lockhart's face where flying glass had sliced open a nasty gash in his cheek. But his eyes were starting to open. In a moment, he'd have pulled himself back together.

The back door of the Toyota had swung open. Steve kicked back with his legs and pushed himself out on to the dusty ground. Within a fraction of a second, he was standing by the side of the vehicle. He saw two men emerge from behind the cover of a rock and start to walk towards them.

Ian and Nick. Ian had his Makarov pistol in his hand. Nick was holding his AK-47.

Ian looked briefly at Steve, nodded, and continued walking straight towards the tipped-over Toyota. He leant into the cabin, the Makarov still in his right hand and pointing straight at Lockhart's head. With his left hand he removed the SA-80 and flicked its mag out so the weapon was disarmed.

'Clunk click, old boy,' he said to Lockhart. 'You should have belted up.'

Thirty-Seven

OLLIE COULD SEE A GLIMMER of metal shimmering in the morning sun. It was a dull grey, coated in dust, and partially obscured from view behind a wall of rock. But unmistakable all the same. A light field gun.

'Christ,' he muttered.

He nudged Chris and pointed upwards. A bullet smashed into the side of the rock, inches from Chris's head, sending sparks and splinters flying, and he instinctively ducked back down. There was sweat pouring off his face, and his expression was a grim mixture of defiance and aggression. 'That's an SPG-9,' he muttered. 'The Russian bastards gave them to Swapo.' He looked at the trenches Ganju and David were furiously digging while the rest of the unit gave cover. 'We're going to take a pounding.'

Ollie fired a couple of rounds towards the artillery team, but from this distance he knew he couldn't do any more than keep them on their toes. He'd heard of the SPG-9, but he'd never heard one fired in anger before. Known as the Kopye, or Spear, it was developed in the early 1960s as a light artillery weapon, and later licensed to the Poles and the Iranians. This one could have been left over from the Soviet invasion, or it could have been bought on the black market in Iran where many of the weapons in the al-Queda camps came from. It had a 2.1 metre steel tube, mounted on a tripod, and could be operated by a two-man crew – perfect for mountainous terrain. With a weight of 47 kilos, it was light enough to be carried by a small unit, and its flexible tripod meant a decent firing position could be established just about anywhere. Its shells were usually fin-assisted, which gave them greater accuracy, and they were fired by a small muzzle charge that gave them an initial velocity of up to 400 metres a second. If necessary, a rocket booster on the shell itself would then kick in. At the right projection, a shell from a SPG-9 could be fired up to 6,500 metres, but it was accurate up to 800 metres, making it a natural weapon for close-range combat. Ollie reckoned they'd set it up about eight hundred metres away.

Their only chance was to get themselves deep into a trench, take the pounding from the artillery pieces, and then, when the enemy figured they were broken and came to check they were all dead, rise up out of the ground and start the counter-attack. It was risky and unpleasant but there were no other options.

Ganju and David had worked quickly, digging five slit trenches eight yards apart, while the rest of the unit kept up a rapid enough rate of fire to hold the assault at bay. For defence, a slit trench was the most effective. It was nothing more than a slim hole in the ground, with a bank of earth around it. The hole was just big enough for a man to drop inside, like a hand slipping into a glove. Shells could be exploding all around you, but unless you took a direct hit, you'd be fine.

'They're about to fire,' shouted Dan. 'Take cover.'

Ollie loosed off two more rounds from his AK-47, firing directly towards the artillery unit. He was stepping back as he did so, and could feel the bullets spitting on the ground around him. He stepped down into the slit trench, aware of the hot earth all around him. He could see the rest of the unit doing the same. He pulled his helmet over his head, then waited.

Suddenly, there was silence as the gunfire stopped. Then a screeching as the first shell whistled through the air.

Ollie reckoned it took less than two seconds for the shell to travel the eight hundred metres to their position but it felt like much longer. Instinctively, his body grew tense and rigid as he listened to the air being ripped open. Next, there was a vicious explosion as the shell struck the ground, breaking open the dirt. Ollie could feel the ground literally shake all around him – it was like being buried alive in an earthquake. He could smell gunpowder igniting, and then earth that had been kicked up by the shell falling down on his helmet.

But I'm OK, he told himself. For now.

Another screech.

This one was even closer. The ground shook, and Ollie slipped half an inch as the ground under his feet gave way. The noise was deafening, and the heat was starting to suffocate him. It was already close to forty degrees outside, but down here in the earth, with fireballs exploding all around, Ollie calculated the temperature was rising way past fifty. The sweat was pouring off him, creating a sodden wall of mud all around him.

And still the shells kept coming.

The metal and gunpowder rained down on them in a ferocious barrage. Ollie counted six shells, but after that he had trouble keeping score. The constant shaking of the ground, the heat, the noise, they were all making it impossible to concentrate. He could feel terror starting to chill him. He had been on a few battlefields and reckoned he coped well with combat. Better than most men anyway. But this was something else. Entombed in darkness, expecting to get blown to pieces any second, he wasn't sure how any man was expected to cope.

And then there was silence.

It took a moment for Ollie to even recognise it. His senses were so shaken, he was hardly even listening anymore. But as two seconds turned into five and then ten, he realised the shelling had stopped.

They think we're all dead. They might even be right.

Ollie levered himself up out of his trench. There were mounds of freshly turned earth lying everywhere, mixed with the charred remains of exploded shell casings. A couple of missiles had slammed into the rock, splitting it open, sending shards of stone into the rubble. Christ, thought Ollie. It's a miracle any of us survived this.

'Bloody noisy buggers,' said Dan, pulling himself out of his trench.

'I won't be volunteering for that job again in a hurry,' said Chris.

Ollie glanced at each man in turn. They looked beaten and grimy, they were soaked with sweat, Dan's beard had mud hanging off it, and Ganju had a shard of rock lodged in the side of his helmet. But they were OK.

'Guns ready,' he said. 'They'll be coming for us.'

Ollie, Chris and David manned one wall, Ganju and Dan the other. Ollie glanced up above the wall. Ten men were advancing towards them, their rifles ready. They looked well drilled. They were marching in a straight line, guns cocked, checking whether the enemy had survived the shelling. If anyone was still alive, there was no doubt they would put a bullet straight through them. This wasn't the kind of battle where prisoners were going to be taken.

'Anyone on your side?' hissed Ollie towards Dan.

Dan shook his head.

'Then move your arse to this wall. We've got bloody Osama's First Light Infantry advancing towards us.'

Ganju and Dan scrambled across.

The column of men was now about thirty yards away.

'Wait . . .'

When Ollie could see the scars on the face of one of the ten men, he lined him up in the sights of his rifle and squeezed the trigger. In the same instant, all five men rose up from behind the rock and unleashed a volley of lethal fire straight into the advancing column.

The man in Ollie's sights fell to the ground with a thick hole in his lungs. Four other men dropped. The six remaining soldiers hesitated, then started to panic.

One man tuned and ran. The remaining five raised their rifles and took aim.

Another volley. Four more corpses fell to the ground.

'Breakout,' shouted Ollie. 'This is our chance . . .'

'Call him sir,' said Steve, looking at Ian with a grim smile.

'You should have belted up, sir,' snarled Ian. 'Now get the hell out of there.'

Lockhart painfully pulled himself out of the cabin of the Toyota until he was standing on the dusty ground. Five yards from both of them Nick was holding his AK-47 steady on Orlena, with Maksim close to her side. Her SA-80 had been flung to the side of the road. Steve was unable to pick it up because of the plasti-cuffs still holding his hands in place, so instead he pressed his foot on it. As he did so, he noticed the IED – improvised explosive device – slotted into the side of the track. It was a brilliantly crafted device. The IRA had invented roadside bombs to attack British Army vehicles; from there, they'd migrated to the Middle East where they came into their own among the insurgents in Iraq. This one was shaped like a cone. A lump of Semtex was placed at the bottom of the cone and dug into the road, with an electronic detonator attached. As the Toyota drove past, it had detonated the device. The cone had directed the force of the blast straight upwards, unleashing enough power to tip the Toyota over and disable the driver but not enough to destroy the vehicle. It was a fine balancing act, and Ian had got it exactly right.

'Well done,' Steve said to him.

'I knew from the start that you couldn't trust the British,' said Ian.

With a sudden movement of his hand, he smashed Lockhart across the face with the butt of his gun. The man crumpled to the ground, clutching his cheek, his face bleeding. He spat out a broken tooth.

Ian walked across to Steve, took a knife from his webbing, and sliced open the plasti-cuffs with one swift movement.

Steve rubbed his wrists where the plastic had cut into his skin. He stooped down to pick up the SA-80. 'Where's the loot?' he said.

'I reckoned there was some kind of double-cross,' replied Ian tersely. 'So I moved it, left a trail and put that bomb on the side of the road so I could deal with whoever was coming after me.'

Steve grinned. 'Maybe I was wrong about never trusting a Provo.'

'Never trust a Rupert,' said Ian. 'At least not in the British Army.'

'How did you know?'

Ian swung his pistol towards Maksim and pointed it straight at his kneecaps. 'Because of him. He's been a plant right from the start.'

Maksim remained mute, staring at the ground.

Steve grabbed the rabbit's foot from around his neck. 'They used this,' he said. He nodded towards Orlena. 'That bitch gave it to me as a lucky charm. It transmits a signal.' He tossed it across to Ian.

Ian took one glance at it and then threw it to the ground. 'That's not strong enough. It'll transmit for a mile at the most. They followed us halfway across the bloody country and over into Pakistan.'

'Then—'

'In my old outfit,' said Ian, 'we had a way of making men talk. We shot their bloody kneecaps off. Now tell me, Maksim, how did you stay in contact with Lockhart?'

In the same instant, Orlena pulled a tiny Raven Arms M-25 pocket pistol from inside her jacket. It was so small that in the US it was known as the 'Saturday night special' because it was so easy to conceal as you stepped into a bar. But its .25 calibre bullet could knock a nasty punch into a man if fired from close range.

Even as she moved, Nick swung the barrel of his AK-47 and hit her hand, knocking the Raven to the ground.

Steve picked it up and smashed it into her face. It was a vicious punch, backed by the 2.3 pound weight of the firearm. The blow would have sent a man reeling. Orlena collapsed, her face covered in blood. She was breathing unevenly as her lungs struggled to cope with the pain.

Maksim spat in Ian's face. 'I'm no traitor, you Irish bastard,' he snarled.

Ian grabbed hold of Maksim's backpack. He rummaged through the kit, then pulled out a small bottle of Russian manufactured 'Brilliant' disinfectant. He opened up the bottle and thrust it under Maksim's nose.

Maksim turned away.

Ian splashed some of it on the back of his hand and walked across to Steve. The smell screeched off him; it was far stronger than any normal European disinfectant.

'I've noticed Maksim putting it on himself every day even though the bastard isn't wounded.' He paused, looking at Maksim. 'Ever heard of the Silver Fox?'

Steve shook his head.

'Well, I can guarantee Lockhart has,' said Ian. 'It's one of the latest generation of predator drones. Nifty little aircraft, its only eight foot long, and you can fold up its wings and fit it inside a golf bag. But it's no toy. The Silver Fox can fly at up to a thousand feet, and it's so tiny you'll never see the thing. All the other drones can take pictures or drop bombs if they need to, but the Silver Fox can also smell.'

'It can smell?' echoed Steve.

Ian nodded. 'It has a device called a SnifferStar. It's a set of tiny sensors, about the size of a pat of butter, connected to a quartz plate. When particles in the air hit the sensors, the plate vibrates. Different types of particles have their own "signature" vibration. So here's what happened. Lockhart sends a Silver Fox up into the air to track us all the way down to Pakistan, and it's programmed to detect the Brilliant disinfectant, which is certainly strong enough to stand out once we got into the wilderness. So Lockhart could follow us all the way and know exactly when to come and steal our money from us.' Ian took a step closer to Maksim, still pointing the Makarov at his kneecaps. 'And that's why you didn't mind leaving some of the treasure behind. You knew you could pick it up later, when Lockhart had killed the lot of us.'

'Is this true?' asked Steve.

It certainly explained why Maksim hadn't put up any resistance when they'd been captured and why he answered Lockhart's questions so meekly. Steve had already been wondering if Maksim was a traitor.

'She put me up to it,' he shouted, looking up, his face suddenly red with fury. 'I didn't want to. Orlena has links to Russian gangsters back home. They'd have hurt my family if I didn't go along with their plan.'

'That's no excuse for betraying your mates,' growled Steve.

'I tell you I didn't—'

'Shut the fuck up.' Steve looked at Ian and Nick. 'Shall we kill them now or later?'

'Later,' said Ian.

Nick and Steve pushed the Toyota upright again. The windscreen was smashed and there was a big dent in the side. Second-hand, you'd be looking at a rock-bottom price, decided Steve. But the tyres were intact and the engine still ran, and that was all that mattered. Nick fished a couple of pairs of plasti-cuffs from Lockhart's kitbag and clicked them over Lockhart and Orlena's hands, then bundled them into the back of the Toyota, along with Maksim. Nick kept guard on all three, his AK-47 gripped tight to his chest, pointing straight at them.

'Is the treasure safe?' asked Steve.

Ian nodded. 'In a cave, fifty yards further up the track.'

Steve pressed down on the accelerator. 'Let's grab it. Then let's see what the hell has happened to Ollie.'

Ollie was running as fast as he could.

The sun was high above him, beating down hard, and the sweat was pouring from his mud-encrusted skin. His feet were covered in blisters, and his clothes were little more than rags. His AK-47 was grimy, and he was no longer sure it would work reliably. Too much dirt could jam the firing mechanism even on a weapon as reliable as a Kalashnikov. And without a gun in your hands, you really were dead.

A barrage of fire blasted open the ground in front of them.

'Take cover,' he shouted.

At his side, Ganju, Chris, David and Dan dived off the track into the rocky scrubland. They had made it five hundred yards down towards the border. The ten-man column that had come to check they were dead had been slaughtered mercilessly, but there were still another ten al-Queda men high up in the hills, and at least one more unit coming at them from around the back.

The bastards are swarming over these mountains, thought Ollie grimly, pushing us into a circle we can't escape from.

He snapped his AK-47 into action, lay down flat on the ground, and looked straight ahead. A unit of three men armed with AKs and an RPG was advancing steadily up the track.

Ollie slammed a fresh mag into his AK-47 and loosed off a volley of bullets, with the rest of the unit doing the same. The first rule of any fire fight was to start hitting back at the enemy as soon as possible. Once you started returning fire, your opponent had to take cover as well, and that at least bought you some time. As the bullets spat across the open track, the al-Queda men hid behind a rock. There were only three of them but they knew what they were doing. They'd taken up a blocking position across the track that would allow them to shoot anyone who tried to pass.

Ollie glanced back. Another ten-man unit was high up in the hills, ready to advance steadily down, while the third unit was probably advancing on them from the east right now. To the west, the mountains were so steep they were impassable: try to escape in that direction, and they'd end up in a dead end, easy prey for their enemy.

Trapped, again.

'We need to get up there and sort those bastards out,' said Dan. His face was set in an expression of implacable determination.

'Who's going?'

'Me and Ganju.'

Ollie looked at the Gurkha. He nodded.

'Then go,' he said, his voice tense. 'And we'll hold these bastards.'

Thirty-Eight

S TEVE BROUGHT THE TOYOTA JUDDERING to a halt. He'd just pulled round a twist in the road and could see the mountain track falling away towards the borderlands.

He could also see the battle raging in front of him. 'Christ,' he muttered.

At his side, Ian grabbed a pair of field glasses. After a moment, he passed them to Steve. He could see Ollie, David and Chris holding a position down the track, facing off against three al-Queda soldiers. They'd be OK so long as the ammo held out, or their guns didn't jam, but if they slackened their rate of fire, the enemy would rush them. A larger group of al-Queda men was advancing cautiously down the mountain, guns ready, preparing to overwhelm Ollie's position from behind.

And Steve could see Dan and Ganju working their way steadily up the side of the hill, crawling through the rocks. It was clear what they were planning. A desperate counter-attack. But it would be two men against ten, and there was no way anyone could feel comfortable with those odds.

'Looks like we got here just in time,' said Ian tersely.

'Dan needs some help,' said Steve.

Ian nodded towards the back of the Toyota.

'Right,' said Steve.

They were still three hundred yards away from the al-Queda column, partially obscured by the turn in the track, and Steve felt confident they hadn't been spotted yet. He signalled towards Nick, and within seconds Lockhart was standing next to Steve on the dusty ground.

'See those blokes down there,' he said. 'I want you to walk straight into them.'

A look of terror filled Lockhart's eyes, the look of a man who knows a sentence of death has just been passed.

'Sodding move,' growled Steve.

'They'll kill me,' stuttered Lockhart.

There was blood and dirt covering his eyes and his body was shaking with fear.

Ian flicked a knife against his chest, cutting open a deep wound. Lockhart cried out in pain.

'At least it will be quick,' said Ian. 'And you'll die like a soldier. Or you can stay here and get cut slowly to pieces like a coward.'

Blood was dripping down the front of Lockhart's shirt. He backed away as Ian flashed the blade again.

'Bloody run,' shouted Steve. 'Maybe they'll take you prisoner. It's your only chance of getting out of here alive.'

Lockhart started to run, stumbling across the open mountainside towards the advancing al-Queda column.

'Nick, get down there and help Ollie,' said Steve.

As Nick steered the Toyota down the track, Ian and Steve followed stealthily in Lockhart's tracks.

Suddenly one of the al-Queda men spotted Lockhart staggering towards them. He shouted something in Arabic.

The entire unit turned to face him, its attention distracted, and in that moment Dan and Ganju saw what was happening and rose up from the hillside. Dan lobbed a grenade into the al-Queda unit and Ganju fired his AK-47 once, then again.

The shots were good ones, delivered at a range of just one hundred yards. Two men dropped to the ground, the bullets piercing their backs and puncturing their lungs.

But the commander hadn't noticed what was happening yet. He shouted at his men to open fire on Lockhart.

A volley of fire ripped across the mountainside. Five of the eight bullets split open Lockhart's face and chest. Another four from the second volley smashed into his legs and arms as he dropped to the ground, a pulped mess of flesh and bone.

But there was no time for the al-Queda unit to savour killing a colonel from the British base in Helmand. Dan's grenade had just exploded behind them.

It kicked up a wave of fire and dirt. Two men fell instantly, killed by the blast. A third was rolling around in agony as pieces of red-hot shrapnel sliced open his face. The remaining five men turned round, only to face a barrage of fire from Ganju and Dan's guns. The discipline and order of the unit was broken, with men firing and running chaotically. Steve and Ian dashed forward to within fifty yards of the unit, then dropped to the ground, slotted their rifles into their shoulders, and picked off what were now the three remaining men one by one.

Steve could see the last man rushing wildly towards him. Blood was already spilling out of a wound in his leg, and he was crying out in agony, but Steve knew from bitter experience that wounded men were often the most dangerous. With nothing left to lose, not even their lives, and with an anger raging inside them, they could fight with a savagery that seemed to have welled up from hell itself. He'd seen it before and, he had no desire to see it again.

He put the man's forehead carefully in the sights of his rifle and pressed the trigger. One bullet. The man dropped to the ground.

The stench of slaughtered men was in the air but this fight at least was over. All they had to do now was get the hell out of here.

Ollie glanced up the hill and permitted himself a brief, tense smile.

He could see that Dan and Ganju had just destroyed the al-Queda column advancing towards them. And Steve and Ian had joined the fight. We're starting to even up the score a little, he told himself. We just need to deal with these bastards right in front of us. And get rid of any units advancing on us from the east.

Right in front of them, eighty yards down the track, the three-man unit had been effectively pinning them down for ten minutes now, putting a constant barrage of fire into their position. Ollie, David and Chris had taken up position behind a rock, but it was only four feet high, and unless they stayed dug into the ground, they were going to get shot to pieces.

Ollie could see an RPG being raised above a man's shoulder. It was pointing straight at them.

His heart missed a beat. An RPG round fired accurately into their position would blast them to pieces. Even if it wasn't a direct hit that killed them instantly, it would blow away their cover, leaving them exposed to a volley of fire that would rip straight through them.

Ollie raised his rifle and put two quick shots into the enemy position. The man ducked behind his cover. But he'd be back, Ollie knew. There was no question about that. These bastards didn't give up so long as there was a single man left standing.

'How long before he gets a shot away?' wondered Ollie aloud.

'Not long enough,' said Chris.

Ollie glanced nervously around. The Toyota was steaming down the track, with Nick at the wheel, edging along the pitted track. It moved closer to their position.

'Cover me,' said Chris.

'What's the plan?'

'An LA-style drive-by,' said Chris, nodding towards David. 'We're getting in the back of that Toyota, Nick's going to drive straight past the bastards, and David and I are going to shoot the fuck out of them.'

'Then run like hell.'

Ollie shifted his position, slipped his last mag into the AK-47, and started to lay down round after round of fire into the enemy position. The bullets were rattling into the rock, forcing the al-Queda unit to keep their heads down. The mag held thirty rounds, so Ollie knew he had to be careful. Once that was empty, he was out of ammo.

He glanced towards the truck. Chris had made it, shouting at Maksim and Orlena to get out.

Ollie paused for a second, watching Orlena climb out of the vehicle. What the hell is she doing here? he wondered. And why the hell has Maksie got plasti-cuffs strapping his hands behind his back? But there was no time to ask questions. The bullets were starting to pepper his position. Ollie swerved, then re-established his aim, putting down another half-dozen rounds. He could see the Toyota accelerating down the track now. One of the al-Queda men stood up, took aim at Nick, but the Welsh boy was fearless when his blood was raised and he accelerated hard into the oncoming fire. A bullet pinged the bonnet, sending a plume of smoke rising upwards but without doing any real damage. Ollie concentrated, fixing the standing man in his sights. He took aim, squeezed the trigger and fired. He hit the man in the left shoulder and he saw him wince in pain, but he was strong, with enough spirit in him to keep firing through a bullet wound. Ollie fired again, then again, but missed both times. Another bullet smashed into the front of the Toyota, Nick swerved, and tried to keep going. Ollie fired again, but could hear only the sickening click of an empty chamber.

'Bugger it,' he muttered out loud.

He watched as the Toyota closed on the enemy position. Chris was hanging out of the back, his AK-47 tucked into his belly, the right position to unleash firepower at high speed. David was tucked in behind him. The engine was roaring as it bounced across the rough surface of the ground.

And then it was level.

Chris opened up, unleashing a volley of fire. The three men fell to the ground, the bullets smashing into them like rain. David loosed off the next volley. Nick swerved, and in the next instant the heavy wheels of the Toyota crushed the three wounded men, squeezing out what little life remained within them. For a few seconds, their screams filled the mountain side, and then they were silent.

Ollie slammed his fists together. The bastards are finished, he thought triumphantly.

He stood up to wave the others back in.

'Hold it right there, Englishman.'

Ollie spun round. Five yards to his right, a man was pointing an AK-47 straight at him. He was five foot ten inches tall, about thirty, with brown eyes that looked as if they were made of rock, a black beard, and a scar that ran across his face.

Ollie jabbed his own gun forwards. 'Drop your bloody weapon.'

'Your cartridge is empty, Englishman.'

Ollie froze.

'So I suggest you drop your weapon.'

Ollie remained motionless. He could remember the discussions they'd had around the campfire. Never be taken alive. Anything was better than that.

'I said drop your weapon,' growled the soldier.

Ollie tossed it to the ground.

'Now put your hands in the air.'

Ollie hesitated.

'I said put your hands in the air.'

Ollie raised his hands.

'And walk slowly towards me.'

Ollie knew that the soldier was going to take him hostage and demand that the rest of the unit give themselves up, or at least hand over the treasure for his release. *We might have been able to rescue David from Salangi, but we won't be able to break a man out of the main al-Queda stronghold along the border territory. If the US Army can't crack them, eight blokes low on ammo don't stand a chance.*

'Now!'

Ollie started to walk. There were ten paces separating him from the soldier, and he intended to take them as slowly as possible.

Buy myself a few more seconds. They might be my last on the planet.

'Faster.'

The soldier was so focused on Ollie he didn't see Maksim start to run. He was standing only a couple of yards behind Ollie, his hands still cuffed behind his back, and he'd edged to the right so that he was at right angles to the confrontation. Maksim was a big man and athletic when he needed to be, with lungs that allowed him to run all day. He bent down like a bulldog, his head thrust forward, his hands behind his back, and kicked forward, accelerating towards the soldier at surprising speed. Ollie was only barely aware of what was happening, and so was the soldier. He started to swivel round, trying to re-position his rifle so that he could get a clean shot at Maksim. If he had managed to press the trigger, he could have put a bullet straight through the centre of Maksim's lowered head, but he had only a fraction of a second to react, and it wasn't enough. Maksim collided with the man with the force of a battering ram. He head butted into his chest, knocking him backwards, and a flick sideways with his head knocked the gun clean out of his hands. The man staggered backwards, a look of shock on his face, struggling desperately to regain his balance. You could see in his eyes that he knew that if he fell over, he was done for. His arms started to flail in the air, then he crashed hard to the ground.

Ollie reached inside his webbing, pulled out the Makarov and took four quick strides forward. He put one bullet through the man's head, then another. He grunted, twitched, then fell back as the blood started to gush out of the wounds.

Reaching down, Ollie grabbed hold of Maksim's bound hands and yanked him to his feet.

'What the hell happened to you, Maksie?'

Maksim remained silent. A cut had opened up on his

forehead when he collided with the barrel of the soldier's gun and blood was trickling down the side of his face.

Steve, Ian and Ganju had rushed down the side of the mountain and were now standing at Ollie's side. Nick had driven the Toyota back up the track, with Chris and David grinning broadly in the back. Suddenly the mountain had fallen silent. The guns had died, the victory won. All you could hear was the light breeze rustling through the rocks. And all you could feel was the sun beating down on your back and the sweat oozing out of your skin.

'He betrayed us from the start,' said Steve.

'Maksie? No one fought more bravely . . .'

Steve nodded in agreement. That was true, but it didn't change the fact. 'When we got down to the road, Lockhart and Orlena took us prisoner,' he said. 'It was a set-up from the beginning. Lockhart used us to get Salangi's money which he planned to take from us when we hit the border. He tracked us using a Silver Fox drone. Maksim had a powerful disinfectant on him that it could smell. He might have fought bravely, but he's a traitor all the same.'

Each man was looking straight at Maksim.

'Is it true?' demanded Ollie.

'It's all the fault of that bitch,' he spat, nodding towards Orlena. 'She tricked me the same way she tricked Steve.'

'Sod it, man, she's your sister,' growled Steve.

'She's not my sister,' snapped Maksim. 'She recruited me in Moscow months ago. She and Lockhart have been lovers from the start, she had it all planned out. But she told me the tracking system was just so they could help us out if we ran into real trouble.'

'In any normal military unit, we all know what the punishment for treason is,' said Ian roughly.

423

Steve nodded. No one needed to spell it out. Traitors took a bullet, usually to the back of the head. It was what they deserved.

'He just saved my life,' said Ollie. He nodded towards the corpse. 'That man would have shot me. Maksie risked his own skin to stop him.'

'That doesn't mean he's not a traitor.'

'There's enough blood on this hillside,' said Chris.

Steve glanced around the unit. He could see the decision was weighing on each man. In normal circumstances, they'd have shot Maksim on the spot. But they'd been through a long journey together. Maksim had fought for his mates when it mattered, and for any fighting man that counted for more than any abstract notion of right and wrong.

'If any of you want to put a bullet in his head, then I'll hand you the pistol,' he said. 'He deserves it, and I won't shed any tears for the bloke. But I'm not squeezing the trigger, and I don't mind bringing Maksie home. I reckon he's earned it.'

He looked around the unit. No one spoke.

'Ian?'

Ian shrugged. It was fine with him.

Steve stepped forward and used his knife to cut the plasti-cuffs off Maksim's wrists.

Maksim nodded his appreciation of the decision but remained silent.

'What about her?' asked Ollie. He was looking straight at Orlena.

She was sitting on the back of the Toyota, her hands still strapped behind her back. Her face was splattered with blood, her clothes were torn, and her hair was matted with sweat and dirt. Her lips were set in a show of defiance but you could see the fear in her eyes: swollen and bloodshot, they were the eyes of a woman who knew she'd gambled with her life and lost.

'Kill her,' snapped Steve. I can forgive Maksim, he thought. But she deceived me from the first moment I laid a hand on her smooth, soft skin. I'm furious with her. And I'm furious with myself for letting her use me.

'I said kill her,' repeated Steve, his voice cold and mechanical.

Ollie walked towards her. The Makarov was still in his hand, and there was a fresh clip in it. More than enough bullets to finish the job. She looked up at him. She was shivering, even though it was well over forty degrees.

Make it quick, Ollie told himself. When someone is about to die, it's the waiting that really gets to them.

He was ten paces from her. At this range, he told himself, it's impossible to miss. He raised his gun.

But he found it was impossible to squeeze the trigger.

'Damn it, man, she's a woman.'

'I said, kill her,' growled Steve.

Ollie turned round, walked the five paces that separated him from Steve. He slammed the gun into his chest. 'She's your bird, mate. You bloody shoot her.'

Steve held the gun tight, then aimed it at her head. He concentrated for a second, lining up a shot that would blow her brains clean out. And yet even as he did so, he could feel the anger in his chest start to fade, like a wave going out on a beach. He lowered the gun.

'Let her go,' he said. 'I reckon she'll die on these mountains anyway.'

David walked up to her and cut her plasti-cuffs with his knife. 'Not this one,' he said. 'She's tougher than the lot of us put together.'

Orlena started to stagger up the mountains, running as fast as she could, not even looking back.

'Get on board, boys,' said Nick from the wheel of the Toyota. 'I'm driving us home.'

Nine men piled into the back of the Toyota on top of the boxes. It was quite a squeeze, they were packed in as tight as commuters on the morning train. Nick pushed the Toyota into first gear. Its engine rumbled and roared, the tyres protested at the massive weight bearing down on them, then slowly it started to roll down the dirt track that would take them over the border.

'Take it away, boyo,' said Ollie.

'Next stop, TGI's,' said Steve. 'And step on it, I'm bloody starving.'

Epilogue

BRUCE DUDLEY PUT TEN ENVELOPES down on the table.

Steve picked his up. It contained a single sheet of paper. He wasn't sure he wanted to open it yet. He looked across at Bruce.

Bruce shrugged. 'It's not exactly Steve West's big payday,' he said. 'But maybe that isn't to be measured in money.'

They were sitting on the veranda of a rented villa in Peshawar. After all the men had climbed in to the Toyota, they had driven straight for the border, then on to the first city of any significance, eighty miles into the interior of Pakistan. The Toyota was burdened down by the weight of the nine men plus the boxes laden with treasure, and its engine struggled to get much above forty, meaning it was into the early evening by the time they arrived. No one bothered them on the way. With their blood-soaked, torn clothes, and their sweaty, stubbly faces, they were far too frightening a mob for anyone to get in their way. An army might stop us, joked Dan on the way, rubbing his hands through his greasy beard, but since the Pakistani Army largely kept out of the lawless badlands along the border, there wasn't much risk of that. They stopped only once on the way, at a filling station, where Ian bought a pre-paid mobile phone and Steve called Bruce Dudley to tell him they were on their way. Bruce gave them directions to the villa, telling them to go straight there. He'd be waiting.

Peshawar is the only significant town close to the border; in the days of British rule it had been the entrance to the Khyber Pass, and it probably hadn't changed much since then. Nick drove down the side streets skirting the town until they found the villa. Bruce had arranged two crates, and a van, and already had an export licence to transport a pair of soft drinks vending machines to Dubai. They loaded the treasure into the two crates, then despatched them to Peshawar International Airport to be loaded as cargo on the Emirates flight to Dubai that left at six minutes past nine in the evening every week. With the papers in order, and a small bribe on the side as well, there was no problem getting the crates on to the plane without their contents being examined.

Bruce promised to be back the following evening and Steve knew he'd be true to his word. Dudley was a hard man but a fair one. Over the course of the day, he unpacked the crates, got the best price he could on Dubai's thriving black market, then deposited the money into the ten accounts he opened at TIFG International, a private Cayman Islands bank that, like most private banks, had a branch in Dubai. That completed, he caught the Emirates flight back to Peshawar International, as agreed.

While he was away, the nine men had been too exhausted to do anything much except sleep. There was hot water and food, and both were welcome after the journey they'd been through. By the time Bruce got back they'd washed, and eaten, and Dan had even shaved off his beard. They were starting to look and feel human again.

And they were ready to open their envelopes.

Steve sliced his open. He looked quickly at the single sheet of paper. The account at TIFG was in the name of Steve West, and showed a balance of £512, 262.58

'Christ,' he muttered to himself. A man died for that. The rest of us could have easily gone down as well.

'It's not what we were expecting,' said Ian sharply. 'We were told three million dollars.'

Bruce stood up and walked towards the window. 'It wasn't what any of us were expecting,' he said. 'But a third of Salangi's money got blown up when you hit the fort. At least half of what you did get out was lost on the journey. Then, when I opened up the crates, it turned out that at least half the dollar bills were fake. The diamonds and the gold were real enough. In total, it was worth about twenty million dollars, but when you fence it on the black market, that comes down to fifteen million. Translate that into pounds, and we were down to seven and a half million, and DEF was owed a third of that for arranging the job. I've divided up what was left ten ways, just as we agreed.'

Well, thought Steve, it will buy my share of the garage, with more than enough left over to keep me in beer money for years to come. That's what I came in for so I can't really complain.

He glanced around the room. You could tell each man's reaction from his face. Nick had never seen so much money in his life, and he'd come along for the ride, so he was thrilled. Maksim was grateful still to be alive. Any money on top was a bonus. Chris, Dan and Ganju all needed the money badly, and half a million quid was still a lot more than they could earn doing anything else. It wasn't going to change their lives forever, but it would dig them out of a hole. David was thinking it was enough to keep his wives at bay for a few years; as long as he could do that, he didn't ask for much more from life. Ian was pissed off. He'd been counting on more, but if no one else was planning to argue about it, there wasn't much he could do. Ollie had been hoping for a lot more. Half a million wasn't going to buy Katie the kind of house she wanted to live in, not the way property prices back home were going.

'Jeff's share goes to his mum,' said Steve, tucking the tenth envelope into his pocket.

No one said anything.

That's agreed then, decided Steve.

Bruce put another ten envelopes on the table. 'I've booked a ticket for each of you on the first flight to Dubai in the morning. You've each got a room for a couple of nights at the Jumeirah Beach Hotel. Then there's a flight back to London. All that's on the house. Tomorrow night, we're booked in at TGI's opposite the Exhibition Hall.' He ruffled Nick's hair. 'I reckon this lad needs feeding up. So we're going to eat and drink the place dry.'

'Bloody fantastic,' said Nick, grinning.

Bruce smiled, then turned serious. 'This is a bloody good unit, and you should be proud of yourselves. I know you didn't make what you thought you would, and I'm sorry about Lockhart. The bastard took us all in. But you finished off a nasty drug dealer, and you shot a few Taliban, and you got decently paid, so there's not too much to regret. And there's another job,' said Bruce, looking at them in turn. 'I know some gentlemen in the mining business. They'd like to see the President of Zimbabwe laid out in a coffin. And they don't mind paying a few quid to make it happen.'

'I'm up for that,' said Ollie. 'But we'll need a whole army for that one.' A broad grin creased up his face.

'Well, you're sodding crazy then,' said Steve.

'You're not coming?' said Ollie.

Steve laughed. 'No bloody way. I've got a garage to run.'

Appendix: The Weapons

T HE WEAPONS DESCRIBED IN THIS book are all in common use by military forces around the word.

AK-47 The AK-47 is probably the most famous weapon in the world. It was designed by Mikhail Kalashnikov, who fought in a tank division in the Soviet Army in the Second World War. While wounded in hospital he started to work on designs for a new assault rifle. It needed to be simple to maintain and simple to fire: Red Army troops had very little training. The result was the Avtomat Kalashnikova of 1947, better known as the AK-47. Its standardised 7.62mm cartridges can hit targets at up to three hundred metres. It was easy to maintain, carried on operating even when it was covered in grease and mud, and was always very cheap to manufacture. The Soviets licensed the technology to the Chinese – they were used by the Vietcong in Vietnam – and throughout Eastern Europe. The result: there are now an estimated one hundred million AK-47s in circulation around the world. There have been better assault rifles built since then but mercenaries still favour the AK-47 because it is cheap, rugged, and because they are so common you can always find fresh supplies of ammunition.

Makarov PM The Pistolet Makarova was designed by the Russian weapons specialist Nikolai Fyodorvich Makarov and was the standard-issue sidearm for the Soviet Army. It was issued continuously from 1951 until the collapse of the Soviet Union in 1991, making it one of the most widely available handguns in the world. It was also manufactured in Bulgaria, East Germany and China. The Makarov was simple to make and easy to use but its main advantage was its exceptional killing power. Its 9×18mm cartridge packed more punch than any comparable handgun, and its clip held eight rounds. After the last round is fired, the slide locks open. When a fresh magazine is inserted, the slide is closed by activating a lever on the left side of the frame or by withdrawing it to release the slide catch; either action loads a cartridge to the chamber. The pistol is then ready to shoot. The PM is fitted with fixed open sights as standard, with click-adjustable open sights available as an option on some models. It is accurate up to a range of twenty metres. There are many more sophisticated handguns on the market, but its combination of economy, stopping power and reliability makes the Makarov a natural choice for mercenaries.

RPG-7 Like the better-known AK-47, the ruggedness, simplicity, low cost, and effectiveness of the RPG-7 have made it the most widely used RPG (rocket-propelled grenade) in the world. The original Soviet RPGs were based on the German Army's Panzerfaust anti-tank weapon, and the Soviet design started with the RPG-1. The RPG-7 was introduced in 1961, and is today used by forty different armies around the world, as well as by many different Middle Eastern terrorist organisations. Although they were initially designed as anti-tank weapons, shoulder-mounted RPGs are so light and easy to fire, they are used whenever a high-explosive force needs to be delivered over a battlefield. A grenade is slotted into place, a booster ignites the grenade and launches it at a speed of 117 metres per second. A rocket then ignites and increases the grenade speed to 294 metres a second. The charge explodes at 900 metres. The launcher weighs just 7 kilograms, and is 95.3 centimetres long.

Arges 84-P2A1 hand grenade Pakistan's state-owned arms manufacturer, Pakistan Ordnance Factories, is one of the main suppliers to the whole region. The Arges was originally designed by the Austrian manufacturer, Armaturen Gesellschaft, and is made under licence by the POF. The grenade weighs 480 grams, even with its light plastic shell, and contains 36,000 splinters. It is the shrapnel as much as the explosion itself that inflicts heavy casualties on the enemy. It detonates four seconds after the pin is removed, and needs to be thrown within thirty metres of the target.

M2A1-7 flame-thrower Armies have been using fire on the battlefield since Roman times, but the flame-thrower was a lethal twentieth-century invention. They were first developed by the German Army during the First World War as a way of breaking through heavily fortified trenches and were widely used by both sides during the Second World War. The American-manufactured M2A1-7 was built out of two green cylinders, mounted on a metal frame, with a tube leading to a powerful metal nozzle which controlled the release of gas through the tube. At the tip of the nozzle was an igniter that set fire to the gas, releasing a jet of flame that stretched for thirty metres. It was widely used in Vietnam, but the horrific casualties and burns it inflicted on civilians led to its eventual withdrawal. By 1978 the US Army had bowed to public opinion and production of the M2A1-7 finally stopped, and the weapon was phased out of use.

SMAW-NE thermobaric Made by the American manufacturer Talley Defense Systems, the SMAW-NE is a device that has come into its own in the wars in Iraq and Afghanistan. SMAW-NE stands for shoulder mounted assault weapon-novel explosive. Thermobaric weapons were first developed by the Soviets but have been perfected by the US. A thermobaric creates a lethal fuel-air mix – a kind of flammable mist – inside a building, then ignites it, literally setting fire to the air. This creates a massive fireball which sucks out the oxygen from a wide area around the detonation. Anyone in the vicinity will be either burned or suffocated, while a building struck by a thermobaric missile will cave in on itself. The US Army used them to devastating effect in the Battle of Fallujah in Iraq; a single trooper could take out a whole building at a hundred yards or more with just one round.

M107 long-range sniper rifle (LRSR) Made by Barrett Firearms Manufacturing of the US, the M107 is the most modern sniper rifle available to American forces and has been widely used in Iraq. It has a barrel length of 29 inches, which is what gives the gun its extraordinary accuracy. In the right hands, an M107 can hit a target at up to two thousand metres, and with its 0.5 calibre bullet it will almost certainly kill anything it hits. In fact, it has a maximum potential range of just over six thousand metres, but it takes extraordinary skill to make a shot hit home over that kind of distance, and probably an element of luck as well. It weighs just a fraction under thirteen kilos, which makes it a heavy piece of kit to carry on to a battlefield, but that is more than made up for by its effectiveness. It comes with a bipod to support it on the ground, and its magazine carries ten rounds. The scope slots on to the top of the rifle.

Vickers K machine gun The Vickers K machine gun was developed before the Second World War for the big bombers of the era, the Bristol Blenheim and the Armstrong Whitworth Whitley. Its ammunition was slotted into big circular drums that snapped on to the top of the gun, and it was the round drum, rather than a more conventional belt-feed, that gave the Vickers its extremely rapid rate of fire. At up to a thousand rounds per minute when it got up to speed, its .303 calibre bullets could shred any opponent within seconds. The gunners manning the turrets on Second World War bombers had only two or three seconds to hit a fighter coming towards them, so a rapid rate of fire was crucial to survival. When the first SAS squadrons were formed in the North African desert in 1942, they took the guns from stricken aircraft and put them on to the back of their jeeps. The Vickers was designed for a big, heavy aircraft, not a jeep, and its weight and kickback were liable to tip the jeep over unless the driver was extremely skilled. But they were lethal, and the Germans learned to fear SAS raiding parties carrying Vickers K guns.

Silver Fox predator drone The Silver Fox is an eight-foot long, sausage-shaped aircraft, with detachable wings and tail fins that can be folded away in a box not much bigger than a golf bag. Built by Advanced Ceramics Research of Tucson, Arizona, it weighs just twenty pounds, and can stay in the air for up to twenty-four hours at a time. It has a total range of 1,500 miles. Plenty of drones have been built in the last few years to hunt out enemy positions and to give soldiers a better view of the battlefield (one of their main purposes is to cut down on deaths from friendly fire). But the Silver Fox can also smell. The Fox is equipped with a half-ounce SnifferStar that uses a series of tiny sensors – collectively about the size of a credit card – connected to a quartz plate. When particles in the air hit the sensors, the plate vibrates. Different types of particles have their own 'signature' vibration. The Silver Fox, which was originally developed to find whales around US Navy ships, can literally sniff out the enemy.

Last of the Good Guys

John Carbone

With echoes of *The Godfather*, *Goodfellas* and *Sleepers*, a new generation of Mafia thriller is born.

In 1970s Brooklyn, it's all about walking tall and making your own luck. Marco Bolzani refuses to get stuck in a dead-end job, so he goes into 'business' with his closest friends. Compared to the guys around them, they're just a group of small-time hoods.

That is, until Marco's Uncle Tony gets involved. Smart, ruthless, respected and feared, Tony asks them to up the stakes and Marco never questions his judgement. But the more Marco tries to break free, the deeper he's dragged into the web of organised crime. And when the whole thing comes crashing down, it looks like no one will make it out alive . . .

Thrilling, moving and intensely powerful – you'll be held rapt by the strong, raw and unique voice which brings this epic tale brilliantly to life.

978 0 7553 3581 7

headline

Now you can buy any of these other bestselling
Headline books from your bookshop
or *direct from the publisher*.

FREE P&P AND UK DELIVERY
(Overseas and Ireland £3.50 per book)

Unspoken	Sam Hayes	£6.99
Envoy of the Black Pine	Clio Gray	£7.99
A Carrion Death	Michael Stanley	£7.99
Dark of Night	Suzanne Brockmann	£6.99
A Mortal Curiosity	Ann Granger	£7.99
The Tomb of Hercules	Andy McDermott	£6.99
The Drop-off	Patrick Quinlan	£6.99
Flesh and Blood	Jonathan Kellerman	£6.99
Bravo Jubilee	Charlie Owen	£6.99

TO ORDER SIMPLY CALL THIS NUMBER

01235 400 414

or visit our website: www.headline.co.uk

Prices and availability subject to change without notice.